OBSIDIAN

OBSIDIAN

JASON O'LOUGHLIN

Obsidian
Copyright © 2016 Jason O'Loughlin

ISBN: 978-1-326-76571-2

Cover design © Gregg Watts 2016

PublishNation
www.publishnation.co.uk

For my beautiful daughter Holly
Every day an inspiration
Book Number One is for you

The troubadour beheld the great-foe standing at his feet, a creature after all, the wretched beast emboldened by its victory. Death brought with it the final epiphany, for his demise had come not from the poison of the sting but the timidity of his Faith. He had never *truly* believed. Thus when the Ankou called his name the troubadour wept, for a life unseeing, a quest unheralded, a song unheard.

—Anonymous Author, *Sub Rosa Tales, Volume IV*

Prologue

The husband sat at the table and rearranged his napkin and cutlery for what must have been the fortieth time. It was his choice not to look up. The other faces in the dining room made him nervous. It was their eyes he disliked more than anything else, the things he saw in them.

He tried to be positive. *You're being paranoid. No one knows you and no one is looking your way. No one cares.*

He had made an effort and worn the navy suit that he had rescued from the layers of dust at the back of the wardrobe. He hadn't worn the suit for some years and could feel his extra pounds pressing against the fabric. The snugness made him uncomfortable but then he had never really enjoyed wearing suits.

The husband glanced nervously at his watch. It was still early, a few minutes after five pm. Time was moving too slowly. He forced himself to look up. The world was dark and outside it was snowing heavily. Despite the early hour the dining room was surprisingly busy.

The restaurant's feat of staying open was something to be admired. It was surviving the ample challenges posed by the weather and the reward for the owner's gallant endeavours was that business was good. It was one of only three or four establishments remaining open whilst so many others had been forced to close temporarily.

They had given him a seat in the far corner and it was certainly one of the more intimate spots for there were no other tables particularly close by. He hadn't waited for her and had taken the liberty of ordering a bottle of the house red. The wine was poor, horribly overpriced, but was a much needed tonic to combat his foul mood. He was already almost finished with his second glass.

1

He sighed quietly. The noise was slight yet full of despair. He had a fondness for this place, it was one of their favourites, and he wondered whether it was a sight he would ever see again.

The husband was starting to wonder whether he would be eating alone when the door to the restaurant opened. She entered quickly from the dark along with a flurry of snowflakes and the sound of the passing traffic moving slowly on the slippery roads. The maître de greeted her warmly and pointed her in his direction.

His wife wasn't smiling. It should have been a special occasion but her demeanour had no hint of romance in it. She sat down opposite him and surveyed her surroundings, carefully examining every face in the dining room with suspicion. When she was finished and content that no one knew her, she turned to her husband.

'Does dinner seem appropriate right now?' she asked curtly. Their time apart had done little to soften the bite in her tone.

He deliberately allowed himself to appear confused. 'It's the second of February,' he said, 'which makes it our anniversary, so I'd go with yes.'

'You have your back to the wall?' she noted, nodding at him. 'Old habits coming back, are they?'

'I'm glad you came,' he said tenderly, ignoring the question. He tried to see past her inhospitable expression. It was pure ice. 'It's lucky they're still open, chap at the door said that a few places across the road had to shut up shop. We can –'

'You probably thought this was cute,' she said, cutting him off. She pulled the note from her handbag and placed it down on the table in front of him like a detective presenting incriminating evidence to a suspect. The note carried the simplest of missives. *Meet me - 5pm – Today - Gianni's.*

He stared at the note and then back at her. He didn't know what she wanted him to say so he chose to say nothing. He could only wait for her to play her hand. She still looked like his wife and to most the change would have been undetectable. Her red hair was tied neatly in a ponytail and she was dressed in a smart grey trouser suit, although he knew that she had been nowhere near the office for the last two weeks. Her brown eyes were focused, all business. But the change existed underneath, resting behind the thin façade. Still, he couldn't help but find her beautiful.

She removed her coat, twisting around and tucking it onto the back of her chair. 'I'm not in the mood for this kind of nonsense,' she said, 'and quite frankly you shouldn't be either. But why do I need to tell you? Sometimes you just frustrate me.'

'Yet you came?' he said. The flicker of hope in his eyes was unconvincing.

'We left more than a few things unsaid –'

'It *is* our anniversary,' he reminded her for a second time. 'I got a cheap red while I waited. Should I order something nicer for when we eat?' He pointed to the wine glass in front of her and grabbed the bottle, ready to pour.

She shook her head and placed her hand over the top of her glass, declining. 'Where is Finn?'

He filled his own glass instead. He took a long sip to ease his building stress. When he was finished he wiped his mouth on his sleeve. She was still waiting. 'He's at a friend's,' he said.

The wife lowered an eyebrow. 'Which friend?'

'Does it matter?'

'I guess not, in the grand scheme of things.'

'None of this seems right,' said the husband. 'You shouldn't need to ask me where our son is. You would know, had you'd been around these last few days.'

'I've been busy –'

'I miss having a wife.'

She said nothing.

The silence made him uncomfortable. He picked up his menu and scanned the words without really taking them in, ready to change the subject, even if just for a short while. 'I'm might go a bit adventurous tonight,' he said, knowing that in reality the food was of little to no importance, 'maybe fish, don't they say fish is elegant? Maybe a sea-bass or a monkfish –'

3

'No! Enough!' The wife swept the menu from his hands and thumped it down on the table. The cutlery rattled. 'Right now who gives any-sort-of-a-damn about fish?'

Her outburst was too loud and a couple of diners afforded a discreet look in their direction. This wouldn't do. She carefully lowered her tone and leaned in closer for more privacy.

'Why are we circling around this?' she said, barely above a whisper. 'I was going to tell you tonight. I've made contact with my Father.'

The bombshell hit him hard. The muscles in his head tightened and he was overcome with a brutal dizziness. He felt closed in, claustrophobic, the world suddenly transforming into the strangest of snow globes, only with his body trapped within the prison of the glass and the snow floating outside, his life shaken by the hands of someone malicious and callous. He expected the glass to shatter at any moment and the storm to course in and consume him.

'We ...' He found it hard to continue. His eyes filled with tears but he forced them back. He was struggling to find the words. 'We ... we said we would wait ... we said we would wait until ... Agatha ... I–'

'Don't. I've always been very clear about the steps forward.'

'But –'

'Can you stop with that word?' the wife said. 'Saying *but* doesn't do anything. *But ... but ... but ...* see ... everything's still the same. Nothing's going to change. I had to act, with or without you.'

'You're wrong. The odds are a million to one –'

'I think you'll find the odds are a damn sight wider than that,' she said. She waited as a waiter moved past their table. When he was out of earshot she found her voice again. 'And regardless, it's done. Father's sending a team immediately. The closest are in Geneva. Now they have a confirmed case they'll move as quickly as they can. They'll be here in forty-eight hours.'

'It is *not* a confirmed case!' He could have hit her. She was so matter-of-fact and it made his blood boil. His voice was starting to snarl. He was losing his composure. 'You don't think your

4

father is going to welcome you back with open arms after what you did?'

'No,' the wife was happy to agree, 'there'll be a punishment. I'm willing to face that. You should be too.'

'I can barely look at you,' he said. 'For the love of God, forty eight hours, what were you thinking?'

There was a long pause. The wife just stared at her husband. Then she picked up her own menu and scanned the offerings idly. 'Maybe,' she said incredulously, 'that question came from the wrong side of the table. What exactly were *you* thinking? You've always been too emotional. That's your biggest weakness. What did *you* think we were going to do with all of this? Perhaps you should consider the answers to your own questions before you ask them. I have my answers. I have no questions. My views *are* and will *continue* to be quite transparent.'

'Stop it,' said the husband angrily.

She dismissed his concerns with a flick of her hand and made a pretend face to show that she couldn't quite decide on what to order from the menu. 'I'm not going to have a starter tonight,' she said, 'but not sure what I want for a main. I hate a cliché but it all looks so good—'

'What's happened to you, Agatha?' he said, choking back tears. 'Did I misinterpret *us*? Did I imagine *us*? Please, this is our son!'

It was his turn to remove the menu from her. The husband took his wife by both hands. He caressed her fingertips.

'You just need to think,' he pleaded, 'and remember what we gave up in the first place. Think about what we gave up for love. It's all going to be worth absolutely nothing if you do this.'

'Peter,' said the wife. A tear had escaped from his eye and she brushed it from his cheek, almost tenderly. 'Don't you see that this is the problem? I don't need to think. I've done nothing but think. It's haunted us for years, you see that don't you? Maybe there was a time where we could fight it but not now. We can't ignore this. And I won't ignore this. You can still come with me. But if you don't, you know what you'll become to me.'

5

'That's your father's voice,' he said. The tears flowed freely from his eyes now, cascading down his cheeks and pooling in the crests of his mouth. He punched his hands into the table, making the cutlery shake once more. A fork fell from the table. There were more stares in their direction.

'Peter, you're making a scene.'

'He is *our* son!'

'You make a mistake,' said the wife. Her stare was intense, burrowing into his soul. 'He is not *my* son. Not anymore. He's one of them. Forty eight hours. Running's no option, not now. I suggest you use such time to say your goodbyes.'

The husband stood. He finished his wine and he kissed his wife on the forehead and walked out sobbing, disappearing into the snowy night. He refused to look back at her. He could keep that bit of dignity at least.

A concerned waiter, noticing the departure, approached the table gingerly. 'Is everything ok, madam?' he asked politely.

'Everything is quite alright,' said the wife calmly, 'and I think I will have the Camoscio in Salmi. Make sure the venison's pink.'

Part One

Chapter One

Finn Carruthers awoke with a violent shudder and a sharp intake of breath. The room that greeted him was pitch black and bitterly cold. *Welcome back to reality old friend.* The memory of his dream faded instantly into nothingness and there was a brief moment of incoherence before the pain, responsible for the interruption to his sleep, became horribly real and reminded him of its existence.

He staggered uneasily from the bed and made his way cautiously through the darkness. He passed the clock on the bedside table that declared in stark and serious red numbers that it was fifteen minutes after midnight. The wooden floor felt like a lake of sheer ice on the skin of his bare feet. The fault was his. His body was naturally warm, often a curse, and he always slept in a thin t-shirt and shorts, even in winter. He would need to rethink his choice of sleepwear. This was the third time in as many weeks that he had been forced from his bed in the middle of the night.

Finn made it to his small desk on the opposite side of the room and he quietly flicked on the desk lamp. With the aid of the modest light he swept his t-shirt off over his head and gazed at the source of his discomfort in the tall mirror that hung on the wall behind the desk. *There you are – you unsightly, hideous thing.* The rash, as always, looked back at him, sitting an inch or so beneath his armpit and on the side of his body.

He looked at the rash with a bubbling hatred and wished that he had the ability to rip out the whole thing with his fingertips. It had started off small and innocuous of course, being nothing more than a curve of tiny pink blisters, but quickly it had grown. Now it had formed and settled into the strangest of shapes. At the top it was formed in a circle, with a horizontal line beneath and then a vertical line of blisters running downwards. It was starting to resemble a ely etched stickman, slapped down rough and ragged, as if nted by an artist performing broad and reckless strokes on a canvas of skin.

The pain was becoming unbearable. Finn started to make noises, winces and whimpers, and he pushed his hands down onto the edge of the desk, clenching the wood with such force that the blood left the area and his knuckles turned white.

Then, by the merciful grace of God, relief came. It always happened this way. Just as it seemed that the agony had reached the highest setting of its vengeful dominance it suddenly loosened its grip without warning. The pain started to ebb away slowly like a tidal wave retreating back to the ocean and over the pebbles and shingles of the beach that it had just devastated.

Finn flicked off the light, put his t-shirt back on and walked out into the hallway. Was his father still awake? The general gloom suggested the answer was no and this was confirmed at the door to his parent's bedroom. There was a tiny creak as Finn edged the door open a few inches and a shape lay in the bed, sleeping. One shape – one parent. His mother still hadn't returned. *Is this what an impending divorce really looks like?*

Finn returned to his room and sat back on the edge of his bed. He was breathing heavily and sweating. He pulled his duvet across his shoulders and hitched his legs up to his chin. He sat perfectly still, bundled up in the dark.

A part of him had been tempted to wake his father but he had quickly decided there was little point. He had tried to describe the condition to his parents before, to share the pain, but he had found that he struggled to do it justice. It wasn't an easy description to master. The pain didn't seem to be on the skin itself, it wasn't an itch or an irritation, but was instead a dull, throbbing ache that seemed to have its origins beneath the surface and somewhere deep inside. When it came on it pulsated, beating in a quick rhythm like a drum and seeming to build and build in intensity as if it were heading towards some form of morbid and fatal crescendo.

His parents had offered little in response. They had completed the minimum, asking to see the rash, examining it closely and then lapsing into silence. Some reassurances were given, customary exclamations of it being *nothing-to-worry-about* and that it was *quite normal for your age*, but there had been something else there, something between them, a look they shared and a flicker of a strange recognition in their eyes.

Unmistakeably whatever the condition was it was getting worse. As such Finn decided that he would have to speak to his father in the morning, regardless of his disinterest. He was tempted to start by asking him why no one seemed to actually care about his wellbeing? He was fifteen and he had seen other children his own age only have to sneeze or graze a knee for their parents to march them off to the Doctors, demanding tests and medicine. They were mollycoddled to the extent of hypochondria. Yet here was Finn sitting at the opposite end of the care scale, afflicted by a strange condition, and if his parents did happen to care they certainly weren't showing him.

Finn considered lying down but something stopped him. The feeling came out of nowhere, a burst of instinct, drawing him to the window. He couldn't resist the urge and he stood, keeping himself wrapped in the duvet and shuffling across to the closed blue curtains of his bedroom.

He peered out. Snow was falling. Cars lined each side of the street and the majority of the houses were in darkness. And there *he* was, standing beneath a single street light. The man was too far away and the night too dark for him to be nothing more than a silhouette. But the outline was familiar, awkward and bulky, and he was looking up at the window.

He saw Finn watching him. Then he took three slow steps out into the road before abruptly changing his mind. He let out a plume of cold breath and then turned quickly on his heels before disappearing into the depths of the night.

Finn stayed at the window ledge for a long while. The man didn't return and when tiredness finally took over he returned to bed and drifted off into an uneasy sleep, dreaming of a strangely shaped rash and the sinister shadows of men who stalk the pavements of the world at midnight.

Chapter Two

Finn used the journey to relax as the Sixty-Four bus slowly wove its way into the heart of town. He lived in the small village of Willowbrook, on the outskirts of Cheltenham in Gloucestershire, and he rarely found himself unhappy to be travelling away from it. He had little doubt that if such an award existed, Willowbrook would easily be crowned the most boring place to live in the whole of England.

St Benedict's Catholic High School was a forty-five minute drive away but today the journey was certain to take a great deal longer. The driver guided the bus along the roads with the greatest care and despite his admirably sensible approach there were outbreaks of mutiny from the passengers. Some groaned loudly and unashamed, others whispered their complaints secretly to one another. The general consensus from the disgruntled mutineers was that the driver was being overly cautious.

Henry Pringle, Finn's best friend, sat with his school bag on his lap, listening to music through his headphones. His head bopped and his knee vibrated every so often with the rhythm, the music no doubt a form of cheesy soft rock by men with long perms and chesty voices.

Finn was tired from the night before and happy not to have to bother with conversation. He rested his head against the cold glass of the window and watched the world pass by.

The bus swerved. The driver took instant action to correct the skidding of the heavy vehicle on the ice. A few passengers gasped but there wasn't any need for such drama, as such occurrences were to be expected and they were not going fast enough to cause any real damage. It only took a split second for the driver to regain total control and he grunted a half-hearted apology.

'Bloody council,' a female voice complained. 'Why are they not treating these bloody roads properly?'

'You're spot on, love,' said an elderly man from the front of the bus. 'Makes you wonder what your taxes are actually going towards, don't it? Actually, I'll tell you exactly what it goes on, expenses for a bunch of Eton toffs who don't know their asses from their elbows.'

The mood of the people was definitely worsening. The weather was the root cause of it of course, the initial novelty having long since mutated into a form of angry apathy and simmering snark. The weather had turned in the early part of January, a Monday evening rush hour, a few modest flakes at first. But six weeks later it was showing no signs of going away.

Finn didn't share the old man's bleak view and had retained the same childlike sense of marvel from day one. Winter was the best season. He remembered the cold nights from when he was young, of standing at the window and watching the glow of the streetlamps, hoping to see the flakes drift in the light. Then the snow really would begin and he would dive into bed and tell himself not to check anymore. He was certain that if he didn't look and he slept the snow wouldn't stop and he would wake the next morning to find that it had settled deeply. But sometimes he couldn't help himself and he would sneak a look. If the snow *had* stopped he blamed himself for not having the discipline to stay in bed.

Yet grudgingly he understood why some were not enjoying the current weather quite so much. England was England, it didn't deal with snow all that well. Roads became impassable, school closures were announced on the radio in their droves, scores of flights from scores of airports were cancelled, and the supermarkets ran out of stock due to apocalypse fearing panic buying. There had been a recovery of course but the memory of past difficulties lingered.

The old man at the front of the bus was still wittering away on his soapbox. He was one of the haters all right. 'We're the only country that crumbles, aren't we?' he moaned. 'Canada gets a hundred foot of snow and they still manage to go about their business. I could do a better job running this country, much better than those useless Eton cretins.'

Finn wished he was braver. He was tempted to say something. Politics wouldn't be one of his A-Levels and he didn't know much about the topic but even so, what exactly were the government supposed to have done? There had been no signs, no forecasts to suggest such a weather event was on its way. No, it hit without warning, an arctic punch into the unprepared paunch of the country. He was sure that the old man would have been complaining just as loudly had the government wasted millions of pounds on treating every single road and then it hadn't snowed at all.

'We're going to be completely late,' Henry said suddenly. It was the first time he had spoken in quite some time. He removed his headphones and checked the time on his phone. 'I wanted to be there like five minutes ago.'

'It's seven-thirty in the morning,' Finn had to remind him. He turned away from the window and enjoyed a long yawn. 'What we going to be late for? Gate's won't open for another half hour.'

Despite asking the question, Finn could already guess why Henry was so keen to get to school. Henry was quiet and he had that look in his eyes. Such ardent desire was *never* due to any deep rooted and commendable lust for learning – certainly not. No, his enthusiasm for punctuality was part of a far bigger plan, a *master plan* that involved a girl. It *always* involved a girl. And that was one fire Finn didn't want to stoke.

Henry was momentarily distracted by a group of girls crossing the road and he leaned across Finn and stared at them intently as the bus moved slowly past.

Finn returned to his own thoughts. Politics was replaced by the memory of the man from the previous night. He was as sure as he could be that he knew who it was who was standing in the street. If he was right, he had seen the man before. He didn't know his name but the man had a face that seemed to be appearing more often than was comfortable. He had seen him outside the school, in the shopping arcade, in the local newsagents. And each time they had made an uncomfortable eye contact.

They had spoken once a few days previously, in the street a mile or so from Finn's house. The man was visibly nervous. He was overweight and he wore a baggy suit, a waistcoat and a Stetson hat, all of which were dark brown. He carried a wooden cane with a golden handle. Although the thing that stood out more than any other was that he had one eye missing.

'I need to speak to you and your father urgently,' the man had said, before declaring that his business was of the highest importance but then disappearing as a group of people came outside from a nearby house.

Finn didn't know him. He had told his father, who asked a few brief questions but then didn't mention it again and seemed unconcerned. He was tempted to mention it to Henry, to get his opinion –

'Man, big day today,' Henry said. Girls gone and out of sight, his mind was back in the bus.

'I bet,' Finn said. His curiosity got the better of him. 'So come on then. Who's the lucky lady this time?'

'*She* is Felicity Gower,' Henry announced proudly.

Finn *was* surprised at that. 'As in Felicity-Gower-who-lives-up-the-road?'

'Yep,' said Henry, 'and she is beyond fit.'

Beyond fit. Finn sighed. *What a line.* There had been times whilst growing up that he and Henry had been mistaken for twins. There had always been physical similarities. They were the same age and had similar builds that were not quite slim but neither were they overweight. They both had blue eyes and had allowed their hair to grow long enough to afford a trendy, swept fringe. They had similar personalities, both being insecure and not massively popular at school. But Finn sincerely believed that their maturity was on a different level. Their use of vocabulary was just one example. He would never dream of saying something like *beyond fit.*

'I'm no expert,' Finn said, 'but I don't think girls respond all that well to being called fit.'

'It's a compliment. They love it.'

'Do they?'

'Yep,' said Henry confidently, 'and I've put off asking her out all year, last chance before half term. Not waiting for next term, no way.'

'I love the way you make out you've liked this one forever,' Finn was already cringing. He paused and thought about the facts for a moment. Up ahead the bus driver pulled into the main road that led to the school gates. 'Actually now I think about it, she's only been at the school a few weeks, not all year. Let's face it. She's just the latest in a very, very, very long line.'

'I'm insulted,' said Henry.

'She lives just up the road from me,' Finn felt compelled to point out. 'Don't show yourself up. Come back to mine after school and go round and knock on for her or something.'

'Are you out of your tiny little mind?' Henry was clearly unimpressed with such a suggestion. He thumped Finn in the arm. 'How freaky and messed up is that? Honestly, go and knock on her front door! That's your suggestion? Man, it's just creepy. No, no, no, I have something a bit more impressive in mind.'

Finn was not in the least bit surprised. Henry had seen too many movies and it had become a curse. Asking a girl out was quite simply not good enough. There had to be a grand, large scale *romantic* gesture to accompany it. He didn't think about how ridiculous it would be or how embarrassing he would look. One day Henry would grow into the type of man who would dash to the airport to declare his love for a woman moments before she was due to jet out of his life forever.

Finn didn't know Felicity Gower personally, despite almost being neighbours. The only thing that he knew about her, or at least so went the rumour, was that the school lunk-head Jordan Tremlett had some sort of caveman-like crush on her and if it was true it wasn't sensible for anyone else to harbour similar feelings. He was tempted to mention it but knew it would fall on deaf ears.

Finn said no more. He just hoped that the last day of term would be as uneventful as possible.

Chapter Three

The form tutor was called Mr Witty. He was a scruffy, thin Scotsman in his fifties and was present in body only, his mind being far, far away. Motivation levels hadn't only plummeted for the pupils. The teacher was leaning back on his chair with his feet on the desk and his nose nestled into a magazine, ignoring his class as best as he could. He hadn't even bothered to call the Register.

Henry was fidgety. They were sat on the high stools at one of the tall desks of Witty's science laboratory. He flicked the rubber gas taps on and off to pass the time and he looked up every time the door opened. Each time he was disappointed to see that Felicity Gower was nowhere to be seen.

Finn was focusing on his notebook. He had already started on the English Literature assignment they had been set for the holiday. He had approved. English was his favourite subject and they had been tasked with creating a short story. There was no brief. It was free reign, anything they wanted. He had already settled on a tale about a pack of small monsters that lived in the woods surrounding a fictional town. The story focused on the town's children, a motley crew of misfits who were employed secretly by the Vatican to fight the monsters and keep the community safe.

He was trying to think of a snazzy name for the monsters. It had to be something cool and droll, rolling off the tongue with ease. The words he had jotted down in the margin were wildly inadequate ... *wildlurks* ... *spludgerackets* ... *dark slugs* ... accidental, onomatopoeic monstrosities that could have counted as crimes against the English language.

No, I'm better than that. He scribbled the words out with his pen. Then Felicity Gower walked into the room. Her arrival was unmistakable by the sudden and urgent whack on his shoulder from Henry's shaking fist.

'This is it,' said Henry. He was pale and looked likely to vomit. He hopped down from his stool and took three deep breaths for courage. 'I'm heading for the trenches. Wish me luck, yeah?'

Finn wasn't overly interested and continued writing. 'You've not told me what you're going to do yet?' He glanced up. 'Care to share? Tell me you're just going to ask her to the cinema or something like that? She can say yes or no and not walk away thinking you're going to murder her one day.'

Henry didn't answer. He was in the zone, the exclusive realm of the poetic romantics. He reached into his shirt pocket and unfolded a scrappy piece of lined A4 paper.

Finn peeked over his shoulder for a look and then his eyes became wide with a sheer, intense horror. He would have been less terrified had a goblin burst out from Henry's stomach and scuttered across the room and embedded an axe in Mr Witty's face.

'Jesus Christ, Henry,' Finn said. He recognised the chorus of a song that belonged to a boyband. 'Are they lyrics? *Lyrics?* Why have you got lyrics written down? You're not going to sing?'

Finn covered his eyes with his hands. He wanted to be invisible. If Henry was indeed heading for the trenches he was tempted to lob in a grenade before he could do any damage. Surely the world would forgive and actually *thank him* for a friendly-fire death in return for not having to witness what was sure to be a horrid serenade that would haunt all witnesses for decades.

'Shut up, will you?' Henry snapped. 'I know what I'm doing. This is going to be epic. Saw it in a film, worked like a charm. Girls love this kinda rubbish. Makes you look sensitive and all that.'

'You really *don't* know what you're doing!' Finn grabbed Henry's wrist. He wanted to wrestle him to the ground and pin

18

him down with as many of the desks as he could carry. 'Come on, please *don't!* These stupid ideas never, *ever* work. You're gonna make yourself look like an absolute div.'

Finn saw it, a flashing vision of impending embarrassment in a glorious sweep of technicolour. It didn't matter that he had *nothing* to do with the conception of this ridiculous scheme. He would be guilty by association. He was *always* guilty by association. Luckily as Henry moved forward the voice of their lazy teacher was heard. The voice saved them all.

'Master Pringle,' Mr Witty called out in his severe Scottish drawl. He rarely said anything that didn't sound like the bark of a huge Celtic hound. Even his charm sounded threatening. He didn't bother to look up. 'As you are standing you can run a quick errand for me.'

The teacher used his foot to push a pile of envelopes to the edge of his cluttered desk. A couple of the envelopes toppled off but he didn't seem to care.

'Pick those up,' the teacher commanded, 'and take them to the bursar and be quick about it. Take your bag with you. Go straight to your first class once you're done.'

Henry made to protest but the teacher pre-empted his aversion to the task.

'Zip it all the way up, Pringle,' Mr Witty shouted. 'Pick it up, like you've *been* told, take your little grumbling bottom off down the hall to the bursar's office, like you've *been* told. The next sound I hear better be you scraping your disgustingly clumpy shoes across the floor and out of my classroom. I'm looking at pictures of a well-known celebrity without makeup so am far too busy to do it myself.'

Finn was relieved to see his best friend go. It was a shame but relief was an emotion that was occurring more and more these days. He quickly returned to his story, a great deal happier to be alone and was just about to finally settle on a more striking name for his pesky, elusive monsters when a voice interrupted him.

'What are you writing?' The voice belonged to Felicity Gower. Without knowing she had been saved from an ordeal, she had taken a seat behind him without him realising it.

Finn instinctively closed the pad as if she was a Russian spy and he had the codes to nuclear missiles written down on the pages. 'Er... its nothing.'

'Really?' said Felicity. 'You started your homework before we've even broken up? That's keen. Me, I'm a last minute-kinda-girl, ten o'clock the Sunday before we're due back, running around panicking. Always happens.'

Finn looked down at his book and opened it up once again. It was a mess. The writing wasn't particularly neat and it slanted dramatically to the right. He had made a conscious decision to write that way. He thought it looked more grown up, certainly more so than his previous efforts, but one of his teachers had advised him to revert back to a more childish style for exams due to the worry that the examiners would not be able to read the scruffier italic form.

'Well...' he paused nervously. He wasn't sure whether he should admit it or not. *Did it make him look like a nerd?* 'Yeah ... well ... it's my English homework. I haven't started any of the others though.'

'Can I see?' Felicity said. 'I could do with some inspiration. I don't even know where to start –'

'No!' Finn said. It was a bark and he was instantly worried he may have sounded rude. He changed to a friendlier tone. 'I just mean it's a bit embarrassing. You'll laugh at me.'

'I won't,' Felicity pressed, 'and embarrassing means it's probably interesting. And why would I laugh at you anyway? Come on, tell me, Finlay Carruthers. What are you writing about?'

Finn turned all the way around, half expecting to see a group of giggling girls mocking him but was happy to see that she was sat alone with her back to the table. She was facing him and dangling her legs off the stool.

Oh no, I'm staring! His mouth went dry and he lost the ability to speak. *Stop staring, you total tool. Stop it, you creepy, creepy man. Say something ... anything. Don't just stare.* He didn't know how long the staring had lasted. It felt like hours.

He had never really seen her up close and the surprise came from realising that she was a great deal more attractive than he had thought. Her hair was long, black and it hung in natural curls across her shoulders and in a fringe on her forehead. Her eyes were big and green. Her style was different to other girls. *Was it called a hippy style?* Most of the girls seemed intent to challenge the school's rules with skirts that were getting shorter, but Felicity didn't, hers being long, black, and pleated. Her coat was made from a mosaic of random patterned material. *No, it's not hippy, bohemian maybe? Actually, is bohemian even a real word?* In a few years he could see her rounding off her attire with a black hat, titled with a casual and effortless coolness, sitting in the evening sun in a muddy field, drinking cider to the sound of fiddles and banjos and watching a quirky music festival unfold.

'You're not much of a talker, are you?' she chuckled. She bit her lip and frowned. His staring had made her a little scared, a little unsure. 'Seriously, you can show me, can't you?' She dropped her voice to a deliberate whisper. It almost sounded flirtatious. 'I won't tell anyone else what it's about, I promise. Your secret's safe with me. And you know what, I'm sure it's really good.'

Finn tucked the notepad back into his blazer pocket. *Pleading over, decision made.* He really enjoyed writing and figured he was pretty good at it but he lacked the confidence for anyone beyond his teacher to see it. He was too insecure and even if they said it was brilliant and that he had potential to write for a living one day he wouldn't believe them and would assume they were just being nice.

'Ok,' Felicity didn't miss the discomfort and she gave up. 'You win, Finlay. I'll just carry on looking at a blank page and crying myself to sleep every night. Sorry. I'm just naturally nosey.'

Finn's cheeks reddened. Great, another thing he couldn't control. *What was happening?* 'You know that's not actually my name?' he said.

'Finn's short for Finlay, isn't it?'

'Only if your name's Finlay, I guess –'

'What's yours then?'

'Just Finn.'

The school bell rang loudly for five quick seconds and the class woke up, the pupils standing and rushing for the exit like seasoned prisoners suddenly presented with an open cell door to the outside world.

'You all have a great holiday and make sure you...' Such was Mr Witty's lack of passion for his well wishes that he didn't even bother to finish the sentence, allowing his words to be absorbed by the sound of scraping stools and moving school children.

'What are you doing tomorrow?' said Felicity. She stood and wrapped her bag onto her shoulder. 'I was wondering if you wanted to do something together?'

'Oh,' he said. The question threw him. *Oh* was the only word he could manage. It was accompanied by a subtle shriek, far too high pitched and very, very uncool. He tried to resist but his mouth rebelled and broke into a little smirk.

They moved towards the door together, hanging back to let the more eager pupils through so they could continue chatting.

'Now, come on,' said Felicity, shaking her head, 'don't you go saying *oh* like that. I don't remotely mean a date so you can get those silly little thoughts out of your head right now, Casanova. I'm *not* asking you out. When I say *something* I did actually have something in mind. I'm talking about you helping me out.'

They were in the corridor now which was chocked full of children and was loud. She had to raise her voice slightly to be heard.

'I'll explain,' she said. 'My foster parents are from the dark ages. I don't get to do anything by myself. They don't even want me going down the shops on my own. I call the dude Commandant. Anyhow I need to visit my Godmother tomorrow and they've agreed to let me go but I'm not allowed to go on my own. That's where you come in. I figured that as we live on the same street you could come with me. Though only if you wanted to, of course.'

Finn shrugged. *Play it cool.* Surely there was more to it than that, despite her protests. He was out of control. Normally he lacked confidence but suddenly he had all the arrogance in the

22

world. He wondered if he would even be walking a little bit cooler once she left him, with a little skip, like he was walking to the sound of hippy-hop music in his ears. *Would it be called a strut? Who cares! I'm just too cool.*

'Can't you take one of your other friends?' he asked her.

Felicity looked to her left and right and squinted as though the answer to that question were blindly obvious. 'These other friends are where exactly?'

Finn briefly debated in his mind whether saying yes would count as a betrayal to Henry.

'Ok,' he said, the debate not lasting very long, 'I'll knock on for you tomorrow, yeah?'

'Nine o'clock would be perfect,' Felicity rustled his hair and started to merge herself into the throng of pupils. But she turned and shouted out one last titbit that she felt was important. 'But don't forget, you're helping me out, Finlay. That's all it is.'

Finn watched her go and the arrogant smirk turned into a larger smile. Of course he wouldn't have been smiling at all had he realised that Jordan Tremlett and his friends were a few yards away, leaning against the lockers. They had overheard the whole thing.

He was thinking about what elaborate lie he would tell Henry when the rash beneath his shirt began to throb urgently. *Not now*, he urged. He turned to look up the hallway, hoping he could make it somewhere private before the pain hit. But a strong pair of hands gripped his shoulders and tried to spin him around. Someone shouted his name. There were other shouts too but he couldn't make out what was being said. He lost his footing and started to fall. The world went dark.

23

Chapter
Four

Finn opened his eyes slowly. His vision was blurry. He was lying on his back and looking directly up at a ceiling with various mounds of wet tissue paper stuck rigidly to the plasterwork. Where the ceiling met the wall there were thick stains of green and black mildew. The air smelt of something rotten and stale.

He sat up and somehow resisted a strong urge to throw up. The effort of sitting had proved far more difficult than he had anticipated. His head started to spin in complaint and when the spinning decided to ease he tried to establish exactly where he was.

It was a toilet, somehow. Fortunately the sight of the stained urinals to his left confirmed that it was a *boy's* toilet. That was one blessing, at least. He recognised the place. The toilets were in the old sports hall, the part of the school that was waiting to be demolished. That of course made little sense and lead to more questions than answers. Quite how he had managed to get over the huge metal fence and the locked gate was something he would think about later.

Finn touched his chest, frisking himself. He could feel sweaty bare skin against his fingertips, despite the toilet having no heating and being extremely cold. There was a brute pang of panic. He was shirtless. *Topless at school is never going to end well.*

He looked in front of him and saw his white school shirt in a crumpled, damp heap on the floor beneath the nearest wash basin.

'Am I invisible or something?' said a voice from behind him.

The voice startled him and it made him jump but Finn turned to see that Henry was in the room with him. His friend was resting on his knees and had a look on his face that suggested he was unsure whether to be concerned or start making jokes. He was carrying Finn's jacket and school bag.

Henry started to speak again but the words were drowned out by a high pitched frequency that spontaneously burst to life in Finn's ears. Finn smashed his fist into the side of his head, a little harder than he had intended but it had little effect. His next thump was gentler and it proved more effective. His hearing slowly returned and the high pitched whine faded into the background.

'All I can say,' Henry said, 'is that you, right this moment, look like a proper fruit loop! What the hell just happened?'

Finn shrugged. He had to get himself up. He suddenly remembered the rash and he really didn't want Henry to see it. He used his hands to cover the area up as best as he could and bolted to his feet. He staggered uneasily for the first few steps like a drunk but managed to make it unaided to the washbasin. He scooped the sodden shirt from the ground and put it back on. He cringed at the feel of the damp fabric against his skin.

He bent down and twisted the tap. It spluttered and complained from a year of underuse, omitted an unpleasant black fluid but then the water ran clear and clean. The water had an unpleasant smell but he nevertheless scooped a handful of it onto his face and looked at his haggard reflection in the cracked mirror. The boy that stared back looked like he had just gone ten rounds with an ultimate fighting champion.

Henry joined him at the basin and pointed instantly to the area on Finn's body that he had been attempting to conceal. 'We can pretend that I didn't see it, if you want,' he said curiously, 'or you can let me ask what it is? It looked proper sore. Why haven't you mentioned it?'

'Am I supposed to tell you every time I get a spot?' Finn said.

'No, but that's not exactly a spot —'

Finn brazenly changed the subject. 'How did you know I was in here?'

'I followed you. Don't you remember? I was calling after you. You ran like the clappers.'

Finn had no idea what he was talking about. He squinted and tried to piece it back together but he couldn't recall anything after his magical conversation with Felicity. *I left the classroom - I watched her go - someone called my name -*

And there it was, *the memory*, sat in a dark corner of his brain and minding its own business. But now he remembered. The rash had started hurting again. There had been agony and then the lights had gone out. That part was new. It was the first time he had fainted.

'I've seen that look before,' said Henry. 'You look like that when you're trying to do trigonometry –'

'Who grabbed me?' Finn asked.

'I was coming back from the office,' Henry explained. 'Tremlett had you up against the lockers. Only saw it from a distance though. He said something to you, you punched his hands away. I think you blacked out. Tremlett didn't know what to do. You just dropped. Then you shot back up a couple of seconds later, dropped your coat and bag and ran off like a madman.'

Finn closed his eyes and took a deep breath. 'Great, not sure I'll be living this one down any time soon.'

Henry pulled a face. 'What was the alternative, fight the school thug and lose? Anyway, my Mum reckons it's the bigger man who walks away.'

There was a short silence as Finn fastened the last buttons of his shirt. He tried to avoid eye contact with Henry. He could sense what was coming.

'So what is that other thing then?' Henry said. 'I mean that thing on your side? It looked a bit like a tattoo.'

'A tattoo?' Finn said. He let out a snort of derision at the suggestion. It was absurd. 'Of course it's *not* a tattoo, you plank. How exactly did you think I would actually get a tattoo, Henry? I'm fifteen and I look fifteen.'

'Are you dying?'

'Yep, because that's the only other explanation of course, I've either got a tattoo or I'm dying. It couldn't possibly be anything else, hey? Honestly, if we just –'

26

A resurgence of unexpected pain stopped him short. Finn screamed violently and he grabbed the taps to steady his body. It was as if his very ribs were pulsating. He took an urgent step backwards and instinctively he lifted up his shirt and with his other hand he flipped the tap back on and splashed water onto the rash. Something else was new. The rash was glowing bright red, a furious and burning red like the hottest of irons. The pain kept on coming and the water did nothing to pacify it.

'Oh my God!' Henry cried. He was heading for the door. 'I'll go now and get –'

'Wait!'

The pain disappeared, so quickly that it was as if it had never even been there in the first place. The angry red glow of the rash subsided, returning to its normal state of small pink blisters. There was no hiding it this time. They both looked dumbstruck at the unusual shape of the rash.

'Why was it glowing?' Henry asked.

'I don't know. That's the first time it's ever done that.'

'Can I touch it?' said Henry. He was already reaching forward with his finger extended.

'No, you bloody well can't touch it!' Finn punched his finger away. 'What a gay thing to say!'

'It just looks so angry and painful! What *is* it?'

'Henry,' Finn said strongly, 'I've already told you, I don't know. Don't tell anyone about this, yeah?'

Henry nodded. The secret was safe.

'I'm going to go home, I think,' Finn said. He quickly tucked his shirt back in for the second time in as many minutes. But he was cautious, fearing another outburst of pain. 'Think I'll skip games. You shouldn't play rugby in the snow anyway. I'll just say I'm ill and sneak out at lunchtime.'

'I'll come with you,' Henry said. He liked the sound of that plan. 'I'll just forge my mum's handwriting in my organiser and say I've got the dentist or something.'

Henry handed Finn his coat and bag and they walked out of the toilet together. The daylight was bright and Finn had to shield his eyes with a flattened hand. Henry pushed a corner of the metal fence aside so they could get out of the cordoned-off site.

As they walked Finn started to worry about a host of things. There was his health for one and that probably should have been his only concern. But there was also the business the one eyed man had with his father. There was the fact that his mum hadn't been home in days. But the thing that troubled him the most was the thought of looking awful when meeting Felicity Gower. Even worse, what if he fainted whilst he was with her? Everything else seemed to pale into insignificance. He had never had a girl show him any sort of interest and it was all he could think about.

'I'll probably get a big spot on the tip of my nose overnight,' Finn said out loud, by accident.

'What's that?' Henry said.

'Nothing,' Finn answered.

Chapter Five

Agatha Carruthers had an important image to project. It was essential to appear professional, calm, and in complete control of her emotions. She had dressed to support this goal with an outfit that was unlikely to stand out, a smart black trouser suit, white blouse, long black coat, and sensible black shoes with a small heel. Her hair was tied up. Little make up. No jewellery. She stood perfectly upright like a soldier at attention. Her expression was cold and professional. It was perfect.

Inside a different tale was unfolding. To her disappointment she couldn't help but be scared, terrified actually, and her heart beat with such a mad and thunderous intensity that she half expected to see it burst through her ribs and deposit itself on the frozen ground in front of her.

The aeroplane had been sitting on the modest runway for what felt like an eternity. It was a cruel spot in which to wait. Midday afforded little respite against the weather and a strong wind roared in across the whiteness of the open airfield, making an already challenging temperature that much more numbing for the limbs. The airport staff had long since been and gone and had attached the external staircase to the fuselage. They had been under strict instructions not to unload the luggage and had instead retired to a little hut nearby for a warming cup of tea.

Agatha's eyes had been focused on the plane the moment it had come to its standstill. Her car was parked behind her and she was ready to move. But there were no signs of movement from the cockpit or anywhere else for that matter. The plane just sat there, not overly expensive, silent.

She couldn't help but speculate. She had certainly travelled in more luxury and style in the few short years she had been jet-setting across the globe and had never landed in such a tiny, depressing airfield. Were the investments failing? Could it be possible that the funding was starting to dry up? No, she shook such thoughts off. Such a notion was absurd.

Agatha finally saw a flash of movement in the cockpit. A strong hiss of escaping air pressure followed and the cabin door opened, creaking slowly upwards.

Six figures, five men and one woman, exited the aircraft swiftly. They moved down the metal staircase with their hand luggage and made their way directly towards her. They were dressed in casual clothing, simple hooded fleeces, black jackets, combat trousers, and dark glasses. They looked like office workers dressing down for a charity day in the wilderness, ill at ease at their excursion away from the usual comfort of their desks.

These were however far from office workers. No, Sir. Office workers were less dangerous. One of them Agatha recognised immediately and another also stood out, a colossal beast that loitered at the back and was so tall that he towered easily above the rest. He had a shaved head and was the most muscular and fearsome looking man that she had ever seen.

The small man she knew led the way, the others funnelling in behind him like dutiful ducks following their mother. They stopped and fanned out, forming a semicircle in front of her. It was the small man who spoke to her first.

'Hello, Agatha,' He said her name with a solitary, unfriendly nod.

'Hello, Theo,' Agatha said back coldly.

Theo smiled. 'Interesting you chose to keep your Christian name. Surname's an interesting choice. Carruthers. Did find myself wondering where that came from.'

She looked at him closely. For most part Theo hadn't changed in the sixteen years since she had last seen him. Her uncle would have been in his fifties somewhere now, perhaps fifty five, but he was still undeniably the little wretch that he had always been. His red hair had thinned a touch and only existed now in overgrown tufts on the sides and his waistline had thickened.

Rumpelstiltskin she had called him when she was a child, a name that she had learnt quickly to whisper so as to not incur his considerable wrath.

One thing that was unmistakeably different was that his left hand was missing at the wrist. The artificial limb that replaced it was stiff and covered with a black glove.

'The years have been kinder to you than they have to me,' Theo said, his voice nasally and annoying. He tapped his fake hand. 'Memento, New Zealand, very much my own fault. Never turn your back on a subject, rule number one, an ever present reminder to be more diligent in my future pursuits.'

He looked her up and down. His expression dripped with distaste as if he had just eaten something incredibly sour that had displeased his palate.

'You look well,' Theo said. 'Better than I expected. Slept well all these years, have you? No demons to keep you up at night? If only all of us could say the same.'

Agatha wasn't going to play his game and she wouldn't allow his taunts to get to her. The kids in the school playgrounds had it right. Sticks and stones had all the power. Names and thinly veiled insults would never hurt her.

Theo looked past her to the vehicle that she had arrived in. It was a black *people carrier*, seven seats, a family car. 'Are we to honour our obligation to the school car pool,' he said, 'before we get down to business?' He started to laugh and the others followed his lead and joined in.

'You don't need to look so worried, Uncle,' said Agatha sharply. 'I've got you a booster seat.'

Theo smirked slyly. His fishing had bought forth his first bite of the day.

'It's the only vehicle I have right now,' Agatha explained bluntly, angry with herself that she had let her uncle get to her. 'It'll carry all of us. I've hired four more cars that you'll find more suitable. We pick them up on the way and one of you can come back for the equipment.'

Deciding that there was no more to say, Theo clicked his fingers and his female assistant passed a small laptop forward.

'Your father wishes to speak to you in private before we begin,' he said.

Agatha took the laptop and headed straight to the car, sliding into the driver's seat and slamming the door shut. She placed the small computer on the dashboard and opened up the screen. She punched the enter key to bring it to life and as the blackness gave way to colour another familiar face awaited her.

'Hello, Father,' she said, the salutation quiet. She had sounded more nervous than she had intended. But then her father was quite the different proposition to Theo.

Her father had also changed little. He still had the stern, almost evil face and the small black eyes that reminded her of a shark. The comparison was apt. He was a predator. His appearance remained impeccable and he was dressed in a crisp grey suit. His hair was still white and long and he was freshly shaven. He was thinner in the face but did not appear a day older than when she had left him. A full bookcase was beyond his shoulders, packed with thick, leather bound volumes and she debated which part of the world he was currently sat in.

'You have grown to look like your mother,' he said. 'This displeases me.'

Agatha said nothing. She could tell from the way he was looking at her that he had chosen this moment to make a decision on her punishment and more importantly as to whether he trusted her. She could only wait for his judgement.

'You have six operatives,' he said, his judgement apparently made and moving directly to business. No tearful family reunions here. 'Another six will join you tomorrow from Cape Town, an additional four from Prague once mobilised, four more from Copenhagen. I'll attempt to secure further resources as quickly as I can. You will lead the teams −'

'I will lead them?' Agatha hadn't intended to interrupt but she wasn't sure she had heard him correctly. 'Father, I haven't been in the field for −'

'You *will* lead them, Agatha,' her father snapped. 'I see your prolonged absence hasn't improved your obedience! That's another thing that displeases me.'

32

'I meant no disrespect,' Agatha said. A part of her was sceptical and sensed a trap. 'It was just unexpected. I didn't expect any leniency. I expected punishment.'

Her father considered that for a moment and then answered curtly. 'Do you feel it would be suitable to be punished right now, considering the challenges that are in front of us?'

'I would expect something, yes.'

Her father was quiet for a time. Then he shook his head. 'Agatha,' he said, 'in our world we're conditioned to discard natural human emotions. Since I was a boy there's always been an unpopular argument against the approach. It asks whether it's realistic that a man or woman can completely discard all the emotions that make them human in the first place? Can we even function to our full capability without our humanity?'

Outside the others were moving. Evidently Theo was not envisaging the reconciliation taking much time and his colleagues had started to remove their ample baggage from the plane and were stacking bags and boxes on the ground.

Her father paused and licked his lips, almost like a wolf surveying a rotting carcass. 'I have no illusions of what *will* and *will not* hurt you,' he said, 'even if you try and make it look like you don't care. I know what will cause you genuine pain. When this is over, if you do your duty correctly, that will be an ample punishment for you. I will say this though. Don't let me down again, Agatha. There are many things in this world that are thicker than blood.'

With that he signed off abruptly, seemingly doing so without pressing a button and the screen went dark once more.

Agatha closed the computer and relaxed in the seat. It felt like the first time she had been able to truly breathe in over an hour. Beads of sweat were pressing against her blouse and a weak part of her wanted to burst into tears.

The passenger door opened and Theo slid in beside her. He reached across and replaced the laptop into a bag that he had bought with him. 'He informed you that you will be leading the teams, I assume?' he said. 'He hasn't changed his mind about that?'

Agatha nodded. She didn't expect her uncle would be particularly pleased about the plan.

'You and I need a moment,' Theo suggested.

'We don't need a moment –'

'Believe me,' Theo said, flashing a wicked smile, 'when I say I only wish that we're true. We have to work together so you need to understand my view. I support your father's decision, as is my duty, but I don't remotely agree with it. *You* are not worth protecting. Even as a small child you had far too high an opinion of yourself. You had qualities too, I can't say you didn't, but you were over confident, disrespectful, and rash.'

'Preaching should be saved for a pulpit,' Agatha said, 'and if you don't have a point then you should probably stay quiet.'

'They saw great things for you,' Theo said. He had no intention of staying quiet. 'Then we had Mendoza. They saw that operation as justifying their faith. I didn't. You see what I think about your betrayal doesn't really matter. What I think about your actions in Mendoza does. That operation was messy, violent, and heavy handed. In fact it was reckless. And it cost innocent lives.'

'Since when are you concerned with the loss of innocent lives?'

'Innocent deaths bring with them unwanted attention,' said Theo.

'I'm in charge,' Agatha reminded him, 'which means you don't question my methods.'

'And I won't,' Theo said, 'from here on in at least. But you do need to understand that The Guild has changed. Today is about calculation and quantification. Your betrayal damaged your father. You see he always knew where you were. He refused to have you eliminated, you and that other traitor. He lost all the credibility he spent so many years building. And I rest all of that blame at your feet.'

Agatha stared out through the windscreen at the frozen airfield. For her emotions she tried to apply a poker face. A lot of what her uncle had said she had expected, the hostility and the criticism, all acceptable, but the revelation that they had known where she was the whole time was a big shock and it sent a sickening shiver up her spine.

'Are you finished?' she asked.

'I'm finished.'

Theo reached across suddenly, almost as if he was going to strike her, but instead he thumped his hand down hard onto the car horn on the steering wheel. A few moments later the back doors of the vehicle opened and slammed and the vehicle was quickly full of people. The larger man was the only one who didn't enter. He remained outside, finishing the organisation of the equipment from the plane.

'Do you have any questions for me?' Theo said as if he had just finished a job interview.

'Only one,' Agatha said. 'Father said we would have sixteen operatives. That's heavy handed for a single subject. Why so many?'

'It's not one subject but three,' Theo answered. He reached into his bag and tossed over a thick manila envelope. 'Two more are in the area. No specific files but their names crop up in other dispatches. One American, Wyatt Eagan, one Frenchman, Gilliam Bèranger, heavy-weights, classical vintage, we believe. Not the kind of targets that come out of the woodwork very often. We were mobilised so quickly because they landed in England two days ago and we were already tracking them.'

Agatha frowned. She opened the folder and gazed at the two men captured in a variety of photos. The photos were blurry and of little help. She didn't recognise either of them. 'Are they Guardians?' she said.

'Highly unlikely,' Theo shook his head. 'Guardian's don't travel in twos. These men travelled separately, met in Kiev, organised by a third party who so far remains unidentified. That's why you have sixteen operatives. They're highly dangerous and will be a far bigger handful than the subjects you secured in Mendoza.'

Agatha shot her uncle a glare and was tempted to bite for a second time. She controlled herself. The mention of Mendoza did affect her, she couldn't deny it. She hadn't thought about the

Argentinian operation for years and had tried hard to block out the memory. The past was the past and she more than anyone else understood the sheer futility of nostalgia. The events in Mendoza may offer her some credibility in the days ahead but right now it had no use.

'That's enough talk, Theo,' Agatha twisted the key in the ignition. The engine roared to life and she started to drive across the airfield. 'I've arranged a temporary H.Q for us and we'll unload there and talk strategy. The aim is to strike tomorrow, once we have an opportunity to gather real intelligence. We compile intelligence ourselves. I don't want any surprises.'

'And your beloved husband?' Theo asked. 'Can we expect any surprises from him?'

'Most certainly,' Agatha admitted. 'You know as well as I do how his mind works.'

'And your son's name?' Theo said. 'You've never said.'

'He is *the subject*, not my son,' Agatha corrected him. She guided the car towards the gates of the airport. The open road awaited them. 'But if you feel you need it, his name is Finn.'

Chapter Six

Jordan Tremlett swept his right leg and the rugby ball sailed towards the posts. His aim – as it had been for most of the lesson – was woeful and wayward and the ball missed its target and landed with an awkward and uneven bounce. It disappeared into the frozen thickets at the back of the playing field.

The lesson had all but finished and now the boys were just milling around, kitted out in shorts and the school colours of a blue shirt with a yellow stripe across the chest. Two boys were fighting gladiator style with the soft rugby pads off the side of the pitch. A dozen or so of the others, *the so called nerds*, were stood in a tight circle and shivering in the cold. The rest were playing a short impromptu game of touch rugby with the one tatty ball that they had been allowed to use, although there was no great structure to the chaotic game. The snow was too deep and the boys could only run a few yards before the effort became too much.

Jordan and his two closest friends, Dean and Oggie, had commandeered the rest of the rugby balls to practice conversions and no one else was allowed to use them. Mr Edmund, the games teacher, had disappeared to get a much needed flask of coffee and the other pupils would pretty much do whatever Jordan Tremlett told them to.

Jordan waited for Oggie to place another ball in front of him. They had smoothed out a circle of snow, trampling it down to make things easier. He attempted a conversion again. This tired effort fared even worse than the efforts that had gone before it, sweeping wide to the left and with not enough legs to even make it to the posts. The ball whistled back to earth and hit an unlucky boy hard on the back. The poor boy grunted in pain. Everyone laughed. Oggie turned back and he too was sniggering.

'You've only got four over,' Dean said unhelpfully from behind them. He was shaking his head. 'My Nan could kick better. She died four years ago.'

Oggie tossed Jordan another ball. 'You're not having a good day, are you?'

Jordan flushed red with anger. He really *wasn't* having a good day and his mood was festering and getting worse by the minute. Just how had it all happened in the hallway? He didn't even know who Felicity *What's-Her-Face* was or where the rumour had even come from. Yes, when he heard the rumour he should have denied it there and then, killing it before it could grow. But the truth was the delectable Jade Fitz-Simmons from the year above was spurning his advances and he wanted to make her jealous. He had figured that leaving the rumour out there could end up being helpful.

Quite how it had all backfired so dramatically and almost turned into a fight was anyone's guess. The planets must have aligned. They had witnessed some sort of uncomfortable flirting, Oggie and Dean were goading, people were watching, and there was a reputation to uphold. And then the little moron, Finn was his name, had been stupid enough to have slapped his hands away, pretending to faint and then running off, making Jordan look like a fool. As such he would have to deal with the humiliation at the next opportunity.

He was wondering what *dealing with it* would look like when something caught his attention in the distance. Two men were walking across the playing field and heading towards them. For a moment he felt his stomach drop, thinking that this was the Headmaster accompanying Mr Edmund, probably to reprimand him for the incident, but as the men came closer he saw that he didn't recognise either of them.

The approaching men split up, one man striding off down the field with purpose towards the boys playing touch rugby. When he got there he simply strolled into the middle of the melee, rudely interrupting the game, and grabbed each child by the shoulders. He surveyed their faces carefully before moving on to the next. On more than one occasion he physically picked a boy up, laboured for a while whilst he studied the face more closely and then not seeing what he wanted tossed them away as if they were little more than ragdolls.

The second man stopped and stood still a little distance away from Jordan, Dean, and Oggie. He wasn't facing them and was watching his companion going about his business.

Jordan was curious. The man closest to them was dressed scruffily. His clothes were dirty and he had long black hair. He didn't work at the school. He could have been a member of the public but that was unlikely as there was a hefty iron fence around the entire perimeter so that strangers couldn't get access.

'Hey,' Jordan shouted loudly so that the man could hear him. More importantly, he wanted everyone else to hear too. It was an opportunity to salvage his reputation. Everyone loved a cheeky student *mouthing off* to an adult. 'Who the hell are you?'

The stranger didn't show any desire to answer. He didn't even twitch.

Jordan looked to his two friends. They both smiled and shook their heads.

The other man was now coming towards them too. He was upon them quickly and he moved through Dean and Oggie first, grabbing their faces as he had done with the others. He pushed them aside with a gruff sigh. Then it was Jordan's turn.

'Get off me!' Jordan complained as the man gripped his chin. They were eyeball to eyeball.

This man was much taller than his friend. He was thin and his cheek bones prominent, as if the skin on his face was stretched too tightly. He was just as scruffy, with a thick grey beard and short grey, curly hair. His eyes were bright blue.

'Are we a no?' the dark haired man nearby asked. He was American.

The tall man shook his head. The answer was indeed no. He slapped Jordan on the cheek. With the random inspection finished the two men walked towards one another and formed a tight huddle, discussing something that the boys couldn't hear.

Jordan again looked to Dean and Oggie and they nodded in the men's direction, seemingly urging him to say something. Today seemed to be the day for goading.

'Hey,' Jordan said once more, even louder this time. 'I was talking to you. What are you guys doing here? Are you deaf?'

The American suddenly snapped around. '*What* did you just say to me?'

There was a long, eerie silence as the question settled in the cold air like a threat.

The tall man omitted a cruel and wicked laugh.

Jordan glanced up the field and gulped. Everyone was watching him, just as he had wanted but it was the second time today that he had ended up the centre of attention for the wrong reasons. There was an aura about these two men that had commanded interest, a sense of the uncomfortable, a sense of the dangerous. The two boys who had been fighting with the pads dropped them and ran away towards the school building like cowards.

'I thought you had something to say?' said the American. 'Where's your voice gone, boy?'

You do have to say something, Jordan. You can't lose face again. But no words formed. His mouth went dry and Jordan didn't say a thing.

'Seeing as you're so keen to talk,' the American said, stepping towards them, 'answer me a question. We're looking for someone. His name is Finn. You know him? He isn't here. That much *we* know. You will tell me where I can find him?'

'Finn Carruthers?' Oggie said without thinking.

'Carruthers?' The American's eyes became wide with curiosity. 'Yes, that's it, Carruthers. Where is he?' He stopped inches away from the boys.

'He's not here,' Dean said, slowly, unsure, less brave now that the man was so close.

'Where can we find him?' The American pressed. He grabbed Dean by the collar of his rugby shirt.

'I don't know!' Dean said. He was wriggling, trying to break free.

The tall man coughed to get his companions attention. When he had it he tapped a watch on his wrist. Time was getting on. Their window was closing. The American held up his hand with a look of frustration but acknowledgment. He let go of Dean's shirt.

From the heart of the school a bell rung, signifying the end of the lesson. The pupils on the school field started to depart, some of them were running, keen to report the strange occurrence to the teachers. Only Jordan, Dean, Oggie, and the two strangers remained. The men however had their *name* and they turned on their heels and they too started to walk away.

Jordan knew he hadn't done enough and that his reputation remained in tatters. He burst forward and with the ball in his hands he aimed a drop kick at the departing men. At this range he would at least hit one of them. And the best bit was he was a child and they were adults. There was nothing they or anyone else could do about it. *That'll show em! They'll be talking about this for months –*

The tall man turned and caught the ball between his fingers, almost casually. He smiled and then squeezed the ball with the minimum of effort and it exploded with a puff of air and torn leather.

'Gilliam,' the American cried out, 'no –'

The boys didn't have a chance to react. The tall man darted forward and aimed a thunderous punch into Jordan's chest. The intensity of the impact sent Jordan Tremlett soaring into the chilled air, high and far and as if he was made of nothing more than feathers. As he flew above the top of the rugby posts and landed with a heavy crunch in the thickets, he couldn't help wondering, even in the drama and fear of the moment, how what the man had just done to him was even humanly possible.

Chapter Seven

Finn ate dinner shortly after eight pm, later than usual, and he was starving. He sat opposite his father at the black granite of the kitchen island, the centrepiece of the room, a variety of cooking utensils hanging from a customised rack above their heads. The kitchen was lit in a way that was dark and intimate, the only illumination coming from the spotlights that had been installed beneath the cupboards.

An awkward silence was present in the room, a silence that emanated from Peter Carruthers. Finn had told him all about the incident earlier at school and his father had barely seemed to listen.

Peter wasn't himself. He had picked up an Indian takeaway on his way home from work but he didn't have much of an appetite. He focused only on the spherical shape of his plate, never looking up, picking through the rice and sauce with his fork without putting any of it into his mouth. He was lost in a dark wilderness that existed only in the privacy of his mind, a wilderness populated with an array of thoughts and concerns that troubled him greatly but that he would not share.

Finn finished the food on both their plates and with the chore of dinner complete Peter stood, grabbing a bottle of wine from the door of the fridge and a glass from a cupboard next to the sink. He headed for the kitchen door, no contemplation of saying a word, let alone a goodbye.

'Dad,' Finn said nervously. His father stopped in the doorway. 'Are you ok?'

Peter answered without turning around. 'I'm ok, Finn, I'm just really tired.'

Finn took a deep breath. He had wanted to ask a question for quite some time and he asked it now. 'Are you and Mum getting a divorce?' he said.

Peter turned. He looked at his son deeply. His face was unsure, flexing into something that could have been a smile or a wince. His eyes were red and moist with tears. 'Why would you think something like that?'

'Why *wouldn't* I think something like that?' Finn said. Now he had asked it, he was instantly braver. 'It's been two weeks. She's not here, Dad, and when she was she barely said a word to either of us.'

'You know your mother gets like that sometimes –'

'This was different. And you look like you've barely slept. I've just put two and two together.'

'And you've come up with fifty six?'

'Sometimes fifty six is the right answer though, isn't it?'

Peter stepped back into the heart of the room and he bent down and kissed his son on the forehead. 'I'm not sure when you got so grown up,' he said. He placed his hands on Finn's shoulders and titled his sons head up so they were eye to eye. 'Your mother loves you, Finn, and she'll remember that, one day.' He walked back to the door. 'I'm going to my office. I've got some work to finish. It's late enough. You should get yourself off to bed.'

Finn checked out the kitchen clock on the wall. It wasn't even nine. He was tempted to follow his father and probe a bit deeper but Peter was already gone. The sound of his office door slamming shut was heard shortly after. As such he could only take himself up to his room, trying to decipher what the last comment had meant. *Your Mother loves you Finn. And she'll remember that one day.* Why did he say that? They hadn't been talking about Finn's relationship with her.

Once inside the bedroom he flicked on a lamp, put on a CD and threw himself face first onto the bed. The mattress was tired and old and the springs cursed and moaned beneath his weight. He wasn't in the mood to sleep and he lay there with his eyes closed. He did this sometimes, taking time to think when he had lots to think about. He spent time thinking about his parents divorcing. It was a strange notion. His parents had always been odd, he had been aware of that from a young age, but despite their oddities they had worked well together. He wasn't sure how they would handle it. Both of their own parents were dead. There were no brothers, no sisters, no aunts, uncles or cousins. There were no real friends. Where would they go?

He only stirred when he realised he needed the toilet. He checked his mobile phone on the way out, no messages, and he was surprised when the display told him it was one o'clock in the morning. It hadn't seemed like he had been led there that long. His mouth was parched dry and the CD had expended its playlist long ago and fallen silent.

He made it to the bathroom and emptied his bladder, humming a tune as he did so, and when he was finished he headed downstairs to fetch a glass of water. He felt sluggish and moved like a zombie, yawning every few seconds. He was already looking forward to heading back to bed and would definitely try to sleep this time.

Finn stopped at the bottom of the staircase. There was an orange light coming from beneath the door to his father's study. His father was still up.

He moved to the door and pushed his ear up against the wood. No sounds from inside. He knocked gently, two sharp raps, no answer. He didn't know why but he was worried. His father had been drinking a lot more lately and he had never been a drinker.

Finn carefully pushed the door open.

Peter Carruthers was asleep at his desk, his face wrapped up comfortably in the arms that were crossed beneath him. His briefcase from work was open on the floor and the surface of his desk was smothered in a mass array of papers, books, and notepads. Three empty wine bottles were nearby on a side table.

Finn stepped quietly into the room, one cautious step at a time, making sure the floorboards didn't creak. The study was out of bounds and this was a new and exciting frontier upon which to explore. He would wake his father, say something mature and caring, like it was maybe time he went to bed. He

44

could get him some water and some aspirin. If it felt right, he could place an understanding, supportive hand on his back. *And the award for son of the year goes to –*

He stopped behind his father and peered over his sleeping shoulders. He reached forward, ready to provide a gentle nudge. He didn't want him to wake with a jolt. The sight of the book stopped him. The clutter seemed to have been strategically placed around one book in particular, the nucleus of his work, the pages resting open. The book was large and very old, the pages stained brown and covered in a thin protective plastic that must have been keeping the material safe. It wasn't an item Finn had ever seen before. They had two book cases in the living room. They were full of titles, fiction and non-fiction, but this book had never graced those shelves.

He leaned in closer and tried to read some of the text but the writing was unusual and foreign. He had dabbled in a bit of French, Spanish, and German throughout school, never mastering any of them but he was certain that it wasn't written in any of those languages.

He pulled a face. *How strange.* His father had a notepad next to him and inside he had been taking diligent notes.

Then Finn saw it, a symbol in the middle of the writing that caught his eye and absorbed the breath from his lungs. His father had copied the symbol onto his notepad from the open book. Inexplicably the symbol resembled the rash on his body, a long cross with a circular head. No, it was more than a resemblance. It was *identical.* Next to it there was printed in English a single word that his father had translated. The word was Obsidian.

Finn almost said the word out loud without thinking. *Obsidian.* He had come across the word in geography a few times in the past. Obsidian was a rock, he was relatively confident about that, but why Peter Carruthers had been translating details about rocks was anyone's guess. His interest piqued, he looked closely at the old book and ran his finger down the page, grazing the plastic. The symbol appeared twice more on each page but the second drawing was actually slightly different.

With the first symbol the circle was complete. On the second the circle was broken.

A phone rang from his father's briefcase. The desk vibrated and some of the papers moved, toppling off the surface. Peter Carruthers coughed, stirred, and started to raise his head with a drunken groan.

Finn almost yelped in shock. He forgot all about fetching his water and ran upstairs as fast as he could. He took the steps three at a time and disappeared into his room, gently shutting the door and diving into bed. He wrapped the covers over his head.

He was expecting to hear his father's approaching footsteps on the staircase but there were no sounds from anywhere else in the house. The phone was no longer ringing. It had been answered. *Could this week get any weirder*, thought Finn. He couldn't think of a tangible explanation for why his father was now taking an interest in the rash and why he would look for answers in such a place.

The front door suddenly slammed and the noise echoed up the stairs. For a second Finn wondered whether it was his mother coming home. He stepped from his bed once more, moving to the window and looking out, expecting to see her car on the drive but instead he saw his father, striding up the path and heading up the road on foot.

Fed up, Finn almost swore and decided there and then not to give this nonsense any more thought. He had endured quite enough *weird* for one day. He needed sleep, lots of it, as he had to look his best for his meeting with Felicity in the morning.

How many alarms should I set? He couldn't decide. *I don't want to sleep through them but I don't want to be lame and feel like I'm too keen.* After a short deliberation he set twenty five different alarms on his phone, spacing them out five minutes apart and got himself off to sleep.

His dream proved to be vivid and he would remember it in the morning. He dreamt of a world in ruins and he walked amongst a host of tall buildings that were crumbling and empty. It was bitingly cold but instead of snowflakes, small books fell from the sky. The books were open as they drifted from the heavens and as they struck the earth hard some stayed in one piece but others slammed shut and disintegrated into ashes.

Finn moved through the buildings without his feet touching the ground, gliding like an angel. He gathered up the surviving books one at a time for a reason he wasn't sure of. He stacked them on top of one another in his arms and very quickly the number was so great that the stack disappeared out of sight, up into the grey clouds, clouds that were crackling with lightning.

When the weight became too much the buildings around him exploded and the column of books swayed dangerously, starting to topple. The column smashed down and spread out for miles into the distance, through a set of rolling hills, piercing the horizon.

Finn realised then that a man was standing in front of him that he hadn't noticed. He couldn't remember the man's name. He had one eye and he started to shout a single word over and over again, waving a wooden cane over his head. At each shout, his face shuddered and started breaking off in big chunks of dust and dirt until he was nothing. The word he shouted was Obsidian.

Chapter Eight

Peter Carruthers moved swiftly along the icy pavements of Waverley Avenue. The street was on the western outskirts of Willowbrook, sixteen modern houses with trademark gables of black and white that provided their fake Tudor extravagance. The residences sat behind identical rectangles of manicured grass and tall trees lined each side of the road.

Everything appeared to be normal, nothing out of the ordinary. The snow fell heavily and settled in thick layers atop the parked cars. The layers were undisturbed, perfectly smooth blankets, showing that no one had come or gone for quite some time. The houses were dark and the world asleep, dreaming and blissfully unaware of any business a man might have outdoors at such an ungodly hour.

In his rush Peter had picked an unsuitable coat from the peg in the hallway, a painfully thin anorak designed to keep out the rain instead of the cold. He was shivering and his bottom lip trembled but there was little point in returning home for a quick exchange. Besides, he had a strong suspicion he wouldn't be outdoors for long anyway. And he had remembered the briefcase. That was the most important thing of all.

He slipped down the narrow alleyway that sat between two houses at the end of the road. The alleyway led to a small courtyard and four modest garages. The courtyard had a single street light and the area was far darker and secluded than the main road. The yellow glow of the light flickered energetically, filtered by the constant sweep of the falling flakes. The drives were clear, the cars tucked up snugly inside. A low wall marked out the perimeter of the drives and sitting on the wall a man was waiting.

Peter stopped a few yards in front of the seated man. He wouldn't get too close. He could see no footprints. It was as if the man had drifted down on the wind, an angel from heaven, determined not to disturb the detail of a world in which he didn't belong.

The man stood up from the wall slowly. He coughed twice, linked his hands behind his back but showed no signs of doing anything else. He was of medium height, dark and bearded, perhaps mid-thirties in age, and handsome in a rugged, scruffy way. He had kind but nervous eyes.

Peter had arranged the meeting so he felt it prudent to speak first. The lack of time wouldn't allow a standoff and egos had no place here. 'You're not Willoughby Carmichael,' he said disappointedly.

'Willoughby isn't coming,' the man answered. His accent was a deep and broad Irish. 'How did you find us?'

'That's not really important,' Peter answered. 'You people are the reason I haven't been able to leave. You've been watching, tried to be discreet, but I've seen you. And I saw Willoughby Carmichael. I know he's here.'

'I'm not denying he's here,' said the Irishman, 'just telling you that he doesn't want to see you.' He gestured downwards. 'What's in the briefcase?'

'Then perhaps,' Peter said, shamelessly ignoring the question, 'I should be talking to the one with all the flamboyance. He's not anywhere near as invisible as he thinks he is. Perhaps I should be seeking out the man with the missing eye?'

'I know exactly who you're speaking about,' said the Irishman, 'but he's not one of us. Don't know his name. He's here alone and has his own agenda. Doubt he knows who you are either, poor guy. So, by all means, have your conversation with him.'

Peter couldn't tell if he was hearing the truth. He was good at sniffing out a lie and the Irishman appeared to be sincere. 'Who are you?' he asked.

There was a pause while the Irishman thought about his reply. 'You can call me Gulliver, if you must.'

You can call me Gulliver. Peter didn't believe a word of it. Where had he plucked that from? It certainly wasn't his real name. It had no doubt come from an obscure memory, maybe belonging to an old acquaintance, a name that had stuck.

A car moved up the street slowly and bathed parts of the avenue in light. Peter tried to hide the panic in his eyes. Someone else could have been coming, snapping a trap, but Peter remained resolute and refused to take his stare away from the man in front of him. That would have been foolish. *Fight one front at a time.* Fortunately the car didn't come near.

'I wouldn't place you as a Historic,' Peter noted when he was confident the car was long gone and they wouldn't be interrupted. *Historic.* He hadn't used such a term in a long time. 'I'd be confident that you're a Post Nineteenth. I'd say we'd have been active around the same time, didn't ever see the name Gulliver on the Lists.'

Gulliver shrugged. 'And that means what? If you had a post box wouldn't the name Peter Carruther's be written on it? If so wouldn't we both be answering to names we weren't born with?'

There was an awkward pause. The two men started to circle one another, pacing extremely slowly like two prize fighters nervously coming into each other's orbit before an important bout.

'I *need* to see Willoughby Carmichael,' Peter reiterated strongly. 'That is my only requirement here. If you can't grant me that I don't see that you and I have much else to talk about.'

'Anything you need to say to him you can say to me,' Gulliver said.

'No, completely unacceptable, has to be face to face.'

Gulliver shook his head. 'Fortunately you finding that unacceptable won't really make a blind bit of difference to anything. This isn't a negotiation –'

'Then this conversation is over,' Peter said.

Gulliver reached forward and grabbed Peter by the arm, stopping him. 'Please,' he urged, 'that's not me being hostile. I don't mean to offend you.'

Peter focused on the Irishman's hand. It was a loose grip and didn't have the feel of aggression but the contact had the potential to be dangerous. *Should I treat this as a threat?*

'The way I see it,' Gulliver explained, 'you don't have many ways to run right now. No friends, no allies. I'm as close to a friend as you're likely to find. I might be able to help you.'

Peter broke himself away. 'You people think I'm the scum of the earth. And help isn't what I'm looking for.'

'Then what are you looking for?'

'Answers,' Peter said. 'I only need answers. Something else is happening here, something I don't understand. It's playing out opposite to everything I thought I knew.'

'I can see how hard this is for you –'

'I don't want your sympathy –'

'Only because your pride won't allow it,' Gulliver said. His eyes became sad. 'You mustn't overlook the magnitude of what is happening here –'

'I told you I don't *know* what's happening here –'

'This storm,' Gulliver said, 'this cold, it's not unprecedented and it's all linked to your son. He's the key. We've felt the same uncontrollable pull to this place, to him and more are going to feel the same thing soon enough and they're going to come looking. They won't have the same desires we do. They're going to want him dead, Peter, you understand that much, don't you? We're the only option here. We want to protect him.'

Peter couldn't help but be absorbed by the words, almost convinced even, but frustrated that they provided him with no more insight. 'And therein sits the problem, Gulliver,' he said. 'I don't know why you want to protect him. I get it, your code, your secrecy, and I get that you're just a grunt and couldn't tell me anything if you wanted to. But Willoughby Carmichael *can* tell me. And that's why I must see him, him alone, before it's too late for me.'

'Willoughby won't ever see you,' Gulliver said resolutely. 'None of us were meant to meet with you. I was the only one who was willing. They either wanted you dead or ignored and left to your fate.'

'Then why did you come?'

'Because I can help your son,' Gulliver said confidently. 'I know how it feels to lose a child and I wouldn't wish that on my worst enemy. All you have to do is trust me and I can make this work for everyone. You need to –'

Peter wasn't willing to continue. Time was up. He had stopped listening and started to walk away. He had decided the man was offering nothing. There would be empty promises and they didn't mean a thing without the answers. All Gulliver wanted to do was take, take, take, securing a mighty prize and basking in the glory.

Gulliver burst forward and moved behind Peter in a flash. The Irishman crouched down, executed his leg into a thunderous sweep and took Peter's own standing legs out from underneath him.

Peter landed hard and the back of his head smashed into the ground. The briefcase flew through the air and plumped down a short distance away. Lying there he felt an immediate sense of shame. Much to his disgust he had been powerless to prevent the assault from happening. *When did you get so old and useless?*

'I had to stop you,' Gulliver was full of apology and already offering his hand to assist him back to his feet. 'Please, don't walk away.'

Peter reluctantly accepted the hand and groggily climbed back up. He dusted the snow off his clothes and touched the back of his head. Thankfully there was no blood. He was dizzy though and he looked up into the night sky. It was a bright night, the sky white even in the darkness. It was still full of snow. The world would look beautiful in the morning.

'I'll need to go back before I'm missed,' Gulliver advised. 'I came here to beg you. I won't lie. We don't reach a compromise and there's a good chance we'll do more bad than good. Give your son to me and I promise I'll protect him.'

'No,' Peter said, 'not until I know more.'

Gulliver sighed. 'I can't give you more –'

'What's obsidian? What does it mean?'

'I *can't* tell you that –'

'Why is the mark acting the way it is?' Peter said. His questions were flowing now. 'Why does it burn red? I've never heard of that happening –'

'Peter … no! Stop it!'

52

Peter walked over to where the briefcase had landed and he pulled it up and pushed it into Gulliver's chest. 'Open it!' he demanded. 'Here's my currency! This'll pay for you to take me to Willoughby Carmichael.'

Gulliver tried to pass the briefcase back. He had a look of horror on his face like the briefcase was liable to explode.

Peter snatched the briefcase back and with one quick yank he pulled it open and held up the one item that had been resting inside it.

Gulliver offered an idle glance at first but then he became serious. His resultant look of shock showed that he recognised the book that was in Peter's hands. In fact the sight had such an impact that he staggered to the side as if he was suddenly drunk.

'It's …it's …' the Irishman was stuttering, struggling to find any suitable words. 'It's … beautiful.'

Peter pointed at the plastic that covered the pages. 'It's a customized silicon resin, not found anywhere else in the world. It's kept the book perfectly safe for the years I've had it but still allows it to be read. It's authentic, Gulliver, and it's yours for the right price. You know the price.'

Gulliver was licking his lips. 'You know that there's only supposed to be one of these books in existence?' He reached forward to touch the book but then stopped himself. He was scared. 'People have been looking for this for, well, hundreds of years. Most people don't even think that it ever existed. Could it be?'

'You need this,' Peter said. 'It speaks of Obsidian but I can't translate it. I can only translate that one word and it tells me nothing. I have to understand what it means. You want me to trust you, you want me to look to you for help, give me a reason to.'

Gulliver reached into his pocket and pulled out a small piece of paper. He passed it across to Peter. The Irishman had grown pale and was sweating.

Peter unfolded the note and read it quickly before putting it into his own pocket. 'When?'

'Tomorrow at noon,' Gulliver said. 'Once they'll see this, they'll forgive me.' The Irishman took the book, cradling it like it was a brittle new born baby and began to walk away. Peter, satisfied, did the same.

'Peter?' Gulliver stopped. He had one last thing to say. 'It glows red because of what Obsidian means. It's a beacon, a message to inform us of something very important. Keep your wits tomorrow. Getting your son away is the only important goal. You and Willoughby digging your heels in and starting a fight isn't going to help anyone. There's already enough chaos heading towards this little village.'

Then Gulliver was gone. This time he left a long trail of footprints in the snow.

Peter moved and didn't remember the journey home. He was in a daydream and before he knew it he was sitting at the end of his son's bed and nudging his shoulder. 'Finn?' he said in a quiet voice. 'You awake?'

Finn stirred and sat up bleary eyed. 'I am now. What's going on?'

'I need to speak to you now,' Peter told him, 'because I won't get a chance in the morning. I have somewhere I need to be. You got any plans tomorrow?'

'No,' Finn answered, 'nothing.'

'Good,' said Peter, nodding his approval. 'That's good. Promise me something. It's going to sound odd and I'll explain when I get home. It's nothing to worry about but you need to promise me that you won't leave the house tomorrow. It's important you stay here. Do you hear me?'

Finn looked confused. 'Yeah but –'

'I will *explain* tomorrow,' said Peter firmly. 'Just promise me that you won't leave this house. Do this for me? I've never asked you for much but I need you to do this one thing for me now.'

'Ok,' Finn said.

Peter leaned in and kissed his son on the forehead for the second time that evening. 'Good boy,' he said and then he headed towards the door. He would find no sleep. There was too much to do.

Chapter Nine

Felicity reached over and unhooked the rusty latch to the wooden gate from the inside. She led them through a pretty garden, the main feature of which was a collection of four large apple trees, their white frosty branches overgrown and interlocking like skeletal fingers. A cobbled path – cleared of snow but still perilously icy – weaved between two lagoon shaped ponds and led to a small, tired cottage that looked as though it was in dire need of some substantial repair.

They stopped at the front of the house. The bright green front door sat behind a neat glassed porch. A set of multi-coloured fairy-lights were on and twinkling in one of the downstairs windows.

Finn hovered behind Felicity as she overturned a small grey rock next to a dying pot plant. She found the key and opened up the porch. It was the first time he had seen her out of school and he liked the way she had dressed, casual but cool, blue jeans, long blue coat, a woolly hat with her fringe poking out, and the familiar long brown boots that must have been her favourites. He had gone casual too, resisting the desire to go *super-smart*, with his normal look of a dark grey jumper, blue jeans, Converse trainers, and the black coat that looked cool but wasn't particularly suitable for the weather.

He was a little tetchy. It hadn't played out quite as he had hoped. Felicity really did *only* need a chaperone. They were visiting Maggie Hemlock, her elderly Godmother and owner of the title of aunt, who lived in the tiny village of Ivydown. Getting there required a train journey, two bus rides, and a perilous trek down a pothole riddled country lane. Their bikes had been locked up outside the small train station in

Willowbrook at nine o'clock and they had chatted the whole way, no uncomfortable silences but enough comments to pick apart any romantic ambitions Finn may have had at the seams.

Felicity Gower was confident and flirtatious, a stark contrast to the quiet, mousy persona she had adopted at school. She was full of jokes and had a strange sense of humour. Had she not been so brutally honest he may had mistook the way she acted with him for some sort of attraction. But no, she had told Finn on more than once occasion that she had almost cancelled the trip, fearing that he had the wrong idea about her true intentions. She then persisted to tell him all about a boy two years above them, a sixth former, who she had spoken to in the cafeteria queue and who she thought was *just dreamy* and looked like a young Marlon Brando, whoever that was.

Finn was surprised to find that he wasn't quite as disappointed as he would have expected. Of course had she suddenly suggested that they kiss or hold hands, he would have agreed in a heartbeat. That was likely because he needed the experience, having so far never actually kissed a girl. Still, clouds were rumoured to always have silver linings and a friendship certainly wouldn't hurt. The cool boys had the attractive female friends, catching movies together, listening to music through shared headphones, drinking lattes and cappuccinos. Friends would do wonders for his credibility.

Felicity guided him inside the porch. There was a small bench to their left with a host of dirty shoes and boots underneath. A fluffy white cat was sleeping on top of the bench. The cat woke and offered a warm and familiar meow, standing and stretching out.

'Why hello there, Richard,' she said, scooping the cat up into her arms. She held him out in front of her and gave him an Eskimo kiss, rubbing their noses together. 'Look at you, boy! You've got soooooooooo fat!'

'*Richard?* Finn tittered. 'Strange name for a cat, isn't it?'

Felicity wrapped the cat up snugly against her coat. The cat purred affectionately. 'Let me guess, you're a Fluffy or a Felix kinda guy?'

'I just think it's weird,' said Finn, 'when people give pets human names. We had a cat called Gizmo.'

'Gizmo?' Felicity cooed sarcastically. 'Sooooooo much cooler!' She knocked on the front door, five sharp, loud bangs. She read Finn's reaction. 'Five knocks,' she said, 'and she'll know it's me. It's like our secret code, impossible to decipher. She doesn't move very quickly these days so she doesn't normally answer the door to just anyone'

Felicity placed Richard on the floor. Finn reached out to the cat and made a clicking noise with his mouth, blundering in for a stroke. Richard wasn't keen on the idea and he hissed and tried to smack Finn with his paw, missing and then running off outside into the snow. The cat sat down near one of the ponds and continued hissing from a distance.

'You're quite at one with nature you,' Felicity was smiling. Then she pulled a sad face. 'I worry about Richard sometimes. He's getting so old and he's Maggie's only real company. She had a dog before, Benji, this gorgeous little bulldog. So cute. When he died she was gutted. So I went out and got her an identical one. I'll never forget what she said to me.'

She became quiet, titled her head and looked like she was about to cry.

Finn was certain it was his duty to fill the silence and he wanted to make sure he looked interested and sensitive. 'What did she say?'

Felicity looked up, utterly serious. 'She said, 'Felicity, just what am I supposed to do with two dead dogs?''

It took Finn longer to get the joke than he was comfortable with and when he realised it was a punchline rather than the end of a sad story he offered a jittery, hesitant laugh.

'Finn,' Felicity said, chuckling to herself, 'if we're going to be friends, you really need to stop believing everything I say. I like to joke, a lot. Just so you know.'

'You mean you lie?'

'Ok,' Felicity said, 'sorry, Mother Teresa. No, I don't lie. I joke. There's a big difference.'

There was movement from inside the cottage. Maggie Hemlock was shouting, telling her visitors that she was coming but that she couldn't find her key.

'Don't worry, take your time,' Felicity shouted to her. She pulled Finn by the collar and whispered. 'I probably should have told you something before we got here. I call her Aunt Maggie but she's not my real aunt, not by blood anyway, she was my mother's best friend. Maggie's a clairvoyant. Do you know what that is?'

'Yeah, means she doesn't eat meat.'

'Very funny,' Felicity punched him in the arm. 'No, she reads palms, tea leaves, that kind of thing. I visit her when I can. She likes to give me a reading. She sees it as a way to make sure everything is ok in my life.'

'It's an important thing to do,' Finn said. 'So many bad things could be avoided if only we took more notice of the creases in our hands.'

'Finn, are you telling me you're a nonbeliever?'

Finn chortled, ready to offer up another sarcastic comment but he decided to wheel it back in. 'Do you believe in that kind of thing?' he said with as serious a tone as he could muster.

'Not really,' Felicity admitted. 'Actually not *at all* but it keeps Maggie happy and she *really* does believe in it. I go along with it for her sake. Some people call her a kook and that makes me want to punch them in the head. People avoid walking under ladders, can't see why that's any different. So be nice ... or ... well ... I might punch you in the head.'

The hallway light came on inside then Maggie Hemlock answered the door. She was short and plump, her hair a brilliant white and tied up in a neat little bun with a yellow pencil holding it all together. A pair of big red glasses dangled on the edge of her nose and her flowery dress was covered with an apron that was stained with splashes of flour.

Maggie whooped with joy when she saw Felicity standing on her doorstep. 'I expected you tomorrow,' she said, dragging Felicity inside and scooping her up into a smothering embrace, straight into her ample bosom. 'The place is a frightful mess! I wish you had said you were coming.'

'Less boob, Maggie,' Felicity said, her voice muffled by the tightness of the cuddle. 'Less boob!'

Maggie let go and she bent down and pressed her thumb into Felicity's chin, pushing her face from side to side, examining her. 'You look thin in the face, young lady? Are these new parents not feeding my little angel?'

Felicity winked. 'No, they're not very nice. They're cold people. They give me a bowl of slop and a bowl of water every night and I eat it with the hounds on the floor. I sleep in the shed. Don't even get a blanket.'

'You little smart-alec,' said the old lady, laughing loud, a booming clamour from the pit of her stomach. 'You know this is the first time I've seen you since Christmas. I thought I'd see a lot more of you, now you're living so much closer.'

'I'm sorry,' said Felicity. She pushed out her lower lip to feign sadness. 'I'm just so busy, you know, shoplifting, vandalising public property and experimenting in recreational drugs. Us teenagers live full and destructive lives, didn't you know?'

Finn was amazed at the way Felicity found a joke in almost everything. She wasn't like a normal fifteen year old. She was smart, she didn't speak like the others and her use of vocabulary seemed to be extensive.

Maggie's face became sad and reflective. 'You know you look more and more like your mother every time I see you. You have her eyes and her sense of humour. I love to see it. It really does make me happy.' She kissed Felicity on the cheek and then straightening back up, suddenly noticed Finn as he closed the door. 'Who's this? Your boyfriend?'

'My husband actually,' Felicity said. 'That's why I've come here today. I've got some news.'

Maggie was happy to play along. 'Isn't he a little short?'

Felicity turned around and surveyed him. 'Yep, now you mention it he is a little short actually. But he's one of the fittest dwarfs in the village, I have you know. You thought Sleepy and Dopey were good kissers?'

'Well you make a lovely couple,' Maggie said. 'Will your husband be staying?'

'If that's ok,' said Felicity. 'Actually we can't stay too long, Aunt Maggie.'

'Oh you children and your wild and busy social lives,' Maggie said. 'Maybe when you get to my age you'll take your feet off the pedal. Let's get started then.'

Maggie led them to her dining room at the end of the hallway. The room was small with a round oak table. The table was covered with fabric from where she had been making cushions, fabric that also seemed to spill out onto the chairs and rested in messy piles on the floor. Numerous *almost-finished* efforts were everywhere but none seemed to be completed. If a bomb had gone off it was a tricky task to determine exactly where it had been dropped.

'So, we're making cushions now, are we?' Felicity said. She picked up the nearest cushion from the table and viewed it. One side remained completely unstitched.

'I saw this young lady making them on this show on the TV,' said Maggie, quickly clearing the fabric from the table so that they could use it and throwing it randomly onto the floor, adding more clutter to the clutter. 'You know the one who's always going on about recycling and organic food and all that guff, I forget her name but she always has such nice hair. It looked so cheap and easy I thought I would give it a go and if it took off maybe look to sell a few bits on that inter-web thing all you kids are using. But I just can't get it right, no matter how hard I try.'

Maggie pulled out three chairs and she gestured for them to sit. Finn sat himself down next to Felicity. Although he didn't believe in this kind of thing he couldn't deny that he was interested. He had never actually seen anyone read a palm before.

Maggie reached forward and clasped Felicity's hands.

'No tea leaves today?' asked Felicity.

'Not if you're in a rush,' Maggie said. 'We'll just do the palms today. We can do tea leaves another time, if you decide of course not to wait so long to come and see your dear old Aunt.'

For the next ten minutes or so Maggie slowly examined Felicity's right palm before moving onto her left. Finn listened to what the old lady said, at first. But very quickly the torrent of mumbo jumbo decimated his interest. It didn't take long until he had heard quite enough about the life line, the head line, and the heart line and his mind started to wander, focusing on some rivets in the skirting board, a dead fly on the window sill, a cobweb high above a book case—

'Your turn,' Maggie said.

Finn looked away from the cobweb. Maggie and Felicity were staring at him. 'Who's turn?' he said vacantly.

'She wants to read your palm,' Felicity explained to him.

'Oh, I'm ok thanks!' Finn said, trying not to sound rude and ungrateful.

Maggie giggled and she reached across, grabbing his hand without his permission. But as soon as she touched him every last trace of colour in her face disappeared. She screamed and she snatched her hands away as if his fingertips were tainted with a powerful acid. She shot up from her chair and looked down at him. There was horror in her expression.

Felicity gasped and stood with her. 'Jesus, Maggie, what's wrong?'

Maggie tried to find her voice but the words stuck in her throat and tumbled back down into the darkness of her stomach. She couldn't stop starting at Finn, entranced, as if bewitched by an evil and malevolent force that would render her forever mute.

Felicity was visibly stuck somewhere between concern and embarrassment and she was already blushing. She went to Maggie and shook her gently by the shoulders. 'Aunt Maggie?' she said. 'What's happened?'

Finn could only sit there and wait. He checked out his hands just in case, not knowing what he expected to actually see and sure enough there wasn't *anything* to see. They were just hands. They were small, *girl's hands* a cruel kid had called them once, and now they were sweating.

Then Maggie broke free of her trance, blinked a few times and seemed to regain a modicum of composure.

'Fliss,' she said very quietly, breathing hard and gripping the back of the chair to help steady her body. She was faint. 'I need a moment with you alone, if I may.'

Felicity laughed nervously. 'Maggie, I —'

'Now!' Maggie shouted it loudly, a blast of anger. *'Right now! Send that boy away this instant!'*

Felicity bit her lip and she looked at Finn anxiously. She nodded for him to leave and Finn rose and started to head towards the door.

When Finn stood Maggie sat herself back down and she held her head in her hands as if she was dizzy. Felicity wrapped her arm around her shoulder.

Finn started to speak. 'I'll wait outside in the hallway —'

'No, you leave my house!' Maggie yelled. 'You wait outside! You mustn't stay here!'

Finn wasn't about to answer back and he had no desire to stick around. He was glad to leave and when he made it outside he was half tempted to leave them to it and head home alone. *What a stupid old kook.*

Richard shot out from a bush, hissed, and smacked Finn on the leg. The cat darted off, happy with his petulantly childish assault, disappearing up the garden to hide. Finn went to give chase but slipped and fell onto his bottom. The morning really wasn't supposed to go this way.

Chapter Ten

'There isn't really much to tell,' Felicity said, 'and it's not all that interesting anyway.'

It was late afternoon, still light, and they walked side by side, pushing their bikes slowly along King George Avenue. A crumbling old wall ran alongside them to their right. On the other side of the wall was sloping woodland and beyond the trees a cycle path that Finn had promised he would show her when the weather got better.

'You don't have to tell me about it if you don't want to,' Finn said kindly. The blame rested with idle curiosity. He already regretted bringing it up.

'Honestly, I really don't mind,' Felicity's smile showed that she wasn't offended and that he hadn't crossed any lines. 'Mum was an author – and I'm not being biased – she was *amazing* – made a lot of money so there's a little inheritance for me at some point. She was a teacher before that.'

'Where was your Dad?' Finn wondered. *God, stop being so nosey,* he thought, reprimanding himself internally.

'God might know,' Felicity said, 'could be face down in a ditch for all I care. Dad's a loser, loved my mum to bits by all accounts, I come along, he's off like a shot.' She smiled morosely. 'Mum got sick … a couple of cancers … beat it … got better … then got sick again … and then she was gone. Then it was just me. Aunt Maggie would have had me but she was never well enough. I don't have any other family.'

'And that brings you here?' Finn said. 'Living with the Wickers?'

'Ah yes, my rock-n-roll life with the Wickers.'

'You don't get on with them?'

'I wouldn't say I do or I don't,' Felicity said. 'I think they liked the idea of fostering a child, you know, tick off one of those boxes that gets you into heaven or something. But their kids are all grown up. They've had time with a quieter house. Now they've agreed to do it I get the impression they see it as a bit of a mistake. They're nice people though, so I can't really complain.'

Finn glanced up the road. It wouldn't be long until they left King George Avenue behind them. It would only take another twenty minutes or so and they would be home. That made him sad. He was enjoying talking to her. And he liked that she had opened up and told him about her mother. He had been beginning to think that all she had inside was sarcasm and weird jokes but already he had seen a different side that he liked a lot.

'I'll tell you what winds me up though,' said Felicity. Her face flexed with a flash of temper. 'It's all the moron's that hear the words *foster care* and think it's something to gossip about. Yep, my mum died and I've no other family … exhilarating.'

'I wouldn't care about what anyone at our school thinks,' Finn reassured her.

'And I really don't,' Felicity said.

'Sounds like my family,' Finn said. 'Anything happened to my mum and dad and I'd have no one. We've literally no family and –'

'Can we talk about something else actually?'

The challenge was there for Finn to change the subject. She stared at him, expectant. *Come on, lighten the mood.* 'You know my friend Henry?' he said. He had just the thing. 'He was going to ask you out yesterday.'

Felicity pouted. 'Is this the boy who once asked a girl out by reading her a poem through the microphone at the school dinner and dance?'

'Yep, that's the one.'

'I've heard about him,' said Felicity. 'I'm not exactly flattered. Doesn't he ask out every girl he comes across?'

'Ah but you don't know what he had planned for you, do you?'

'Would I have been impressed?'

'More likely disturbed and it may have scarred you for life.'

64

She laughed loudly and Finn was a touch smug. He loved making people laugh. It was one thing that he was confident about. He was funny and according to Cosmopolitan, a magazine he had thumbed through once at the hairdressers, humour was the main thing that women looked for in a boyfriend. If he could find a way of buying a Porsche and sculpting a six pack, he'd be beating off the chuckling admirers with a big stick.

'Felicity, I don't think you realise what a lucky escape you had,' he said.

'Hey,' Felicity pulled an unimpressed face, 'come on now, I'm only called Felicity when I'm being told off. Call me Fliss, yeah?'

'Oh, right,' he said. He paused and then did as he was told. 'Ok, Fliss.'

She rolled her eyes to heaven. 'Don't call me Fliss straight after I've told you to call me it! Oh my God! That's soooooooo weird! Why would anyone do that? Sooooo awkward!'

It was Finn's turn to laugh and he laughed too hard and omitted a little snort. 'You know you don't come across as a normal fifteen year old,' he stated, hoping that he could move on quickly and she wouldn't notice he had sounded like a pig. 'You don't speak like a normal fifteen year old either.'

'What does a normal fifteen year old talk like?'

'Not like you.'

'Not enough *innits* and *whatevers?*' said Felicity. 'Sorry, my mum had a bit of a thing about English, so does Aunt Maggie actually, so I picked up a lot of stuff from them. Got to speak *proper, dun't I?*'

Finn smiled and looked forward. The entrance to the cycle path was close. He could just make out the metal railing, in place so idiots on mopeds couldn't get through and joy ride. Maybe he could take her walking on the cycle path now. He certainly wasn't ready for the day to end just yet. Would she notice that he was taking her on a detour?

'Speaking of your Aunt,' he said whilst he tried to make up his mind, 'what did she say to you when she kicked me out of the house? I thought you would say when you came out but you didn't.'

Felicity scrunched up her face into a tight ball of discomfort. 'Do I have to tell you?'

'Of course you do.'

She mulled it over for a few seconds. 'But it's going to sound mental. You'll either laugh your head off or run a mile.'

'I promise not to laugh.'

'Ok,' Felicity said, 'but you really have to remember that I told you I don't believe in any of this stuff, yeah? Right ... don't freak out ... but she said that when she touched you she saw something. She said I had to stay away from you. She was dead serious too. I thought she was joking at first. Never seen her like that.'

Finn didn't understand. 'She saw something?'

'Now that's the bit I really *don't* want to tell you.'

'Go on —'

'Well,' Felicity nodded to herself, plucking up her courage. She decided she may as well just say it. 'She said ... and these are *her* words ... that you were surrounded by the greatest of life but a far greater force surrounded that life, smothering it, trying to kill it.'

Finn shivered. It was the weirdest thing he had ever heard in his life. He had to ask. 'What force?'

'She said the force was death,' Felicity cheeks went a little red at the revelation. 'She said that you were dangerous and made me promise to never see you again.' She saw the hurt in his eyes at that last comment and she touched his arm reassuringly. 'Don't worry, Finlay, I may have promised her but a little white lie doesn't hurt every now and again, does it?'

'I don't know,' said Finn, 'I think I'm kind of offended.'

'Don't be, she's a kook —'

'Thought you said you hated people calling her a kook?'

'I hate *other* people calling her it,' said Felicity, 'but she's *my* kook and I love her to bits. Doesn't mean she doesn't go a little bit crazy every now and again. Honestly just ignore it and don't think about it. Let me tell you this, one time when I was like six or seven she came to—'

She didn't finish.

66

There was shouting, *urgent shouting*, a single voice bellowing from behind them.

Finn and Felicity both spun around at the same time to see who it was. A man was running in their direction, waving a wooden cane with a golden handle in the air, trying to get their attention as if his life depended on it.

Finn almost dropped his bike. It was the man who had been watching him, Mr Flamboyant, the strange gentleman with one eye. Running didn't agree with him and beneath his hat his hair was already matted with sweat.

'Please,' the man was urging desperately. He stopped in front of them and grabbed Finn's arm. He was out of breath, erratically unfocused and looking all around the street. 'You have to come with me right now! You must! We have no time! I don't know why but they're here!'

Such was his close proximity that Finn couldn't help but detect the hot stench of liquor, brandy perhaps, although he was no expert in such things. He must have been drunk and certainly looked uneasy on his feet.

Felicity was looking to Finn for an explanation. 'Aren't you going to introduce me to your mate?'

'You must, must, must!' the man said. He wasn't listening and whatever he wanted he was resolute. He was trying to physically pull Finn away with him.

Finn smacked his arm away, hitting it hard. 'What do you think you're doing?'

'I'm sorry,' the man said. He held his cane out in front of him, balancing it loosely between his fingers to show that it wasn't a weapon. 'I'm scaring you. My name's Edwin Cavell. Please, we're not strangers now. I beg you, please, come with me!'

'Edwin Cavell?' Felicity said. 'That's like the coolest name I've ever heard.' She rolled the name off her tongue in a purr. '*Edwin Cavellllllllllllllll.*'

'You've been following me?' Finn said. His original curiosity now turned to outrage. He was embarrassed too and he had already decided to give this Edwin Cavell character a severe piece of his mind. In fact he was going to do a damn sight more than that. He was going to give him both barrels and then stop, reload and pop off a few more rounds.

'I have been following you,' Edwin admitted, 'yes, yes, you're quite right! I'm your Guardian, I'm sorry to do it like this. They've forced my hand! Who are they? I don't know. I thought we had more time—'

Felicity couldn't help but get herself involved. 'Why have you been keeping an *eye* on him?' She had over emphasised the word *eye* and she sniggered, amused at her own joke.

Edwin didn't get a chance to answer. Instead he nudged them both out of the way and took two steps forward. He gazed worryingly up the road as if something very dangerous was out there. But as it was, there was nothing. 'It's too late,' he said, closing his eyes. 'They're here.'

Felicity eased closer to Finn and she flicked him with her finger. She held her hand over her mouth and whispered. 'Do you know this dude? *Who's* here? You think he's talking about the men in white cloaks?'

Edwin turned and directed his words to Finn. 'You need to listen to me … you need to get off the road … now. Then you need to get yourself home as quickly as possible and lock the door.'

Finn shook his head, lost. 'What are you talking about? What the hell are —'

A black car slowly emerged from up ahead, turning the corner of King George Avenue. The windows of the car were tinted and blacked out. A second car pulled onto the road behind them, same make, same model, same dark windows. Both cars stopped. They kept their distance and their motors running.

Finn was aware that the world had suddenly become eerily silent. He hadn't noticed it before but they were alone in the street with only Edwin Cavell and the newcomers in the cars. He couldn't lay his eyes on the drivers and he wasn't sure he wanted to. Instinct made him look again to the entrance to the cycle path. They needed somewhere to go. Going over the wall wouldn't be possible, the slope was too steep. The path was the only option. He gripped the handlebars of his bike tightly.

'I've failed,' Edwin said gravely. 'Over time I hope you find it in your heart to forgive me.'

The black cars revved their engines, two roars, a warning –

Finn went to speak. 'Listen, Mister, no offence but –'

Edwin made the sign of the cross on his forehead and chest. 'Dear boy,' he said, 'we really should have had so much more time together. They're coming for Obsidian. Don't let them have it. I only wish I knew of the tale earlier.'

Edwin strolled out into the middle of the road. He tipped the rim of his hat, addressing no one in particular, his cane dangling by his waist. He moved almost like a matador, approaching a fearful, wild beast –

The two black cars, two wild metallic bulls, screeched forward.

Chapter Eleven

The realisation that something truly bad was about to happen hit Finn like an invisible punch to the jaw. 'Quick!' he shouted to Felicity. 'There!'

He pointed to the entrance to the cycle path, a dozen or so yards in front of them. He was already climbing onto the saddle of his bike. If they could get onto the sloping path they would be safe. The cars wouldn't be able to get through the metal barrier without sustaining serious damage.

Felicity didn't question or mock him and they appeared to be on the same wavelength. She mounted her own bike and tried to pick up as much speed as possible over the short distance they needed to cover. They both rode standing up, pedalling furiously with the snow spraying up from their tyres.

Finn looked left as he rode. Edwin Cavell was still striding forward with great purpose. The two cars were bearing down fast, threatening to sandwich him.

Felicity was quicker and her bike moved out in front. She made it to the entrance to the path and was forced to jump off her saddle. It was the metal barrier that had stopped her, made of two parts, one allowing a bike, the other a pedestrian, impossible to pass whilst seated. The bike went first, then her body and she disappeared down the slope and out of sight, running with her bike.

Finn tried to pick up his own speed – the final push – and he pulled a pained face at the sudden effort his body was asking him to expend. He was in the wrong gear and in his panic he couldn't think how to change it. His legs were trying to work quicker than the peddling would allow and his thighs burnt with building lactic acid.

Out in the road, Edwin launched his cane into the air like a javelin. The cane smashed through the windscreen of the car in front of him and then Edwin dropped to a knee and thrust his hands outwards.

The first car was only inches away. Edwin spun to this left and aimed a punch, making contact with the side of the vehicle. It should have been a mismatch of heavy metal against flesh and bone, but the car came off worse and it flipped up, spinning high into the air and landing on its side with a sickening clamour, skidding across the road and pavement, leaving a trail of broken metal and glass behind.

Edwin turned as quickly as he could. The second car was upon him. Still on his knees, he extended his shoulder and stiffened his body. The vehicle hit him hard and lurched up onto two wheels as if it had sped up a ramp, thundering past.

Edwin Cavell rose slowly but he screamed out in pain and within a few seconds collapsed to the ground.

Finn almost screamed too, if not in solidarity for Edwin's pain then in fear for his own safety. The second car was out of control and was heading his way, remaining on two wheels and careering onto the pavement. He was inches away from the entrance to the path and dismounted as quickly as he could. He pushed himself through the gap. The vehicle clipped his back wheel before zipping past and angling into the wall with a violent smash. Finn hit the ground.

The world was silent again. Nothing was moving.

Finn sat instantly up. His bike was in its last resting place, a mangled mass of twisted metal, spokes, and rubber, wedged uncomfortably in the entrance. Beyond it he could see the mechanical carnage out in the road.

Edwin had once again got to his knees. He was wounded and he tried to stand but pain forced him to give up. Realising the futility of doing anything else, he abandoned his efforts and sat cross legged in the road. He took off his Stetson hat and placed it in his lap, rubbing the material affectionately with his finger. He noticed Finn watching him and smiled. He hadn't however seemed to notice the man who had appeared next to him. The man had climbed from the wreckage of the first car. He was scruffily dressed and had dark hair. He stopped and stared down at Edwin.

Edwin met the man's stare and he blessed himself once more. With the sign of the cross complete, he tilted his head down and stared into the ground, awaiting his fate.

Finn was almost sick – whatever was about to happen was going to be serious. He wanted to turn away but found that he couldn't. The dark haired man wasn't happy, yet he looked almost sad, but regardless he placed his hands on both sides of Edwin's neck and started to violently twist –

A face suddenly blocked the view – a second man – the second driver. He was growling and blood escaped from a cut on the side of his head, spilling down and running into his thick beard. He was tall and looked awkward crawling on his knees, disorientated from his own escape from his demolished car.

Finn shrieked and jumped to his feet. He started to run down the path, through the trees, a desperate escape. But his leg was almost dead and he moved with a painful limp that slowed him down. He thought he would get away at first. But then he felt a hand on the hood of his jacket, yanking him backwards. The tall man had already caught him up and the grip that held him was hard, powerful, and unlikely to let go.

'Got him!' the man shouted triumphantly in a strange accent. 'Stop your –'

'Duck!' a female voice shouted.

Felicity flashed out from beside a tree, swinging a huge broken branch she had acquired towards them.

Finn was lucky enough to react to her urgent instruction and he forced his head down, breaking free of the grip a split second before the tree branch made contact with the tall man's nose. There was a loud thump, the crunching sound of broken bone, and a scream of agony.

The tall man fell backwards. He writhed on the path on his back, cursing and clutching his face.

'Bike?' said Finn urgently, scrambling back to his feet.

Felicity pointed into the trees. 'There! You're too heavy for a crossbar though!'

Finn looked back up the slope. Where the path had snaked he could no longer see the obliterated entrance and he couldn't see if the other man was following. 'Quick,' he said. 'Run!'

'One sec'!' said Felicity. She darted forward and aimed a well-placed kick into the tall man's groin. More grunts, more pain. Then she ran past Finn as quick as the wind. 'Ready now!' she said almost casually as she fled the scene of the crime.

He followed her into the woods. There was no plan, only to make it as far away as possible. The terrain was uneven and his knee throbbed as his footing seemed to slam and slip against every rock and bump. But he couldn't stop. He lost sight of Felicity and was just starting to worry when she reached out from behind a tree and dragged him down into the undergrowth.

Finn's face made contact with snow, twigs, and soil. The ground was cold and the snow was damp.

She pressed her finger to her lips and pointed out into a clearing that stretched out in front of them. They could see part of the tarmac path. The two men had regrouped and they were stood there, looking for their prey.

'You know them?' Felicity whispered, careful not to be overheard. 'They been following you too?'

'No,' answered Finn. 'You recognise them?'

She shook her head, serious now. 'What the hell just happened?'

Finn said nothing and focused on the men. The tall man was bleeding from both his head and his nose now. His face was red and angry and he reared his head back and bellowed an almighty roar towards the heavens, a scream of anguish and frustration. Such was the volume of the outburst a host of birds nearby were startled and they flew from the trees and took flight.

The dark haired man grabbed his companion by the shoulders and spoke in an American accent. 'Compose yourself!' he demanded.

The tall man showed no signs of complying and the two men grappled as if ready to fight. The American seemed less hungry for conflict and he took a step back.

'Your fault,' the tall man said. 'Your stupid rules!'

'Crying about it won't help,' the American said calmly. 'I told you, you keep it hidden –'

'*He* didn't keep it hidden, did he?' The tall man said. He pointed in the direction of their wrecked cars and was spitting his words out furiously. '*You* didn't either!'

'What's that accent?' Felicity said. 'Spanish or something?'

'French,' Finn said. 'I think –'

The American held his hands up. 'I had no choice –'

'I would have had him – '

'And the world may just have seen it,' the American said. 'What then?'

There was the sound of barking. The sound was close. The two men heard it too and they moved and were gone in seconds. A few moments later a tennis ball whizzed past, chased by two sprinting dogs. The dogs were quickly followed by their owners, an old man and an old lady. The dog owners were talking about the large set of crashes they had just heard in the distance and speculating as to what it could have been.

Once the dog-walkers were gone, Finn and Felicity stood up and emerged out into the clearing. Finn bent down and pressed his fingers into the point of his knees that hurt. He could feel the swelling and his knee felt twice the size than normal. There was a sound of sirens in the distance.

'That really just happened, didn't it?' he said. He didn't only want to convince Felicity. He wanted to convince himself that it hadn't all been some strange dream.

Felicity was taking it all in her stride. 'What exactly are you involved in, Finn?'

Finn was already trying to apply some of his own logic to that very question. Put simply he didn't know. It was all becoming a puzzle, the many strange things that had started happening, the pieces floating around his mind but none of them seeming to be able to interlock. Could they all be linked?

'There's things you're not telling me, isn't there?' Felicity said. 'But either way, what do we do now?'

'We go home,' said Finn, 'and tell someone what we just saw.'

'What *did* we just see?'

'I don't know – '

'What happened to that Edwin-guy?'

Finn couldn't bring himself to say it. But Felicity saw the truth in his eyes. She reached into her coat pocket and pulled out her mobile phone, ready to call the police.

Finn stopped her and took the phone from her hands. 'No,' he said. 'I need to get home first.'

Felicity almost laughed, such was her confusion. 'Tell me why we shouldn't be walking towards the sounds of the sirens?'

'Because my Dad knows something,' Finn explained, 'and I think it's time he started talking. Something really messed up is going on here.'

Chapter Twelve

It had started to snow again around three o'clock, another blow to the credibility of the weather experts who had optimistically forecast a thaw. Evening was only a whisper away and night was stirring from its slumber and slowly creeping down from the hills.

Finn and Felicity moved with purpose and dashed past a group of children playing in their street. The youngsters were screaming with glee and lobbing poorly made snowballs that fell apart long before they found their targets.

He escorted Felicity to her door and when he was satisfied that she was safely inside he returned home, carefully crossing the street and weary of seeing the two men who had chased them. He didn't want her to go home but she had insisted. She made it clear that she would have to check in with the Wickers. If she didn't, all hell would break loose. But she promised that she would come over to his house as soon as she could get away.

His father's car wasn't on the drive and he entered a dark house. He didn't turn on any lights, not wanting anyone to know that he was there. He sprinted along the hallway, thankful that the swelling in his knee had already eased substantially and headed straight for the living room, taking a position near the window so he could look out into the street. He plucked his mobile phone from his pocket and clicked on his father's name. It connected directly to his voicemail. He didn't do as the voice told him, and refused to leave his name, number, or a short message.

He sighed deeply and tried another number. This time it connected after a single ring. There was no greeting, only silence.

Finn shook his head. 'Mum? Are you there?'

There were muffled sounds, two voices it seemed, a man and a woman. Someone had their hand over the receiver.

'Finn?' said his mother suddenly. The connection wasn't great. It sounded like she was in a moving vehicle.

'Mum?' he said. He was relieved to be speaking to her.

'Something's happened. Don't even know where to start. I was walking – '

'Finn,' she said, '*where* exactly are you?'

'Don't you want to know – '

'I want to know where you are?'

'I'm at home – '

'Lock the door! Do as I say and do it now! Don't let anyone in! And I mean no one!'

Finn was barely keeping up with events. *Why was everyone telling him to lock the door? Did she already know? How could she?* 'I've rang Dad,' he explained. 'His phone was off and – '

'Do not let your father into the house,' she said sharply. 'You hear me, young man?'

'Mum ... what's going on?'

'You're not listening,' she said, 'and you need to understand what I'm telling you right now. Lock the door and wait for me. ETA – ' she paused and changed her terminology. 'I'll be there in thirty minutes. I'll explain everything to you when I get there. You understand?'

'I guess – '

'I need to hear you say it. Say I *understand*.'

'Yes, I understand!' But he didn't. He didn't understand any of this. 'But Dad I can surely – '

'You keep your father out most of all,' said his mother. She was calm now, matter of fact and firm. 'You're in great danger, Finn!'

Finn ran his spare hand through his hair. 'Mum, have you ever heard of Obsidian?'

There was a brief pause, an intake of breath, and then she hung up abruptly. He threw the phone onto a side table in frustration.

Finn sat down on the sofa, alone in the gathering darkness. A series of words kept flashing through his mind. *Keep your father out most of all.* Why could she have possibly demanded such a peculiar thing? Was his father involved with the men who had chased them? Had his mother left because of all this? Just what was it that he was involved in? He had been acting so weird and –

No, he stopped his mind going into overdrive and urged himself to see sense. Peter Carruthers worked in an office dealing with claims on behalf of insurance companies. He didn't wear a suit to work, only a cheap shirt and a cheap tie. He ran four times a week. He read a lot. He was just a normal man. He couldn't have been into anything strange or criminal. There was just no way it was true.

There was the sound of the front door opening, shattering Finn's troubled trail of thoughts. There were footsteps echoing from the hallway. He swung his head around and was relieved to see Felicity sliding through the doorway. 'Haven't you heard of knocking?' he said, angrier than he had intended as he was actually happy to see her.

'Haven't you heard of locking doors?' she shot back. 'Don't worry, I locked it for you. At least one of us is using our brain.'

'Dad's not here,' Finn said, 'and his phone's off. I don't know what to do.'

She sat down next to him on the sofa and he told her about the phone call he had just had with his mother. Then without realising it he went one step further, then a second and third step, spilling his guts about all the other things, the rash, the blackout, the peculiar book with the peculiar words.

Felicity listened and when he finished she gazed at him blankly. 'I don't know what to say,' was all she could offer. 'Finn, I get that there's a lot of strange stuff going on but we *have* to call the police, you realise that, right? Something really bad just happened to that Edwin guy.'

'He took out two cars, Fliss,' said Finn, 'with his bare hands –'

'I don't believe that happened,' Felicity said. 'It can't have done. You can't have seen it right. There was a lot going on –'

'I saw it –'

'A man's dead –'

'I didn't actually see *that* –'

'But we both think those men murdered him,' she said slowly. 'And *you* want to do nothing?'

Finn couldn't bring himself to answer.

'We're talking about murder, Finn,' Felicity said, 'it's not like you just saw someone fly-tipping.'

They stayed in silence for a long time, each alone with the mystery. The room was now dark enough to require a light.

'Finn,' she said eventually, 'you just *have* to call the police. Not being funny but if you don't, I'm going to, right now.'

'Please, I need to – '

'Need to what? Speak to your parents? No offence but if what you've told me is true they might just be involved with whatever's going on.'

'My parents aren't murderers, Fliss!'

Felicity already had her phone and she was resting it in her palm. She popped in her password, unlocked the screen and tapped three nines on the keypad. Her finger hovered over the green key that would push through the call –

A set of headlights flashed through the closed curtains and a car rolled to a stop on the driveway. The lights went out and the engine died.

Felicity didn't press the button. Finn's father was home.

Chapter Thirteen

Peter Carruthers watched the snowflakes that were slowly covering his windscreen. He needed to move but he had been moving all day. Night had fallen and his body was shutting itself down, overcome with fatigue and stress. The snowflakes proved a lovely distraction, endlessly graceful, effortlessly beautiful.

Fatigue wasn't the only thing responsible for the slowing of his wits. Knowledge had taken its toll too. Willoughby Carmichael had given him the answers he had sought and it had been a bitter pill to swallow. He had never believed in their superstitions and he wasn't about to start now. But belief had little importance. Others *would* believe it – hell – most of them already *did* believe it, and it enhanced the danger of a situation that already had enough danger in spades.

He caught his reflection in the rear view mirror. A tired faced stared back at him, a stranger with bloodshot eyes and a forehead wrinkled with the deepest slipstreams of worry. There were more wrinkles on his head than there had been in December. He had looked good in December. Now, he looked every one of his forty four years.

Peter rolled down the driver's side window. He was nauseous and needed some air. The small black box he had swallowed hadn't gone down easily and he could feel it sitting uncomfortably somewhere inside his stomach. Knowing his recent luck it was probably pressing against a vital organ.

His knuckles were hurting too. The punches had split the skin, the blood already drying into awkward scabs that gave him shooting pains every time he bent his fingers. It was annoying for the fight itself had been over in seconds. The *tail* had followed much too closely and when Peter slammed on the breaks and burst from his car the man looked like he was going to have a heart attack. He had left him tied up and gagged in a place they were unlikely to find him. He would wake up with the worst headache of his life and the stark realisation that no one was coming for him.

The man belonged to his wife, a member of The Guild, not an Operative, only an observer. An Operative would have never given up so easily. The main party would be close behind.

Peter closed his eyes. He was thankful for the snow on the windscreen as it meant he couldn't see the house. It was no longer a home to him but a coffin and when he looked he could almost see his name ingrained in every one of the bricks. *Damn you, Agatha! Damn all of you!*

Enough – it was time for action. He forced himself up, leaving the car, noting the two sets of footprints in the snow on the path. The footprints were fresh, someone *was* inside. He made his assessment, noting the minor details, the dark house, the children still playing in the street, the lack of screaming, the lack of sound, the lack of approaching sirens. Agatha hadn't returned. The play hadn't started yet and the curtain was still down. It wasn't too late and there was plenty of time for him to take his seat and start changing the script.

He looked up and down the street as he walked towards the house, using his key and moving inside as he heard the sound of an engine in the distance – *two cars* – coming from the end of the street. Then the others, *two more*, coming from the opposite direction.

Peter made his way directly to the kitchen and pulled the blinds of the window down, twisting the cord so that if he squinted he could see out but anyone who happened to be outside could not see in. He had left the spotlights on in the garden and a subtle light came in through the blinds in shadowy streaks.

He crossed over to the fridge, helping himself to a bottle of beer and opening it with his teeth. He took a long, stressful swig and then closed the fridge door. The fizzy liquid was cold and refreshing. He leaned back and drank again.

He surveyed the kitchen, neat and tidy, undoubtedly *his* domain. His wife was a terrible cook, even managing to burn the simplest of microwave meals, whereas he was accomplished and slightly pretentious in his culinary exploits. He saw the frying pan that she had bought him for his last birthday, hanging on the utensil rack above the kitchen island. Two hundred pounds was the cost, accompanied by a proud boast that nothing would ever stick to it, and a forty year guarantee. It once had an easily identifiable value but not now. Nothing did.

'I know you're there,' he said loud enough so that those hiding could hear him. The time for nostalgia was over. 'Out you come.'

No answer.

'They're coming for you right now, Finn,' Peter said. He popped up onto the worktop island and sat waiting. 'If you're hiding from me I guess it's safe for me to assume you've spoken to your mother?'

The door to the larder slowly opened and Finn peered nervously out. His son didn't speak at first.

'Finn,' Peter said, 'how could you ever think that I would do anything to hurt you?'

'You lied to me,' Finn said. 'About the rash – '

'I lied to you about the rash,' Peter wasn't denying it. 'I lied to you about other things too.'

'Mum knows too, doesn't she?'

'Your mother knows,' said Peter. 'She said you need to keep me out, didn't she? Am I right?'

He watched as his son walked cautiously out of the larder. A young girl followed him. He gave her a surprised, curious glance but he didn't question her being there. Ultimately it didn't matter who she was. She wasn't his responsibility.

'I'd give you answers if I could,' Peter said, 'but we don't have time and I'm not the person to tell you.' He hopped down from the worktop and rolled his sleeve up. He clicked a switch on his wrist, starting his stopwatch. The clock was ticking. 'Do you both have phones?' he said. 'Show them to me. There's a chance they've been traced.'

He was surprised when both Finn and the girl handed them over without any complaints, although not as surprised as they were when he threw them forcefully into the wall, breaking them into pieces.

'That was an I-phone!' shouted the girl. 'Honesty if I had a knife I would stab you in the heart right now!'

'You don't use phones from here on in,' Peter said. 'It's the easiest way for them to track you.' He gestured for them to join him at the window and pointed outside for them to look. 'Careful, make sure they don't see you.'

Peter hadn't forgotten how it all worked. Protocol rarely changed. Scouting party, three members, two around the back, the last through the front door, the other's hanging back for the time being.

Finn was leaning into the front of the sink and focusing. The Carruther's garden was long, flat, and separated into two sections. The first section was closest to the house, the raised patio area with the cheap plastic patio furniture. The second section was accessible through a narrow path that led through an arched trellis towards the ample allotment and the large garden shed.

And there they were – two figures dressed liked soldiers in winter fatigues, clothes of purest white, faces covered with white balaclavas. In their hands they carried black rifles. They were treading carefully towards the house, weapons at the ready, covering the many angles as they went.

Finn gasped. 'What the hell?'

'Jesus,' the young lady said. She was even more horrified than Finn was. 'What the hell are this family involved in? People are supposed to come with cakes or biscuits, not freaking assault rifles!' She grabbed a spatula from a jar by the sink and waved it in front of her.

'And you're going to do what with that exactly?' Finn said. 'Make an omelette?'

'Shut it,' said the young lady. She smacked Finn on the arm with her makeshift weapon. He yelped and she went to hit him again –

Peter caught the spatula and threw it to the other side of the kitchen. Ignoring her dirty look, he removed a small plastic switch with four grey buttons from his coat pocket. The device was secured together crudely with masking tape. He was embarrassed at how amateurish it looked but was confident that the wiring and signalling would be effective. He pressed three of the buttons simultaneously –

BOOM! The shed outside exploded. The blast threw the two advancing men high into the air, the trajectory forcing them backwards, knocking down a fence as they went. When they hit the ground they stopped moving and were still. The flames climbed high into the sky before coming back to earth. Smoke billowed, fences everywhere were on fire. The blast was so loud that a series of car alarms were blaring far away, out in the street.

'Oops,' Peter said, chuckling to himself. He pouted comically at the sight of the chaos and noticed that both Finn and the girl were on the floor. 'Nita and Tony won't be inviting me around for a Christmas sherry this year! May have misjudged that one a tiny little bit.' He paused for a moment and had to steady himself by grabbing the nearest worktop. His stomach was complaining again, the sensation of sickness returning. *Stay in there box, I need you to stay in there.*

Finn was getting to his feet and was already pale. 'Did you just kill those men?'

'They'll live,' Peter said, 'more's the pity. Scouting party, needed to be neutralised before we move. Get –'

The kitchen door behind them opened. An outstretched arm carrying a handgun appeared –

The girl screamed and staggered backwards.

Peter showed no signs of panicking and he moved like a ghost, grabbing the intruder by the wrist and sweeping the weapon from his hand before dragging him fully into the room. The intruder was dressed exactly the same as the others, the same white, the same mask, the same concealment of his identity.

Finn shepherded the girl behind him, protecting her as the fight erupted.

Peter was already blocking the intruder's flurry of furious punches. His opponent was tough, well trained, younger, and fitter. But Peter had been the same once and his own skills were only dormant, far from dead, and when the opportunity presented itself he grabbed the intruder by the throat and launched him over the kitchen island, his head smashing into the dangling utensils. Then he went to work, picking up the discarded handgun and dismantling the weapon in three swift, puzzle-solving moves. Rendered useless he threw the parts into the washing up bowl. He turned to see that the intruder was on his feet again, dazed but ready for round two. The intruder bolted forward, arms and hands swishing this way and that.

Peter swept the fridge door open, smashing it into the intruders face and halting his advance before it had any chance of gaining momentum. The intruder flew through the air for a second time and crashed into the cupboard beneath the sink.

Peter strolled over and removed the intruders mask. The man's hair was blonde and damp with sweat. 'Don't know you!' he noted, examining his face.

'But I know you, Wilhelm!' said the intruder. He was dizzy and his speech slurred.

Peter didn't like that one bit and his mouth twitched with anger. It had been over sixteen years since he had last been addressed with that name. Wilhelm was dead, a phantom, he didn't exist. Even Carmichael had spared him that insult and it bought out the petulant side within him. As such he reached into the fridge and grabbed the first items he could find, a carton of milk and a tray a berries. He clutched his foe by the hair and opened the milk, tipping it over his head. The berries went up the nose of the intruder, five or six up each nostril. His victim tried to resist, struggling and snorting but he was too weary and Peter was too strong.

'Finished,' Peter said. He punched the intruder in the head, knocking him out. 'Let's see how she reacts when she finds you like that.'

'That's a novel form of torture,' the girl said through a nervous laugh. 'Is it wrong that I'm both horrified and amused right now? Hands down, strangest way I've ever seen anyone make a smoothie!'

Finn shook his head and looked at her. 'Seriously? What is wrong with you?'

'I'm scared, Finlay, ok!' she shouted. 'I say stupid things when I'm scared.'

Peter wasn't listening. He didn't need the distraction. He peered out into the hallway. The front door was resting open but he couldn't see that anyone else was approaching. Satisfied that they still had a little time, he pushed the kitchen door shut and gripped Finn by the shoulders. 'We're leaving,' he said, 'right now.'

He stopped. The look in his son's eyes was killing him. Finn was utterly lost and he was scared out of his wits. A parent's job was to protect their children. It was a duty, unconditional, and he was failing and the likelihood was that he was leading his son into more danger. But what hurt most of all was that his own son didn't trust him.

'Where are we going?' Finn asked.

'Somewhere where I pick the ground,' Peter answered. 'I still have a few tricks up my sleeve.'

Finn was reluctant but he allowed his father to guide them out into the garden. Peter checked on the felled men. They were unconscious and bleeding but alive. Next, he examined their weapons. The triggers were only usable with fingerprint recognition, making them utterly useless to him. Angry, he tossed them away, high into the distance and into a neighbour's garden.

'Imagine that knock on the door?' the young girl said. 'Sorry to disturb you neighbour, but can I have my assault rifle back?'

Peter smiled. He couldn't quite comprehend how anyone would see it as a time that was suitable for jokes. But he believed in the foresight of first impressions and his view of the girl was a good one. 'What's your name?' he said.

'Her name's Felicity,' Finn said, answering for her, 'and we need to get her home as – '

'She comes with us,' Peter said. 'She can't go home now! We need to move!'

Chapter Fourteen

Finn was running like he had never run before, through the gate, into the narrow alleyway behind his house, across roads, and in and out of housing estates. The world flashed by in the darkness, a blur of images made incoherent by haste and surreal by his mounting sense of dread.

They found the Operatives vehicle a good distance away from the house, parked in a small layby that jutted off from the main road, out of view from any overlooking houses. The spot was deliberately private with no streetlamps nearby. The car was dark in colour and had five seats. There was no one inside, all three passengers being unconscious somewhere else from the hand of Peter Carruthers.

Finn had no idea how his father had found the car so easily. There had been no missteps on the way, no stopping or debate of taking a different route. He had simply known where it had been parked all along.

Peter thumped his elbow into the driver's side window. The glass shattered but no alarm sounded.

'Jesus, Dad,' Finn said. He was worried that somebody might have heard the smash. 'You're going to get us arrested!'

His father reached inside and pressed a button on the dashboard, popping the boot mechanism. Then he ran to the back of the car, lifted the boot open and proceeded to unzip and search through the contents of a number of bulky black bags that were stored inside.

'Why did that guy call you Wilhelm?' Finn asked, joining his Dad at the back of the car.

'That was my name once,' Peter answered. 'Not anymore. Wilhelm died a long, long time ago.'

'This might sound odd,' said Felicity, 'but you're starting to sound like we should be calling you Obi Wan. When does Finn get his laser sword thingy?'

'Is Agatha even Mum's real name?' Finn said to his father, ignoring her.

'Yes, she kept her first name –'

'Where is she?' Finn said. 'She said she was coming back.'

'She's somewhere,' said Peter. He barely seemed to be listening.

Finn narrowed his eyes. 'Just *who* are you?'

Peter didn't answer. He was still moving between the bags.

Finn stared into the boot, annoyed that he wasn't commanding his father's full attention. 'What you looking for?' he asked.

'Anything of use,' Peter answered. He found and held up a large black rifle, examining the weapon closely. He smiled, approving. 'No print recognition, old school, this comes with me in the front.'

Finn was still breathing hard from the escape and struggling to compose himself. The cold air was pulsing painfully in his lungs and it reminded him of why he despised cross country running so much. Felicity in contrast looked as fit as a fiddle and she hadn't seemed to have broken a sweat. Instead she was quiet and transfixed by his father in a curious, cautious way.

He wondered what it was that she saw. Did she see a saviour or a monster? For his part he barely recognised the man in front of him. His mother was the dominant one in his parent's relationship, stubborn, incisive, and decisive. His father was laid back, happy to go along with a host of things for an easy life. He rarely questioned her, never stood up to her, often looking weak in the process. This was a different man entirely. He was cool, strong, fluid and unflinching, in complete control.

Peter tossed a bag into Finn's arms and a flashlight over to Felicity. The bag wasn't large, a little smaller than a rucksack but Finn struggled with the weight all the same. Whatever filled it was uncomfortable and had jagged edges that stabbed awkwardly into his palms and chest.

'Cartridges,' his father said, 'we'll need plenty. I'll need some light too!'

Peter kept them moving, shepherding Finn and Felicity inside the car, his son taking the front passenger seat. He passed the rifle over to Finn and reached forward, breaking off a section of the interior beneath the steering wheel and revealing a set of wires. He hot-wired the engine with ease as if he had been stealing cars forever, reversing the car into a sharp turn and then guiding it down the road, all the while keeping a careful eye on his rear view mirror.

Silence filled the car. All was calm and there hadn't been an opportunity for such a luxury for some hours. Peter drove quickly, going through the gears aggressively, but never too far above the speed limit so to be noticed. He travelled along quiet lanes at first, then into the centre of town and onto roads that were busier, before eventually taking a sudden left that took them out towards the country and onto roads that were all but deserted.

Leaving Willowbrook and Cheltenham behind, there was little light in the rural areas. Finn could see next to nothing beyond the glass, only a thick darkness and the odd splash of brightness from distant cottages or the sparkle of the cat's eyes in the middle of the road that were illuminated by their headlights as they passed.

No one was in the mood to talk. But Finn found the silence uncomfortable after the brute loudness of the chaos they had just witnessed. So he spoke, filling the silent void, telling his father all about the savage attack by the cycle path. He offered a brief description of the two men and disclosed what he thought had happened to poor Edwin Cavell.

'Not your mother's people,' Peter told him. 'They belong to something else, something worse. There's other's out there too, looking for you, although thankfully they've got better intentions, if they're to be believed.'

'Why me?' Finn said. 'What's so special about me? What have I done wrong?'

'You must have a hundred questions,' Peter said. 'I can't answer them. What you need to understand, what you need to know … it isn't for a place like this and isn't for me to tell you. I've never been on this side of things, Finn. I'll do what I'm good at, and I'll take you to someone who can explain all this.'

There was another silence, longer this time. The car moved past a country pub, a sudden burst of light, gone in a flash.

Finn hadn't been at all satisfied with his father's response. A hundred questions was a woeful estimate, he had a damn site more things to ask than that, and his impulse was to let them all spill out, one after another in torrents, but he could tell that his father wasn't in the mood to play ball. He wouldn't push.

'I need to go home,' said Felicity from the back.

Peter shook his head. 'You can't –'

'I can!' Felicity said angrily. 'Just drop me off here and I'll walk back. I don't want to be here.'

'None of us want to be here,' Peter said, 'but you're involved now, whether you like it or not. They find you – you'll say you'll never tell anyone about what happened if they let you go. You'll swear, you'll promise, you'll beg. But it's never true. People *always* talk and they won't allow any loose ends. The moment you go home the list of their targets just widens.'

'But I don't know anything,' Felicity said.

'Doesn't matter,' said Peter. '*They* don't know that.'

'So, what you're saying,' Felicity said, 'is that I'm just going to disappear?'

Peter said nothing. There was light coming through the back window. Finn turned around to look. Behind them on the road were other cars, still a fair distance away. There was an initial pang of fear but he quickly told himself that this wasn't anything out of the ordinary. It was a road. Cars travelled on roads.

'That's them,' said Peter, dashing his son's hope in an instant, 'four cars, fourteen Operatives, standard pursuit force.'

Finn kept his eyes on the cars. He wanted to judge their distance but he couldn't gauge it. 'How'd they know where we are?' he said.

'Tracking system,' Peter said. 'Somewhere in the car, wasn't going to waste the time trying to find it. And all in all, I didn't want to find it anyway.'

Finn's mouth lulled open and he looked at his father with bemusement. *How are you so unconcerned?*

'Let's just say,' said Peter, 'that escape isn't the only part of the plan.'

The road slowly started to curve to the right and on the left was a sign signifying that an exit was up ahead. When the exit came into view Peter steered left, taking a road which was narrow and flanked by hedges. The road ran on for a few hundred yards and came to an end at a huge set of metal gates.

Peter pushed his foot down harder on the accelerator, smashing violently through the gates and breaking the flimsy lock with ease. With a quick swerve he brought the vehicle to a skidding stop, spraying up the loose shingle and snow that covered the car park surface. 'Out now!' he barked like a determined drill instructor.

Finn climbed out of the car to see a large complex of clustered buildings looming above him. The main part of the building was dominated by a square brick structure with an abundance of passageways and walkways poking out from it in all directions. Where the passageways and walkways led was a mystery, their destinations having long since been demolished, leaving the building to resemble a giant concrete spider. The site was abandoned, no security, no signs of life.

'We move inside,' Peter said urgently, leading them across the car park. He wrapped the bag of cartridges onto his right shoulder, the rifle hung from his left. Everything else was left behind.

Finn shot a look back at the gate, out to where the road rested behind the long rows of hedges. He couldn't see the road itself but he could see the approaching lights, shining through the branches, heading their way. His father was right – there were four of them – the vehicles flying along the concrete like fireflies.

'Finn?' Peter said, getting his attention. 'They still don't know you're here. They'll assume I've smuggled you away. They're coming for me, not you. It needs to stay that way.'

Finn didn't need to be told twice and they were running again, inside the structure, through an open space where there had once been a door. Immediately they were met by the metal of an industrial staircase and up they climbed without thought, the metal creaking beneath their weight, higher and higher into the ruined heart of the neglected building.

'What is this place?' Finn asked as they ascended.

'Old metal factory,' Peter said, 'been abandoned for about ten years, won't be disturbed here.'

After three flights the staircase came to an end, leading out into a vast open space. On the far wall the room had its own internal staircase, rising up to a foreman's office that had once overlooked the former factory floor. The glass in the office had been removed. On the factory floor were random gatherings of stacked crates, boxes, and furnishings, sitting amongst abandoned machinery that was old and riddled with rust and dust. High up above, the roof was lofty and made of glass but the panels were riddled with dozens of holes and cracks. Snow crept inside, leaving drifts on the ground and cloaking the air with floating flakes that danced with one another in the atmosphere.

Finn watched his father, reading his body language. It wasn't the first time his father had seen the room. Peter knew exactly where everything was and he paced over and stopped in the centre of the space, next to a semicircle of shoulder high boxes and pallets that conveniently faced the door and would provide him with cover. There was a crate nearby, full of a random assortment of products from home.

'Young lady,' Peter said to Felicity. 'Can I have the torch, please?'

She threw it across. He used a roll of masking tape from the crate and taped the torch to the muzzle of his rifle. He flicked the flashlight on, directing the beam around the room to make sure it wouldn't fall off.

Peter looked at his watch. 'You both go up there,' he instructed, nodding towards the office staircase. 'There's a small fire exit at the far end. It leads outside to the woods behind the building. You get out that way, find the road, and head back towards town the way we came. There won't be anyone following you but if you do hear a car coming, hide by the side of the road until they pass.'

He handed Finn a folded map from his pocket. Finn unfolded it, seeing a standard map of Cheltenham. On one of the grids, an area that showed the eastern edge of town, Peter had marked a small red X.

'Find a place called the Ellis Moran Hotel,' Peter said.

'Why?' Finn asked. 'What hotel? Where are you going?'

'I'm not going running in the woods,' Felicity stated firmly. 'My boots are made of suede. I'd take a bullet to keep them safe.'

'I have a prior engagement with some old friends,' Peter said to his son. A small smile hinted that there was at least a part of his father that was relishing this and looking forward to what was to unfold. 'I'll buy you some time. Find the hotel, Ellis Moran, find room one hundred and forty eight. Don't stop at reception. You'll find a man called Willoughby Carmichael. He already knows who you are. He'll tell you everything you need to know.'

Finn made a mental note in his head, *Ellis Moran Hotel, Willoughby Carmichael.*

Peter placed his rifle on top of the nearest crate. He removed all of the cartridges from the bag and positioned a selection on top of his makeshift base and the others into the pockets of his trousers and jacket. With the final cartridge he slammed it into the rifle, priming it for action.

Finn moved closer to his Father. He didn't want to go and he could feel his eyes flooding with tears, desperate to come out.

Peter gripped his son by the shoulders and looked at him deep in the eye. 'I've never said it enough,' he said sadly. 'But I love you, Finn, so much. I wish I could have given you a better life away from all this, away from –'

93

There was a crash, something metal being disturbed and falling, the stark impact echoing upwards. They were no longer alone in the building.

'Go now!' Peter said. He bowed his head and pressed it up against Finn's. 'Don't look back.'

Finn broke away and grabbed Felicity by the hand. They sprinted for the internal staircase, making it half way up when Peter's voice stopped them.

'Finn,' his father shouted from below. 'Promise me one thing. Promise me you'll believe. No matter what you're told, no matter how unlikely it sounds, believe what you hear.'

Peter turned and faced the door. He raised his rifle, ready.

Finn and Felicity continued up into the old foreman's office. There was no door. The office was a crumbling wreck and the wall beneath where the window used to be had gaping gaps in it where some bricks had broken away. The whole wall looked like it was ready to collapse at any moment. The fire exit was where his father had said it was, the doorframe covered in cobwebs.

Finn stopped and staggered to the wall, falling to his knees.

'What do you think you're doing?' Felicity screamed. She was already hovering near the fire exit.

'I have to see this – '

'We have to get out of here –'

'I have to see what's going to happen!'

Finn angled his body so that he could peer through the gaps in the wall. In that position, they wouldn't be able to see him. The view was perfect – there was his father – where they had left him. He felt a sudden burst of love and affection for the man and hoped with all his heart that he wouldn't come to any harm.

Chapter
Fifteen

Peter had one final task to carry out before the curtain came up on his particular brand of theatre. He removed his I-Pod and speaker from his bag, slotting them together and placing the unit carefully next to the cartridges. He turned it on, rolling the volume up to its highest setting. He couldn't exercise without music and he didn't see any reason to break with the tradition.

He stared at the dark doorway, waiting. The torchlight strapped to the end of his rifle illuminated the entrance in a perfect circle, the spotlight, waiting for the introductions to the cast.

There were sounds out there, down below, sounds of people moving. He pressed play on the player. His favourite song – a fast cover version of Bad Moon Rising – was loaded and ready to rock and roll. He had always liked the lyrics. They were dark and foreboding. The sudden blast of music would throw them, stopping them in their ascent, unsure of what was happening up on the third floor.

Peter caressed the trigger of the rifle with his finger. Fourteen Operatives, give or take, he saw no reason to change his calculation. He had to make sure that their images didn't merge into one. That was the key. In a fight it was important to not become disorientated, to know exactly who you were fighting, seeing the enemy as individuals instead of a collective. Every enemy was different. They moved differently, aimed differently, and even in the chaos of a firefight it was possible to make quick, accurate notes to gain an advantage. His current enemy would be dressed in a universal way. He would give each of them a number.

There was rattling up above, someone scrambling across the roof, drawing near. A distant shout from below sounded out, a command. It was go-go-go. They would come in heavy and hard. In an abandoned warehouse in the middle of nowhere, there was no need to hide their existence.

A face covered by a mask appeared in one of the holes in the glassed roof.

Peter grinned. The slight caress of the trigger became a very deliberate squeeze. It was perfect timing – the song building towards its first chorus.

'Hello, Number One,' he said.

And so it started. The thin rope came first and then a lean figure dropped down through the roof void, abseiling towards the floor. The figure was dressed all in black, face as always concealed by a balaclava, head protected by a steel helmet. He was firing wildly, carrying a Heckler and Koch G36 assault rifle, German made, a serious gun meant for serious business. The bullets fizzed into the clutter on the factory floor.

Peter rolled to his left, avoiding the bullets with relative ease. He squeezed off his own shots, three well aimed efforts that thumped directly into One's chest. One's body went limp. He fell from the rope, crashing into a crate beneath him.

Two, Three, Four, and Five appeared in the doorway, spreading out and moving quickly amongst the furnishings that provided ample cover for both defence and assault. Shots rang out, sweeping by in all directions, the flashes from the gun muzzles lighting up the room as though a celebrity lurked within and that a thousand paparazzi were desperate to capture.

But Peter very much had the advantage. He knew where every last bit of cover was placed and he moved with a potent grace, light footed, ducking and diving. He fired short, controlled bursts. Within seconds Two and Four were down and would trouble him no more.

Three was pinned down behind a piece of chunky machinery and they exchanged frantic fire. As Peter's ammo was about to run dry he grabbed his next cartridge from his jacket and Five, who he had lost momentarily in the drama, was upon him in a flash. Five was quick and strong and he knocked Peter's rifle away. They started to trade punches.

Why didn't he just shoot me? Peter wondered. And then he realised. They wanted him alive, at least at first. He almost laughed as he broke Five's arm, allowing him to scream and then knocking him out to silence him.

More were coming now – Six and Seven came through the door – Eight down through the roof. Three had escaped and was approaching opportunistically, firing towards Peter's legs and trying to take him down. But the aim was poor. Peter was unarmed and he leapt into action, diving himself across the floor and rolling forward towards his lost rifle. When it was retrieved, Three had taken cover once more.

Peter fired towards the heavens. Shattered glass fell, forcing Three out into the open. Peter used a single bullet, hitting Three in the shoulder. The voice that cried out was female but Peter knew it wasn't Agatha. She was better than that. She would never have been so sloppy.

Six, Seven, and Eight were joined by Nine, Ten, and Eleven and they were a great deal more experienced than those that had come before them. Their fire was heavy, accurate, and superior, preventing Peter from firing back. They moved forward, aggressive and professional, and then Seven flanked Peter's cover and held his gun to his head.

'Drop it,' Seven commanded.

Peter did as he was told. Seven pushed the muzzle of the gun harder into his head, forcing him to walk forward.

The music was coming to the end of the song.

Seven was searching for the source. 'Someone turn that off – '

Peter cracked his head back, making contact with Seven's chin. He grabbed Seven's arm, pulling it forward and then down against his shoulder. The arm broke at the elbow and incapacitated he deprived Seven of his gun and used it to fire into Nine.

The rest rushed forward and Peter fought like a lion. He was slower than he used to be but the extent of his training came back. Although he suffered blows to his head and body it didn't take long until the rest of his foes were sprawled out on the floor with more broken bones and bloody noses.

More gunfire prevented a sense of victory, the final collection of the enemy were entering the fray.

Peter scooped a gun up from the floor and saw the next area that he wanted to use for cover –

He fell to the ground with a sudden shriek of pure agony. The two bullets hit him hard, the first pushing into his thigh and the second into the hip. He landed on his stomach but managed to spin around so he could still see out into the room. He wouldn't even bother trying to stand. He already knew he couldn't.

The music abruptly stopped. His resistance was over, he knew then. He couldn't feel his legs. Flashlights were flicked on in the gloom, shining in his eyes. He could hear the whir of small machines and he recognised the noise. They were using their tools to comb the area for explosives. They already sensed a trap.

Agatha Carruthers emerged from the darkness and stood calmly in front of her husband. She wasn't wearing the same clothes as the others. She was dressed normally.

Peter let out a long, tired breath. 'Hello, Agatha.'

'Peter,' she stared at him with pity and dropped the MP3 player in his lap, 'this was the very definition of futility.'

Peter looked at her fallen comrades all around him. 'Was it?'

Agatha shook her head. 'Where is my son? My man didn't check in this morning. You didn't want him to see where you were taking him.'

'I'm surprised really,' Peter said, 'you're bothering to ask a question you know damn well I'm never going to answer.'

'Why fight it?' Agatha said. 'You've got just as many demons as I do. I've seen the sleepless nights –'

'Caused from the paths I used to walk,' Peter said, 'not the ones I ended up on.'

'That's poetic,' said Agatha, 'But a lie.'

The rest of the Operatives funnelled into the light, three of them, making the total attack team fifteen. Not a bad guess. Peter saw their grudging respect, identifiable by their nerves. He was no longer a threat but still their guns were aimed squarely at his chest, despite his wounds, despite him being unarmed.

Although hiding behind a mask, he would have recognised Theo anywhere. There was another he knew too, a huge man, he couldn't remember his name, Grogan or Rogan or something of the sort. But he recalled meeting him once before. He had been a boy of sixteen and was already towering above his contemptories. They were related, fourth or fifth cousins –

'How are you, Theo?' Peter said.

'Don't you even talk to me!' Theo spat back.

'Still holding a grudge then?' Peter said.

'We're wasting time here,' Theo said to Agatha. 'He needed eliminating, he's eliminated. The boy won't be far. He's not had time.'

Peter tried to make sure they could read nothing in his expression. They were giving him too much credit. The truth was he had been slow. There had been reasons, not least the sudden appearance of a host of men like Willoughby Carmichael, but by far the most prominent reason for his slowness was the power of hope.

Hope was responsible for his mistakes. He still loved his wife and even though he could see that her love for him was gone, he could never hate her. He wanted her back, still, always, and a part of him still thought that she might love him again. None of this was her fault. She had been corrupted from the moment she was in her mother's womb. He wished with all his heart that things could have been different, that she had the opportunity to see the error of her ways and walk away from The Guild for the final time. Perhaps he could convince her in Hell. He would have eternity to work at it after all.

He could feel nothing below the neck. The bullets had run through or clipped something vital, paralysing him. He was thankful for that in a way, for it spared him the pain.

He was disappointed however that he couldn't look at his watch. The timer was counting down to zero. He would guess there were a hundred seconds or so to go before the black box he had swallowed would omit a wave, reaching the devices that he had stored in the far corners of the factory, out of range of their detectors, devices that would blow the whole building to smithereens. It was a sensational design and of his creation, customised from a hybrid model he had invented years ago but never shared. They wouldn't know what hit them.

Agatha moved forward and dropped onto one knee. She held her husband by the side of the face, softly, almost lovingly. 'Does it hurt?' she said.

Peter smiled weakly. 'It doesn't tickle.'

'Peter,' Agatha said sternly. 'Tell me where Finn is.'

'If I could move my arms,' Peter said, 'I would break your neck.'

'No,' said Agatha, 'you wouldn't. And that's why you fail.'

Peter said nothing. *Keep talking.* He was happy for her to waste as much time as possible.

'I guess this is that moment in the story,' said Agatha, 'where the villain tells the hero their plan before the good guys break in through the door and save the day.' She gave her husband a long lingering kiss. 'Not this time. Real life doesn't do happy endings. In real life the bad guys prosper because they're willing to do the things the good guys won't. '

'Finish it!' Theo said. 'You do it!'

Agatha stepped back and removed a small pistol from her pocket. She raised it up.

Peter saw it then, in her eyes, the devastation she was feeling. It was hidden from everywhere else, hidden by the coldness of her expression, by the robustness of her voice, by the unflinching, confident posture – but the eyes couldn't be anything other than honest. She showed off to the world her lack of emotion about what she had to do. But he could see that it was a mask, a mistruth.

He closed his eyes as if he was drifting off into a beautiful sleep. Sixty seconds or so and it would all be over.

Chapter Sixteen

Felicity Gower was surrounded by colour. She stood on a small hill, the grass thin and patchy, burnt a striking yellow by the simmering heat of a summer sun. A cherry blossom tree was growing on the summit in full bloom, defying the seasons, the branches covered in the sweetest of pink flowers. A fast flowing river moved past the base of the hill, the hill splitting the blue water into forks, the water cascading over damp grey rocks. A hundred butterflies filled the air, a hundred different shades, flying past her nose.

Finn was there too, a little distance away from her, lying on his stomach on the grass. He looked asleep, peaceful.

She closed her eyes. The wings of the butterflies were floating close to her face, soothing her with a breeze. The sound of nature had a soothing quality too, the click of the crickets far away, the serene whistle of birdsong in the air, the rhythmic tune of the rippling water going on its journey from spring to sea. It was ambient. It was beautiful. But then there came a rumble of thunder, a distant storm was gathering –

Felicity opened her eyes. The butterflies were gone, replaced by flakes of snow drifting aimlessly in front of her. There was no hill, no cherry blossom, and no river. The expressive colours had been devoured by darkness and paled into nonexistence. Cold had eaten the warmth. And Finn was no longer asleep. Instead he was lying on a filthy floor, peering out through a small gap in a wall that was derelict.

She was still standing in the doorway of the fire exit. The stress had forced her to go to a different place in her mind. She was no guru of meditation. She had just always had the gift to let her thoughts go to somewhere calming. The gift had been indispensable during her mother's illness, allowing her to escape from the monotony of depressing hospitals and dreary funeral homes, exchanging them for sepia toned vistas and stunning landscapes. But the fantasies never lasted long, the lure of the real world too strong.

Felicity was firmly back in the real world now. A song she didn't recognise was playing from the factory floor, the lyrics becoming unintelligible as they were interrupted by bursts of clattering gunfire.

She ducked down, making sure she couldn't be seen and joined Finn on the floor. She nudged him, trying to convince him in urgent whispers the main reasons why they shouldn't be there. But her new friend proved to be a stronger brick-wall than the one he was leaning up against. She may as well have not existed.

Felicity wasn't about to go running off on her own. She was terrified. It was dark and she didn't have a clue where she was. Without a wealth of other options, she could do nothing else but join Finn in witnessing the carnage down below.

It didn't take her long to conclude that Peter Carruthers was a savage maniac. He wasn't always in sight, disappearing from their vantage point from time to time as he took out the intruders one by one, but when he was visible he was tough beyond belief and impressive in a methodical, violent way.

Curiosity took over. What was happening below was horrific, people were dying after all, but it was a series of shocking images of the like that she had never seen before and would likely never see again. She never understood the car crash analogy, figuring that if she saw one she wouldn't want to see some poor motorist gory and in tears. But if men were spilling out of the crashed car, firing all over the place and taking one another out with some form of martial art, she had little doubt that she wouldn't be able to take her eyes off it.

She looked at Finn. He was suffering badly. His chest was beating furiously and he was sweating heavily. His hands, pressing into the wall, were shaking with rage. More worryingly he wasn't in control of his emotions and if his expression carried a message it was that he was more than a little tempted to go down there and assist his father.

That message became more real when they saw the two bullets knock Peter Carruthers off his feet. Finn jerked forward, made a loud noise that was covered by the sound of the action below, and he was on his way upwards, getting to his feet, desperate to head for the staircase.

Felicity dragged him back down and they struggled there, rolling on the floor, their clothes getting filthy with muck and grime. It was only when he caught sight of his mother that Finn stopped and composed himself. Her emergence turned him pale and he was back to the gap, watching her step forward. They couldn't hear everything that was said below, only the odd raised voice.

She didn't know what to do next. The covert observation had given her the first time to think in quite some time. What exactly was she involved in? Before today she hadn't really known Finn Carruthers. He was a commodity that she needed to use, she *had* been surprised by him, he was more handsome and better company than she had thought, but it didn't change anything. He was nothing to her. She didn't *want* or *need* a boyfriend. She had seen friend potential, but even friendship had its boundaries and they didn't extend to tolerate gunfights, strange family mysteries and running away from platoons of heavily armed lunatics.

Felicity heard her inner voice. It spoke to her a lot and it always sounded like her mother. *He's just some random boy. Get home, Fliss. This has nothing to do with you. It's not your problem. Get home, tell the Wickers, call the police. Run, Felicity Gower, run.*

Part of her didn't like what the voice was telling her. It was too callous, cruel even. She surely couldn't leave without giving him a chance to come with her.

She tapped him on the shoulder. 'Finn,' she said as quietly as a mouse, 'I can't tell you how much we need to leave right now.'

He ignored her. He didn't even blink.

'Finn!' she said, a little louder, prodding him in the back. 'Look at what's happening! We need to leave!'

Again, there was no response to her plea.

This was it. Her mind was set, chance given, chance thrown back in her face. She was going to leave him. *Run, Felicity Gower, run.*

Fate must have had other ideas. Finn suddenly shot up, exposing his presence, his head popping up above the wall, clearly visible to anyone down below who happened to be looking.

Such was her shock Felicity found herself rising with him and she didn't realise her mistake until it was too late. She looked down, seeing the reason why Finn had been so reckless. Finn's mother was standing above his father, aiming a gun at his head, her intentions shockingly clear.

'Noooooooooooooooooooo!' Finn screamed.

His mother looked directly at them. She shouted an order. A large man with her immediately disappeared into the darkness – a second smaller man joined her and they sprinted towards the foreman's office. The last man stayed behind, taking a few steps closer to their captive, taking over.

'RUN!' Peter Carruthers bellowed. The final masked man struck him in the stomach with the butt of his rifle.

Felicity tugged at Finn's jacket but he was rooted firmly to the spot, reluctant to leave. She shouted, cursed, urged, physically pulling him away from the window but when they made it to the dark of the fire exit he seemed to come to his senses, his resistance easing. The pitch black passageway devoured them, their footsteps echoing on the metal of the steps.

The pursuers were making their own noise, calling to one another in excitement, the voices getting louder as they gained on them, adults moving faster than children –

Felicity hit a heavy door in front of her and she was out in the open, her feet making contact with something softer – grass – snow. There were trees, a forest. She looked down to the small drop of a hill leading to a slim stream of water.

Finn had stopped. He was a mess, crying, spitting out saliva, pacing back and forth, a spirit torn, one side wanting to escape, the other desperate to confront his vile mother.

Felicity staggered backwards, almost toppling down the drop of the hill. She was shaking her head, realising that she couldn't influence him anymore. Her mother's voice had returned. *Ten seconds and he's on his own. Run, Felicity Gower, run.*

She started her countdown. *One, two, three –*

Finn's mother and the shorter man emerged from the exit. Finn dashed forward without fear, fuelled by rage, lashing out with punches and yelling a series of words that were drowned out by the erratic bluster of his tears. The smaller man stopped Finn, grabbing his from behind and pinning his arms tightly against his chest.

Four, five –

Felicity wanted to help, the emotion strong, instinctive. She searched the ground beneath her feet, for any random piece of nature she could use as a weapon, but there wasn't anything of use.

The hand gripped her by the collar and lifted her off her feet. The larger man had appeared from nowhere. The desire to resist was powerful, the ability not so much, and all she could do was kick her legs out in front of her like an angry child being removed from a playground by her parents against her will.

Six, seven –

Felicity could do nothing to break free. The larger man was taking her back towards the factory. She was screaming, demanding to be released, calling for Finn to help her, begging her late mother or God himself to intervene.

Eight, nine – was there any point in continuing to count – time was running out.

'Get them to the vehicles,' Finn's mother was saying. 'We move in–'

There was a bright, blinding flash, followed by a horrific thunderclap of noise and a brutal gust of sizzling wind. The light of the world went out and Felicity was flying, weightless, blessed with a floating freedom. Her stomach dropped. She was falling.

She landed in the stream at the bottom of the hill, shattering the ice. Her head snapped back and collided painfully with the pebbles on the bed of the stream underneath.

The blow to her head almost knocked her out. There was the hot metallic taste of blood in her mouth, warm and sticky against her tongue. She opened her eyes to spinning, as if everything in the world, every image and memory that ever existed, sat in the grooves of a perpetually rotating roulette wheel.

Felicity got to her feet, forcing herself to focus. She looked back up the hill to the factory. The building was a mass of broken brick and furious flame, the structure appearing as though it had been physically lifted from its foundations and slammed back down with fury. The skeleton of the factory had survived but everything else had been distorted, deformed and shattered by the strength of the explosion.

It had been Peter Carruthers' plan all along, she realised with a sense of looming disbelief. That was why he had looked so panicked at the end. He was dead, having sacrificed himself, blowing the building up and trying to take as many of these hideous people with him as possible, giving Finn time to get away. The factory had been Peter Carruthers Alamo.

Felicity looked all around her. Finn was lying next to his mother, thrown clear by the blast, both of them unconscious and face down against the bank of the stream. The larger man she found on the opposite side of the bank, his feet poking out beneath a blanket of bricks. The smaller man was nowhere to be seen.

Felicity couldn't force her brain to click into gear. She had frozen, unable to think of anything sensible to do. Every part of her body ached.

The countdown, which was stopped by the rude interruption, started once more.

Nine, ten –

More explosions, up above. Parts of the building were falling down.

She turned and saw the tall trees of the wood.

Run, Felicity Gower, run.

Part Two

Chapter Seventeen

The body was resting in the metal drawer, eyes closed and lips blue, the skin having taken on a ghostly white sheen that made it resemble the alabaster of a sleeping statue. The marks were visible on the neck, the harsh bruising where it had been broken but despite the signature of a violent demise the man looked at peace.

The morgue was a small and sterile room, one wall dominated by identical rows of drawers, four high and six across. The lighting was bright – more so than a normal room to aid the requirement for detailed examinations. There was a single window and two metal tables that were used for autopsies. Three wooden desks, belonging to the coroners who were off duty, were situated at the back of the room near the door. The desks were covered with a variety of surgical instruments.

James Devery was riddled with discomfort as he looked down at the dead man, not least because a man had the right to privacy, never more so than in death. He had never dealt well with such matters, ever since his father died all that time ago in Ireland. His father had been a proud, strict, and religious man and in his last weeks was reduced into something unrecognisable, regressing into a frail and shrunken skeleton, his pride eroded away by the disease that was eating him up from the inside. He recalled kissing him on the head in the funeral directors in Dublin. His father didn't feel real, his skin having the feel of cold, hard wax.

The years had done little to soften the pain of that memory. His relationship with his father had been fragile and fraught with a series of disagreements. He had rebelled against the strictness, incurring wrath and eventually banishment, only returning when his father's days grew shorter and the opportunity for reconciliation was dwindling. It had been too late. Things were left unsaid, bridges left unrepaired, grudges left unresolved. And it had haunted James Devery every day since.

'What time is it?' Willoughby Carmichael asked. He was stood on the other side of the drawer, his eyes expectant and impatient.

'A few minutes after two am,' Devery told him, dropping his bag carefully to the floor.

'Then we mustn't linger.' Willoughby said. 'Is it him?'

'Don't know for sure,' Devery looked carefully at the body, 'Not seen him in a long time and only met him once. Looks like him.'

Willoughby wasn't willing to deal with uncertainty and he had no such qualms with spending quality time with the dead. He reached into the drawer and removed the plastic cover, the body naked underneath. He checked the man over from head to toe, searching and examining the skin for the evidence he required, before tucking his hands underneath and tilting the body onto its side.

Devery watched in silence. He resisted the urge to say something about the rough treatment of the corpse. It wasn't worth the argument. Willoughby would say their relationship was strong, and he was right to an extent. He owed his brother in law much, some would say everything, but no matter how hard he tried he couldn't bring himself to trust him. Willoughby was the wisest man he had ever met, blessed with a shrewd brain and an admirable passion. But there was little denying that he was a fanatic and there was little in life where it was healthy to be fanatical.

There was caution there too, not enough to be scared, but certainly enough to be wary. Physically, Devery was his superior, Willoughby not being an athletic man. Willoughby was not particularly tall, neither fat nor muscly but naturally bulky. He was sixty five, his hair for the most part black and thick, with subtle streaks of grey that were distinguished. No, it was his cunning that generated the caution, his mind and knowledge compensating for his lack of physical imposition. Knowledge truly was power and Willoughby wasn't afraid to use his power to manipulate those around him.

'Found it,' said Willoughby, pointing down to the area on the back above the body's buttocks. On the skin there was the mark he was looking for, a black cross with a circle on top of it. He gently placed the body back down, satisfied.

'Have him as John Doe,' said Devery, reading the small notice that sat above the drawer. He bowed his head solemnly. 'I'll say what no one else will. You rest yourself in peace, Edwin Cavell.'

Willoughby said his own prayer, closing his eyes, his words kept silent and personal to himself.

Devery waited for the prayer to finish, at one with his own thoughts. He had never wanted to come to the morgue in the first place and he had been the soul voice of opposition. Getting in had been easy enough. There were no alarms and the security guard on duty was an old man who seemed content to sit behind the monitor at his desk and read a book. But there were too many risks involved and not enough gains to justify the endeavour.

'I thought it before,' Devery said, 'and I'll say it now. This is pointless. He's too far gone. Isn't like his heart stopped beating while reading the paper. They broke his god damn neck, Will. No one comes back from that –'

'We're successful,' Willoughby reminded him, 'and he leads us to the boy. He *is* the Guardian. We're drawn to this place in a broad fashion but he was drawn to the boy specifically. That makes him invaluable. You'd be surprised, just how far a body can go, how much punishment it can take. Never give up hope on anything in this world before trying.'

'He's been dead two days –'

'Bought someone back after five before –'

'I'll believe it when I see it.'

Devery picked up the limp wrist of the corpse and let it go to illustrate his point. The arm landed with a lifeless plump. It was just so very pointless.

'Watch the door for me, please,' Willoughby asked, ushering him away. 'Don't want you hanging over me while I do this, with all your doubt.'

Devery was happy to move away from the drawer. There wasn't a single part of him that was looking forward to what was about to happen. He had seen it twice before and still hadn't gotten used to it. Willoughby called it a gift, his wife a calling but to Devery it was nothing short of old fashioned witchcraft.

Willoughby got to work, caressing the dead man's wrist with his fingertips where he would normally find a pulse. He next moved his hand to the corpse's heart, again softly massaging the skin, trying to generate a response.

Devery could tell from Willoughby's expression that it wasn't working, meaning there was only one option remaining. Willoughby called it the *kiss of death*, fully aware of the ironic contradiction. He bent forward, pushing himself into the drawer a little further and placing his lips onto those of the body. Then he took the deepest breath he could and exhaled, sending the generated air deep into the cold depths of Edwin Cavell's lungs.

A cold tingle shot up Devery's spine and the hairs on his neck stood on end. The body moved – only slightly – but it *definitely moved* and in an instant a wealth of colour burst back into the dead man's cheeks and chest. The eyelid's flickered, opened, and the fingers on his left hand twitched. The corpse shuddered once, vibrating violently in the metal drawer, the drawer rattling on its casters. The brightest of lights emanated from Edwin Cavell's eyes, from his mouth, growing and growing, brighter and brighter –

The colour faded away as quickly as it had arrived, the light dimming into nothing, the body still, lifeless, and dead once more.

'Maybe we should have had a wager,' Devery said.

'I don't think you're funny,' Willoughby said, disappointed at this failure.

'Neither do I,' said Devery, 'but at least now maybe we can give him the respect he deserves and leave him be.'

112

'Don't talk to me about respect,' Willoughby said with a sudden surge of anger. 'It's all you talk about, James, morality, morality, morality, regardless of the risk it puts on the rest of us. Some things have to suffer if we want to achieve our goal and if it's to be our morality then so be it.'

Devery longed to retaliate but he managed to resist. Willoughby and the others still hadn't forgiven him for his secret rendezvous with Peter Carruthers and he would have to show remorse for a while yet. They blamed him for the predicament they now faced, even his wife. The way they saw it, if he hadn't got involved, there was a very good chance they would have the child in their possession.

He didn't however regret his actions and not that he would admit it to the others but he would do the same again given the chance. They had told the tales of the Monster, of the dark deeds, the unforgiveable wickedness, of the despicable man who fully deserved the strange twist of fate that had fallen upon him. But that night out in the snow by the garages, Devery hadn't seen a monster. No, he had seen a father, desperate to protect the child he loved while the walls closed in all around him. He saw regret there too, the need for a redemption that Peter Carruthers knew in his heart would never come.

Devery hadn't used his real name, he had been sensible enough to take that precaution. Gulliver had come to him, off the cuff, clutched from the memory of his favourite book by Jonathan Swift. Twenty four hours later Peter Carruthers was dead. He would never get a chance to make a real introduction and to apologise for assaulting him. All he could do was take a secret oath that he would *find* and *protect* his son. He only hoped that Peter Carruthers could hear the oath in the afterlife and take at least a little solace.

Willoughby pointed to Devery's bag on the floor. 'Let's get this over with, please, if you will.'

Devery bent down and removed the small can of petrol from the bag. He loosened the cap. 'This is also wrong,' he said. 'I'm not sure we have to do this.'

'The others will come here too,' said Willoughby, 'and if they don't, someone will start asking questions about Cavell's mark. The body needs to be destroyed.'

Devery hesitated at first but then he tipped the petrol over the corpse, attempting to cover it from head to toe.

Willoughby smiled reassuringly. 'Believe me when I say –'

The sentence went unfinished. The door to the morgue creaked open and a man walked inside. The man saw Devery and Willoughby standing over the drawer and he gasped and then turned to run.

Devery leapt into action, stopping the departure by throwing the petrol can into the visitor's back before thundering across the room and slamming the man into the wall.

Willoughby took a few steps forward. He couldn't hide his smugness at his prediction having been proven right almost immediately. 'Hello, Jared,' he said.

In the short melee, Devery hadn't realised who it was that had entered. Now that he knew, he felt the instant burn of a familiar hatred. Jared De Mornay was a weasel, small and skinny with long dark hair and a metal piercing through the bottom of his nostrils. A colourful tattoo crept out from beneath his shirt and ran up the side of his neck. They had been acquaintances once, *never* friends, but members of the Brotherhood, back in its infancy and when it was little more than a club and long before it had evolved into the bunch of murdering scumbags it was today.

'You alone?' Willoughby asked the gate-crasher to the party.

Jared wasn't about to answer. He was still writhing, struggling to break free.

Devery was strong enough to restrain him with one hand. With the other he eased the door ajar and looked out into the corridor. The security guard was gone.

Jared stopped his wriggling, abruptly, becoming perfectly still. He slowly rotated his head so that he was eyeball to eyeball with Devery. His eyes became wide, not with fear or shock, but something else, something that could have been a demented form of happiness. He opened his mouth wide to reveal his rapidly diminishing set of yellow, rotting teeth, and then broke out into a crazed cackle.

'What you finding so funny?' Devery said. He feigned a punch.

Jared blinked but his laugh remained wild. 'Not alone,' he said.

Devery glanced back out into the corridor. There was no one out there. 'You're lying,' he said.

'Look closer!' Jared said. His noises of amusement turned into whoops of joy.

It gave Devery pause for thought. Could he have missed something? No, he couldn't have done, the hallway *was* empty, he was sure of that. Still, he checked it once more, refocusing on the details. The hallway was narrow, blue linoleum on the floor, the guard's small desk at the far end in front of a set of automatic doors activated by a movement sensor. Fluorescent lights ran down the centre of the ceiling, making it well lit, no shadows. There was no other furniture, no other doors, nowhere else to hide –

The doors to the hallway suddenly opened. There was no one on the other side to have activated the sensor.

Devery turned back to Jared.

'Gonna kill ya, he is,' Jared said, 'rip your heads off your neck! Both of ya! Kill ya bad!'

Devery was incredulous to the warning. 'I'm faster than –'

'He's faster!' Jared shouted. 'Don't matter how fast you is! He's faster! Rip ya arms and head off he will!'

'Who will?' Willoughby questioned. For his part he was taking the warning seriously. 'Who are you talking about?'

Jared dropped his voice to a whisper. 'Tobias,' he said. The name stopped his laughter. Now Jared looked scared and it was back to struggling, the polar opposites of his demeanour suggesting a man who had lost his mind.

Devery tightened his grip and went to speak but no words formed. He afforded himself a little laugh, although he wasn't sure what he found funny. That name – Tobias – was absolutely absurd, a joke surely. Even Jared De Mornay wasn't that insane.

115

'You're talking about a myth,' Willoughby said.

The lights out in the hallway flickered.

That commanded Devery's attention. He saw them, one by one, the lights starting to rupture and go out. It began above the automatic entrance doors, sending sparks and broken plastic towards the ground, leaving the areas behind them to fall into darkness, a darkness that seemed to be alive and was creeping towards the morgue.

'Will,' Devery said, 'something's coming!'

Smash – smash – smash - the final light in the hallway died.

Devery slammed the door shut, locking it from the inside. He let Jared go and paced backwards into the centre of the room. The door handle moved downwards. Someone was trying to come in. Three times the handle moved. The lock held.

'You dead men!' Jared said. He had retreated back into a corner and was covering his head with his hands. 'We all is! Don't trust me, he'll think I with you! We're all dead men!'

There was a sound a lot like thunder, then the door smashing away from its hinges, the force from the other side sending it flying across the room and smashing into the window, taking out the glass. The overhead lights in the morgue glowed bright and hot and then they too exploded. There was darkness, brief and horrifying, until a set of sparks ignited the spilt petrol around the discarded can. The ignition started in a pool before running across the floor and coursing into Edwin Cavell's mortuary drawer.

Jared stood up on the other side of the wall of fire, screaming like a madman once more, asking them to help him.

Devery dragged Willoughby towards the window, the flames growing with fury and burning up towards the ceiling. Together they fell through the gap, two floors up, landing with a painful thump on the snowy grass outside. The morgue detonated with an explosion, the fire shooting outside above them.

A shouted name echoed out from inside, from the lips of Jared De Mornay – *Tobias* – *Tobias* – *Tobias* – over and over again, before falling silent.

Chapter Eighteen

Felicity Gower surveyed the bedroom with disgust. The bed was unmade and the shag-pile carpet concealed by a collection of pizza boxes, chip shop papers, and most shockingly of all dirty underwear. To compliment the visual grime was an aroma that smelt like a dead animal that had been left in the summer heat for a long weekend. *Would you like to try our new fragrance, Madam? It's called Roadkill.* The room had all the trappings of a teenage boy and was what made most teenage boys such disgusting little rats.

It was early evening and Felicity flicked on a lamp. She stood up on the bed and checked out the DVD collection that ran along a shelf above it. Without knowing why, she had always taken an interest in people's bookcases and shelves. Tonight she was greeted by a collection of butch and brutal movies about killer cyborgs, maverick cops, master villains, and Kung-Fu masters. Yet hidden in the corner were four of five romantic titles, not male-friendly romantic comedies either but unabashed, frothy monstrosities that no teenage boy would ever admit to liking, let alone owning.

Felicity picked one up and started to read the sleeve before remembering where she was and placing it quickly back where she had found it. She wasn't here to be nosey. Instead she sat down on the bed, picking up a newspaper that she had stolen from the table of the kitchen downstairs.

She flicked through the pages. The paper was The Gloucestershire Echo, a local periodical, one day old. She ignored the uninteresting articles about the weather, about residents protesting against the planned building of houses on greenbelt land, of the new proposals for an elaborate new shopping centre in Cheltenham, and the small fire that had gutted the hospital morgue. She only stopped her idle browsing when she got to page twenty-three.

Felicity read the headline of the page out loud. 'Local Man Loses Cancer Battle!'

The accompanying photo showed the Carruthers family, Peter, Agatha, and Finn posing in happier times and smiling for the camera at some birthday or anniversary. The article was short with ten lines, the information confirming sadly the end of Peter Carruthers short but brave battle against bowel cancer. It finished by confirming that Agatha and Finn had departed to Malaga, Spain to recover with the support of their family during what was sure to be a difficult time.

Felicity wanted to tear the page out. She wasn't stupid and the extent of the nonsense infuriated her. This wasn't news. It was a manipulation, orchestrated by Agatha Carruther's *people*. It had no right being there. Her own mother had died and it didn't make the paper. People died every day, always tragic, rarely newsworthy. No, the article existed because it needed to be there. The world needed to know that Peter Carruthers was dead and that Agatha and Finn were no longer around, embraced by loved ones that didn't exist. That way, there would be no questions about any of their absences.

She finished the rest of the paper without having to stop again. She found no mention of a car crash and death in King Edward Avenue, no dramatic pictures of a massive factory fire on the outskirts of town, no stories telling the reader that in the quieter corners of Gloucestershire, in the darkest of the shadows, a body count was mounting. What's more there was no article covering the worrying news of a young girl called Felicity Gower going missing.

Felicity crumpled up the paper in a temper and threw it on the floor with the rest of the garbage. She doubted the owner of the room would notice. She stood and made her way to the window, easing the curtain back a touch and looking down into the drive. No one had come home. She would have to continue waiting.

She returned to the bed and threw herself down, stretching out, closing her eyes as the fatigue from the last few days hit her like a sledgehammer to the forehead. Sleep was just one of a host of things that had the potential to make her feel better, along with a much needed shower and a change of clothes.

A line from a nursery rhyme drifted through her head and prevented her from getting too comfy. *Who's been sleeping in my bed?*

No, Felicity thought. She forced herself up. *You can't sleep, despite how much you want to. You have to be alert. But my God I'm tired.*

She looked around the room once more, trying to find something to focus on to keep herself awake but nothing really appealed to her. Instead she decided to think hard about her quest so far, casting her mind back to gaining entry to the house and her efforts to make sure it went unnoticed.

She was confident that she had done well. The backdoor had been locked but someone had foolishly left one of the small windows to the pantry open for the cat, wide enough for her to squeeze an arm through and open the larger window beneath it. The newspaper was the only item she had disturbed. Everywhere else, the hallway, the staircase, there were no traces.

There was a sound from down in the darkness of the house, of a door opening and a set of keys being thrown onto a work surface.

Felicity took herself quickly back to the window, still no car, still no adults. This was paramount. Adults would most certainly call the police. There would be no talking, no chance to put her case across. All they would care about was the trespassing.

More sounds, someone coming up the stairs. This *someone* was heavy footed.

It was time to put her plan into action. Safety first, she retreated into the only place she could think of, into the double wardrobe, closing the door carefully behind her. She left a slight opening so that she could see out a little into the room. She had to make sure that she had the right person before making her presence known.

The bedroom door opened and in walked Henry Pringle. He was singing a random tune to himself, completely unaware of the intruder lurking inside his room. He threw a rucksack into the corner and plucked the controller of his game console from the floor. With his other hand he flicked his little television on.

Felicity's could only see him side on. She saw him step back to the bed and was about to sit down when he stopped what he was doing, standing perfectly still.

She held her breath. Did he sense something? Did he know she was there? How could he? This wouldn't do, if he ran and raised the alarm, all would be scuppered.

Henry farted. The fart was *loud and proud*, not once, not twice, but three times in quick succession, a cacophony of putrid, full bodied, squelchy wind. After the last effort he evidently approved and laughed out loud. 'Don't remember eating that,' he said crudely.

Felicity had to put her hand over her mouth to stop herself from laughing. It wasn't easy and things got that much harder when Henry decided he was going to get comfortable for the evening and took his trousers off, revealing a pair of grotty old boxer shorts with a huge hole that provided an ample view of his left bum cheek.

The sound of a whimpering squeal escaped through her fingers.

Henry spun round and gazed at the wardrobe as if a poltergeist was hiding somewhere in his room. He only needed to use one of his senses. He heard that alright. 'Mummy?' he asked nervously. 'Is that you?'

That turned something that was already difficult into something that was borderline impossible. She could barely breathe and had an abundance of comebacks locked and loaded, ready to be unleashed. She could picture Henry wearing a patterned wool jumper, playing hide and seek with his *Mummy* and then skipping down to the kitchen for hot chocolate with marsh mellows and then a great big, snuggly cuddle and an afternoon of Disney classics.

Say something, she urged herself. That was what she needed to do, to get everything started. It had to be sensible, something that would make him calm and not scare him away. She needed him, which meant she needed to be grown up and not allow her whacky and silly side to get the better of her.

Failure was inevitable. She burst from the wardrobe and shouted. 'SURPRISE!!!!!'

Henry screamed. The scream was horrendously high pitched and he fell back in shock, falling into the bed with such a force that most of the DVD's toppled from the shelf and landed on top of him. He wasn't down for long, screaming even louder, diving from the surface and attempting to disappear under the bed. The space beneath the bed wasn't big enough for a fifteen year old and within seconds he had got himself stuck and was wriggling, trying to force himself further under.

Felicity stared down at half-a-body stuck there, the bum cheek peeking out at her from the hole in the boxer shorts. 'Henry,' she said, 'it's me, Felicity Gower –'

He started to yell. 'Help! Help! Help –'

'No one's coming to help you, moron,' She kicked one of his legs. 'Henry! Listen to me!! It's Felicity!'

He stopped wriggling and was a little calmer. 'What?'

She repeated her name for a third time and with a little venom in it. She didn't like repeating herself that much and didn't feel *that* guilty for scaring him.

'Felicity … Gower?' he asked warily.

There was a long silence.

Henry's voice became quiet. 'You scared the hell out of me.'

Felicity nodded. 'Yeah, I kinda saw that. Sorry, didn't mean to.'

'Can you see my bum?'

'Only half of it,' said Felicity. 'It's a nice bum, Henry, well not nice, but it's not a bad one either. No offence, you should really get some new boxer shorts.'

It took Henry a while to answer. 'I farted … didn't I?' he said, clearly embarrassed. If she could see him she was sure he'd be blushing.

'Yeah, you did,' Felicity chuckled. 'Don't feel bad. We all fart, Henry. I fart. The Pope farts. David Beckham farts. Mother Teresa probably used to enjoy a guff from time to time. It's nothing to be ashamed of.' She sat down on the bed. 'Henry, are you going to come out? I really need to speak to you properly. I haven't got too much time.'

'I'm not sure,' said Henry. 'Felicity ... can I ask you ... what the hell are you doing in my bedroom?'

'That bit's simple,' she said calmly, 'but a bit of a long story. I need your help. And you're the only person I can turn to.'

Chapter
Nineteen

Finn Carruthers sat through the early hours of the cold morning in a dreamlike trance, staring at the rotting walls of the wooden treehouse. It was a miserable place that he hadn't left in three long days. If such a thing existed, the treehouse would have been somewhere at the lower end of the treehouse market. It rested amongst the branches of a stoic oak tree, four crudely assembled walls of pine that let the wind in, capped off by a flat felt roof that had once belonged to a garden shed. A ladder led to a trap door and a small window had been carved untidily into one of the walls.

His body had reached the miserable levels of exhaustion but his mind remained annoyingly alert, dwelling on the lies and complexities of his parents and haunted by the memories of the bloodthirsty savagery that had unfolded in the factory. He bore a selection of scars, both physical and mental, and was certain that he would continue to do so for years.

Felicity returned a couple of hours before dawn, poking her head through the trapdoor and bringing with her a large pizza. He was tempted to complain. Their clothes were dirty and damp, having not been changed in days. She had also been gone far too long and time seemed to have stood still during her absence, but the smell of the food destroyed the fleeting desire for conflict.

'I'll say grace,' she said once safely inside, picking up the pizza box. 'We thank you Lord, for giving us fat people who demand fast food at ungodly hours, thus requiring takeaways to stay open twenty four hours a day. And we thank you for Henry Pringle, the pennies from his piggy bank, the generosity that paid for this fine feast.'

'Amen,' said Finn.

Felicity explained as they ate that she had made it to Henry's house, confident that she hadn't been followed, and had succeeded in securing Henry's help without mentioning Finn's involvement and scaring him off. Henry had her cashpoint card, her pin, and strict instructions. The reason for the delay was simple. As she was about to leave an ominous car had parked on the opposite side of the street. It sat there for three hours, no one coming or going. *They* were watching Henry's house and she suspected that had Peter Carruthers not made such a good job of killing most of the resources, they would have watched it all night. She waited for the car to disappear before heading back.

Finn understood that he owed Felicity Gower *everything*. She had admitted that she had almost left him behind but the important fact was she hadn't, dragging him painfully through the woods, as far as she could manage before his dead weight became too much and she had collapsed in an exhausted heap. She had told him that flashlights had shone through the trees, searching for them, only going out when the sirens of the fire engines sounded in the distance.

Finn had no memory of the escape or of coming round. All he could remember was suddenly being awake and the hours of walking silently through the deep snow of the forest, then the relief when the trees finally thinned out and they found the treehouse. A large house was close by, the treehouse surely belonging to the owner. It was fortunate that treehouses were a summer activity and so far they hadn't been disturbed or discovered.

When he was finished with the pizza he gestured for Felicity to join him and they huddled together, pulling the bed sheet tightly around their shoulders. The morning was dark and bitterly cold and they both understood that they couldn't stay there much longer, at the risk of freezing to death. Felicity had *borrowed* the sheet from a washing basket at the back of the nearby house, rewarding the homeowners for their unwitting hospitality by stealing their laundry. The thick duvet was missing from inside and it provided little warmth.

She placed an arm around his back and nestled into his stomach. There was no shyness, the need to share body warmth far more important than any awkwardness of cuddling up to a boy.

'Can I ask you something?' she said. Her voice was quiet and she was sleepy.

'Go on,' Finn said.

'Why haven't you cried yet?' she said.

'Does that matter?'

'You just lost your Dad,' said Felicity. 'I know I make fun out of lots of things but I wouldn't make fun of that. We're friends, Finn. You don't need to worry about doing that kind of thing in front of me.'

Finn considered what his response might sound like, it being a question that he had asked himself on more than one occasion. Whenever his father's name was mentioned something *did* stir inside of him, hinting that tears were not far away. But something prevented them from coming, other emotions that were stronger, confused feelings of hate and resentment that created the thickest of dams that stubbornly kept the waters at bay.

'All I can think about is *her*,' was all he could say, 'and just how much I hate her.'

Felicity didn't say anything. She had wanted him to talk to her and she seemed happy to listen. But when Finn didn't add to the statement she took the hint that it was time to change the subject.

'So,' she said, 'what we going to do from here? We going to find this Willoughby dude, like your Dad said? Maybe find out what this obsidian thing means?'

'Nope,' said Finn, 'we're going to meet up with Henry, get the hell out of town and never look back.'

'And ... what we going to do when we get wherever-it-is-we're-going?'

'I kinda figured we'd work that out when we got there.'

'Sounds like a well thought through plan,' Felicity said with a little chuckle. She had closed her eyes and was drifting off. 'I'd love some answers though, but can't help but think that running away is probably a better idea.'

'Good,' Finn said. 'You get some sleep ... big day tomorrow.'

'Big day tomorrow,' she said, concurring.

She became quiet and slept solidly for a few hours, letting out a cute little snore throughout. Sleep didn't find Finn, the same way that it hadn't found him the previous three nights. His brain lacked the ability to shut down, refusing to relax, continuing to ask a million questions, most of them speculating, trying to reach some clarity as to why all this was happening to him.

By the time morning broke his body was in an awful state, ready to declare war on the restless mind that had refused it much needed succour. He ached from head to toe. The walk into town that followed, a trek of only four miles, may as well have been a marathon in the desolation of the arctic tundra. Felicity thankfully took the lead, choosing the route, checking the roads for any sign of the strange enemy that was looking for them. Finn was nothing more than a passenger. All he wanted to do was lie down on the curb, crawl up into a ball, and close his eyes and never wake up.

They reached the Kingswood Shopping Centre shortly before noon. Finn's fatigue had reached its miserable zenith, his mood nosediving into the foul depths of despair and agitation, accentuated by the endless array of patisseries and sandwich shops they passed. They had no money and his stomach rumbled like thunder. He was relieved that he didn't have a shotgun, certain that if he did he would have marched into one of the shops, holding the staff at gunpoint and demanding they empty the oven and make him a bacon and sausage sandwich.

Felicity took him by the hand and guided him through the crowds. The centre was busy. England really was in full recovery from the weather by now, no shops being closed and the appetite for bargains re-established.

They moved up the lower two floors of the shopping centre, speeding past the brunt of the popular stores, the entertainment outlets, the jewellers, perfume shops, and mobile phone providers. The agreed rendezvous point was on the third floor and as they made it off the escalator it was a great deal quieter. The top floor of the centre was dominated by empty shop-fronts, large *to let* signs stuck to the inside of the windows. A few open stores were nestled here and there, a small dingy place selling exotic crystals, a rough and ready establishment selling antique vinyl records, a tiny shop selling customised T shirts with strange slogans.

Finn positioned himself at the glass barrier at the edge of the floor. She had chosen a good spot, with lots of exits. There were two escalators, a glass elevator, and a staircase for the more energetic consumers. He observed the rest of the centre that stretched out below, seeming to see more from the high vantage point, despite the height sending him a little dizzy. He focused on two large lagoons all the way down on the ground floor, fed by ornate waterfalls and used as wishing wells, the hopeful collection of coins sparkling from beneath the water.

Felicity joined him at the barrier. 'He's late.'

Finn shook his head. Henry *was* indeed late and it added another surge of heat to Finn's already boiling blood flow.

'I love people watching,' said Felicity.

'I'm not people watching,' said Finn, 'I'm looking out for anything suspicious.'

'I've seen something suspicious,' said Felicity seriously. 'There's a chap down there, very dodgy, something about him I really don't like, seen him talking to loads of people and asking questions. I don't like what he's wearing, sticks out like a sore thumb –'

'What?' Finn was instantly on edge and trying to zero in on what she was seeing. 'Where is he? Do you recognise him?'

'Not sure,' Felicity pointed downwards. 'There … see him? He's stood outside that little hut thing on the first floor, can't miss him, young chap, dark hair, wearing a red hat and carrying some sort of weapon in his hand. The rest of his clothes are really weird too.'

When Finn saw what she was referring to he wanted to punch something. The man she pointed at was indeed wearing a hat, a large sombrero, and the weapon was a yellow maraca. The hut behind him was a food stand and he was handing out leaflets, trying to drum up business.

'The Mexican?' he said. 'The guy dressed like a fajita?'

'Actually,' Felicity said, smiling, 'I think technically you'll find he's a chimichanga –'

'Is there anything you take seriously?' he snapped.

'Not really,' she answered warily, noting his tone, her smile gone. 'Don't you think life's serious enough without us making it more so?'

'No, I don't,' said Finn strongly. 'I *really* don't actually. You know what I think, sometimes things *are* serious and we *should* take them seriously, like right now. Do you think after what's happened in the last week I need you making fun of me?'

'I wasn't making fun of *you*,' said Felicity. 'I was making fun of the chimichanga man –'

'My Dad was blown to pieces –'

'I know, Finn –'

'It's starting to really get on my nerves –'

'Finn,' said Felicity. 'Come on, you know I didn't mean to –'

'Maybe sometimes you should just grow up –'

He stopped himself, the guilt insidiously instant, not enough to diffuse his mood and apologise but enough to see that he had gone too far. No one liked being told to grow up. He retreated away from the barrier and sat down on the step of a coin operated toy helicopter meant for children. Felicity was glaring at him.

'What the hell are *you* doing here?' said someone from behind him.

Henry's voice startled Finn and he shot up. They hadn't even seen him approach – so *much for keeping a close watch*. He must have come up the glass elevator and was now stood behind them, wheeling two bikes, a ruck sack attached to his back.

'I thought you were in France,' Henry said. 'I tried to call you. What are you two fighting about? What's going on? Finn, why are you here? Why are you with *her?*'

'Spain,' Felicity corrected him, walking across. 'He's supposed to be in Spain, *not* France, learn to read maybe? But then he's obviously not in either of those countries, is he?' She glanced at the small bikes he had brought for them. 'I thought we agreed that you would bring bikes for us to borrow?'

'Huh?' Henry said. 'What you mean? These are bikes –'

'For who?' Felicity was taking her temper out on Henry. 'Three year olds? Midgets? Hamsters? Did you get them from the circus?'

'We're talking BMX,' said Henry defensively. 'They're worth a fortune, my brother's cost like six hundred quid, if he finds out I've taken it he'll crucify me.'

'I'll happily supply the nails,' said Felicity. She held out her hand. 'You got my money?'

Henry stood the bikes up against the helicopter. He unzipped one of the side compartments of his bag, pulling out a wad of notes and Felicity's cashpoint card.

Felicity snatched the money and card and then without providing any words of thanks stomped off towards the escalator.

'Where you going?' Finn called after her.

'Downstairs,' she answered without turning around. 'Going to check out train times, as planned, like a grown up!' She stepped onto the first metal step of the escalator.

'Fliss,' Finn shouted. 'Come on –'

'Bite me!' she said before disappearing from view.

Finn looked to Henry. 'Mate,' he said, 'thanks for this but you need to get away from here.'

Henry moved forward, scooping Finn up into a huge, caring hug. Finn could only stand there, Henry attached to him like a sympathetic leech.

'I'm so sorry to hear about your dad,' said Henry.

'Thanks,' Finn said, 'but you're cuddling me. You realise that right?'

Henry let go and took a red faced step back. They were breaking new ground. Fifteen year olds didn't normally have to deal with the aftermath of grief. Their parents normally took care of that kind of thing, the condolences, the uttering of optimistic pearls of wisdom in the face of a loved one's death.

'I'm a little bit lost here,' said Henry, 'What the hell's going on?'

'You know,' said Finn. 'I'm not sure you'd believe me, even if I told you. And it's probably safer if I don't.

Chapter Twenty

Her anger had subsided a little by the time she found herself at the doors to the internet café on the ground floor. The café was a pokey little place, nestled between a clothing store and a calendar shop, overlooking the larger of the lagoon pools in the main precinct. She had forgotten that internet café's even existed and wasn't overly sure they really needed to anymore. Her mobile phone, now sadly deceased, had all the internet capability she would ever need, power on the move and in the palm of her hand.

Felicity made her way inside. There were two computers mounted on desks in the window, old and battered, neither being used. She understood it now, the term 'internet café' was a loose and outdated term, no longer the unique selling point. The customers were drawn to the establishment by the large array of delicious looking homemade cakes and pastries and the shelves of organic produce from local farmers, the computers being relegated to a corner like a naughty child.

She paid the assistant for half an hours surfing time, a custard mille-feuille, three stunningly intricate pink macaroons, and a cappuccino with cream and chocolate sprinkles. She was far too ravished to count calories, calories could go to hell, and she took a seat at one of the stools in the window, placing the cakes and coffee next to the computer. She logged on using the ID the assistant had provided her with, scrawled on a piece of notepaper.

The computer didn't respond immediately and while she waited she stared out the window, bending her head a touch to see past the large red and black letters of the cafés logo that were stuck on the glass. She automatically looked up towards the highest floor. The escalator was empty. From this distance she couldn't see Finn or Henry.

She reverted back to people watching, envying those who strolled past the window, jealous of their right to move around aimlessly without a care in the world. They would claim their lives were far from trouble free, of course they would, but their troubles wouldn't be real, not in comparison to what she and Finn had to face. Working out the best way to pay for a holiday you don't really need *wasn't* stressful. Considering what model I Pod to upgrade to *wasn't* stressful. Trying to plan on how to fit into a size-fourteen-dress instead of a size-sixteen *certainly* wasn't stressful. Solutions were simple. Save up! Be happy with what you've got! Lose some weight!

Her solutions and options however were far from simple. Everything was against her. There were real dangers out there, genuine perils, and an enemy she didn't know or understand. They had decided that it was best to run, not to trust anyone, but she had no idea whether that would work or what the future would look like as fugitives. They were entering a different world, one where everything they knew would be new and challenging, and that was terrifying.

Felicity used her fork, breaking off a large chunk of the mille-feuille. She cooed at the taste and it made her feel a little better. My god, it was the *best thing* she had ever tasted, so good that she could almost feel a pound of sugary fat protrude out from her waist. She had the impulse to be petulant, to run up after she had finished and tell Finn all about the food in great detail, burping in his face to bring the tale to life. But she quickly told herself off. She would fetch him a mille-feuille-to-go. She hadn't forgiven him for telling her to grow up but deep down she understood why he might be a little tetchy and she wouldn't hold it against him.

The computer screen flashed blue, bringing her attention back to the desktop. She got straight to work and tapped away furiously at the keys on the keyboard, keen not to waste time in getting the information she needed. The computer had other ideas and was embarrassingly slow, making her increasingly inpatient as she waited for the page to load.

Finally, the website for British Rail came up on the screen. She clicked on the tickets section and selected Cheltenham Spa in one tab and then paused as she realised she didn't know where they were actually supposed to be heading.

She took another big bite of cake and a long swig of coffee while she thought it over. After a few seconds she made her selection - *All London Stations.* London made the most sense as they could easily *get* lost and *stay* lost in the capital. She pressed enter, nervous to look at the prices. Henry had kindly withdrawn her two hundred pounds, the limit for daily withdrawals from her account. She had healthy savings and could withdraw more but she didn't want to wait twenty four hours. She was relieved to see a train leaving Cheltenham Spa at three o'clock that afternoon, a three hour journey to London and the price comfortably within their budget.

Felicity glanced at the time in the bottom right hand corner of the screen. Fifteen minutes past twelve, she still had plenty of time. They could hop on Henry's embarrassing bikes and cycle like little hamsters and be at the station in no time.

She went to close down the browser and log off but hesitated. She tapped in the name of her mother into the search engine and clicked on the first result, the website of a publisher called Mainstein and Roth. On the list of their authors she found the picture of her mother, black and white, sitting at an old wooden desk with an ink jotter, tapping away on an old fashioned typewriter. The synopsis's for her three books were underneath, short overviews of the trilogy of stories about a girl called Fliss and her adventures in the magical kingdom at the bottom of her garden full of fairies, unicorns, and the Goblin King Zentaur.

She came here often, never finding herself upset, only feeling a strong sense of pride for her mother's achievements.

She clicked the X in the corner of the screen and the image disappeared just as a clumsy customer moved past her and accidently knocked her stool. The piece of paper with her log-in information floated to the floor. She reached down to pick it up and when she sat back up she froze.

The two men from the cycle path were standing on the other side of the glass. Mr Yank and Mr Frog were facing away from her and looking out into the heart of the shopping centre. Mr Frog had a large plaster across his nose where she had broken it. They shared a few words with one another and then strode away, stopping at the wooden barrier in front of the lagoon, in between two large flower pots filled with fake foliage

Felicity moved almost without thinking, leaving the last of her sensational cake and coffee behind. The macaroons she scooped into her hand, eating them whole as she sneaked outside, positioning herself on the other side of one of the flower pots. She was nervous, hoping that she wasn't too close to be discovered but close enough to overhear their conversation.

'Not yet,' she heard the American say. 'Need to be cautious. We're talking about hundreds of people –'

'I say we go up,' said the Frenchman, 'and toss him off the balcony. Then it's done. No more of this sneaking around.'

'If only it were that simple,' said the American.

'Screw the ritual,' said the Frenchman. 'If he's dead, he's dead –'

'We choose to believe in this,' said the American, 'and we believe it all. No short cuts.'

The Frenchman huffed. 'I'm more than happy with certain shortcuts.'

'And we're happy with a hundred witnesses, are we?'

'I would be very happy, yes.'

'I'm not,' the American said sternly. 'And your thoughts about them?'

Felicity sensed the American was pointing. She looked out across the water, nothing standing out.

'Deal with them too,' said the Frenchman coolly.

'They know we're following them,' the American pointed out, 'and they'll be ready.'

The voices abruptly went silent, vanishing.

133

Felicity frowned, waiting a few seconds before pushing a few plastic branches of the plant aside and peering through. The men were gone. She couldn't see where. She wanted to move but found that she was rooted to the spot, the panic setting in. Just how had they been found? What had they done wrong? Then she realised. It was all her fault. They had traced the cash withdrawal and then followed Henry. *Just who are these people?*

Instinct made her glance to the escalators, to see Henry coming down and a man going up. The man wasn't Mr Yank or Mr Frog. It was a man she didn't recognise, short and strange looking, probably someone looking for a nifty t-shirt or an obscure crystal –

The knowledge hit her straight between her rapidly widening eyes. No, she *had* seen him before. Not his face, that had been concealed behind a black balaclava, but he had been in the factory and on the hill outside moments before it had gone up in flames. She had thought he had been killed but the man heading for the third floor was very much alive. He was no ghost.

Think, Felicity, think. She ran out into the middle of the crowds, looking up at the shop fronts, erratically searching for anything to give her a spark of inspiration, to tell her what to do. She bumped into a security guard who was walking idly through the crowd.

'Easy tiger,' he said. 'Shops ain't gonna run out of stock, little one.'

Felicity stared up at the guard, focusing on his crisp white collar, neat black tie, black vest with *Security* emblazoned across the breast, the walkie-talkie attached to his belt. That was it, their way out.

'Please help me,' she said, her face showing a fear that didn't need to be feigned. 'How many of you guys are there in this centre?'

Chapter Twenty-One

'No,' the small man pleaded. 'There's no need to run.'

An invisible force tugged at Finn's shoulders, stopping him. He stared back at the man. The moment he had emerged from the escalator they had made eye contact, the stare lingering too long to be considered accidental or meaningless.

The small man raised his hands. 'Please,' he said in an outwardly friendly tone. 'I've come here as a friend. You really don't need to run from me, Finn.'

There was a twinge of annoyance burning in the pit of Finn's stomach. He wasn't at all comfortable with the man knowing his name. They all seemed to know exactly who *he* was, yet they were strangers to him and strangers didn't have the right to use his Christian name without his permission.

'You've been through a lot,' the small man said, 'and you're right to be cautious. But you can trust me. You have to trust someone.'

Finn turned again, a longing look to the staircase, the escape route.

'Think where those steps take you,' the small man said, reading his thoughts. 'What are you realistically going to find at the bottom? Certainly not answers, no, only a dark corridor, another road, another place to hide from the truth. I *can* give you answers.'

Finn went to say something but stopped. He narrowed his eyes. A notion suddenly occurred to him, a notion born by the talk of answers. 'Are you Willoughby Carmichael?' he asked excitedly.

The small man didn't answer straight away. He smirked. 'Yes … I am.'

Finn hadn't spent much time thinking about Willoughby Carmichael, mainly because they had decided early that they were not going to seek him out. He had no expectations, no preconceptions of how he would look. His father informed him only of his name.

'Finn,' the small man pressed, 'unfortunately time isn't really a commodity we can rely on. We need to leave.'

'You were supposed to be waiting for me at the hotel?' Finn said nervously. He wasn't ready to sign away the rights to his trust just yet.

'But you didn't come to the hotel,' said the small man. 'Hence I was proactive and sought you out. The stakes are so high that I couldn't just sit and wait for you.' He extended his hand, urging Finn to take it, to submit to a leap of faith and come with him. The hand was covered with a black glove. The limb was stiff and strange.

'Let's get back somewhere warm,' the small man said enticingly, 'get a hot meal inside you. We can talk more then. Hotel does a wonderful steak, creamiest peppercorn sauce you've ever tasted.'

The lure of food was a powerful bargaining device and Finn was slowly becoming convinced. A wonderful steak with the creamiest peppercorn sauce he had ever tasted sounded so very good. He ambled forward –

'Noooooooooooooo!' Felicity appeared with a hollering scream, stopping next to Finn with such force that she almost knocked him to the ground.

The small man eyed her appearance with an unfazed curiosity. He said nothing, rubbing the thumb and forefinger of his good hand against the stubble of his chin.

'Don't trust them!' Felicity shouted, trying to catch her breath. 'He's not who he says he is!'

'Bad timing,' the small man said through a hefty sigh, 'and just as we seemed to be making some form of progress. Young lady, you're proving to be quite the thorn.'

An extremely large man emerged from the darkness of the staircase. He had been lurking there the whole time, hiding from them. It all suddenly slotted together and Finn closed his eyes and reprimanded himself harshly for being so stupid, for not having the wit to see it. He could have blamed it on fatigue but he should have realised that this man was *not* Willoughby Carmichael. He hadn't made an introduction, Finn had been the one to say the name, and the small man had latched onto it like a disease. These men were his mother's people.

The man who had claimed to be Willoughby Carmichael started to pace.

'Saw you in the factory,' Felicity said. 'Never forget a scumbag.' She pointed to the larger man. 'Freak of nature was there too. They killed your father, Finn.'

The shorter man chuckled to himself and shared a look with his companion, seemingly unsure how to proceed.

'Okay,' the short man said. He stopped pacing and folded his arms. 'My name is Theo. My companion goes by the name of Rogen. I'm not Willoughby Carmichael, you're quite right. The masquerade would have made this all run a bit smoother. Not sure any of us are in the mood for running.'

'Nice to meet you, Theo' said Felicity sardonically.

Theo stared at her and then he spoke like he was reading from a dossier. 'Your name is Felicity Gower, born the fourth day of June, 2001, to Evelyn Gower in St Peter's Maternity Hospital, Cheltenham. Mother dead, full inheritance waits at the age of eighteen, in the meantime incremented amounts from mother's estate paid into your account every year until that day, current bank balance just shy of forty-three thousand pounds, minus the two hundred pounds a young chap called Henry Pringle withdrew for you today. Have to say the master plan was disappointingly illogical, even for a child your age. I'm not sure why you thought your little friend using your bank card would have a different outcome. I think you can cite naivety as an excuse, as it's likely you very much don't understand the world you're now a part of.'

Finn watched her reaction. For what he suspected was the first time in her entire life, Felicity Gower had been left speechless.

Theo wasn't finished. 'Lives with foster parents, a lovely old couple called David and Elaine Wicker –'

'Nice trick,' Felicity snarled, rediscovering her voice. 'What you gonna do next? Ask me to pick a card?'

'Oh, it's no magic,' said Theo. 'Magic's something that died out to folk like you and I many years ago, although it can still be found in the darker corners of the world, if you know where to look. No, there's another word for it. I would call it a *violation*. You'd be appalled at just how easy it is to obtain every last detail of someone's life. All you need is a little bit of funding.'

Finn was aware of Rogen moving. He was now half way between the elevator and the staircase, close enough to reach either exit should they choose to run.

'You work for my mother, don't you?' Finn said.

'In a way,' Theo said. He was smiling. 'Your mother and I are related, which makes us related too.'

'Is she here?' said Finn.

'Unfortunately not,' Theo said. 'We were lucky to be close by when the trace we put on your little friends account pinged. There wasn't time to report it.' He allowed his smile to fade, serious now. 'But time for idle chatter is over, I'm afraid. You'll be coming with me now.'

Finn and Felicity looked at one another, the fear in their expressions showing that they both understood that there was so little they could do. He wanted so much to conceive a plan, something masterly and clever lie they did in the films, but nothing came to mind. Seeing that plotting was fruitless, he was overcome with a desire to protect *her*, to save Felicity before anything else, and it was this desire that allowed him to find his voice. It was time to grow up. It was time to be decisive.

'I'll come with you,' he said, 'on one condition. You let Felicity go.'

'I can fight my own battles,' said Felicity.

Theo shook his head. 'I'm afraid things aren't as simple as that–'

'Then make it simple,' Finn said. 'Refuse ... I'll kick and scream and spit so that every last person in this place sees what you're doing to me!'

'Noble,' said Theo, 'and as much as I love that little feeling that comes with being merciful, our little lady here with the big mouth isn't going anywhere. She knows a little too much, Finn, which means I have no choice but to bring her with us on our little expedition.'

'No!' Finn said firmly.

'No?' Theo frowned. 'What do you think gives you the power to say no to me?'

'I've told you,' said Finn angrily. He was growing in confidence. He had realised that he *did* have cards and he was going to play them. 'I come with you *only* if she walks in the other direction. Right now, that's the only thing that interests me.'

Theo looked to Rogen. He was uncertain, or at least it looked that way.

Finn was beginning to tingle with hope. In the confusion of the factory he had spent the whole time looking at his mother. She had been ruthlessly cold, resolute, and robotic, but the man in front of him seemed to have the smallest trace of humanity. It looked as though he had perhaps gotten through to him. He was listening, he had a conscience –

Theo thrust forward and grabbed Finn by the neck, pulling him close so that their faces were only inches apart. 'Tell me this,' Theo hissed, his cheeks going ruby red, 'what currency do you think you have here? You do what I say, when I say it!'

Rogen wagged a finger at Felicity, making it clear that it wouldn't be good for her health to rush to Finn's aid. Despite never being one to follow instructions, his sheer size made her heed the warning and she didn't move an inch.

Theo dragged Finn across to the glass barrier by the escalators, pushing Finn's cheek against the glass. 'Look down there,' he said. 'There! Second floor! You see those two men looking at us? They followed us here.'

Finn was trying to shake free but Theo was surprisingly strong and he could only do as he was told. He did see them, the two men that were indeed watching the whole exchange. The faces belonged to the murderers of Edwin Cavell, the American stern and focused and the tall Frenchman nursing a large plaster on the nose that Felicity had broken with a tree branch.

'That's the true enemy, son,' Theo pointed out, 'the enemy to all of us. Understand this, we're *not* nice people but they take sadism to a whole different level. I'm led to believe that our French friend in particular is fond of a good bit of old fashioned torture –'

'Sir,' a strong voice said. 'Put the lad down and step away from him! Right now, please!' The voice belonged to a policeman, standing in the middle of a congregation of uniformed security guards. There were six men in total, the noble and welcome cavalry, a group of men who had crept up the staircase unnoticed.

Theo surveyed the policeman. He pulled Finn away from the glass but showed no signs of releasing his grip from his neck. 'I know how this must look,' he said, 'but is it a crime nowadays to discipline your own child, Officer?'

'Yes,' the Officer replied calmly, 'the way you're doing it would be. But then he's not your son now, is he, Sir? Let's go and have a little chat downstairs and maybe get to the bottom of what's happening here. Trust that's ok with everyone?'

'Of course,' Theo said. He let go of Finn and nodded at Felicity. 'This would be your doing, I assume?'

Felicity grinned proudly. 'The look on your face.'

Finn stepped backwards, his neck throbbing immensely. He was tempted to rush to Felicity, taking her hand and running away from them all. But Rogen was still in close proximity and so far the policeman hadn't seemed to notice him, perhaps mistaking him for an innocent bystander.

Theo pointed a finger at Felicity. 'I hold you responsible,' he said, 'for what happens to these gallant fellows. You think you're clever but all you've done is create more victims.'

140

The policeman bellowed out a firmer warning, identifying Theo's statement as a clear threat and he stepped forward, the security guards spreading out around him. One of the guards said something into his walkie-talkie –

'You know what they say,' Theo said casually. He clicked his fingers. 'Pigs will fly!'

Rogen was amongst the approaching men before they even had a chance to realise it was happening. He plucked the policeman up with one hand and walked him easily towards the glass barrier. The policeman lost all his composure, squirming and squealing, hitting out with the truncheon that he had acquired from his belt. Such was the extent of Rogen's reach the truncheon didn't even come close to making contact.

Theo was smirking at Finn, his face crumpled up into an expression of macabre amusement that was pure evil.

Rogen got to the glass barrier of the third floor of the Kingswood Shopping Centre, raised his arm up and tossed the policeman out over the edge.

Chapter Twenty-Two

The scream was so loud that it could have curdled blood, filling the shopping centre from floor to ceiling, the noise echoing off the rafters. The policeman dropped like a stone, landing in the water of the lagoon. A host of shocked fingers pointed up, some people ran for the exits, a woman dived into the water and pulled the policeman to safety. He was injured but thankfully alive.

Theo tilted his head to the side. The six guards were stood perfectly still, pale, a collection of ghosts in uniform. 'Your turn,' he said, taunting them. 'Confident?'

The guards looked to one another. No, they were not feeling confident. No one moved. Rogen observed them like a powerful predator waiting to pounce, straight faced and emotionless, ready to suck the flesh, sinew, and marrow from their bones.

A muffled transmission blasted from a walkie-talkie. Two of the guards jumped in shock, one lost his mind and sprinted forward. It was all that was needed for Rogen to spring to life. He punched the bravest of the men in the face, the man falling unconscious before he hit the floor. Then Rogen got to work on the rest of them.

Theo went for Finn's throat again but Finn kicked out hard, making a crunching contact with Theo's groin. His tiredness was gone, replaced by a rage that was bubbling. He was fed up of being pushed around, fed up of the lies. He wanted to hurt someone.

There was a grunt of pain and Theo dropped to his knees, shaking.

'Grab the bike,' Finn barked. He was all authority.

Felicity was already running but Theo recovered enough to scramble painfully across the floor, grabbing her by the ankle.

She hit the ground hard, Theo's artificial hand plopping off from the stump with the impact and skidding a few feet in front of him. The hand rotated in a circle like a spinning coin.

She pushed herself instantly up, taking the hand and lobbing it far into the distance. It struck the edge of the glass barrier and dropped down three floors.

The escape that followed was frantic and desperate. They cycled away, slipping past Rogen who was finishing off the final guard, a pile of broken and crying men resting at his feet, before riding down the staircase at pace, their bottoms vibrating and bouncing uncomfortably in their saddles. A group of people blocked the bottom of the staircase, forcing them to exit out onto the first floor.

'Plan?' Felicity said, riding up alongside him. Cycling was proving difficult. They had to weave this way and that like slaloming skiers to avoid colliding with the shoppers.

'Haven't thought of one yet,' said Finn.

'I'm gutted,' said Felicity. 'Know what I should have said back there when I chucked that idiot's hand over the side? *'Watch out for the hand grenade'*, or something like that, would have been hilarious!'

'You're a sick girl, Fliss,' Finn stood up on his pedals, trying to go faster. He spotted something useful. 'There's another staircase –'

The staircase he was referring to loomed up ahead. But he soon realised that the American was standing in front of the entrance, blocking the way.

Finn took evasive action, swerving into a sharp left, heading towards the escalators. He made it a split second before Felicity but the steps of moving-metal were a different proposition to concrete and they fell instantly, the bikes twisting and wedging into the narrow space, Finn and Felicity slamming awkwardly over their handlebars.

His first thought was to look back. The American was behind them, at the top of the escalator and making his way downwards. Felicity was on the step below and trying to force the bikes free but the handlebars had twisted at odd angles and they were stuck hard.

'Leave them,' Finn said. He hopped up onto the smooth metal in between the flights and slid down to the ground floor. Felicity did the same, close behind.

They broke into another sprint, hustling their way through the crowd and finding a walkway between two shops that lead out to the street. It was occupied by a trio of loitering teenagers, two of whom were huddled together and kissing, the third-wheel-friend doing solitary tricks with his skateboard. Two policemen were running towards them, their squad car parked on the curb of the road, the lights flashing like a wonderfully warm and enticing beacon. The first policeman was calling out, the second transmitting words into his radio.

Finn and Felicity halted to a stop as Rogen slipped out from a concealed fire exit. He gripped the back of the policemen's vests, affording them one hand each, and pushed his arms outwards, sending them smashing through the shop windows on either side. The glass shattered, cracking sideways into a chain reaction that destroyed every panel along the length of the walkway. The alarms started to blare. The teenagers took flight, running out into the road.

The big man stopped, completely still, blocking the way like a devoted troll protecting the integrity of a beloved bridge.

'Ok,' said Felicity, 'I'm calling it, the dude's Superman!'

Finn had to think again and he considered the direction they had just come. People were gathered there, observing, some with hands over their mouths, others taking pictures and videos on their mobile phones. A single face stood out more than all the others, the face of the Frenchman, jostling his way forward, desperate to get close.

'This way,' Felicity said. She jumped through the missing window to their left and trampled over the items in the window display. Finn followed without question, moving past two gasping members of shop staff who had been alerted by the smashing and were now watching the action unfold.

Once inside it was clear that they were in a health store, brightly lit, with high rows of shelves choked full of bottles and boxes. Felicity took them to the back of the shop. There was nowhere else to go and they dropped to their knees, trying to hide.

'What do we do now?' she said, breathing hard.

'Don't know,' said Finn, 'got to hope someone calls the police.'

'Do we?' Felicity gasped. 'So Superman can come and use some more of them as punching bags?'

Finn peeped out from their hiding place, seeing the deserted aisles. They were alone, for now. He checked out the rest of the surroundings, seeing if there were any other potential escape routes that didn't involve them going back into the shopping centre. The only option was a single door behind them but it was locked with an electronic keypad.

He pointed to the door. 'If we can find a way to get in there –'

A loud, sharp crash interrupted his suggestion. It was followed by a series of huffs and grunts, the sounds of fighting men. The shelving unit next to them shook as if wracked by a powerful, destructive earthquake. A large box of stock fell from the top of the shelf and thumped into Felicity's head. She cried out from the shock of the impact.

Finn pulled her close, brushing the hairs from her face and caressing the skin of her forehead where the box had hit her. She was dazed but there was no blood.

'What's happening?' she said. Her eyes were damp with tears.

He hadn't the time to answer. Rogen broke violently through the shelf to their right, falling backwards, smashing into the back wall and leaving a massive hole in the plaster. He landed on his back, his eyes closed, not moving.

All was eerily quiet. Finn placed his ear next to the shelf, trying to hear anything from the other side –

A hand punched through the wood, making a horrible contact with Felicity's chest. She went the same way as Rogen, the force strong, her body colliding with the wall. The hand that had viscously burst through gripped a part of the wood of the shelf and pulled. The unit toppled down, landing with a plume of dust.

Finn stood up. He was now face to face with the Frenchman.

'Now,' the Frenchman said, 'you die.'

'Why?' Finn said. 'What have I done?'

'It's not what you've *done*,' said the Frenchman, 'it's what you *will* do. You're too dangerous to –'

Rogen slowly sat up, his strength returning like a robot reenergised with a burst of power. He got to his feet and looked forward, reminded of where he was. His size wasn't simple window-dressing and he was strong enough for another frontal attack. Taking a series of quick steps he was back in the centre of the shop and trading punches with the Frenchman once more. The Frenchman seemed to toy with his prey. He didn't move his arms, keeping them by his side and pirouetting easily, flashing his head side to side to avoid the ferocity of Rogen's lunges.

Finn seized his opportunity, pulling Felicity up and wrapping her arm around his neck. She was conscious but only just and was coughing erratically. He couldn't help but shoot a glance back and he saw Rogen's punch connect with a chin. Affronted, the Frenchman ended the fight, catching Rogen's next effort and holding on tightly, scrunching the bones so that they cracked, and then hitting Rogen with such a brutal uppercut that Rogen struck the ceiling, the plaster coming down on top of him as he hit the ground. This time Rogen wasn't going anywhere.

Finn didn't hang around and they escaped through the newly formed-Rogen-shaped hole in the wall, a few bricks breaking away as they passed through a deserted staff room and through a fire exit. The cold hit them as they emerged outside.

'He's coming!' Felicity said as they ran. 'Finn! He's coming!'

Finn looked out at the area in front of them. They were at the rear of the shopping centre, a tarmacked area covered in snow and full of high stacks of pallets and static delivery vans. There was not another soul to be seen, no one to appeal to for help, no more victims to create. A huge brick wall penned them in, preventing them from going any further. It was much too high to climb.

But then he saw it – the most glorious sight – a small metal gate just sitting there, enticingly open. Finn gobbled the opportunity up, dragging Felicity through and slamming the gate shut behind them. He wondered if fortune was finally favouring the brave when he saw that a padlock was wedged in the metal grating. He pushed it down, locking the gate.

'We're safe now,' he said confidently as they made it out into the street. 'There's no other way of him getting to us! I've locked the gate!'

'I'm in agony,' Felicity complained, 'I can't breathe –'

A bright orange Volkswagen camper van was on the road in the distance.

'I'm going to try and flag that van down,' Finn said. 'See if we can get –'

A black shadow swept overhead and the Frenchman dropped down in front of them, blocking their way, falling down from the heavens. He landed on one knee, the knuckles of one hand smashing into the concrete. The concrete fractured beneath his fingers. He raised his head.

Felicity spoke with a stunned stutter. 'Did … he just … *jump*... the wall?'

'That's impossible,' said Finn. He ushered Felicity behind him although he wasn't sure what protection he would be able to offer her.

'Stop this running,' the Frenchman said. 'Not going to tell you –'

The Frenchman saw the camper van a heartbeat before it hit him from the rear. He managed to react, flipping his head around and spreading his weight. But the impact sent him skidding across the ground, disturbing the snow with the sweeping brush of his body. The driver slammed the brakes late, thundering forward before changing gear quickly and reversing backwards.

Finn had dived to the side to avoid the van, taking Felicity with him. They were on the ground when the door to the van shot open. 'Get in!' a woman was yelling frantically, stretching her arm out across the seat.

Finn hesitated, dumbstruck by a new fear, events moving too quickly for him to process. Every corner they turned seeming to throw up another fresh wave of tribulations and riddles that needed to be solved.

'He'll be back on his feet *any* second,' urged the woman, 'so I suggest you get in now!'

The Frenchman was indeed slowly getting to his feet. Despite the strike, somehow he hadn't been killed.

'He should be dead,' Felicity said, horrified.

Finn bundled her to her feet, pushing her inside the van and next to the woman. The woman started to reverse, the tyres screeching on the tarmac. The Frenchman was running forward now, eating up the ground. He leapt onto the bonnet, clamping on tightly. The woman cursed and pushed down harder on the accelerator.

'Get him off,' Felicity was screaming. She started hitting switches on the van's dashboard in her panic, the woman trying to swat her hands away. The lights flashed, the horn sounded, the indicators flicked on and off and then the windscreen wipers came to life, the lengths of plastic slapping into the Frenchman's face – a rhythmic *slap – slap – slap*. For a moment everyone froze, silenced by the absurdity of the scene, slapstick taken to the brink of the ridiculous.

'What … the … hell?' Finn said, tittering nervously.

Enough - the Frenchman moved his arm back, ready to punch through the glass.

'Hold on,' said the woman. She twisted the steering wheel sharply, the van manoeuvring into a dramatic turn so that they suddenly faced forwards. The Frenchman couldn't hold on and he toppled off into the road, spinning across the concrete.

'What the hell was that *thing?*' Finn said. He peered out of the back window, glad to see the Frenchman reducing into nothing more than a distant, decreasing black speck.

'Not a *thing,*' said the woman, 'just a man.' She too was keeping a close eye on the rear-view mirror. 'Was blind luck I found you, heard the commotion over the scanner. So lucky I was close. Hate to think what might have happened.'

Finn noted the police scanner mounted on the dashboard, the voices still crackling through the static. He looked across at the woman. She would have been around the same age as his mother, pretty with straight brown hair and big blue eyes. 'Who are you?' he asked.

'My name's Cora,' she answered. 'Doubt anyone's thought me important enough to mention. But you may have heard of my brother. His name is Willoughby Carmichael.'

.

Chapter Twenty-Three

'The rarest of red Sancerre,' The Politician said proudly, watching his butler carefully pouring the bottle of wine into tall crystal glasses. The bottle was one of a dozen that rested on the table. 'The bottle hails from 1648 from the vineyards of the Château de Goulaine in the Loire, a truly excellent year. I trust you'll be able to appreciate the aromatics on the tongue.'

Wyatt Eagan waited quietly for the butler to pass him his glass, staring out the window and trying to catch sight of the powerful snowstorm that raged amongst the darkness. He had been inside the Stately Home on many occasions but only ever been permitted to enter The Great Hall. It was never a place in which he felt comfortable and he was always keen to escape with the first opportunity that arose.

The Great Hall itself was an impressive room, with high ceilings complimented by exposed wooden beams, tall gothic windows covered by blood red curtains of velvet, and elegant tapestries adorning the walls. The main feature was a large solid oak table – medieval in origin – that ran the length of the room. The table had a total of thirty six chairs placed around its edges, although only seven were currently occupied. On the western wall was a large marble fireplace, firewood burning furiously within and bathing the room in an ambient glow of warm orange.

The Politician, as always, was seated at the head of the table. Wyatt Eagan and Gilliam Béranger were the only visitors who had chosen to sit together. The remaining guests, justifiably cautious, had taken their seats as far away from one another as possible.

Wyatt was well acquainted with each man. They were the driving forces behind the latest incarnation of the Brotherhood, most of them hailing from different countries. Benedict, the volatile Scotsman, was seated with his back to the fire. The Englishman Noakes, stout and serious, was seated opposite him with the German Kruger a little further to his right. Ekström, the striking Swede with the flowing blonde locks and thick beard, sat closest to the door. The final man in the room was The Politician's assistant, seated away from the table and resting in an arm chair. The assistant wore a black cloak and had an ugly, pale face with a hooked nose.

The wine glasses were handed out and the butler quietly left the room, locking the door behind him. Wyatt sipped from the glass. It was strong and scented like perfume, not at all to his taste. Vintage it may be but he had tastes that were more drawn to beers and ales.

'We drink not in celebration,' The Politician said, 'but in solidarity. The first phase of our plan has failed. But tonight we regroup, reenergise, moving forward together, stronger and more determined.'

Wyatt listened carefully. He had never understood The Politician. He looked exactly like he did on television, moving with the same effortless pizzazz, the same confidence, the same skill and prowess at addressing a crowd. He was striking in a black Armani suit, hair parted neatly down the side, eyes innocent and absorbing. He was recognisable and where the rest of the Brotherhood spent their entire lives trying to stay hidden, The Politician had crawled out of the woodwork and done the complete opposite. There must have been a reason to be so visible, a meticulous end-game and goal that none of them could comprehend. He was too well known to simply disappear when the time came.

'The greatest outcome of a setback,' The Politician said, 'is the opportunity it gives to prevent the same mistakes from happening in the future. More of our kind will feel the pull to the boy and more of us will be coming. The scrutiny will increase.

We need to be prepared and god willing, resolve this before they get here. Tonight, we discuss the next phase.'

Wyatt fiddled with the curls of his black hair, fantasising of being somewhere else. He was sick of this country. He had always hated England. He hated the weather, he hated the food and he hated the people. He longed to return home to America, to be on the ranch again, to finish the day by cleaning the dust, muck, and sweat of the prairie from his hands.

'I don't trust this man,' Gilliam whispered in his ear.

'And you shouldn't,' said Wyatt, equally as quiet.

The Politician explained how he had cleared up the messes that had been created. There had been no witnesses to Edwin Cavell's demise. The same could not be said for the melee in the shopping centre but they had been fortunate enough that no one had seen the more rash moments. Witness statements had been deliberately lost in a bureaucratic trail of paperwork, all CCTV footage confiscated and destroyed. History would note that the people of Cheltenham had simply seen an outrageous fight between criminal fraternities, nothing more and nothing less.

Gilliam kept his head bowed shamefully throughout. He was in bad enough shape without adding a feeling of guilt to his ailments. He was battered and bruised from being run over by the van and still suffering from a broken nose that was showing no signs of healing.

Wyatt had his own guilt. He had been ill at ease from the beginning. He had no other choice but to kill Edwin Cavell but it didn't mean that he had wanted to. The fact had been keeping him awake ever since.

'What about the girl?' Noakes asked the group.

'We eliminate her,' Benedict said, 'when we get the chance –'

That made Wyatt instantly angry. 'She is just a child –'

'As is the boy,' Benedict shot back. 'Or are your views on such matters dictated by how the deed benefits you?'

'Fortunately,' said The Politician, 'for the time being there's no need to be quite so barbaric. The girl's foster parents have been paid off, sold a story of her running away, the pay off a compensation that they'll be far too embarrassed to mention to anyone. Mr Benedict is correct however, in that at some point we will need to deal with the girl. My recommendation is –'

'I'm afraid, gentlemen,' Kruger said, the German speaking for the first time, 'that you will have to continue on this journey without me.'

Wyatt closed his eyes. He had always been fond of Kruger and he feared for him now. He was a noble, honourable, forthright man in his late fifties but that didn't matter. The Brotherhood was not well known for its mercy towards those who changed their minds.

'I wish you luck,' Kruger continued, his English perfect, 'but I was lured to this undertaking on the understanding that none of us would risk our identities coming out into the open –'

'And they're not in the open,' Ekström said.

'Not yet,' Kruger said. 'Let's not forget, The Guild are here. They'll regroup and become stronger, same as us. Then we have the knowledge that Carmichael has the child. It means we have two enemies to fight, two fronts, and it will be absolutely impossible to do so quietly and without taking many risks.'

Wyatt watched carefully, absorbed but trying not to make it obvious. Kruger's points were interesting and not anything that the rest of them hadn't considered in secret. He didn't know whether to admire the German's bravery or pity his rashness.

'I think you need to consider what you're saying,' The Politician said. 'I can tell you that Tobias won't be happy.'

'Ah,' said Kruger, 'but none of us have seen Tobias, have we? All we have is your word that he even exists. I believe in Obsidian, I always have, but Tobias is another matter. I can't deny the pull to this boy. But I've come to believe that what will be, will be, and what's more, that I don't have it within myself to hunt down a child.'

There was a part of Wyatt that wanted to break out in applause. He agreed whole heartedly with some of what the German said, not least the doubt in Tobias being involved. He had been suspicious from the beginning about that particular claim and was getting more doubtful with each passing day that the elusive Tobias failed to make an appearance.

The Politician rose from his seat and began to pace around the outline of the table. 'There is a little known battle,' he said, 'that took place in a dark corner of an empire, long ago. Fifty or so Roman soldiers found themselves facing a horde of over a thousand barbarians. They understood that they faced certain death.'

Wyatt didn't like the sound of this. The story was surely going to be anecdotal. He wondered where it would go.

The Politician grabbed the nearest bottle of wine from the table and refilled his glass. 'I sometimes wonder,' he said, 'what would a modern army feel about being designated such a task? *Certain death!* Would they refuse? Would they rebel? Death is such an inconvenience in the modern world.'

'Is this necessary?' Kruger asked. 'I've made my point and –'

'But did these noble legionnaires complain?' The Politician said. 'No. And why? I see two reasons. First, they believed in the power and the glory of Rome and all its ideals. Second, they had utter faith in their capabilities and skills. And so they fought the hordes, hour after hour, one impenetrable unit and by the end of the second day they had defeated the barbarians. Of course, history has a habit of honouring the losers, the men who fight against insurmountable odds like the Spartan's of Thermopylae, but true bravery comes in the guise of those that succeed and don't throw away their lives.'

The Politician stopped behind Kruger and pulled a small dagger from his dinner jacket, thrusting the blade into the German's chest. Kruger grunted in both pain and shock, looking down at the pool of blood that was rapidly growing on his white shirt.

Wyatt burst back out of his chair. The others stood too, pushing their chairs back against the wall.

The Politician retracted the blade from Kruger's flesh and casually picked up a napkin from the table and cleaned the blood from the metal before placing the dagger back into his pocket. Kruger gargled and then plopped forward, his head smashing into the table. He moved no more.

'Tell me this,' said The Politician, 'had a legionnaire at the corner of the unit suffered a crisis of faith, would there have been a different outcome? Had he doubted the power of what he was fighting for and the strength of his own capabilities, would they all have died? *Our* power comes from our unity, gentlemen, from our beliefs, from our drive to succeed towards our one true goal. We can't have any doubt.'

Wyatt stared at The Politician with the deepest of disdain. The man was an animal, a pure killer, hidden behind a sharp suit and a sharper tongue.

'Is this to be our fate if we ever disagree with you?' said Ekström.

'That question wouldn't be for me to answer,' The Politician said. 'Tobias *is* in charge here. He has made *his* intentions *very* clear, through me. Withdrawal is *not* acceptable. If any of us turn against the Brotherhood, you should hope it's me who catches up with you, not Tobias.'

Wyatt wanted to run around the table and wipe the smugness off The Politician's face with his fist. He was sure now. He was using Tobias's name for his own advantage. He cursed him for the manipulation. It was something he didn't need to do. They were all scared enough of the boy on his own.

The Politician pointed to the man in the dark cloak, who had remained seated throughout. He clicked his fingers and the cloaked figure walked to the door, pulling a large set of keys from his pocket and pushing one into the lock, before disappearing from the room.

'The child has the mark of Obsidian,' said The Politician whilst he waited for the man to return. 'There is no longer any doubt. And Mr Kruger did raise some valid points. We do need to be very careful and as such I propose we approach this in a different way, a way that protects our desires to stay in the shadows.'

The door to the hall reopened and the cloaked figure reappeared, dragging a large crate on a heavy pallet-truck into the room. The crate was bigger in height than all the men present. The wood was thick and old. A huge iron chain, secured by a sturdy lock, ran along the outside. He bought the pallet truck to a stop in front of the fire.

The Politician smiled at the cloaked figure. 'My good man, would you be so kind as to dim the lights for me?'

Everyone made their way curiously towards the crate. The lights in the room were dimmed as requested, the crate illuminated by the glow of the fire, sending a long rectangular shadow across the floor.

'You will all know,' The Politician said, 'that I have a vast collection of antiquities, items that I ensure will never see the inside of a museum. This is what I bring you.' He pointed to the cloaked figure. 'My man Lorcan here protects such antiquities.'

Lorcan made his way back to the crate and selected another key from the set on his chain. Unlocked, the chain around the crate went loose and fell to the ground. One side of the crate collapsed with a loud thump. Lorcan placed the lock on the table and then retreated to the back of the room. His job was done.

Wyatt furrowed his brow. Inside the crate – at least on the face of it – was nothing but darkness. A cold shiver found him. *What did the darkness hide?*

Benedict was leaning closer. 'Isn't this a curiosity?' He dropped to one knee in front of the crate and reached forward, grasping.

'Not advisable,' The Politician cried, the seriousness of his tone making the Scotsman flinch and stop in his tracks. 'A host of virtues exist in this world, Mr Benedict, but believe me when I say that in this moment patience will by far be the one that serves you best.'

Benedict was puzzled but he took a few steps back all the same.

'Thank you,' said The Politician. 'Please, give her a little time. She will come out when she's ready.'

There was a subtle sound in the darkness, almost quiet enough to be undetectable. It was a scuttering like the sound of a large rat moving. And then s*omething* started to emerge. It was small, black, and scrunched up in a tight, ball-like shape – *a shape with legs* – its face concealed by an overgrown mop of dark, knotty black hair. The animal, if that's what it was, had its eyes closed and it slowly made its way across the floor and onto the rug in front of the fire, its movement most resembling that of a crab.

Wyatt couldn't quite come to terms with what he was seeing and he heard himself gasp loudly. The creature wasn't an animal at all but a small woman. She moved on her hands and feet, her back nearest the floor, her chest facing the ceiling. Her head was twisted, the neck lowered at an odd angle so that the head lulled flaccidly against the chest. Each of her limbs, the arms and legs, jutted and contorted at strange and severe angles.

No, Wyatt thought. *She doesn't move like a crab. She moves like a giant spider.*

The Politician spoke to her. 'Stand.' he demanded. The woman did nothing so he pulled a small wooden locket with a hemp necklace from his jacket pocket and with more authority he repeated the command. 'I said *stand!*'

The woman stood, slowly but surely, her back straightening with an agonising crack, her feet taking all the weight from the effort. The limbs and bones crunched back into a place that became more human. Her head slowly rotated around so that it faced the right direction. She was naked and skinny, her hair hanging loosely across her small breasts and waist, covering her modesty. Her chest pulsated in and out dramatically as if she was ready to lash out. Her arms dangled at her side and on the end of her fingers were nails that were so overgrown they had curled into sharp claws. Her skin was smeared black and covered in an oil-like substance that flowed from various random pores and fissures. The strange black tar dripped from her body and claws, staining the rug beneath her.

'What new kind of devilry is this?' Ekström asked.

Wyatt already knew. He had read about such a creature but never seen one.

The Politician nodded, proud with himself. 'She is the Dragwich.'

The woman twitched at the mention of her name and something very odd occurred. There was a voice, a whisper that echoed throughout the room but did not belong to any man within it. The voice, quiet and demonic, repeated the strange name in a chant – *Dragwich* – *Dragwich* – *Dragwich* – over and over. The flames of the fire swayed erratically as if buffeted by an invisible wind.

The Politician smiled. 'I love it when that happens. Always sends a shiver down my spine.'

The Dragwich opened her eyes, revealing pupils that were a furious, angry red. The eyes were small but they glowed like torches, bright enough to be detectable through the thick hair that concealed the majority of her features.

'That's impossible,' Ekström said. 'They've been extinct for hundreds of years –'

'I should correct you,' said The Politician. 'They were *hiding* for a thousand years to avoid becoming extinct. Still, hide as they may, this, my friends, is the last one.'

Benedict spoke next. 'Is she not utterly magnificent?'

'I would choose a different word,' said Gilliam.

'Me too,' said Wyatt strongly. 'The Dragwich is an uncontrollable being. Uncontrollable unless –'

'*Unless* you have her locket!' The Politician finished the sentence for him. He held up the locket in question and ran the hemp through his fingers. '*This* locket, gentlemen.'

Wyatt stared at the small sphere of wood, beautifully carved and riddled with an ancient enchantment.

The Politician stepped away from the crate and sat back down in his chair, leaning back like a King addressing his subjects. 'The man who possesses her locket,' he said, 'is the man who can command her to do his bidding without question. Make no mistake, she is the perfect assassin. And she will bring us the boy. All I have to do is give her his name and she will leave this place and will not sleep until she brings us her prey.'

'She will bring us the *corpse*,' said Noakes, 'and it will be spoiled. I want to be certain that the boy really is the one we fear. I want to see the mark of Obsidian with my own eyes.'

The Politician addressed the Dragwich. 'Come to me!' The Dragwich stepped forward.

Wyatt could not hold his tongue. 'Please, reconsider this –'

The Politician ignored him. 'You will bring us the boy. Finn Carruthers –'

Wyatt was looking to the others for support but could see that he was on his own. He had to be careful. He didn't want to end up like Kruger. He wasn't questioning their cause, only the way upon which they were going about succeeding.

'You must ensure that the boy does not die,' The Politician said, 'you leave him in a condition where he can be identified and where the ritual can be performed. His companions, you can kill as many as you like. Do you understand?'

The Dragwich hissed like a snake and then burst suddenly upwards, leaping high into the air and then thumping down onto the table, sending the rare bottles of wine and the crystal glasses smashing into the floor. Then in one further movement she used the table as a springboard and careered out through one of the tall windows, the glass shattering and the red curtains blowing out into the snowstorm.

Wyatt rushed to the window, quick enough to catch sight of the small woman bounding across the lawn of the estate like a wolf. Then she disappeared into the blackness of the night. His heart was awash with sentiments of horror and disgust. *God help us all. What have we now unleashed on the world?*

Chapter Twenty-Four

Finn awoke to the sound of a fierce wind, a haunting wail that buffeted the glass of the windows and whistled through the eaves at the top of the building where it had breached the brickwork. The building seemed to stretch and creak, its only way to complain about the punishment it was suffering from the might of nature.

His dreams had been poisoned by the vivid dominance of a nightmare. Now back in the real world he couldn't remember a single detail of what his dreams had shown him, only knowing that it had terrified him and caused him a restless night of tossing and turning. Sitting up, he enjoyed a long, chesty yawn and unzipped his sleeping bag.

The room had been left in a miserable state, unremarkable, unloved, and unremembered. The wallpaper had been stripped away, the walls of plaster underneath cracked and crumbling. The carpet and underlay had been removed, exposing the rough wooden floorboards and the rusty nails holding it all together. Furniture was at a premium, with only a scraggily arm chair, a moth bitten sofa, a small trestle table, and an empty bookcase remaining. There was no running water and no electricity. The fire place was the one source of welcome comfort, a godsend that had been lit and was sizzling away happily at least.

Finn had taken the arm chair and he shuffled to the edge, moving his hands closer to the flames of the fire, toasting them lightly on both sides. Felicity was nearby, fast asleep on the sofa with her body smothered by a series of blankets and her own sleeping bag. The last few days had been one long ordeal but she was warm and snug for the time being.

He walked to the window and spent some time watching the morning storm. The wind was immense, sweeping the flakes into the deepest of snowdrifts across the tarmac of the abandoned carpark. Outside an old children's playground was falling apart, the long logs of the timber structures broken and jutting out of the white ground like the carcass of a prehistoric beast. The road from the car park funnelled into a narrow country lane of loose gravel, the road curving into the distance and disappearing into a tall wood of horse-chestnut trees.

The building once had a name, *The House in the Tree*, a quaint country pub that had closed during the recession. Most of the windows and doors on the ground floor had been boarded up with thick sheets of plywood every day since. It was too rural and remote to have had problems with vagrants seeking shelter or bored teenagers seeking something to vandalise and as such the building wasn't in the worst condition. The bar area and optics of the ground floor were still intact and the upper levels were stripped bare but in most past weathertight. In the severe cold of a late February morning, it wasn't the worst place in the world to be. Yet the storm was happy to test the notion.

The choice of hideout had been Cora Carmichael's idea, the building having been scrawled onto a mental note in her head during a previous reconnaissance of the area. Much to her dismay, she had needed to get back to the Ellis Moran Hotel to fetch the others, whoever these *others* were, but Cheltenham was too hot a zone for Finn and Felicity to travel and the forgotten public house proved a useful alternative in the meantime.

Finn returned to the arm chair and tucked himself under his blanket. Cora's promise had been heartfelt – she would return within twenty four hours. That had been two days ago. He had spent long periods staring at the distant trees, waiting to see some sign of her, but now he only looked fleetingly. He had seen too many trees recently, the woods and forests that he had either ran into or been chased into. He longed to once again look out of a window and see the spires and chimneys of civilisation.

He had also become somewhat indifferent to her absence. At first the company of an adult had reassured him. She had shown both of them ample kindness and had provided sheets and sleeping bags from the van and had the resourcefulness to get the fire going. But very quickly it became clear that she wouldn't tell him anything tangible about their dilemma and when he had asked she had become coy and irritable.

He let out a long trail of chilled breath, watching it rise into the air and dissipate into nothing.

'I think it's getting colder,' said Felicity. She had woken up without him realising, peeking out through the small opening in her sleeping bag. She hadn't moved an inch and didn't show any signs that she was likely to.

Finn yawned once again. 'At least we're inside.'

'I'm really cold,' she said. 'Like *really* cold, right down to my bones.'

'It won't be long,' said Finn. He moved across to the sofa and sat himself on the end. He gently moved her legs onto his lap and placed his own blanket onto her body. 'Cora will be back real soon and then this will all be sorted.'

'If you say so.'

'She's coming back −'

'Regardless,' Felicity said, 'think we need to think about what's going to happen if she doesn't.'

Finn wouldn't admit to her that he had harboured similar concerns. The truth was he didn't know what the consequences of Cora not returning would be but he was sure that they would not lead to anywhere positive. She had left them with a modest bag of provisions, the bag containing a single egg-mayonnaise sandwich, two torches, a basic first aid kit, and four small bottles of mineral water. They had already finished three of the bottles, the sandwich having been shared and devoured the previous day.

'Come on,' he said, 'why do we need to start talking about things like that?'

'Don't know what that punch has done to me,' she said. 'Can't see why it's done so much damage.'

'Wish it had been me −'

'I wish it had been you too,' Felicity said. There was a brief smile that swiftly faded. 'Promise me something? And I want you to be serious.'

Finn was quiet, fearing what she might say.

She coughed. 'If I die first –'

'Don't,' he said sharply, shaking his head, a genuine spasm of annoyance at even the slightest thought of such an idea.

'*If* I die,' Felicity repeated, 'you have to promise me that you'll eat me.'

Finn sniggered. *Typical Felicity.* Even in her condition she hadn't lost the strange sense of humour that set her apart from others. 'Shut up!' he said.

'I'm serious,' Felicity persisted, 'always thought I'd make a decent Fliss-burger. Not sure how I'll taste, maybe have me in a bap or something with some fried onions. I'd take it from the thigh, don't go for the ass, I don't work out enough, be full of fat and gristle. Stop laughing, I don't –'

The fit of coughing stopped her, a series of barks that were full of phlegm and pain.

Finn had nothing more to smile about. He watched her carefully. The coughing was getting worse, much worse. He glanced down, trying to check on her breathing but he couldn't see anything through the thick layers that were covering her.

'How's it all feeling this morning?' he asked.

'Well, Doctor,' she said flippantly, 'the cough's gone.'

'Fliss?' he said her name through a grimace, like a parent seeking the truth from a child who has just refused to give it.

Felicity shrugged through the tightness of the sleeping bag. 'You want me to be honest or lie?'

'Guess that's up to you.'

'Ok then, feels a lot better.'

Finn was silent for a long time. She had chosen to lie and he didn't need the skills of a polygraph machine to read it. He had been worried from the beginning, a worry that was quickly growing. Cora had checked on her injuries before she had left, insisting on Finn leaving the room whilst she did so, and when she emerged she had said nothing but her expression was visibly grave.

'Can I check on it?' he said finally.

Felicity dropped an eyebrow. 'Check on what exactly?'

'Your chest?'

'Oh, that's smooth,' she said. She coughed again, a dozen or so in a row, the effort taking the energy out of her. When she finished, she attempted a flirtatious smile. 'You're like a pervy Romeo. I'm going to go with no. *No*, you can't see me taking my top off and *no* you can't have a sneaky peek at my boobies.'

Finn smirked. He wasn't even going to bother defending himself. They both knew it wasn't what he meant.

'Being serious,' she said softly, 'what would be the point anyway? You don't know what you're looking at. You're no Doctor.'

He wished with all his heart that he *was* a Doctor. But there were other things that he wished for too, not least that he was someone bigger and tougher, so that next time the despicable Frenchman crossed his path he could dish out a much justified beating, fulfilling a growing desire for vengeance.

Finn was uncomfortable with such a thought, knowing that he truly wanted to hurt the man, a strong, burning emotion he had never experienced before. He wanted to kill him. Trying to shake off the feeling, he led himself down beside Felicity and nestled gently into her back. She writhed a little but she didn't complain. The feeling of shared warmth was welcome for both of them in the cold room.

'Finn,' she said, closing her eyes, 'you won't leave me, will you?'

'Never,' he said.

'I don't want to be alone.'

He waited for the joke but the joke didn't come. He could feel her laboured breathing against his body, dangerously weak.

Acting on instinct, he bent forward, tucking a few stray strands of her hair behind her ear. He kissed her softly on the cheek. She twisted her head and opened her eyes with an expression of puzzlement on her face. He instantly regretted the gesture, sure that a torrent of sarcastic mocking was heading his way. But surprisingly she pushed her face closer, her eyes intense and transfixed on his, and then she kissed him on the lips. The first kiss was brief, nothing more than a glancing peck, but then she kissed him again, longer, before breaking away.

'I love it when you call me Fliss,' she said, before tilting her head back into her original position and closing her eyes. Within a few second she had drifted back off to sleep.

Finn wasn't sure how long he stayed there with her, it could have been hours. He was sure that the kiss would have been *no big deal* to her but for him it was something monumental, signified by the arrival of the butterflies that fluttered enthusiastically into his stomach. The age of fifteen was far too old an age to have your first kiss. Everyone else was doing it or had experienced it, but it was a rite of passage that had so far eluded him.

The memory of the kiss stayed with him for the rest of the day, a day of boredom and endless pacing inside the prison of the room, sometimes sitting in the window seat and watching the snow, other times lying in the arm chair and staring into space. The thoughts regularly returned to that moment. It hadn't happened the way he had imagined it. He smiled to himself every now and again, a morbid amusement that the first time he kissed a girl properly the only requirement was for her to be near death's door. *If you're fit and well, go and kiss Jordan Tremlett. If you're literally about to snuff it and no one else is near, Finn Carruthers will do but only as the very last resort.*

It was some time later that he found himself standing once again at the window, realising that the room had become dark and the fire was quietly dying. He debated whether he might tend to the fire but it was a quick debate, stalled by the realisation that he didn't have the first idea where to start. He was thinking he could perhaps trek out into the woods, lopping some branches off some horse chestnuts, when he noticed something in the distance.

A light had appeared, funnelling through the tall trees, creating tall shadows in the snow. As the source of the light came closer it was identifiable as two spheres, the headlights of an approaching vehicle. A car was on the road, heading in their direction.

'Fliss,' he said, 'looks like we've got company.'

Felicity didn't answer and she lapsed into another coughing fit, waking with a violent shudder and convulsing on the sofa.

Finn almost tripped and fell as he scrambled across the floor, scooping up the final bottle of water on his way. He wanted her to drink after the coughing subsided but this time the coughing didn't stop. Indeed it got worse, intensifying, sending her to the edge of the sofa and almost falling off. She frantically unzipped her sleeping bag, struggling for breath. She covered her mouth and when the fingers came away there was blood staining the fingertips.

'That's it,' Finn said, 'I'm getting you to a hospital —'

'No ...' she said, the word pained and almost unintelligible. She was crying now. 'Finn ... please ... you can't ... they'll catch you if you —'

Finn was adamant. 'I don't care —'

She knocked him away, pushing her face into the sofa, the fabric muffling the sounds of her struggles.

He staggered back, urging himself to act, but he didn't know what to do. What *could* he do? His offer had been real. He *did* want to rush her to the hospital, to push her into the hands of people with white coats and clipboards, the people who could genuinely help her. He didn't care what it meant for him. But he had no mobile phone and the landline in the pub would have long since been disconnected. He could drag her but how far would he get?

Finn froze, his soul chilling to a temperature far harsher than that outside the window. The truth settled in his head, stinging, terrible. Felicity Gower was dying.

The devastation hit him in waves, one after the other, slamming into his body and making it shake. The world went dark and silent, the image of Felicity lying there cast in a stark spotlight, the rest of the world fading into a blur around the circumference. He didn't feel the bodies pushing past him, didn't notice the room suddenly fill with people.

It was the man's voice that sucked him out of his trance. 'Quick,' the man said in an Irish accent. The Irishman carefully lifted Felicity from the cushion and cradled her in his arms. He was speaking to the others that had arrived with him, ignoring Finn as if he didn't exist. 'She needs room, the bed upstairs. Will, you need to help her right now.'

Chapter Twenty-Five

'This needs careful consideration,' Willoughby Carmichael had a voice that was deep but quiet, almost a mumble. He was moving slowly back and forth in a creaky rocking chair. 'Can be fraught with danger, get the wrong area, accelerates the true injury. Only get one shot. Get it wrong, she dies in a great deal more pain.'

The Irishman, introduced as James Devery, was there too and he had been the one that had taken control. Seeming to know exactly what to do he had scooped Felicity gently into his arms and dashed up the narrow hallway that led to a room at the top of the house. Inside was a converted loft space with two sloping ceilings, skylights on each face, the room furnished sparsely with a rocking chair and a double bed. The four legs were missing from the bed so that it rested flat against the floor and a stripped, lumpy mattress rested on top. It was here that Felicity now lay.

Finn had gone with them. He had already forgotten the names of the two men who had stayed downstairs. His only focus was Felicity. The colour of her skin had changed from a pale white to a cold blue and a situation that was already alarming was now evidently critical. He was troubled as to why they had climbed *up* into the house instead of running down and heading to the hospital.

The plan wasn't the only thing to trouble him. Willoughby had eyes only for Finn and Willoughby watched him intently with a stare that sat unblinking and serious above a dour, passionless expression. Where Devery had moved with purpose and genuine care Willoughby came across as very different. He was unmoved by Felicity's condition.

Finn could do nothing but stare back, a staring contest. *What do you want with me? What's going on inside your head?*

Cora entered the room in a hurry, the door thumping loudly against the wall, the noise enough to break the uncomfortable staring contest. She carried with her an armful of blankets and two candles. She got to work immediately, wrapping Felicity up as best as she could before quickly lighting the candles and placing them on the floor at the head of the bed.

'Up you get,' Devery said to Willoughby. The Irishman was leaning up against the wall. 'Way I see it, there's no alternative. You do something, risk or no risk.'

Cora took her place next to Devery and she directed her question to her brother in the rocking chair. 'What do you think it is?'

'No way of knowing for sure,' Willoughby said with an idle shrug. Then he thought about it for a moment, pressing two fingers and his thumb to his bottom lip. 'Best guess, I'd say something like a flail lung. Our French friend probably damaged a fair few of her ribs. Complicated injury, not sure it's within my power to fix.'

'Not within your power to fix?' Devery said. His shock and annoyance at the statement was visible. 'Funny how your confidence changes in the situations where the outcome doesn't benefit you.'

Cora blinked and discreetly nudged Devery on the shoulder. The comment had been cutting.

'No, it's true,' said Devery, unashamed. 'Wasn't any hesitation with Cavell in the morgue and that was a lost cause from the beginning. This isn't a lost cause.'

Willoughby's expression changed and he rose and paced across the room menacingly. He stopped a few inches in front of the Irishman. 'Sounds like you have something to say to me, James?' he said.

'Yeah and I just said it,' Devery said. He had no intention of backing down and he eased away from the wall, standing up tall. The two men were almost touching, forehead to forehead.

Willoughby cleared his throat. 'We have bigger things to deal with—'

'Not bigger than this,' Devery said, shaking his head. 'She's dying, Will. And she deserves a damn sight more than your selfish, tunnel-visioned apathy.'

Finn watched in silence. His father had always endorsed the power of first impressions. And right now, he had already taken a dislike to Willoughby Carmichael. Devery by contrast he already liked. The Irishman had a kindness about him, a warmth radiating from his strong blue eyes, a strength from the softness of his controlled voice.

'Come on, boys,' Cora said. She was acting as peacemaker and she pushed her arm in-between the two flexing men, looking closely at both of them. 'We get it ok, you're big strong men. But can we play nice, please?'

Finn shuffled uneasily from one foot to the other. He was itching to speak, desperate to interrupt the ridiculous display of testosterone and force these people back to the matter at hand. His silence so far had been fuelled by his lack of confidence but finally, he found his voice.

'She needs a hospital,' he said quietly.

Willoughby turned around. 'That's completely out of the question. It's too risky. I won't allow it.'

'I don't care what happens to me,' Finn said.

'You would,' said Willoughby,' if you understood what they'll do to you.' He moved away from Devery and crouched down by the bed.

'You're not a doctor?' Finn said. His tone was doubtful but even so he hoped that he might be contradicted.

'Not quite,' said Willoughby, 'but then I don't need to be.'

Finn went to join Willoughby at the bed but Devery raised his hand, shaking his head and stopping him.

'Probably best to stand back a bit,' said Devery.

Willoughby looked over Felicity's lifeless body, his eyes intense and his stern demeanour un-cracked. There was uncertainty. 'There's little belief in the concept of the soul anymore,' he said, making it clear that he would move at his own

170

pace and wouldn't be rushed for anyone. 'There was a time when it was the only school of thought. I maintain it's by far the most important part of our existence. You see the soul grows more determined as we grow older, getting used to its home, comfortable even.' He caressed Felicity's cheek tenderly. 'Yet in the young the soul is so often unsettled. It leaves at the first sign of trouble.'

Finn didn't like the way he was talking. People didn't speak like that. There were ominous undertones, making his words take on an almost sinister, supernatural form.

Willoughby hummed a little tune and pouted. He opened up his palm and allowed his fingers to hover over Felicity's forehead, tracing a careful route downwards, running his fingers over the bridge of her nose, past her lips, down her neck. He stopped at her chest, titled his head back, and closed his eyes.

Finn, puzzled, looked to Cora and Devery, both of whom avoided his stare. Devery in particular looked most uncomfortable, his head bowed solemnly, transfixed on the fabric of his boot laces.

Then a light appeared as if from nowhere, its origin coming from the skin of Willoughby's fingertips, which now glowed. The light started to move as if alive, spreading up and down Felicity's body and growing brighter and brighter until its dominance filled the room from floor to ceiling. Willoughby's eyes cracked open and he writhed with a sudden pain. His eyes then started to glow too, furiously, two opal spotlights, the eyes of *something* or *someone* that science had yet to write a thesis about and that the world had not seen before.

Finn didn't want to look away but the strength of the glare forced him to use his forearm as an urgent shield. Sound then took over, the clamour of the glass in the skylights shattering, the whoosh of the gust of wind that swarmed into the room and brushed harshly against his face. The wind itself was painfully loud, a terrible roar that sounded like a group of men crying out in unison, the ghostly choir singing a tale of woe and agony.

He was tempted to look again, so tempted, but fear stopped him. What was unfolding in front of him *was* supernatural, he had not a single shred of doubt, and he knew that if he witnessed the scene it would haunt his nightmares for the rest of his life. It was an opinion that worsened as his body was suddenly hit repeatedly, the strange wind funnelling into him as if he was in the centre of a moving crowd and dozens of bodies were brushing past aggressively, their shoulders clipping him as if he wasn't there.

Then everything stopped. The wind died in an instant and without warning the pained voices of the choir became eerily silent, their pain and suffering over. The light was gone as quickly as it appeared.

Finn cautiously removed his arm, his eyes taking a moment to adjust. Felicity was sat up on the mattress, breathing hard, her neck dripping with sweat. All around the mattress were shards of broken glass. Snow floated into the room from the shattered skylights. Willoughby was a few inches in front of her and looking at her, checking over whatever work it was that he had carried out.

'Fixed?' Devery said, finally looking up from his boots.

'I would say so,' said Willoughby. He waved his hand in front of Felicity's eyes and clicked his fingers. 'You back with me, young lady?'

Felicity didn't move an inch. It was as if whatever happened had left her with a paralysis that would be hard to shake.

'Difficult to tell though,' noted Willoughby, 'it felt like it went well. Could feel a warmth behind the –'

Felicity screamed and slapped Willoughby hard across the face. A thwacking noise echoed through the room. Her eyes rolled towards the top of her head and she fell back into unconsciousness, plopping down on the mattress.

Devery snorted with a laughter that quickly became hysterical. 'Oh my god,' he said, having to bend down and press his hands into his knees to compose himself. 'Without doubt the funniest thing I've seen in years. I swear I almost wet myself.'

Finn darted to the bed and kneeled. He was confused. 'I don't understand. Is she ok?'

172

'She's fine,' Willoughby said, returning to the rocking chair. He sat down, nursing the cheek that was already starting to swell up with four thin red streaks. 'Finn, people normally find being healed to be an odd experience. But I must say that's never happened before.'

'Meet Felicity Gower,' Finn said. 'If you knew her, you wouldn't be surprised.'

The relief washed over him and Finn caught himself grinning. The snowflakes that had fallen onto Felicity's cheeks were starting to melt, absorbed by the heat of her returning health. He pressed his flat hand to Felicity's forehead. It was already warmer, like a hot water pipe that has been turned on for the first time in winter. Her breathing was more controlled.

'She needs to rest,' said Devery. 'I'll move the bed to another room, one that's a bit more weathertight.'

Finn turned back and looked at Willoughby with something that sat somewhere between awe, bemusement, and terror. 'How did you just do that?'

'That's just one question,' Willoughby said, rocking forward, 'with one of many wondrous answers. She'll be out for a couple hours. Come, let us go downstairs. Think it's time we had a bit of a chat.'

Chapter Twenty-Six

The vehicles that approached did so in convoy, single file, eight dark shapes that descended the hill and from their outlines appeared to be jeeps of some shape or form. The headlights illuminated the dark road, making it look like a long snake slithering down out of the bosom of the dark horizon.

Agatha watched them in silence. She was dressed all in black, wrapped up warm with a long thick coat and thick gloves. Still, the cold attacked her ears and she wished she had worn a hat.

The lights of the factory glowed behind her. There had been no particular reason to choose Gloucestershire as the place to settle down. It had been Peter's choice, picked completely at random. She had never liked the area, finding it too quiet, too serene, and just too damn polite. But one thing it did have was an abundance of rural areas and quiet, empty factories like the one she was stood in front of. The factory they had rented for their headquarters required an element of tact during the day, the neighbouring buildings still occupied and in use, but at night it was deserted and there were no signs of life for miles around, meaning no interruptions, no witnesses.

She was struggling to shake the anger from her thoughts. It had been two days ago, the debacle at the shopping centre. The trace on the girl's account had pinged and Theo and Rogen had moved without her instruction or her permission. There had been no plan, no strategy. The men had made it up as they went along. They *should* have notified her. Moving without the Operation Leader's say so was one of the worst sins.

'Dwelling on it's pointless,' said Theo. He walked down a small slope, the tall building of brick dark behind him. The metal roller-shutters were rising, Rogen and the three other surviving Operatives coming outside to join them.

'You think it wrong to audit a disaster?' said Agatha sternly. She watched her approaching subordinates, all of whom had suffered and were bruised, Rogen in particular having taken a violent pummelling at the hands of the French subject. Her husband had, at one point, incapacitated the other three but luckily they had survived. She had now remembered their names and she watched them as they stopped a short distance behind her. The girl was called Saria, the two men Udo and Brahms, and she wasn't overly impressed with any of their performances thus far.

Theo started to speak again. 'You've been out of the field a very long time and –'

'I know what a *failure* is, Theo,' she spat back. 'That kind of thing remains easily identifiable irrespective of how long one has been out of the field.'

Theo removed a metal hip flask from his pocket and took a long drink. 'We had a window of opportunity and we took it.'

'You took nothing,' said Agatha. 'We lost the subject –'

'And we'll track him again,' said Theo confidently. 'That's what we're good at after all.'

Agatha didn't answer. She looked again at the road. The vehicles were perhaps half a mile away now.

Theo took another swig from his flask. He lowered his voice so the others couldn't hear him. 'You've changed vastly, you know. Dramatically so, more so than I had imagined.'

'In sixteen years everyone changes,' Agatha said. She shrugged. "Is that why none of you trust me?'

'I don't trust you, Agatha,' Theo said strongly, 'because I don't know what it is you've changed into.'

'Theo,' she said calmly. 'Let me make something abundantly clear to you, something I have no issue with you filtering to the others in whatever way you deem fit. You ever undermine me again, in *any* capacity, and I'll kill you. We're talking medieval justice, having your head, that type of thing. I make no qualms about that.'

Theo didn't react and they shared a long stare with one another. 'You have some bigger fish to fry,' he said, pointing to the approaching cars. 'Those that are coming, they'll try and relieve you of your command.'

'Will they?' Agatha said with surprise. 'Even against my father's wishes?'

'Has no clout,' said Theo, another drink of warming liquor. 'Told you before, he's lost his status. Man in charge of this cell's called Rattigan, won't take kindly to even the smallest suggestion that he's to work under a traitor's direction.'

'I see,' said Agatha, 'then we'll just have to find a way to politely convince him.'

The vehicles parked up on the drive. They were not jeeps at all but black pick-up trucks, made by Mitsubishi, five seats in two rows in the front, the back full of equipment that was covered up with a tight tarpaulin. The doors to the vehicles opened and the passengers disembarked onto the tarmac, their hands in their pockets, spreading out in no particular order.

Agatha counted the relevant points of the scene in front of her, *eight vehicles, twenty-four Operatives.*

The leader took a step forward. He was broad across the shoulders and wore multiple layers of clothing and a wool hat. His chin and forehead were large and his features were chiselled and grizzled, almost handsome. He had brown stubble and brown eyes and although he could never hope to compete with Rogen in terms of size he was certainly bigger than anyone else in the vicinity.

'You the deserter?' he said with a nod of distaste.

Agatha narrowed her eyes. 'Cut that nonsense out from the offset,' she said. 'I'm in charge here and you'll address me with the proper degree of respect.'

The man smiled, rubbing his hands together to generate warmth. 'Is that right?'

She looked at the other newcomers, wanting to read their intentions. They all stared at her, everyone a stranger, their looks conveying their emotions. Few emotions were friendly. She turned back to the leader of the pack. 'You're Rattigan?'

Rattigan ignored the question and stared to the side to her. 'Long time no see, Theo.'

With surprising solidarity, Theo ignored Rattigan. It was all a game.

'I welcome your skills,' said Agatha. 'We have a lot in front of us and –'

'Been on the road since Pavlodar,' said Rattigan. 'Haven't the patience for speechifying. Bring us some food.'

Agatha pointed towards the building. 'Food's inside.'

'Perhaps I wasn't clear,' Rattigan said. An order was coming, pure and simple. '*Prepare* us food. And then when you're finished have them unload the trucks and set our equipment up in the far corner of the warehouse. We check the equipment and you'll brief my people with the intelligence you have so far.' He turned to walk away, back towards his truck, but her voice stopped him.

'Rattigan,' said Agatha. There were no nerves evident in her voice, its pitch perfect with authority. 'Guess you're under the impression that you're to give *me* orders. You're *my* reinforcements.'

Rattigan turned back and watched her curiously. Then he glanced at his colleagues and he laughed out loud. His colleagues joined in, a chorus of childish mocking.

Agatha glanced discreetly to Theo. None of *her* people were laughing. Rogen looked as though he was just waiting for the command to break forward and snap someone in two. She hadn't uttered a mistruth, they truly did *not* trust her, but still, in *this* situation and *this* stand-off, they were very much on her side.

'Put up a flag,' Theo whispered out the side of his mouth.

'I'd say you can't have heard of me,' said Rattigan when he was finished laughing. 'You don't know what I've done, what I'm capable of. Maybe I'll forgive your lack of respect. But understand this, sweetheart, I *am* in charge now. You've lost too many men. Your operation's been an embarrassment from beginning to end. And what's more, I don't take no orders from a *woman* and I certainly don't take no orders from a disgusting, dirty little deserter.'

Rogen took a quick step forward, a movement that didn't go unnoticed.

'Careful now, Big Un!' said Rattigan. Two of his colleagues, a woman to his right and a man to his left, drew pistols from their belts and held them up, their threat evident.

Rogen stopped and looked to Agatha for direction.

'It's ok, Rogen,' said Agatha. She waved him backwards with her hand and turned her attention back to her so called *reinforcements*. She wouldn't admit it but she was touched by the big man's show of dedication.

She allowed herself some further analysis, pushing beyond the numbers and starting with Rattigan's obvious strengths. He was approximately six foot, seven inches. His clothing rested tightly against his skin but didn't show a single bulge of fat, meaning it was all muscle. His arms were long and would have a useful reach. Despite having not moved far, his movements still suggested that he was agile and confident in his abilities. It was all positive ... *for her.* He would be overconfident, slower than her, easier to chip away at.

'My father isn't going to be happy with all this,' she said.

'Daddy isn't here,' Rattigan shot back. 'Besides, even your father, in all his wisdom, will understand the prudency of having the most efficient cell in charge of this. And what's more, he doesn't scare me.'

'I was talking about something different,' said Agatha with a cool detachment. 'I meant that my father will probably be angry at the example you've forced me to set.'

Rattigan raised an eyebrow and flashed a wicked smile. 'And what's that supposed to mean?'

Agatha then showed him *exactly* what it meant. She thundered forward, targeting the two armed people first. The gun arm of the man was broken before he had time to think let alone react. She used his own finger to fire two shots from his weapon into the armed woman's thigh before depriving him of the gun. The woman fell sideways, dropping her gun and clutching the fresh wound, attempting to stem the blood that was spraying onto the snow.

Behind her Theo drew his own weapon. Rogen, Saria, Udo, and Brahms followed his lead, using their handguns to cover the grouped number that was far greater than their own.

Rattigan's smile was gone but his confidence was not. He came at her, his first punch knocking the gun out of Agatha's grip and the efforts that followed raining down. But Agatha was no slouch and she avoided the majority of the assault, until one punch came too close and almost connected with her chin. Noting the warning, she evaded the next punch and kicked out, making a sharp connection with Rattigan's groin. Seeing that this wasn't enough, she followed this up with a brutal kick to his kneecap. The bone twisted and cracked. Rattigan fell to his one good knee.

Agatha stood upright, straightening her ruffled clothes and then picked up the gun that had fallen near her feet. She addressed the rest of the newcomers with a loud shouted announcement. 'Are we going to have a problem now?'

They said nothing. Nothing was diffused. They still didn't respect her, still didn't trust her, each of them still unwilling to submit to both her will and her authority. It was the O.K. Coral all over again, guns at their hips, the charge of electricity before the violence of gunfire and death resting in the air.

'Was my example not strong enough?' Agatha said.

Rattigan was grasping for breath. He reached out at her ankle. 'You stupid little –'

She casually aimed the gun at Rattigan and without turning around squeezed off two shots into his chest. Rattigan's body shuddered and he slumped onto his back, struggling for a moment, creating a bloodied snow angel. But then he stopped moving and he showed no more discontent, no more mutiny. *Dead men are always more obedient.*

Agatha shrugged. 'How about now?'

Still there was no audible answer. But the newcomers fanned out slowly and made their way towards the open building. That was answer enough.

Rogen helped the injured man and woman up, taking one under each arm and into the warmth of the warehouse. Saria,

Udo, and Brahms got to work, moving amongst the pick-up trucks, killing the lights and the engines. Theo remained by Agatha's side, peering over the fresh corpse that she had just created.

'When I said put up a flag,' he said, 'that wasn't quite what I meant.'

'Will I cause ripples with this?' Agatha asked.

'Potentially,' said Theo, 'Rattigan was an idiot but an excellent soldier. He was a favourite and will be a loss, might put a few noses out of joint. Still, I'll report what I saw, for what it's worth. My view, such as it is, is that I don't think there can be too many complaints. Although I doubt anyone's witnessed such an old fashioned brand of justice in quite some time.'

'Where's Pavlodar?' Agatha asked.

'Don't know,' said Theo, 'think it's somewhere in Kazakhstan. It's a long way to come just to die in the snow.'

Agatha pulled off her glove and stared at her hand. It was shaking erratically. She knew she wouldn't be able to put it down to the cold.

Theo saw it too. 'You ok?'

'I haven't killed anyone in fifteen years.'

'No, I don't suppose you have.'

She slipped her glove back on. 'This Carmichael character won't keep him here. There's too much heat in this town for that and he knows that it'll be getting hotter. We have enough people now to cover most of the exit roads from Willowbrook and Cheltenham.'

Theo nodded his agreement. 'I'll get them dispatched at first light—'

'Tonight,' Agatha said. 'Feed them and get them dispatched. Enough of this sneaking around, we need to find them, hit them quickly and hit them hard. We think about the mess afterwards.'

Theo wasn't about to question her. 'I'll get someone to come out and dispose of the body —'

'No,' said Agatha coldly. 'Leave him out here. There's plenty of vermin roaming around. Let them have him. Someone finds the body later on and they won't be able to identify it anyway.'

Theo didn't say anything but his expression showed that even he was shocked at such an unceremonious instruction. 'You think me a little cold?' she asked. 'More than a little,' he answered. 'You were right earlier,' said Agatha. 'I *have* indeed changed. And I'll be honest with you. Even I'm not sure what I've changed into.'

Chapter Twenty-Seven

Finn rested back into the soft leather of the chair, watching the group of people go about their work with purpose around him. It was close to midnight and they had furnished the room with a selection of old chairs and tired sofas that they had scrounged from the other parts of the house, placing the furniture on the rug around the fireplace. The fire in the hearth was reinvigorated and a rack set atop the flames, a small black pot of coffee bubbling away on the iron wires. A variety of bags and boxes had been brought inside from the van, some of which were filled with food and provisions.

Now that the sense of urgency had passed, he had made more of an effort to remember each of their names. Edgar Bloom stood by the window enjoying his coffee and watching the falling snow, a black man in his forties, tall and muscular, his beard dark and shaved short. Hamish Ives, a Scotsman with a mop of brown hair and his own impressively thick beard, was a little younger and he sat on the floor in front of the fire, fiddling with a variety of small, metal toy soldiers that he had removed carefully from a tartan sack. Cora had passed everyone a blanket and she took a seat next to Willoughby on one of the sofas. Devery, who had been revealed to be Cora's husband, was seated nearest to Finn in a tall backed armchair, leaning over a map of the area that he had unfolded out onto a box.

'I should perhaps start by apologising,' Willoughby said. 'We couldn't get back to you any earlier, despite our best efforts. The roads are being watched. Your father did a good job reducing their number but there are others out there. And more will be coming. On that note we –'

'What did you do to Fliss?' Finn asked it too bluntly. He was anxious to *get-the-show-on-the-road* and didn't really care for any apologetic notions.

'*He* saved her life!' Cora pointed out, picking up on the tone and defending her brother. 'Perhaps you should remember that, young man?'

'Yeah,' said Hamish sarcastically, 'and I'm sure the way he went about it didn't look strange at all and leave him with some questions.' The Scotsman pulled a small paint pallet and brush from his pocket. He held a soldier up to the light of the fire.

Willoughby afforded himself a moment and he surveyed the room that he was sitting within with a look that almost hinted at sadness. When he was finished, he shuffled to the end of his seat and reached down, picking one of Hamish's soldiers up from the floor, a sweeping romantic figure of metal with a tall hat and a horse striding beneath him. 'A Russian Hussar,' he noted, rotating the soldier between his fingers. 'Can't help but bring to my mind a day one July, think it would have been 1807, where a different meeting took place between a little Frenchman and a naïve, young Russian Tsar. Was something meaningful, that event, something historic that would have huge repercussions for the whole of Europe later on down the line. And the setting befitted the significance of that meeting of course, a small raft with a small pavilion on the Neman River. I would imagine it was quite beautiful.'

None of the others said anything or made to interrupt but Devery sipped from his coffee mug and was shaking his head as he continued pawing over his map.

'Doesn't seem right, does it?' Willoughby said. 'Is our meeting here any less significant than that one? Is it any less important? No, put frankly, it isn't. And what do we get? We get a cold, damp, grey room in an abandoned and forgotten pub in the middle of an English winter. Hardly seems deserving but then I shouldn't be surprised. History has always had a knack of dealing us a crappy hand.'

'You'll have to excuse, Will,' said Devery, finding his voice. 'He's always enjoyed story-time a little too much.' He looked up and made a face at Willoughby. 'Personally, I think the boy's probably been through enough and might favour something a little more direct.'

Willoughby was still focusing on the soldier. 'There are some,' he said, smiling to himself, 'who just fail to appreciate the power and the potency of stories.' He then tossed the toy soldier to the floor, much to Hamish's dismay, who groaned in complaint at his lack of care.

Finn drank from his own coffee, wincing at the bitter taste. He was no coffee drinker but the warmth it afforded his chest was at least welcome. He pulled his blankets a little bit tighter around his body. The room was growing colder, despite the strength of the fire.

'There tends to be things I like to avoid,' said Willoughby. 'Not least the talk of prophecies or of things that were written down long ago.'

There were a few laughs, a few more snorts and groans, suggesting that such a statement was wildly inaccurate.

Willoughby continued, unperturbed. 'Most prophecies aren't prophecies at all but nothing short of pure guesses. You write down that it'll rain tomorrow and it rains, doesn't make you a prophet. Just makes you lucky.'

'And today,' said Hamish jokingly, 'makes you a weatherman, oddly enough.'

'But in this case,' said Willoughby, 'talk of prophecy is unavoidable. And there is one in particular that proves important, the one that has bought us all together in this room.' He cleared his throat and began to recite a passage he had long since stored to his memory. '*From the storm of ice and crystal the child will be born, coming forth, the first of his kind, the last of his kind, the end of the circle, the last circle, the completion of the promise of obsidian.*'

There was a lurch in Finn's stomach. There was that word again. Obsidian. And spoken from the lips of a man who appeared to know what it meant. He was both nervous and excited about what he was about to hear.

'Translations vary,' Willoughby explained, 'but that's my favourite incarnation, fluid and to the point.'

'In short,' said Cora, 'and as crazy as it might sound, this strange weather, this cold, is all because of you.'

'Or,' Hamish said as he painted the tunic of one of his British soldiers in a lush red, 'it could all just be a great big coincidence.'

'Mr Ives serves as our resident doubter,' said Willoughby, 'the devil's advocate, not known as a man of faith –'

'Oh I have my faith,' Hamish said, 'but this is something different.'

'Finn,' Willoughby stood up tall before the fire and rested his coffee mug on the mantle-piece, 'would you be able to tell me now, to dispel any doubts, do you have the mark?'

Finn didn't need an explanation as to what he was getting at. He knew exactly what they meant and as Willoughby turned he saw the truth in Finn's eyes. The others saw it too and they looked away, at one with their own thoughts at the revelation.

'Wow,' Willoughby smiled widely and his face shivered with excitement. 'You do have it.'

'So,' said Finn, 'it's not just a rash? Just like I thought?'

'Well, it never was a rash,' Willoughby corrected him. 'It's a mark – or a symbol if you'd prefer. May I ask, if it's not in too private a place, whether I might see it? It's not that I don't trust you but once I explain its meaning, you'll understand why I'm inclined to seek a bit more confirmation.'

Finn considered the question for a moment, his natural bashfulness aghast at the thought of getting his chest out in front of a room full of strangers. But the promise of *answers* was too intoxicating a concept and despite the coldness of the room he slowly pulled his jumper up, his chest peeking out from beneath his blanket, revealing what was now apparently to be known henceforth as the *mark*.

It was enough to make Edgar Bloom turn fully around from the window. Cora rose and joined her husband in the chair, forcing herself onto his lap. Devery turned away from his map studying, wrapping her up into his embrace. Hamish stopped painting and sighed loudly, running his fingers through his long brown hair.

'Well, there goes any chance of a peaceful life,' the Scotsman said before returning to his painting.

Willoughby took a few small steps from the fire and extended his arm. But he didn't allow himself to touch the mark, allowing his fingers instead to hover as close as he dared. 'You see it now, Mr Ives,' he said quietly, 'with your own eyes, the truth of it all?'

'I see it,' Hamish replied, not looking up.

'I could look at it all day,' said Willoughby.

'Which sounds more than a little weird,' said Finn. He pulled his jumper back down. 'And I'm no nude model. So ... what is it? Everything in my life has gone wrong since this thing appeared.'

Willoughby appeared unsure and he looked to his companions as if looking for support or at least a clue as to how best to proceed.

'It's time,' Devery said.

Willoughby sat back down. 'The mark,' he said, taking a sip of coffee and finishing the last drops in his mug, 'signifies something that we call The Settling. The term's relatively unopposed, used widely amongst us. The mark appears on day one, until it does there's not really any way of you knowing what it signifies. That, of course, is why the role of the Guardian becomes so important.'

'I've heard that term before,' said Finn excitedly, feeling as though he at least had a snippet of information to contribute. He frowned, the feeling being short lived when he realised the extent of his knowledge. 'What exactly is a Guardian?'

'All of us are spiritually linked,' Willoughby explained, 'a spirituality that exists exclusively for us. You'll be able to feel our presence, when one of us is close, sometimes feeling it from far away and other times maybe only a split second before you get a tap on the shoulder. But with the Guardian, it's very different. The Guardian shares an unbreakable bond with the one who Settles.'

'There's no reason to it,' said Edgar, who had returned to peering out beyond the glass and into the snowy night. 'No explanation, so don't seek one out. It just *is*. Never know who it's going to be, who gets chosen for The Settling. One of us *Settles*, the other feels it like a punch to the gut, which turns into an irresistible desire to find that person –'

'It's the most important role,' said Hamish, 'at least in the beginning. The Guardian will know where to find you, they feel it, and when they find you they tell you everything. When you accept the truth, the mark turns black, never changes again. Any pain you've had from it will also be gone, thankfully.'

Finn looked at each of the faces before him. Logic made a question form in his head. 'Is one of you my –'

'No,' Willoughby jumped in, pre-empting the query. 'Poor Edwin Cavell was your Guardian, which in its own way was a cruel twist of fate. He wasn't really known to any of us. James only met him once and only briefly. I've never even heard his name mentioned amongst friends. I suspect he had no idea why so many of us appeared. Had he known of the significance of *this* Settling, he would have been a very useful ally.'

Finn winced. His mind was torn, not helped by being a natural cynic. He had known he was a cynic long before he had come to an age to even know that a term existed to describe his lack of faith in people. He had been given no reason to think any differently. His father had said that he needed to have more confidence but whether they were self-fulfilling prophecies or not, generally when he feared something bad would happen it did and when he mistrusted someone they usually let him down. He was already mistrusting his new friends, wondering why they would be telling such lies and why they would make such things up. Their claims, still not formed into any sort of tangible answer, were of the most odd. But a counteracting argument existed. *They* had sought him out. And if he couldn't quite see the truth in their eyes he could see their belief. What reason would they have to lie outright?

'Ok,' he said. 'Let's go with this then, assuming this is all true. What is Settling? Who am I?'

'It's not a question of *who* you are,' said Cora, 'but *what* you are.'

'Actually,' said Willoughby, 'it's a question of both *who* and *what* you are. Finn, tell me, are you truly ready to hear what I am about to tell you?'

Finn nodded. 'Yes, I'm ready.'

Willoughby reached down and yanked his trouser leg up. There, on his shin and as clear as the day itself, was a familiar shape, the shape of a black cross with a circular head at the tip.

It was Finn's turn to position himself at the edge of his seat. He immediately noticed that the mark was not identical to his own. Willoughby's words rang in his ears – *the circle completing.* Willoughby's mark was *not* complete. The circle had a gap.

The others followed Willoughby's lead – one by one – Cora rolling up a sleeve to reveal the mark on her left wrist, Hamish inching the collar of his jumper down to show the mark on his neck. Devery had to show a similar degree of bravery to Finn, his mark placed in the centre of his chest. Edgar stayed at the window and without turning he eased his shirt upwards, showing the tip of the image on the lower part of his back.

'These are the marks of our kind,' said Willoughby. 'Your father had a very rare book that he passed onto us and it's one of many that mention the marks. You'll note that yours is just that little bit different to the rest. The marks that we all share have had a host of different names over the ages. We like to use the name from ancient Egypt.'

'We call it the ankh,' said Devery.

'But yours,' Willoughby said, 'has but one name –'

Finn thought back to the night in his father's study. 'Mine is called Obsidian, right?'

'Quite right,' said Willoughby. Everyone in the room slowly put their flesh away, smothering the marks with clothing. 'Yours is inexplicably unique and –'

'Will,' said Cora quietly, 'maybe get back to the Settling stuff?'

'Oh,' said Willoughby, stuttering, 'Yes, you're right. Settling, Finn, signifies the day that each and every one of us steps forward, the day we stop growing, the day we stop ageing, the day we freeze in time. It signifies the day we no longer get sick, the day that we no longer suffer at the hands of any germs or bugs.'

Finn frowned. He heard the words and he recognised the sequence of how they were all put together. But he wasn't sure he understood. 'What?' he said. It was all he could say by means of a response.

Willoughby flashed a wry smile, 'Settling, Finn, is the day that we become immortal.'

There it was again, Finn's cynicism, gnawing away like a dog with an old bone. The complaints wanted to form on his tongue, the *what-you-talking-abouts* and the *don't-talk-such-rubbishes* but despite the strength of the desire to snort his derision, something stopped him dead. It was if a switch had been flicked on somewhere deep inside of him.

'I …' he stuttered, 'I … I don't know … it's so weird … it's as if –'

'I know,' Willoughby nodded. 'It's as if you've *always* known. There's no disbelief, only acceptance.'

'Yes, that's it,' said Finn. Yet he wasn't ready to concede his rationality just yet. 'But that's impossible.'

A heavy silence fell upon the room. There had been a birth. The birth had been a realisation, cast by the omitting of a single word – *immortal.* The word spilled from Willoughby's mouth and deposited itself there on the patterned rug. It sat there, fully formed, looking up at those present, shrugging idly, a strange, powerful truth. It was challenging them and one of them in particular. It was challenging him to believe. It was challenging him to take a leap of faith.

'I Settled,' said Willoughby, proudly breaking the silence, 'at the grand old age of fifty-nine.'

'Thirty four,' Cora disclosed.

'Forty three,' Hamish announced.

'Forty five,' Edgar said.

Devery smiled. 'Thirty eight,' he said.

Finn listened carefully. Still no hint at a ruse, they were all utterly serious, no humour evident. 'If I've got this right,' he said slowly, almost embarrassingly, 'You're telling me that's the age you Settled, but not *actually* how old you are?'

Willoughby, enthused by Finn's positive response, went first. 'Willoughby Thomas Carmichael,' he said, 'born in the village of Mornay, England, the year of our Lord 1316.'

Cora went next. 'Cora Juliet Carmichael, born in Mornay, the year 1312.'

'I have the dubious honour,' said Hamish, 'of being the oldest. I was born Hamish Donald Ives in a little place close to Stirling, around about 1252. It's not there anymore.'

'Hackney,' said Edgar bluntly, '1960.'

'Edgar's the newbie,' Devery said, 'took over that honour from me.' He leant down and kissed his wife on her hair. 'I'm probably the world's most disgraceful toy boy. I was born in a place called Corofin in Ireland in 1831, the same day the Tithe War started. I go with Will, not the biggest believer in most prophecies, but was oddly prophetic that I was born on that day, as let's just say I've had a bit of a taste for rebellion ever since.'

Finn wanted to do the mathematics based on the disclosures but it was too much to deal with all at once. Besides, his curiosity had been breached by something else, a looming sense of eeriness. It was just the simple thought of it that unsettled him, the thought that the people sitting in front of him had been walking the earth, some of them for hundreds of years, hiding in the shadows. It was a notion strong enough to chill even the sturdiest of souls.

'Put simply,' said Willoughby, 'and without debate, which will come later, immortality is a gift, a gift that we believe was given to us by God himself. Again, there's debate about the purpose but I see no reason for us to burden ourselves with that right now. What you do need to understand though is that immorality is *not* the extent of our gift.'

'You've seen us do things,' said Cora.

'Wonderful things,' Hamish added.

'We're blessed with a further ability,' Willoughby explained, 'a capability to do something physical which mortal men and women can't. To give you an example, I have the ability to heal, you've seen it. The men who murdered poor Mr Cavell had the ability to harness enhanced strength and power, as did Mr Cavell himself we believe. As a rule, abilities tend to fit nicely into six categories. Categories tend to be enhanced strength, enhanced speed, enhanced wisdom, the ability to heal, the ability of telekinesis, and the ability of foresight.'

'Six categories,' said Devery, 'with the odd exception. But those stories would just confuse matters right now.'

Willoughby gestured his hands outwards, to the others in the room. 'Yet far be it for me to speak for others.'

Cora was blushing. 'I'm not a fan of talking about this kind of thing, feels a bit too much like we're living in a comic book. I can sometimes move things with my mind. *Sometimes* is the key word in all of that. Can be frustratingly intermittent and it's not like there's a user manual.'

'I'm quick,' said Devery.

'You're not *that* quick,' Hamish said by means of a quip.

Devery sighed. 'I'm quicker than you, Hamish.'

'Some contest,' said Hamish. 'Settled at forty three, didn't I, had it been thirty three is might have been closer.' The Scotsman looked to Finn. 'Anyway, what use is speed when you've no idea what you're running into? Me, I have a little teeny weeny bit of foresight. Don't go asking me to tell you the lottery numbers, it doesn't work like that. No, it's the same as Cora, a bit unpredictable, comes to me in visions.'

Finn glanced over at Edgar, assuming he would speak next, but the big man said nothing.

'I wouldn't expect much from Mr Bloom,' said Willoughby. 'I was given the honour of being his Guardian yet so far he's never revealed the nature of his extra gift. We of course all have our suspicions.'

Edgar made a gruff noise in his throat. 'My business, ain't it! And it ain't ever going to be none of yours.'

'Which is annoying,' said Willoughby, 'yet undeniably clever. It's these little gifts that have a habit of getting us into trouble. Revealing them, if of course you ever choose to do so, risks attention, risks focus, risks a scrutiny that leads us down a road than only ends with darkness.'

Finn suddenly thought of himself and he almost fell from the chair as an excitable realisation hit him. 'What can I do?' he said urgently. 'I haven't felt anything.'

'That will come with time,' Willoughby reassured him. 'Some of us gain access to these abilities before we Settle, some after. But something you do need to understand, Finn, is that you are just that little bit different to all of us. You see, a child has *never* Settled before. Never. This is the first time in all of history. And it was prophesised that when this happens, the child will be born with a mark that shows the complete circle and that he or she will have *every* gift. They will be strong, they will be agile, quick, they will be able to heal, see things that are yet to pass, everything. I believe that you are that child.'

Finn fell back in his chair. 'I'm invincible,' he said to himself.

'*Never* make that mistake,' Devery said strongly, 'although you wouldn't be the first to do so. Don't have illusions of invincibility, immortality fine, but not invincibility. You're flesh and bone, Finn, nothing more, nothing less. You get shot in the heart, you die. Head gets chopped off and it's not going to grow back. Your power, our power, stops with time and time only.'

'Knew a chap once,' said Hamish, 'nice enough fellow, a fair few hundred year's old, immense wealth, very careful. Goes and gets drunk one night, strolls out the carpark, mistakes a boulder for his car and then topples off the edge of a steep little cliff. One broken neck and one broken back later, he's a corpse and there wasn't nothing he could do about it.'

'I read this in a book once,' said Willoughby. 'It said that we are the dust. We float around time, Finn. Every now and again we settle somewhere, in a house or a town or a village, and we coat these places, but it doesn't take long for us to be disturbed and then we move somewhere else and start the process all over again.'

'Dust is a poetic way of looking at it,' said Edgar gloomily. 'But I would say we are the ghosts of this world.'

Willoughby enjoyed a long, lingering yawn and did not go to say any more. Finn realised that it was the end of his tales, yet it was not the end of Finn's questions and he went to speak but Willoughby cut him off by standing. There was one thing they hadn't even touched upon and he didn't consider it arrogant to speculate. *Why am I so important?*

'No more questions now,' Willoughby said, heading towards the door. 'Not for tonight at least. There's more to tell, Finn, quite a lot more, not least where your parents come into all of this and why they've been hunting our kind for a very long time. And we haven't even begun to scratch the surface of just why you being the first Settled child has so much importance and why it's bought so many demons out to play. But tomorrow is tomorrow and we need sleep and rest. To be continued, young man, you have my word.'

Finn watched Willoughby and the others as they rose.

'I'm heading outside,' said Devery, finding his coat, 'keep an eye on things.'

'I'll come with you,' Edgar said. 'There's been enough of this sitting around lark.'

Devery kicked Hamish in the legs. 'And so will you.'

'Will I, now?' Hamish picked himself and his soldiers up from the floor. 'I can sense that this little task is going to be a barrel of laughs.'

Finn watched them go, some out into the dark morning and others to find makeshift beds. He was happy to be left alone, alone with his thoughts and he sat there for quite some time, barely moving, the embers of the fire slowly dying and daylight creeping through the woods and back into the world.

Chapter Twenty-Eight

She had been allocated the small box room for her recovery, a room as slight in size as it could be before officially being classified as a cupboard. There was only enough space for a single bed and one small bedside cabinet. The only light came from a small square window on the slanted roof that jutted out at an odd angle above the bed.

Felicity had woken to the light of morning and to the sight of Finn, perched at the bottom of the bed like a man waiting for a loved one to come round from a coma. At first she had been relieved to see him, welcoming the warm hug, the peculiar explanation of how Willoughby Carmichael had saved her life, and the caring question of how she was feeling. But she was less enthused at how swiftly he moved on and started talking about what appeared to be his new favourite subject – himself.

He was in as excitable a mood as she had ever seen him, a giddy, restless schoolboy, a far different Finn to the one she had left behind before the darkness had set in. His speech moved at a thousand miles per hour, an erratic rat-a-tat-tat, struggling to finish one snippet of information before moving quickly onto the next. The information came in barrages and it was hard to keep up.

She listened dutifully to every last word that came out of his mouth with a strange look on her face that he didn't seem to notice. She didn't ask any questions, not that she would have had a chance to, and when he was finished he sat in silence in front of her, staring, blinking, and waiting eagerly for her reaction. He was breathing hard and his eyes were wide.

She rolled her own eyes from left to right and then back again. She shrugged, not knowing what it was that he expected of her.

'Say ... something?' Finn implored her.

'What do you want me to say?' she asked.

'Well,' said Finn, 'what do you think for starters?'

'I don't think anything.'

'I meant about what I've just told you –'

'I know what you meant,' Felicity said, 'and I don't think anything about it.'

'Nothing?' said Finn. The surprise in his tone showed that he was annoyed. 'How can you *not* think anything? Come on, it's like the single most amazing thing I've ever heard in my entire life.'

Felicity afforded herself a wry chuckle and a shake of the head. She did for a split second ponder whether Finn was actually trying to win some sort of award for being a prize idiot but alas no, he was blissfully unaware of how he was coming across to her.

'Ok,' she said, 'if you say so.'

'Come on, Fliss,' he said, keen for her to see his point. 'It *is* amazing ... in like *every* single way ... you have to admit that. I just can't get my head around it all, I couldn't wait for you to wake up, I couldn't wait to tell you, when I –'

'I need to sleep some more!' Felicity said. She closed her eyes and turned her back to him to give a less-than-subtle weight to her point. For his part he didn't say anything more but he did stay a short while, presumably with a bemused look on his face. Eventually, and no doubt fed up, he dragged himself up and closed the door gently behind him.

She lay there for a long while, happy to be alone, her eyes closed but awake. She didn't need any sleep, satisfied that she had been afforded enough sleep to last a decade. Now was the time for mulling it over. Her first thought - did she even believe him? She wasn't so sure that she did. Had she been presented with such information four weeks previously she would have had a field day, tearing apart every last word with a sarcastic and bombastic relish. But by the same token, the openness of her mind *had* changed, as had her interpretation of what was real and what was not. It had changed the moment the Frenchman had fallen from the sky and shattered the concrete beneath his knuckles.

Finn clearly did believe it, that much was clear, and his excitement had truly annoyed her. *Amazing* was the word he had used but it wasn't a word Felicity would have chosen, mainly because such a delighted adjective missed a whole heap of other more valid factors and points. Just what was so *amazing* about his insane mother murdering his equally insane father? Was it *amazing* to watch his whole world fall apart? What was so *amazing* about having to run away from an army of lunatics with guns and very bad attitude problems? But most of all, the thing that annoyed her the most, was that he couldn't see that it wasn't only his life that had changed. He had no consideration for anyone else who may have been dragged along for the ride.

She decided to distance herself us much as she could against such thoughts, for they were not helpful. There were other things that concerned her too. The explanation was not complete. They hadn't denied that, making it clear that more was to come, yet Finn hadn't seemed to think about what else they might need to tell him. Just why were these people all here in the first place and more importantly what was the significance of Finn? She had her own ideas about that.

A gentle knock at the door stirred her. Her eyes slowly opened and she sat up in the bed. She could already feel that the time alone had done little to soften her mood and she could detect that the flippant side of her character had turned itself on and was ready for an argument.

Cora moved gingerly into the room, bringing with her a small tray. 'I've got some nice bread,' she said, 'with a little bit of butter and jam and a big pot of tea. You can't hang about with it though, we're moving as soon as possible, as soon as the chaps downstairs get everything ready. Try and be a bit careful though, it's my china from the van.'

Felicity enjoyed a long, loud yawn. She glanced at the tray. 'I'm not hungry.'

'You must keep your strength up,' Cora advised her.

'Why?'

Cora placed the tray on the bedside table and popped herself down at the end of the bed at Felicity's feet. 'Did he tell you everything?' she said. 'He was up here for a while.'

Felicity didn't answer. Instead she looked up at the window, examining the intricate webs of frost on the other side of the glass.

'My thoughts are with you,' Cora said. 'I honestly don't know how all of this must seem to someone like you.'

Felicity bit her lip, tempted to offer her first little bite. 'Someone like me, hey?'

'Yes, someone like you,' Cora said, happy to repeat, unashamed of her choice of words. 'Where's the benefit in me pretending that we're all the same when quite clearly we're not?' She licked her lips, curious. 'Felicity, do you believe what he told you?'

'Honestly?' Felicity answered. 'I'm not sure I care. But since you asked, does all sound a little bit weird to me. Was thinking maybe you guys are part of some nutty cult, something like that. Give it a week, I reckon you'll ask for Finn's bank account details or ask him to strip down naked and howl at the moon or adopt a rock or a pebble or something. Yeah, week sounds about right, and I'll find Finn chatting to a piece of cheese.'

Cora was quiet this time. She stared at Felicity and then stood, turning for the door. 'Try and eat, please,' she said. 'You're old enough to know why you need to eat and drink.'

'You don't want to be immortal, do you?' Felicity said suddenly. 'And you see Finn as the answer, don't you?'

Cora stopped dead in the doorway, her grasp on the handle, the door slightly ajar. She didn't turn around. 'What makes you say that?'

'He hasn't worked it out yet,' Felicity said.

'There's no way you could know –'

'It was a guess,' Felicity admitted. 'Well it was a guess up until about thirty seconds ago until your reaction pretty much confirmed it. I had a few theories actually, that was just one of them. I kept thinking, why are you all here? There has to be a reason. Way I figured you're already going to live forever so I couldn't see how he would make anything better. But then maybe, just maybe he could take something away.'

Cora smiled to herself and nudged the door shut, turning to face Felicity. 'You're a very smart girl.'

'Not really,' said Felicity. 'I don't get it. Why would anyone not want to be immortal?'

Cora stepped back into the room and retook her previous spot on the bed. 'Can I tell you a story?' she said.

'Harry Potter?' Felicity said with a fake hope in her eyes.

'You ever heard of the Black Death?'

'Sounds tempting,' said Felicity, 'but just so I know, we're definitely not going to go with Harry Potter?'

'I wonder,' said Cora, 'whether I'll ever get to know you well enough to find out what pain it is that makes you cover everything up with your so called humour?'

Felicity found herself both stung and silenced by the rebuke. She was used to making people mad, accustomed to seeing their blood slowly boil, but Cora's one sentence was by a great length the best *come back* she had ever encountered. Name calling and curses she could handle, they were easy to deflect away, but breaking into the psyche of her character was something she was never comfortable with.

'I try quite hard not to look back,' Cora said. 'I'm not sure why I would choose to, not sure what good it would do me. But sometimes I can't help it. There's triggers, some obvious, others not. Do you remember much from your childhood?'

'Bits,' said Felicity, 'silly things mostly.'

'I don't have much of it left,' said Cora, 'only flashes, short, blurry. I remember it being cold, dark, and wet. I didn't live in Mornay when the plague came. Mornay was too remote for me, there was no reason to go there and I wanted more. No, I had married by that time, my first husband –'

198

There was a little rumble in Felicity's stomach and she peered down to the tray resting on the bedside table next to her. Cora noticed and she reached across, bringing the tray over and resting it on Felicity's lap. Felicity immediately grabbed a thick slice of bread and started to chew. The bread was smothered in a rich butter and a sweet strawberry jam. It tasted wonderful and she was glad that her stubbornness had given in.

'His name was William,' Cora said, continuing as Felicity ate, 'a veteran of Crecy none the less, a landowner. God I was lucky he even looked in my direction let alone think of marrying me. He was a good man, kind, especially for the time. We lived with his parents after we were married, along with his sister, her husband, and his two nieces. It was a bit cramped to say the least.'

'No offence,' said Felicity, eating ravenously so that the crumbs tumbled from her mouth. 'But is this just going to be a running commentary of your life? I mean it's interesting and all that but you were the one who said we didn't have much time.'

'The plague hit our town hard,' Cora said, ignoring Felicity's comment. 'Like a god damn sledgehammer. I wasn't in any danger, I'd already Settled but of course I didn't know it at the time, my Guardian not finding me until many years later. The townsfolk started to die, one by one. We nailed the door shut, barred the windows, we hid and we prayed. I realised then that God didn't answer prayers, even the most powerful and desperate. The children, they went first –'

Felicity stopped mid-chew. She was regretting her jokes and hostility now and hadn't realised that the story was of such a sad nature. It didn't take a genius to realise it wasn't going to have the happiest of endings.

'William's parents were next,' Cora said. She spoke without showing any signs of getting upset, with a robot like expression at the recollection. 'Then his sister, then her husband a day later. William went last of all. I was lying with him when he died. I watched the last breath leave his lungs. I watched the colour fade away. And then I did nothing. For days, weeks, I just lay there, holding his hand, waiting for death. It was a monk that found me in the end, from a nearby monastery. He only realised I was alive when I twitched as he threw me onto the funeral pyre. I was the only survivor in the whole God forsaken town.'

A sombre silence followed. Felicity didn't know what to say but she wanted to say something, to fill the awkwardness that hung stale in the air. 'It sounds awful,' was all she could offer.

'It was,' Cora agreed. 'When Willoughby discovered I was alive he came for me. Mornay was remote enough to have suffered little. I mean there were deaths but nothing like those in the highly populated towns. He was married at the time, three children, a wife, and a mother in law crammed into a tiny little cottage that wasn't much more than a hut. How they survived I still don't know. It must have been blind luck.' She laughed at the memory but then quickly became serious. 'They were already whispering. Oh, I'd hear them, the names. Sometimes it was witch, devil another, occasionally penitent, but witch was the one they liked the best. Why had this girl lived whilst so many others had perished? And that's all they were at first, questions, insults, slurs, at least until Willoughby got older. Until his wife got older. Until his children got older, to the extent that we appeared to be the same age. It was then that name calling simply wasn't considered a strong enough reaction to my clear devilry.'

'What happened?' Felicity asked. She couldn't help but be intrigued.

'They came to their conclusions,' said Cora. 'That's what happened. It was a pact with the devil, apparently, the exchange of a soul for everlasting life. There's many things that have changed over the years but one that hasn't is that people still destroy the things they don't understand. They all turned against me, even Willoughby. I was beaten, whipped, spat at. Should they hang me? Burn me? Some thought both were a good idea. I was lucky that my Guardian turned up at the perfect time. He saved my life. You see he was from a foreign land, I never learnt where, his skin black. Most of the villagers had never seen skin that colour. They thought he was the devil himself and so they ran. But he wasn't the devil. No, he took me away from that place.'

'How can you even stand to talk to your brother?' said Felicity. 'I would hate him forever, for what he did.'

'I did hate him,' Cora admitted, 'for a long time. But you mustn't judge my brother. He didn't know any better. You can't apply modern scrutiny to ancient behaviours. He was in no position to help me, even if he'd wanted to. And trust me he ended up with it worse than I did. He Settled a few years after I was driven out, in his sixties. And he had exactly the same fate. But he was forced out of Mornay by his own children. He had company at least, his favourite granddaughter, who refused to leave him, but he spent his time on the road and eventually he buried her on the road. That's something we all do if we choose to open up our hearts. We bury those we love on the road and the road, well, that's never-ending.'

Felicity had finished the plate of bread and she wished there was more. She decided to make do with a mug of tea and started to pour.

'The silly old fool,' said Cora, 'spent the rest of his time trying to find me. Just kept searching and searching and searching. He shouldn't have found me in reality but one day he walked quite randomly into a bookshop in a narrow alleyway in Copenhagen and there I was, sat by the fire, reading Don Quixote. It took him four hundred and fifty seven years to find me. I barely recognised him.'

There were sounds from outside, down below, the sound of a vehicle turning on gravel before parking to a stop. Then there came the sounds of voices, of men getting ready to leave, shouting instructions to one another.

'You see, that's all we have,' said Cora, 'all we have to cling onto, stories, memories, most of them painful.'

Cora's coolness had slipped a tad and Felicity caught sight of something that had not been there before. She knew that look. She had seen it enough times staring back at her in the mirror. It was a look of personal loss and tragedy, a wounded, silent pain that was rarely spoken of and that few people could understand.

'You've lost something else, haven't you?' Felicity said softly.

'Excuse me?' said Cora, blinking.

'Something you're not telling me,' Felicity said. 'I can see it, in your eyes. There's something else that bothers you, more than being exiled, more than losing your first husband.'

'You're right,' Cora said slowly, 'James and I had a daughter.' She stared at Felicity for a short moment and then shook her head. 'You really are quite a clever one.'

'How did she die?' Felicity said, taking a sip of tea. 'Would she have been immortal too?'

'No,' said Cora sadly, 'they never are, the children.' She stood, straightening her clothes. 'Anyway, I should go out and help the others and –'

'Why did you tell me all of this?' Felicity said, pressing. The story was fine but she didn't see the relevance.

Cora nodded, remembering that the story had a point. 'Because wisdom would have you believe that we're surrounded by life,' she said. 'We're not. We're surrounded by nothing but death, pain, and anguish. It gets to the stage where you wish … just wish … that the person you lost was never in your life in the first place. You wish that you had never met them, never loved them, that you had never given birth to them. If they never existed, you can never feel that pain.'

'I don't want to sound harsh,' said Felicity. She paused, wanting to choose her words carefully but realising there was no way of asking it politely. 'But why don't you just kill yourself, if living is this hard? I don't understand.'

'We can *never* do that!' said Cora, affronted by such a suggestion. 'Whether we see it as a burden or not immortality is unmistakeably a gift from the very fingertips of God. You don't destroy that, complain yes, become bitter maybe, but never destroy. I can tell you this, eternity on this earth for people like me can be a curse but I have no doubt that it's nothing compared to an eternity in Hell. You'll never find one of us who would ever contemplate suicide.'

The van outside was beeping. It was time.

'Felicity,' said Cora, a slight tremor of nerves in her voice. 'My point ... and I'm sorry if this seems callous or cruel ... is that there is no place for you in Finn's story. What we'll ask him to do could take a hundred years if not longer. You'll be long gone. I've seen the way he looks at you. He cares for you deeply, that much is obvious, and that makes you dangerous. He'll risk his life for you, he'll make mistakes for you, and he'll risk everything for you. And the only thing you'll leave him with is a cursed memory. You'll haunt him and then one day you will become his biggest regret.'

Ouch. That truly hurt and Felicity felt tears build in her eyes and a little venom in her throat. She didn't know many people like Cora, people who could shatter and maim with the power of their words instead of the power of their fists.

'I don't tell you that to hurt you,' said Cora, reading the reaction. 'But when we get a chance, you must leave. There's nothing here for you. You mustn't come on this journey with us, despite how much Finn may beg you to.'

With that Cora stood, took the tray and planted an awkward and strange kiss on Felicity's head before leaving the room.

The horn of the van outside sounded once again. It didn't make Felicity move. She did nothing but sit there, a numbness setting in. Whatever her intentions had been Cora had failed and in actuality it *had* come across as cruel and callous. She wanted to react, at least in some way, to cry or to lash out, but she didn't do anything. Once again the word *amazing* floated into her mind and once again she couldn't see what was so amazing about the predicament she now found herself in.

Chapter Twenty-Nine

'You sure the bridge will take our weight?' Cora asked nervously, picking up on one of the more obvious flaws in the plan. She was driving the orange camper van along a tight, narrow lane, and tall hedgerows whizzed by on both sides. Her brother was sat next to her in the passenger seat with everyone else tucked up comfortably in the rear of the vehicle. It was only an hour after midday and already the light was weak and dwindling.

'Honestly?' Devery said from behind her with his nose nestled in the pages of his map. 'Don't really have a clue. Best case scenario, we hit it at enough speed and get across to the other side before it gives way beneath us.'

'You install such a confidence in me,' Cora said. She shook her head. 'And on that note can I just put it on record that I'm not as sure as the rest of you that this is a good idea.'

Finn knew of the bridge they were heading towards. Nettleton Bridge enjoyed a modicum of local fame, having been designed by its namesake, the Victorian architect Cornelius Nettleton. Once upon a time it had served an old wool mill but that had closed many years ago. He had seen the bridge before, when his parents had taken a wrong turning during a country excursion, and he remembered it to be a thin, unremarkable stone structure linking two extremely steep banks. The water below was relatively deep and fast flowing. What's more he remembered that due to a pressing need for substantial repair, the bridge had been shut for quite some time.

'In theory this isn't a possible route,' Devery reminded his wife, 'not with the bridge closed. It's nothing but a dead end. It's the least likely route to be watched.'

Cora wasn't reassured. 'If *you* can decide that the bridge is a worthwhile risk,' she said curtly, 'then I'm sure other people may just reach the same conclusion.'

Finn was inclined to trust the Irishman's judgment and besides it was good to be moving again, but also to be warm and have some company. Felicity was sat next to him but she was quiet, Edgar seated in front but he said even less and to talk to Hamish or Devery meant talking over Edgar, so he had spent long stretches watching the road, catching glimpses of what he could when the hedgerows provided an odd break. They had seen no other vehicles, no one else, no trace of the enemy.

'A word of advice,' said Willoughby, twisting in his seat up front so he could face Finn, 'and especially as you're likely to come across quite a lot of us on your travels, it would be wise to take most things you are told with a hefty pinch of salt.' He saw the doubt in Finn's eyes. 'No, no, I don't mean what I told you last night. That was all completely and utterly true.'

'Put simply,' Edgar said, joining in the conversation, 'most immortals are outright liars. Gets very, very tiring, listening to it all.'

'Heard it all over the years,' said Willoughby, 'all the bold, unbelievable claims. I call it the I-Was-There syndrome.' He impersonated some voices of people he had once known. '*I-was-there in the cathedral the day Thomas Becket was murdered. I-was-there and sprinkled the first grain of salt on the battleground of Carthage. I-was-there and sold Lincoln his theatre program a few minutes before he was shot in the head.*' He allowed his voice to return to normal. 'One guy, I forget his name, once claimed he had been out drinking with Alexander the Great the night before he caught the fever that killed him.'

Devery started laughing. 'And don't you go thinking that all of the people in this van are any different.'

'Ah, for God's sake,' said Hamish, knowing full well the barb was aimed at him. 'I *was* at Stirling Bridge! I was born in bloody Stirling–'

'Fought with William Wallace,' said Devery, 'if you can believe that –'

'Fought at Stirling,' said Hamish, defending himself, 'ran away at Falkirk, sat out Bannockburn, not that I saw much of Stirling anyway, bloody arrow hit me smack bang on the helm and knocked me out in the first sixty seconds –'

'God,' Edgar complained with a hefty growl, 'will you give it a rest, man? No one believes you, Hamish!'

'You know it's not impossible,' said Willoughby. 'He was born around about the right time –'

'So he says,' said Edgar, 'don't humour him, please, for the sake of my sanity –'

'You remember old Jonathon Nesbith?' said Cora, laughing loudly from up front. 'He had the best load of old nonsense I ever heard. There was a time –'

Finn peered forward, wondering if she would finish the anecdote but something had caught her eye and it now commanded her full attention. She was focusing on the rear view mirror next to her head and she adjusted it a touch to get a better look at what troubled her.

'Problem?' Devery said. He turned himself around and afforded a glance out of the back window.

'Maybe,' Cora confirmed. 'Two vehicles behind us!' With that stark revelation everyone then turned, trying to see exactly what it was that was behind them.

Finn pressed his face against the glass which was cold against his nose. He squinted. They were there alright – two large black shapes on the road in the distance. There was enough room on the road for them to drive alongside one another, although the sides of the vehicles must have been brushing mere inches past the reaches of the hedgerows.

'How long they been there?' Devery asked, taking the threat seriously.

'Not sure,' Cora said, 'but not long –'

'Could be a problem,' Edgar noted.

Devery was trying to keep calm. 'It's not a problem until it's a problem!'

'What?' Hamish said. 'What's that even supposed to mean, Dev?'

'How far are we from the bridge?' Willoughby said.

Devery glanced down at the map and shrugged, then gave his best estimate. 'I don't know, a mile and a half, something like that, not too far. If we go –'

Hamish suddenly shot up from his seat, staggering violently into the aisle as if he was drunk and forcing his hands into the top of the seats on either side of his body to steady himself. He urgently covered his eyes and his body started to convulse. He fell to the ground and started retching as if he was about to vomit.

Finn went to say something but Willoughby cut him off.

'No,' Willoughby said. 'Wait! He's seeing something!'

Hamish started to control his breathing and then he got back to his feet and rushed forward, snatching the map from Devery's hands as he went. 'There's a crossroads up ahead,' he screamed. 'Speed up! Now! We're heading straight into a trap!'

Cora didn't have to be asked twice, trusting Hamish's gift of foresight, and she pressed her foot down hard on the accelerator. The camper van roared and complained but started to pick up some real speed.

'What are we looking at?' Devery said, joining Hamish at the front seats. 'How much did you see?'

'Four vehicles,' Hamish answered quickly. 'Maybe five, the two behind us are going to try and pin us in, the others are on each lane of the crossroads! Quicker! You need to go quicker!'

'She's going as quickly as she can!' Cora shouted, looking down at the rising speedometer.

Finn shot a look forward and through the windscreen. He couldn't see any sort of crossroads up ahead. If it was there, it was hidden well, the road seeming to just be long and straight. But then it *was* there. There was a sudden flash of bright light as the hedgerows disappeared briefly on both sides and the campervan thundered over the heart of the crossroads. At the same time a harsh black shape appeared as if from nowhere to the left and came within inches of colliding with the back of the van. The black shape, a pickup truck, beeped its horn furiously as the driver slammed on the breaks, the vehicle skidding, almost losing control.

Cora ignored the beeps and kept going and when she looked again in her rear view mirror she could see that they were now pursued by four vehicles, four pickup trucks, speeding forward together like a pack of black panthers, a united, hungry pack at that, seeking out their prey. The convoy moved perfectly, two by two, Noah's assassins.

Finn watched with a sense of looming horror. 'Can we outrun them?' he gasped. He *hoped* they could but the chasing vehicles looked sleeker and faster than the van.

'They belong to your dear mother,' said Hamish, 'which means life is going to get a hell-of-a-lot more complicated.' He pointed forward. 'And there my wee chums comes enemy number five.'

Out there in front the fifth black truck was heading straight towards them and bearing down fast.

Cora took immediate action, sweeping the steering wheel hard to the left. The campervan thumped directly into the hedgerow. There was a smash and crunch of thickets and branches and the windscreen cracked in two or three places. But they made it safely through and found themselves moving recklessly through a field choked full of winter wheat that dropped visibility to zero. The terrain became abruptly uneven and uncomfortable.

Quickly the wheat gave way to a vast, open field. The ground was deep with snow and noticeably rougher than before, the campervan bobbling violently this way and that and tossing the passengers around like ragdolls inside.

Finn again turned his gaze backwards and was relieved to see that they were alone. But such relief was mightily short lived when the five chasing trucks screamed out from the tall crop. They were still feverishly in pursuit and were a damn sight closer already than they had been out on the road. What's more the trucks started to fan out, three sweeping to the right and two sweeping to the left.

'Oh my God,' Finn said, 'what the hell is that?' He had to close his eyes and then open them again to make sure that what he had seen was real. Sadly, it was *very* real. On the back of two of the trucks, one on the left and one on the right, a man cladded in combat fatigues had climbed out into the pick-up section. In their hands the men carried a weapon that was so heavy they had to rest them rigidly on their shoulders.

'You won't get a make or model,' Hamish said, laughing morbidly to himself. 'But to the layman I think they are known as rocket launchers.'

Edgar was on his feet. 'Russian,' he noted. 'Ain't gonna be all that accurate at this speed.'

Finn looked around the van. Only Felicity was still seated. She wasn't even looking out the window and was just sitting there as if nothing of interest was happening. Whatever it was that she was sulking about, he was surprised that it stretched to her not being at least interested or terrified by this.

'They're going to try and blow us off the road,' Cora shouted. She turned to her brother and was already squeezing herself out from the driver's seat. 'Quickly Will! Take over for me!'

Willoughby did as he was told, sliding across into the driver's seat whilst Cora fell back clumsily into the aisle, the vehicle losing only a little speed in the process. Cora fixed her gaze firmly on the two trucks with the launchers, left, right, left, right, changing her attention intermittently between the two. She was deep in thought.

'Missiles gonna be coming at you quick!' Devery said, reading his wife's plan from the focus of her expression. She was planning, or at least hoping at the very least, that she could use her telekinesis to divert the impending fire.

'Won't be looking for a direct hit,' Cora said, 'only to knock us over. They'll want to take us alive and disorientated and –'

Whooooosh! The first rocket screamed in from the left, its high pitched whistle the only warning.

Chapter Thirty

Cora smashed her husband out of the way and with her fingers extended she swept both her hands towards the trajectory of the rocket and then pushed them away from her chest with a brute urgency.

Finn could only watch in a dumbfounded horror as outside the rocket moved a touch in the air and blasted quickly into the frozen ground nearby. The explosion shook the van, blowing out the glass of the back window into a billion pieces.

'Jesus Christ!' Felicity screamed as the glass rained onto her neck and back. She couldn't maintain her calmness any longer and realising her position near the back was particularly precarious bolted forward, sliding into the seat in front. She was shaking.

The second rocket came a moment later, this time from the right. Cora again attempted to use her gift as a countermeasure and again the missile changed its trajectory. This time however the impact was a little close for comfort and the explosion lifted the camper van into the air and for a few seconds it coasted along on two wheels before slamming back down to earth.

Felicity screamed again. 'They're going to blow us up!' she yelled. 'Why don't we fire back?'

'With what?' Devery said.

'Haven't we got any weapons?' Felicity shrieked.

'Weapons encourage violence,' Willoughby shouted from the driver's seat. 'We're not violent people!'

'Great,' Felicity said, pointing out into the field. 'But they are!'

'I need you to watch for me,' Cora said frantically to all inside the van. She pointed at each truck in turn. 'Right now, there they are, Trucks One, Two, Three, Four and Five! Watch them! Let me know what's coming!'

Finn counted them off. Truck One and Truck Two were the ones to look out for. They were the ones with the launchers, launchers that were being quickly reloaded. But it was Truck Three that accelerated forward and pulled up alongside the campervan. A tall man climbed out from the back window, carrying a large machine gun.

Devery leapt into action and without announcing his intentions he opened the sliding door of the van and threw himself out into the cold air, clamping his grip onto the roof bar of the truck and vaulting up into a gymnastic flip so that he landed inside the pickup section. Within a split second he was wrestling with the armed man, who looked genuinely shocked that he was being assaulted so quickly into his offensive endeavours. Bullets were fired aimlessly into the air. The driver inside instinctively swerved away and took the Irishman with him.

Truck Four entered the fray, moving up on the right flank and making contact, forcing itself into the side of the camper van with a sickening screech of metal on metal and a shower of bright sparks. But Willoughby kept the van moving.

Finn moved to the door and tried to pull it shut but due to the speed it wouldn't budge easily. Hamish came to his aid and together they slammed the door back into position. He stared out, trying to see what was happening with Devery, catching sight of the Irishman fighting gallantly, the truck hitting bumps and making things difficult. One misstep later and Devery was able to snatch the weapon from his opponent, before gripping him by the shirt and throwing him off and out into the field. The man hit the cold ground hard, rolled a few times and then was still.

Devery, machine gun now in hand, opened fire on Truck One, which was closest to him. The bullets thundered down and into the tyres, blowing them out in a violent hiss of hot air and shredded rubber. Then the truck hit a convenient bump and was launched high into the sky before twisting and turning over and landing upside down with a crash.

The Irishman was far from finished. Ammunition expended and not having a fresh cartridge to hand, he punched through the back window, gripping the driver by the back of the neck and attempting to pull him outside. The car, unmanned, went into a sharp spinning spiral and disappeared momentarily from view.

Finn looked forward. Up ahead he sighted a small cottage and a short distance away from the house was a large wooden barn. Willoughby was guiding the van in-between the two structures.

There was the hiss of another projectile, an effort Cora again deflected. This time she really got hold of it and the rocket whizzed past the camper van and flew directly into the heart of the wooden barn structure. The resultant explosion was brutally impressive, with debris of wood roaring out in all directions, some of it landing on the windscreen, cracking it some more.

'I won't keep getting away with this!' Cora announced to the others. She was sweating profusely.

Finn's whole body seemed to be shaking. By far it was the scariest experience yet. But at least this time he had people with him and clearly these people were no slouches. Yet it was he who saw the next rocket before anyone else. He should have cried out but he decided that this was the moment where he would see if the powers the others said he was born with were really true. He copied Cora's example and aimed his outstretched arms at the rocket and then he tried to sweep it away with the power of his mind.

It didn't work and nothing happened, other than the rocket hitting the ground a few feet behind the back of the speeding camper van. The explosion was the closest so far and it shook the vehicle, the blast ripping off the back door in its entirety. A variety of bags were instantly aflame and falling out from the back.

Truck Four came again, gaining distance. A woman climbed out into the back and she opened fire immediately with her own sub-machine gun. Her aim was careful and considered and she targeted the windows on that side, knocking out the glass.

Finn pushed Felicity to the ground and dived on top of her. Hamish and Cora were forced to do the same and even Willoughby had to duck out of the way as he struggled to keep the vehicle on a steady course. Edgar was the only one who moved without a sense of panic. He was on his knees, peering out of the fresh holes in the van.

There was a noticeable bump and when Finn looked up the woman with the machine gun had leapt across and dived in through one of the missing windows. She had wasted no time and was already stood upright with the gun directed at Hamish's chest, her finger flexing the trigger. Hamish could only close his eyes and await his fate.

Felicity came to the rescue and dropped her shoulder instinctively into the intruder's stomach. It shocked her enough to force her shots awry and to drop the rifle. This gave Hamish an opportunity to bolt forward and engage the intruder himself.

'You should never hit a woman!' Hamish shouted before disproving his own rule and punching her square in the face. The woman's head rocked back but she was strong and she kicked out, smacking Hamish in the groin. The Scotsman fell to the ground and she then aimed a second kick into his stomach. She started searching for her gun and then froze.

Edgar had retrieved the weapon from the ground and he casually fired off three shots into the flesh of the woman's thigh. She screamed out in pain.

'Hold onto something!' Willoughby urged from the front. Up ahead they were coming to the end of the field and the boundary was marked by another tall and hefty hedgerow that sat at the summit of a small but steep slope.

Finn had enough time to see it and he threw himself down, wedging himself in-between the seats on the second row. Willoughby picked up as much speed as possible and smashed straight through, the impact harsh and the slope forcing a sharp flight. Such was the violence of the impact that what was left of the windscreen crumbled and all in the back of the van fell backwards. The female intruder, in too much pain to resist, tumbled out of the missing back door but as she went she grabbed Felicity's shoulder and took her with her.

Felicity scrambled for her life, managing to grip the handle of a bag as she fell. The woman had already let go and was rolling painfully along the floor of the field.

Finn dived forward, managing to desperately clutch the handle on the other side of the bag and stop Felicity from falling. Felicity dangled there, her legs and knees scraping across the speeding ground.

'I can't hold you!' Finn yelled.

Edgar prevented anything bad from happening, rushing across and bending down and clasping onto the grip that Finn was losing. Using all of his strength he dragged Felicity back inside the relative safety of the van.

The three remaining trucks moved into an attack position. Truck One loitered behind, launcher primed, Truck Two went left, Truck Five went right.

Cora staggered forward and thumped the seat behind her brother. 'Brake!' she hollered. It was a sudden command that seemed to make no sense.

Willoughby didn't question it and he slammed his right foot on the break, as hard as he could. The camper van screeched and started to halt, making contact with the truck directly behind them, bringing both vehicles to a stop. The other two trucks shot off out in front and Devery, behind the wheel of the vehicle he had acquired, appeared as if from nowhere, the truck moving across the ground at a hideously unsafe speed a few inches in front of the camper van.

Finn almost felt compelled to rub his eyes in disbelief. The Irishman had his driver's door open and had wedged something down onto the accelerator. With one hand he steered and with the other he was holding onto the open door, standing up in the foot well. He slammed straight into Truck Two and as it connected he threw himself clear, rolling like an acrobat and in one movement pushing himself back to his feet and into a desperate run. The Irishman's claim was clearly accurate, he truly was exceptionally quick. Truck Five managed to avoid the collision and was still in action. There was a deafening explosion as the two colliding vehicles burst into flame.

'Drive!' Hamish screamed!

Willoughby thumped the accelerator, the interlocking mangles of metal from the collision with the truck behind breaking free from one another.

Finn hoped to see the first truck staying where it was but no, they were not that lucky. Truck One, its tyres screeching from the driver's impatience, started to move once more.

Devery was sprinting alongside the van now and when Truck One closed in he arched back and jumped, clamping his hands onto the side of his next target. The driver shot out the glass, trying to hit him, but Devery completed his manoeuvre, gaining access to the pickup section and face to face with the man armed with a familiar rocket launcher. The fight that followed was different to the last, his foe this time a much sterner test and a great deal stronger than what had gone before.

Hamish was ready to offer some sage advice. He pointed out into the distance, past the hedgerow on the road side. 'There,' he said. 'I can see the road and I can see the bridge!'

Willoughby saw it too and he bought the camper van up to speed and turning quickly right he thumped through his final hedgerow, getting the van back onto the smoothness of the main road. The bridge was indeed close up ahead and the brightness of the council's orange barriers were clearly visible, barring the way.

Truck One and Truck Five joined them on the road, breaking through the gap the van had made for them. They travelled single file this time, the road that much narrower, and Devery was still grappling with the man with the launcher, wrestling over the launcher itself, which was now facing upwards.

'I know what he's going to do!' Cora said urgently. She slapped the back of the driver's seat again, harder and more eager this time. 'Push, Will! Push! Push!'

Through the plastic of the barriers they went and out onto the bridge, which although made of stone creaked and groaned beneath the vehicles sudden weight. Importantly, the bridge did not collapse.

Devery saw them go and he squeezed off a shot from the rocket launcher and aimed it out high in front of him and up into the heavens, leaving a trail of smoke behind it. Cora watched the rocket go and using her power she attempted to control the trajectory.

Truck One roared onto the bridge and in that very moment Cora bought her hands down hard to her knees. The rocket flew into the heart of the truck. Devery threw himself into the air and down into the water, the bright explosion casting his desperate, falling silhouette to anyone who happened to be watching. The bridge collapsed violently and downwards with a sprawling ball of flame.

Truck Five had no chance. It was too close and moving too quickly to avoid the carnage and it could do nothing but smash into the fire and then down into the water below to its inevitable fate. It too exploded, creating an even bigger, second fireball.

Willoughby bought the camper van to a stop and they all shot out, although Cora was the most concerned and moved the quickest. As they neared the bank of the river everyone was relieved to see Devery climbing up the steep bank on their side. He was alive, bleeding from the side of his forehead, but alive all the same.

Edgar was the one to offer him a hand and pull him safely up onto terra firma. 'You're a lunatic,' he said by means of a compliment. 'You do know that, don't you?'

Devery smiled and then threw himself down onto the floor. He was exhausted. But there was no rest for the wicked. In the distance and on the road on the other side of the bridge a sixth vehicle, one that they had not seen before, was slowly getting nearer.

Chapter Thirty-One

Agatha Carruthers climbed out from the truck, idly sidestepping the chaotic debris around her as if she was out for nothing more than a pleasant drive in the country. She was unarmed and dressed in a navy-blue trouser suit and matching heels. She wore her red hair in its trademark ponytail and had on a pair of thick-rimmed glasses.

Finn watched his mother take a few paces forward and stop at the edge of the steep bank. She peered down. With the bridge in ruins there was no easy way across, short from wading through the water. The snow had been disturbed and replaced with a host of black burn marks and chars, exposing the green of the grass underneath which hadn't seen a glimpse of the sun since the cold weather had set in.

Edgar, the machine gun he had acquired warily in hand, aimed the weapon squarely at Agatha's chest. 'Are you alone?' he bellowed like a strict drill sergeant. 'Anyone else in the car?'

Agatha raised her hands above her head, submitting. 'You're in control, Edgar Bloom. I'm alone and unarmed. Do I need to keep these up?'

Edgar blinked, not comfortable with the fact that she knew his name. He looked at Willoughby for further instruction. Willoughby nodded and Edgar cautiously lowered his gun.

Agatha rested her hands at her side. 'Thank you.'

Standing there on the bank and with his mother in sight, Finn was affronted by an array of conflicting emotions. Anger did battle with sadness, revulsion competed against devastation. There was fear, hate, and rage. But there was also something else that he would never have anticipated. There was love. It still existed. He could feel its power, resting in his heart like a powerful infection amongst a host of healthy blood cells. Love had no right to be there and love wasn't helpful. Love had the capability to blinker, to prevent from seeing straight and to make mistakes.

Willoughby shuffled himself closer to Finn so that he could whisper. 'Be very, very careful, young man. Make no mistake, there stands a jackal. She'll manipulate and lie with every breath she can muster.'

'We should be walking away from this, Will,' said Cora.

Finn turned to look at the others. Cora was pale, mightily uncomfortable. Devery was sat on the ground, stemming the blood from the wound on his head. Felicity, Hamish, and Edgar were stood together. The atmosphere was weighty with fear.

Agatha gestured to the smoke that was climbing into the sky from the obliterated barn in the distance behind her. 'This place is remote,' she noted, 'but not remote enough for *that* to go unnoticed. I'd say we've ten minutes at best.' She bent down and picked up a small section of wrecked metal, examined it briefly and tossed it down into the water. Then she looked back up at her son. 'Finn, are you ok? Are you hurt?'

Finn's mouth opened, the angry reaction ready to be unloaded, but no words formed. His mouth had dried up. He hadn't had time for a rehearsal, no practice for speeches and stark condemnations. But he wanted to swear his heart out, call her terrible things, find some way to make it across the river and thump his hands into her chest and ask her why she had done such terrible, unforgiveable deeds.

'I'm really sorry for all of this,' Agatha said, her tone tender. 'None of this has played out how I'd hoped. I wanted to get to you first, so I could sit you down and explain, make you understand before the others had a chance to poison you against me. You need to be very cautious about who you're listening to.'

Willoughby gave out a sarcastic, booming laugh. 'You almost sound sincere,' he said, 'but then the biggest monsters are often those who speak with the softest voices.'

Agatha wasn't impressed at the interruption and she fixed Willoughby with a distasteful stare. 'I had a feeling you'd take this route, Mr Carmichael,' She kicked some loose clumps of earth off the side of the bank. 'Man who spotted you is down there somewhere, last resting place and all that. Hardly seems a fitting reward for someone just doing his duty.'

Cora was becoming more agitated by the second. 'Will, please,' she pleaded, 'we need to leave!'

Agatha turned her attention back to her son. 'Finn,' she said, her eyes turning sad and haunted, 'please, if you can just tell me if you're hurt? I've been worried sick. I've barely been able to sleep –'

'Why do you care?' Finn said.

'Why?' said Agatha. She pressed her hand to her chest, showing that the question hurt her. 'I care because I'm your mother.'

Finn shook his head. He didn't know this woman. It was strange. It was almost like she wasn't his mother at all. Agatha Carruthers had always been a cold person. But this was a different version of her. Willoughby might not believe she was sincere but she certainly appeared to be. Her concern appeared real.

'What have they told you?' Agatha said.

'It doesn't matter what they've told me,' said Finn. His chest was starting to beat hard, rage ready for its turn behind the wheel. 'You killed my father –'

'Technically,' Agatha said, 'he killed himself.'

There was moisture building in Finn's eyes. 'I saw you –'

'He didn't die from my hand,' said Agatha.

A tear rolled down Finn's cheek which he quickly flicked away. 'Doesn't matter, you killed him –'

'Maybe there's truth in that,' said Agatha, 'and maybe it's time we all stopped trying to outrun the truth. What good's it doing any of us? You've seen me, why don't you see him? What utility is there in protecting and preserving the memory of a man who spent the entirety of *your* life lying to you and the remainder of *his* life lying to himself? Peter Carruthers wasn't real. He didn't exist.'

More tears now, running freely down both of Finn's cheeks. 'I know he lied to me, but he loved me –'

'Yes, he did,' Agatha agreed, 'and I love you too –'

Finn swallowed a large lump in his throat. 'But you're trying to kill me –'

'Who says I'm trying to kill you?' said Agatha. She laughed as if it were the most absurd suggestion in the history of man. Then she pointed at the companions, Willoughby by his side, the others behind him. 'Them? People you've known for all of five minutes? The fact is we only have to come in so heavy and hard *because* of them. I told you, they're very, very dangerous people and if we didn't come in all guns blazing we would die. If they weren't here, no one would have died.'

Finn leapt to their defence. 'These people saved me –'

'These people secured a commodity,' said Agatha, 'what that commodity is, I'm not sure yet. I'm sure they haven't told you either, not everything –'

'You don't know what you're talking about,' said Willoughby.

'I don't know why so many have come for you,' said Agatha, 'it must be because you're unique, as these types of people don't appear without a very good reason. It's because of them that you've become our number one target. They've made it clear that if you're so important to them you're probably going to be important to us.'

Finn glanced across to Willoughby. Willoughby didn't look comfortable or confident and it was the first time he had seen him appear that way. Finn had no idea if what his mother was saying was true but from Willoughby's obvious discomfort it was clear that some of it wasn't far off the mark.

'So what comes next, Mum?' he said. 'You going to ask me to come with you? Am I supposed to forget everything that's happened?'

Agatha shrugged. 'You trusted your father. Why not trust me?'

Finn had a long sniff through his nostrils.

'We were cut from the same cloth,' said Agatha, 'your father and I. Wilhelm was a cold, calculated killer, impressive in the field, utterly peerless. Wish you could have seen him for what he really was, not what he became. In a strange way I think you would have been proud of him.'

'His name was Peter!' Finn pointed out angrily.

'His *name* was Wilhelm,' Agatha corrected him sternly, a stiff rebuke. 'He was already a legend when I met him. He was the most determined man I had ever come across. He was the same as me, trained from the moment he could walk, turned into a ruthless specimen.' She was quiet for the briefest of moments, a sadness creeping into her expression. 'We fell in love in a place where love should never have been found. We ran away, disappeared, tried to reinvent ourselves and live a normal life, away from the Guild. We tried to convince the world we had changed. But no one changes, not really. I kept my first name, he went so far as to change his, but no matter what, underneath we were always different people. We were always pretending. What we were born to do stayed with us.'

There was a small explosion from down below as some previously untouched petrol from the vehicles was ignited and a spiralling flame shot upwards, intertwined with a spray of dirty river water. Everyone jumped, watching the flame reach its highest pinnacle before retreating back down into the wreckage and spreading out along the riverbed.

'I'm here to rescue you,' Agatha said, 'but more importantly I'm here to make you look at these people closely. They're an enticing proposition, aren't they? That's because they've spent centuries honing their little stories. They're master-manipulators. And you don't know anything about them, only what they've told you. You think so negatively about me because of the things that have come out of their filthy, lying mouths. You need to consider how you feel–'

'I feel like I hate you,' Finn said, suddenly keen to oblige her, 'more than I've ever hated anyone. I feel like I wish you were down there, dead. And I hate feeling like that and I don't know why I hate feeling like that.'

Agatha listened intently. 'And do you feel that way without question, without any trace of doubt? Do you truly think I am the monster they make me out to be?'

Finn didn't reply but he didn't need to. His poker face was poor and his expression made it clear. He was in doubt. He was confused. He didn't know what to think.

'Let me talk to you,' said Agatha. 'These days, people judge based upon actions, giving no consideration to motivations. It's so much easier to condemn what you see rather than take the time out to understand the reasons behind it. In the past people understood *our* actions. We were respected, we were honoured, celebrated. Let me explain to you why we do what we do.'

Willoughby laughed again. 'You broker an articulate argument –'

Agatha raised her voice for the first time. 'I'm talking to my son, not to –'

'Mankind has never celebrated murderers,' said Willoughby strongly. 'Murderers are the only ones who celebrate murderers –'

Devery tried to stop things escalating further. 'Will, don't get involved –'

'The rest just condemn you for what you are,' said Willoughby. 'Might they understand your motivations? Perhaps there's some that might. But once you chase your goals with no respect for life your motivations become utterly reprehensible.'

Agatha took the insult in her stride and then flashed a wicked smile. 'Says a man that has never taken a life?'

'We're talking about very different times,' said Willoughby.

Agatha gave off an idle shrug. 'Why don't we look at the carnage below? Still no blood on your hands?'

'That's different,' said Willoughby. 'That was –'

'Self-defence?' said Agatha. She was getting more self-assured by the second. 'See, there it is, there's *your* motive, there's *your* justification. Do you not understand what I'm trying to show you? You have your reasons to do the things you do and so do we.'

Willoughby shook his head and sighed. 'Your point would be good if not for one fundamental flaw.'

'Enlighten me?' Agatha said.

'What *we* just did *was* self-defence,' said Willoughby. 'It wasn't cold blooded but it *was* murder. And we're not trying to justify it. There's a big difference between one who kills out of necessity to one who kills for pleasure. There's *never* a legitimate reason to take another life. And people like you and I, we'll all have to face God one day and explain away the things we've done. For our part, we try and do everything in our power not to kill and perhaps that will be enough to save us from Hell. Will you have that luxury?'

Agatha cackled like a witch, throwing her head back. 'Oh, what a stark divide we face! The eternal battle of Good against Evil –

'Don't mock us!' Finn urged her. 'You don't know –'

'Oh, there is no *us*, Finn,' said Agatha, 'there's only their desires. And I'll tell you this now in case I don't get the chance to later but I can assure you that when the time comes they will commit just as many atrocities if it looks like they're not getting their way.'

Finn lapsed into silence. He couldn't help but pay attention to the things his mother was saying. She wasn't presenting herself like he would have expected. When he had observed her in the factory, standing over his wounded father, she had been a ruthless and cold proposition. But now – what was she? She launched her arguments effectively and she had an answer for everything and was very convincing. She was luring him in. There was power to her words.

Willoughby, visibly concerned, stepped forward so that he was next to Finn. 'Don't listen to her, Finn,' he said. 'Her whole twisted logic stems from her ancestors. That story needs more time but I'll give you the grimy highlights. There once lived twins, hugely wealthy, royalty of a country swallowed up and forgotten by history–'

'That isn't your tale,' said Agatha.

'One was immortal,' Willoughby continued, 'and the other wasn't and he became consumed by his jealousy and one night he dragged his brother from his bed and sliced him up to try and understand the magic that was inside of him. He took his heart —'

Agatha was shaking her head. 'You know nothing —'

'He took his brain,' said Willoughby, 'took his liver and his kidneys and his pancreas and his intestines. He drained his blood, hacked away his arteries, sucked out every last bit of fat from the marrow. When his Guardian came he did the same to him and he learnt nothing, other than that there were others out there who were the same as his dead brother.'

There were sounds drawing closer, growing in volume in the distance, nearing the scene. Finn saw the shapes appear, a fleet of trucks weaving through the hedgerows, the reinforcements, heading towards Agatha, their figurehead.

Willoughby saw them too and he quickened up his tale. 'And so they've scrambled on ever since, investing their fortunes, operating under the radar so they can have these little illegitimate quests to hunt us down and pick at us with scalpels.'

Edgar was nodding. 'Master investors too,' he said although his tone didn't suggest a compliment. 'No one's heard of them but they have their little rat fingers in everything. Chance is you buy your latte from Starbucks, a percentage of what you spend goes straight to the Guild.'

Hamish found his voice for the first time. 'And here's the fruit of that labour,' he said, pointing at Agatha, 'a child brainwashed from the womb and rotten to the core.'

Agatha showed no signs of responding. She had eyes only for her son. 'You have this ability, Finn,' she said. 'You will live forever. You will never get sick. You will never die. But everyone else around you will. And I mean everyone. The point you're missing is that you have the ability to stop that from happening. You have the ability, if your power can be understood and can be harnessed, to *prevent* death. Do you appreciate the enormity of that? You can *stop* death, Finn. And not only death but disease, pain, and suffering —'

'And if you go with them,' said Edgar, 'they'll strap you to a bed and cut you open –'

'This is the twenty-first-century,' Agatha said, 'things are far more advanced than that.'

People were starting to move. Edgar returned the butt of his gun to his shoulder and again aimed it at Agatha. Devery and Cora were already making their way towards the camper van.

'I guess that's us running out of time,' said Agatha, 'but think of this. A research scientist sits at his desk, staring through his microscope and he sees, sitting there in front of him the cure for cancer –'

'Time to get going,' Hamish said, keeping his focus on the advancing vehicles. 'These chaps are definitely going to be armed –'

'Not just one cancer either,' said Agatha, continuing with her speech, 'but every last flavour of it. And then he does nothing. He takes the slides, takes the data, and locks it away forever so that no one can ever find it. What does the man who has the power to save lives but makes the choice not to become? He becomes a murderer, Finn, the biggest murderer in history. And that's all these people are, murderous, selfish, deplorable cretins who have a very real chance to do real good but turn their back on it so they can look after themselves.'

Willoughby gently nudged Finn's elbow. 'Come, lad,' he said tenderly. 'It's time to go.'

Finn nodded and started to turn.

'Finn, I am begging you!' Agatha was full of passion now, desperation even. 'Come with me, please. I'm your mother. Does that count for nothing? I look at you and all I want to do is come to you and hug you and tell you that everything will be ok. I'll never lie to you again. You have my word, my word as a mother that I'll never let you come to any real harm. We'll do this together, Finn, together. We can change the world.'

Finn started walking, turning his back on her. Hamish and Willoughby started jogging, Edgar covering their retreat.

Felicity was smiling widely. 'So are we going to shoot her now?' She held her hand out to Edgar excitedly. 'Do you want me to do it?'

Edgar smirked as he went past, appreciating the humour, but he didn't hand the gun over, just in case she was serious.

Finn reached out and grabbed Felicity's outstretched hand.

'You did well,' said Felicity, 'you know, considering everything.'

Finn pulled a sad face. 'Then why do I feel so dead inside?'

Agatha was still talking from the bank, having to raise her voice as they moved away. 'This makes me sad, honey,' she shouted, 'really sad. I hate the idea of not seeing my little boy again. Maybe I'll see your little friend instead?'

Finn froze. He had still been listening. It was simply four little words. *Your little friend instead.* He slowly rotated around.

Agatha now had a wicked smile on her face. 'If you can't find the mouse,' she said with a snarl, 'then you make sure you get his favourite cheese to lure him out.'

Felicity frowned. 'Is she calling me ... cheese?' She looked at Willoughby, who had also stopped walking. 'Should I be offended?'

Agatha took a step closer to the edge of the bank. Any sense of warmth she had displayed previously had quickly disappeared. The cold, calculated monster had returned. 'This will be much harder if you turn against me,' she said, 'and we will not stop chasing you. And the more we're frustrated the more we will hunt down those you love. We will make you come to us. And I can assure you that *she* will suffer, eventually.'

Finn's eyes widened, fuelled by horror. The provocation worked brilliantly and he went to burst forward, enraged, spitting and cursing, ready to make his way across the water by any means possible and rip the skin and flesh from his mother's body. Edgar got in the way and even with his bulk he had to break into a sweat to stop Finn from getting away from him.

'Easy!' Edgar urged.

'I'll kill you if you hurt her!' Finn screamed. 'I will kill you —'

Willoughby held his head in his hands. 'We were so close.'

'Think it's safe to say,' said Hamish, 'that she's found his weakness.'

'Will?' Cora shouted urgently. She was inside the van and reversing so that it was closer to those who had lingered behind. 'Come on, will you! They're getting closer!'

Edgar started to physically drag Finn away from the scene. For Finn's part the struggle was tiring his body but his anger was showing no signs of abating.

Agatha just stood there and smiled. 'Thank you, Finn,' she said, 'and I'll see you soon, poppet.'

Finn could feel it, the grip of Edgar's hands behind his back, the feeling of being lifted and gliding across the ground, a weightless force. He could hear it too, the voices, some whispering, others loud and proud. That's how they came now, his emotions, a tirade of voices, some zinging out of his brain and others pulsating up out of his stomach. The voices told him how to feel. They told him to hate her. They told him to seek vengeance. They told him to shout and to scream and to lash out. They told him that he could never, ever forgive her. The voices wanted him to ask questions too. How could she be like this? How could she have done all these vile things? How could she have acted without remorse, without pity, without reason or decency?

The voices though told him something else. It was a quieter voice, sitting beneath the rage, a whisper, a reminder. But the voice told him, despite all the other clamouring and dominant noise, that he still loved her. And that was why it all hurt so much.

Part Three

Chapter Thirty-Two

The snow was falling heavily in London, thick and luscious, a constant deluge of flakes that hammered down with a bitingly cold wind as a wintry accomplice. The road was clogged with the traffic of the city, moving uneasily through the gathering slush, sending up dirty sprays onto the pavements. The pavements themselves were choked with people, commuters and shoppers, moving in every direction. The air was filled with a thousand different noises, combining into one frenetic din, the soundtrack of a city in full flow.

Wyatt Eagan watched it all whizz by around him, leaning up against the stone pillar of a shopfront, unmoved as the snow slowly settled in his hair and melted. His focus was the tall building on the opposite side of the road, a structure of flash glass and black granite cladding. His chosen vantage point, partially obscured by a host of buses and taxis that had parked nearby, showed him what he needed to see. The entrance, at the top of a long flight of steps, was guarded by two policemen, armed with guns, ear pieces, and a desire for action that was unlikely to ever come. A long cordon on the pavement kept at bay a congregation of eager paparazzi.

He looked at his watch – a few minutes after three pm. He was still in there, no doubt embroiled in some form of high power meeting or pow-wow. But as far as Wyatt was concerned The Politician was already over an hour late for his more important appointment.

'You couldn't do me a massive favour?' a female voice suddenly said.

Wyatt glanced to his left to see a young lady had stopped next to him. She was shivering beneath her umbrella and fumbling with her handbag. She was dressed smartly, perhaps twenty-one years of age, and wore a little too much makeup but was attractive enough.

'You wouldn't be a love and hold my umbrella for one second?' she said. Her smile was flirtatious and well-rehearsed. She understood its power all too well. 'Just while I get myself a smoke? I've kinda ran out of hands.'

Wyatt didn't smile back and he stared at her blankly for a moment. He hated distractions but regardless he couldn't help but instinctively take the umbrella from her. He ensured she was covered from the weather while she searched through her handbag. She found her cigarettes and quickly lit herself one.

'Thank you,' she said, blowing a trail of smoke into the air. She wrapped her handbag back over her shoulder and snatched her umbrella back. In her right hand she had left the cigarette packet open and offered it across. 'Want one?'

Wyatt said nothing. He didn't smoke anyway.

'You have to travel far to get into the city?' said the young lady. 'Have a hunch you're not a local.'

'No,' Wyatt said curtly, 'not far.'

'You American?' said the young lady, noting the accent. 'My boyfriend's from the States, whereabouts you from?'

Wyatt turned, sighed and looked her up and down, 'Somewhere down South.'

'Oh, wow,' the young lady was smiling again. 'Boyfriend used to live in Chicago.' She blew another long trail of smoke into the air. 'So what brings you over to the UK then?'

'Lady,' said Wyatt abruptly, 'what makes you so interested in asking so many questions about me?'

The young lady flushed an instant shade of deep beetroot, taken aback by the bluntness of the question. She quickly discarded the half-finished cigarette into the road and taking the less than subtle hint walked away as quickly as she could, out into the passing throngs of people.

Wyatt wasn't proud of his behaviour but he chose not to dwell on it. Ordinarily he hated rudeness but he wasn't here to indulge in idle chit-chatter and he wondered – if he had been coerced into conversation – if he would have missed the sight of the bus pulling away from the curb and of The Politician's assistant watching him from the other side of the road.

Lorcan was loitering next to a public phone box. He had made no effort to amend his appearance to blend into his surroundings and was hunched down, covered by his long black cloak, hood pulled up around his head. He had the look of the Grim Reaper taking a short break, watching the flights of the living he so dearly wanted to claim. Still, no one seemed to pay him any attention.

Wyatt started to move and when Lorcan saw him heading in his direction he moved too, evidently wanting the American to follow. The hunched figure covered his ground surprisingly quickly, gliding across the pavements, weaving in and out of the crowds.

The pursuit itself did not prove to be a long one and within a few minutes Wyatt found himself pacing into the darkness of a narrow alleyway. He stopped, having momentarily lost sight of his target, Lorcan nowhere to be seen. But then he sensed his presence and at the end of the alleyway, which he could now see led to the frozen River Thames, he saw the hooded figure gesturing him to come forward and join him.

Wyatt walked forward slowly, suddenly cautious and aware of how alone he was, and he emerged from the alleyway and out onto the slippery wooden boards of a deserted quay. There was a small hut sitting on the dock that in better weather sold refreshments and boat rides but the door was shut and locked with a secure metal chain. Six decent looking speedboats were tied up to iron hooks on the boards, encased rigidly in the river ice. A gangplank supplied a route both left and right, leading to other deserted quays and other business that were currently closed, having not yet reopened from the winter challenges.

The Politician was coming, slowly waking down one such gangplank towards him. He was dressed as always in an amazing suit, a deep black this time, with a sharp blue tie and finished off with a long grey coat. He held onto a huge umbrella that kept his amazing suit impeccably dry.

'I can't apologise enough for the short game of follow the leader,' The Politician said. 'And I must offer the same sentiment for my lateness. Unfortunately my *other* life does sometimes have the habit of dominating my time, as you'll appreciate.'

Wyatt stopped where he was on the dock. The wood moaned a little beneath his weight and when he looked down he could see the murkiness of the moving grey water, imprisoned beneath the ice. Then he looked out into the centre of the river. There was no sign of life anywhere nearby, save the few moving specks walking across the distant bridges on the other side of the shore.

'You still don't trust me?' The Politician said, reading Wyatt's discomfort.

'No,' said Wyatt honestly, 'but I'm the only one here. So let's talk.'

'I truly appreciate you coming,' said The Politician. 'The Brotherhood is falling apart, my friend. We can't allow that to happen, not with so much at stake. Yes, we've had a setback –'

'It's more than a setback,' Wyatt pointed out. 'Situation's become impossible.'

The point had been made directly and with little dressing up. The Politician was instantly digesting the comment.

Wyatt had been fearful of the meeting for days and on more than one occasion had decided he wouldn't even attend. The truth was that The Politician scared him. But a different man was standing in front of him now. This man was nervous and despite Wyatt enjoying seeing him so uncomfortable he didn't actually know how to deal with this type of gentleman.

The Politician showed him eyes that were full of pleading. 'We mustn't give up hope –'

'It's not a question of hope,' said Wyatt. 'We have realities to face. The child's gone. If you've summoned me here for a post mortem then I don't see how it's going to be remotely beneficial. We lost. We have no leads. We don't have anything. The Guild made a holy mess and that's it.'

'Do we think The Guild have him?' The Politician said.

'No, we don't believe they do.'

'That's a pity,' said The Politician, 'I despise those people but although they don't realise it, we have the same end game. They would have killed the child for us. The absence of the ritual isn't ideal but maybe we –'

'Do you know why I came here today?' Wyatt said, interrupting. 'It isn't because I want to fix things. I'm leaving for home as soon as I can. I'm going to lay low a while, let the heat die down. But I wanted to see you first because I don't want any unfinished business between us. I know the kind of man you are. I don't want to be your enemy.'

The Politician offered a tired smile. 'You have more to worry about than that,' he said, 'don't you see it, Mr Eagan? The child has come forth into this world –'

'And I've heard that sermon,' Wyatt said, 'and more than once. Yes, he came forth, and now he's gone again. Now he's escaped that grotty little town it's like looking for a needle in a stack of needles. And The Guild struck like a bunch of maniacs. They used rocket launchers for God's sake. I can guarantee you it's not gone unnoticed.'

'That's what I'm here for,' The Politician argued. 'I can make these messes disappear, theirs as much as ours. Do you want to consider –'

'I'm three hundred and two years old,' said Wyatt, interrupting once again, 'which means I'm old enough to have been investigated on more than one occasion by a variety of agencies. The American program was closed down years ago, you know that, after the massacre in Siberia. They get any hint that they've a chance to catch some of us again and it'll re-open just like that. I'll be a prisoner in my own God damn country and I've worked too hard and I'm damned if I'll go through that again. Looking for the boy is one thing, fighting The Guild another, but we can't be having governments reopening files on us too. That's too many fronts to fight on, Sir.'

'I'm not sure I see your point,' said The Politician, 'or why you've told me that. We've all faced similar challenges over the centuries. It's all part of the game.' He paused for a moment, collecting his thoughts. 'Have you heard from the others? I had hoped Mr Béranger would be with you.'

'Gilliam is around,' said Wyatt, 'but like the others I doubt you'll see him again. They're scattering. They feel the same way I do.'

'So you've heard from them?' The Politician asked.

'Most of them,' said Wyatt, 'apart from Ekström, who seems to have disappeared off the face of the planet. But then I suspected you might have had something to do with that. Tell me I'm wrong?'

The Politician was quiet once more, thinking. Then he looked across to his assistant. 'Lorcan,' he shouted, 'would you be so kind as to leave us, please?' Lorcan did as he was told and departed down the same alleyway that he had arrived from. Now that they were alone The Politician stared out across the Thames.

Wyatt broke the silence. 'You still have the Dragwich,' he said.

'She hasn't come back to me,' said The Politician sadly. 'I've tried using the pendant. It's no use. I've no idea where she's gone.'

'If I had been locked up in that crate for hundreds of years I might just have done the same thing.'

'*Do* you trust me, Wyatt?' The Politician asked suddenly, uttering the same question for a second time.

'No,' said Wyatt. 'I've already told you that –'

'Have you ever seen me afraid?'

'Never!'

'I'm afraid now,' said The Politician.

'I'm afraid too,' said Wyatt, 'but we have to move on. Look, the child shows his face again and just maybe we –'

'Yes, the child scares me,' said The Politician, 'as does the thought of losing this gift. But no, I'm not speaking of that. I'm talking about Tobias. He is most unhappy.' He moved himself closer and stopped just in front of Wyatt so that they were face to face. He started to whisper. 'He came to me, Wyatt. He's scared of the child too. He uses an ancient spell to stay invisible, such is his fear. And he wants us to do his work for him and if we don't, he's going to kill us, one by one. There will be no mercy for any of us.'

Wyatt smiled, almost as if he pitied him. 'You've used that name for leverage before but –'

'It is *not* leverage,' The Politician grabbed Wyatt by the collar of his coat. His umbrella fell to the ground, the snow instantly filling his hair. There was a wild look in his eyes. 'I am nothing to him without the rest of you. Don't you see that?'

Wyatt could see the power of belief in The Politician's eyes but then he had met a thousand different men over the years that had a habit of believing in the impossible. He wasn't afraid to admit that the first time he had heard Tobias's name mentioned it had knocked him off his stride, regardless of the fact that he didn't believe in him. As a child he didn't believe in the bogeyman but still, sometimes the mention of his name was enough to give him a sleepless night.

'You're talking about a ghost,' he said. 'Tobias is nothing but a story. He's a myth. He's not real, not anymore. He probably died a long, long time ago.'

'And you're so sure about that?' The Politician asked.

'No one has seen him in a thousand years –'

'I asked if *you* were sure?'

'I wasn't,' Wyatt said. 'I wasn't for a long time. But I am now. If he was real, he would have intervened by now –'

The Politician raised his voice. 'I told you, he's scared –'

'Tobias *doesn't* exist,' Wyatt said angrily. 'You bluffed, it's been called. As I said, we move on.'

'You're wrong –'

'It's over, Sir –'

There was a sharp sound of a revving motor behind them.

Wyatt turned to the direction of the noise and saw that one by one the engines of the six speedboats attached to the dock were coming to life. Somewhere beneath the water the propellers were rotating, or at least trying to, as they had to battle against the ice that was currently encasing them before breaking free.

The Politician's countenance became grave. He stepped backwards, shaking his head. 'He's here,' he said.

A pain started to build in Wyatt's neck, a brute and sudden pressure that was wrapping itself around his throat and getting tighter by the second. He clutched upwards but an invisible force stopped his fingers from finding his own neck. *Something* was there, *something* indeed invisible, a phantom hand that had clamped down mercilessly and was cutting off the air supply to his body. He could feel the slippery skin of the fingers responsible but he couldn't see them. He desperately wanted oxygen. He was slowly being strangled.

He managed to flip his gaze painfully back to The Politician. The Politician was shouting something but he couldn't make out the words.

The *strange* changed into the *perilous* as Wyatt's whole body started to float high into the air, ascending like an angel and moving out over the bank and high above the water's edge. Below the propellers of the speedboats finally broke through, churning up shards of shattered ice. Then a force seemed to deposit its weight at the front of the vessels, pushing the bows beneath the water so that the sterns reared up, exposing every last angle of the propeller blades above the waterline.

The boats broke free from their moorings. The ice cracked out in sprawling fractures and the sterns of the boats started to move. The propeller blades formed into a circle, the odd spark as they occasionally touched, a whirlpool whipping itself into a bubbling frenzy in-between.

Wyatt's body was still climbing, being lifted. He still desperately clutched for breath, catching the odd glimpse of the propellers that were now directly below. He could fight no more and he embraced his fate. He stopped struggling and his arms dangled by his waist. He rotated his chin upwards so that his face looked towards the sky. He felt the cold slap of the snow on his cheeks. The world was growing dark, the invisible grip tightening.

He was thankful that he was lucid enough to still think. He had always wondered how he would finally die and had he been able to, he may have laughed as death by speedboat had never crossed his mind. But still, with his imminent demise nearing, he found himself fascinated by one single realisation. He knew who it was that was attacking and didn't need to see him to understand. *Tobias is real after all.*

'Stop!' The Politician pleaded from down below. 'Please! Tobias! Don't do this! We need him! We need him to bring them all back together.'

The air suddenly surged back into Wyatt's lungs, shortly before the grip loosened and the drop took it away again. He was falling, twisting in the air so that he was directed towards the water face first and heading with speed towards the fizzing circle of propellers. He closed his eyes as quickly as he could. He really didn't want to see it. But then the freefall abruptly halted.

Wyatt opened his eyes. He was still alive. The closest propeller was an inch from his forehead. He then realised that he was floating in mid-air, levitating above the water.

The propellers started to shut down, stopping their spinning and grinding to a halt. All was eerily quiet. The boats returned to normal, the propellers moving away from Wyatt's head, the front ends of the boats re-emerging out of the water and levelling off. The boats bobbed away happily in the gap that had been made in the ice, like hypnotised clients still dizzy at the end of the strongest of trances.

The Politician was running forward now. 'Let him go!' He pleaded to what looked like the fresh air.

The invisible force let go.

Wyatt plopped down into the water. The water was freezing and the impact painful. He could feel his body slipping away, dragged under by the hidden strengths of the current. Before he knew it the darkness of the ice was above him, the world on the other side blurry. It seemed so strange to him, Tobias saving him from the shredding only to let him perish beneath the ice. He started to beat against the frozen surface.

The Politician was there, striking out and coming to the rescue. He punched through the ice, pushing his hands into the water and dragging Wyatt to safety. A few seconds later they both fell back onto the damp wood of the dock, out of breath, but safe.

Wyatt coughed out what felt like a gallon of water and reached for his neck. He could feel the indents in the skin caused by the invisible man's fingers. Composure regained, he looked at The Politician's suit which was soaked through. 'Well that's ruined,' he noted.

The Politician looked at him with genuine worry. 'Are you ok?'

'No,' said Wyatt.

'I told you Tobias was real,' The Politician said. 'I've never lied to you about that, Wyatt. I told you, he's cast some sort of spell on himself of the like I've never heard of. He really doesn't want to be seen.'

Wyatt pushed himself up onto his knees.

The Politician touched him on the shoulder. 'We need to get everyone back together and complete this mission.'

Wyatt watched his freezing breath climb into the air. He pushed a hand out in front of his face, noting the severity of his shivering skin and considered whether he would ever feel warm enough for it to stabilise. And then he realised that for the first time in his life he and The Politician were in complete agreement. They had a child to go find and kill.

Chapter Thirty-Three

The library operated from inside a grand heritage building of Grade Two Listed stature. With its tall stone tower at one end, the vast array of tall, arched window frames, and the selection of beautiful stained glass within, it resembled a church and indeed it had been one, once upon a time, in a previous life.

Inside it was modest in size compared to some of the other more popular libraries in the city of Bristol. The ground floor, a large open space punctuated only by the intrusion of the chunky original stone pillars, had aisle after aisle of differently shaped bookcases, each one seeming to be made from a different wood. The aisles themselves had been arranged with little logic, the bookcases placed at random here and there, the routes for eager readers weaving this way and that like a strange maze of literature. At the far end and opposite the entrance was a balcony area, accessible by a staircase with a stark blue carpet, with rows of desks and lamps up high and out of the way for vigilant study. On the far wall of the balcony was something that dominated the attention in the room, a sprawling window that was shaped by a perfect circle of glass.

Finn was stood with the others at the customer service desk, quietly waiting for a staff member to return, all except Hamish who seemed to prefer a bit of isolation and had thrown himself down into a comfy chair nearby, where he appeared to be sleeping.

It was four thirty on a Friday afternoon. The sky outside was rapidly darkening and every electric lamp in the library was on, yet the bulbs were not overly bright and there were still lots of dark corners to be found. The library was shortly to close for the day, with only a few customers lingering.

Finn was happy to be inside and out of the cold. After they had left the chaos of the bridge behind they had travelled west for what seemed like the longest of hours, heading into Wales, despite knowing all along that the intention was to end up somewhere else. It was part of the plan of course, a simple deception in case anyone happened to find the abandoned camper van, which they had no choice but to leave behind. The poor vehicle had taken a hammering during Agatha's brutal assault and it had been close to dying throughout the journey.

The memory made Finn glance across to Cora who was still in mourning. Her eyes were red and blotchy from where she had been crying. The camper van was her baby and she, like the rest of them, had to watch it slow to an ominous halt with smoke puffing from the engine. Twenty minutes later it was aflame and burning away in what would be its last resting place. He didn't have the heart to tell her that he was actually relieved to see it go. For a motley crew of people on the run and operating beneath the radar, quite frankly a bright orange camper van just wasn't at all practical.

Afterwards they had set off on foot, carrying what they could and walking into the chilled depths of the snowy night. It was some time before they found a small taxi rank in a small town with a name they didn't care to remember. The drivers had attempted to quote themselves out of the job, not fancying a trip across the bridge and into England, but Willoughby didn't blink and paid them what they asked, calling their bluffs.

Being inside in the warm wasn't the only positive for Finn. There had been no more explanations on the journey, no more unravelling of the puzzles. Everyone had been too tired. That status however, here in the library, was apparently about to change.

'I do hope she's here,' said Willoughby, growing impatient with waiting.

'She's always here,' said Edgar. 'Relax.'

The *she* in question was Bronwyn Pettigrew. She was the Head Librarian and Willoughby had said that libraries were sacred places to all immortals. An unwritten rule existed, one that was only occasionally broken, in that immortals would not bring any conflict through the doors. In turn the Librarian would always remain impartial and ready to provide access to any book that an immortal might require.

'What makes this place so special?' Finn said.

'All being well,' Willoughby said, 'and you'll see. Let's just say there might be a few things in here that you're unlikely to find elsewhere. And even here, they're not things that are shown to any old person.'

Over in the chair Hamish jerked awake and omitted a loud snort, which echoed unkindly up in the high ceiling.

Finn glanced across at Felicity, wondering if she might make a joke but she stayed silent. It was another little slice of evidence to support his fears. At first he thought it might just be paranoia but he was becoming more certain that something had changed between them, a shift in the dynamic of their friendship. She hadn't been rude to him or said anything too harsh but she had been very quiet, rarely saying more than a few words whenever they had a chance to chat. What's more she seemed to have taken a liking to James Devery and she spent most of her time talking to the Irishman. For his part Devery seemed to like her back and he had told Finn that he liked her wild nature. Ever since, he had looked at her like a protective father.

There was some movement from the balcony. A member of the library staff was heading back towards the customer service desk.

'Word of caution,' Willoughby said to Finn, 'if you happen to speak, choose your words very carefully around this man. He has a habit of being a bit temperamental.'

'Amen,' said Devery. Hamish had picked himself up from the chair and was quickly joining the rest of the group at the desk.

With the ominous warning, Finn wanted to take a closer look at the man that approached. The man was black, had a slight body, was short in height, and had a neat, short haircut. He wore glasses, a royal blue jumper with a crisply ironed white shirt collar poking out from underneath. He moved with what could be described as precision, his posture perfect, neither rushing nor dawdling. He didn't look particularly threatening.

Finn nudged Willoughby. 'What do you mean?'

'He means,' Edgar said quietly, the staff member now close enough to be within earshot, 'that it's best not to get on the wrong side of him.'

Devery nodded. 'Which Will always seems to manage.'

The member of staff slotted himself behind the customer service desk. 'I'm sorry to keep you waiting,' he said apologetically. The badge clipped to his jumper announced his name as Kemi. 'How may I help you, this evening?'

'We're looking for a specific book,' Willoughby said. He didn't look too pleased to be asking his question.

'We do actually close in about ten minutes,' said Kemi, glancing at his watch. He tapped a password into the computer and the screen in front of him unlocked. He looked up and smiled warmly. 'But I can see what I can do for you in the time we have. What would the title of this book be called, Sir?'

'The book is for the boy,' said Willoughby. 'And he looks for a very old and rare book called Sub Rosa Tales, volume four to be precise. I'm led to believe you may have a copy.'

Kemi made a humming noise of consideration and shrugged. He tapped the name into his computer search facility and pressed enter. The computer program started its search and then made a short, sharp beep. The beep didn't sound encouraging. 'No results unfortunately,' he said sadly, looking up with a smile that had changed to be more sympathetic. 'I confess I've never seen such a title on the shelves either, Sir. But then we are a very small library in reality. Perhaps you would be better looking for it in one of the larger libraries in the city? I can point them out to you on the map, if you wish?'

Willoughby shook his head. 'They won't have it. There's only three or four in existence.'

'Then I'm sorry again,' Kemi said.

Willoughby gave a tired smile. 'Perhaps you would be kind enough to search for me again?'

244

'I need to close up,' said Kemi, 'but it will take me ten minutes or so. You're welcome to have a look around and see if you can find anything else that may help.' He started to walk away.

'Might it be in a very specific section?' Willoughby called after him. He pointed to his left. 'Maybe somewhere at the top of that staircase?'

Finn followed the direction of Willoughby's finger. He was pointing at a dark staircase that sat behind a small, red cordon within one of the pillars. He hadn't even noticed it until it had been pointed out. It was as if it had magically appeared from nowhere.

Kemi stopped walking and turned. 'Can you stop pointing, please, Sir?' he demanded.

'Why must we play these little games every time?' Willoughby asked stressfully. 'I understand, you despise me, but I'm sure Bronwyn will be happy to see me.'

Kemi noted the position of the few customers that remained inside the building. He strolled back to the desk, reaching over to a tannoy system. He pressed a square button and spoke into the speaker, all the while keeping his stare levied at Willoughby. 'The library is now closing,' he announced, his voice broadcast out from the speakers. 'With regret we must close on time this evening due to a scheduled stock take so if I could kindly ask you to head towards the nearest exit now that would be most appreciated. Thank you so much and we hope to see you again.'

Finn and his group stayed where they were.

Kemi waited for the customers to funnel out into the snow and when the last patron was gone and they were alone he spoke to Willoughby again. 'Her name would be *Miss Pettigrew,*' he said. 'And *Miss Pettigrew* is always happy to see everyone, such is her nature. That is what I am here for, to ensure she doesn't get taken advantage of.'

Willoughby lowered an eyebrow. 'It's not for you to say who does or doesn't get access to this place, Kemi. You can't just say no due to your pathetic prejudices and grudges –'

'No,' said Kemi, 'but it's my job to identify the vultures. And you, Sir, are a vulture.'

245

Willoughby looked at the African closely. 'Why do you hate me so much, Kemi?'

Kemi didn't care to respond to the question. 'You shouldn't be here, Carmichael,' he stated instead.

'Is the library not open to all our kind?' Cora pitched in cautiously. 'It's supposed to be a haven for us all.'

'In ordinary times perhaps,' said Kemi, 'but these aren't ordinary times. I know why you've come here. I know what you're going to ask. I know what is going on out there in the snow. It's Miss Pettigrew's duty to stay impartial to all your little quests and adventures. Yet you come here, not with any discretion or class, one big group of you, risking all that, jeopardising her integrity.'

Willoughby pointed to Finn. 'Do you know who this boy is?'

Finn cringed at that. *Do you know who this boy is?* It sounded a tad desperate, like a vain celebrity relying on one of the many members of his entourage to remind the world of their supposed fame and clout. Which was fine but he would had much rather such efforts went towards maybe getting a free steak or hamburger or a Porsche – not a book.

Kemi wasn't buying it anyway. 'The library is closed,' he said again, allowing the fake smile and persona of the customer service clerk to return to his expression. If anything he was even more robotic than before. 'Please accept my sincere apologies again that we do not have the book you are looking for. The exit is behind you. Have a pleasant evening. Goodbye now.'

All that was left were bemused stares, Devery staring at Willoughby, Willoughby staring embarrassingly at Finn, Finn staring at each of them in turn. Where were they supposed to go from here?

Felicity afforded herself a little laugh. 'Kinda like this chap,' she said, 'he's kinda no nonsense.'

Willoughby took action, unhooking the satchel from his shoulder. He pulled out a book from inside, the very book that Finn had seen on the desk in his father's study. He placed the book carefully onto the desk and stepped away from it, allowing the old volume to speak for itself.

For his part Finn tried not to look at the book. The book had been on the journey from the beginning and bought back memories of when he had sneaked a peak over his father's sleeping shoulders at the pages. It had been the last night they had been together as father and son, before the violence and the chaos. *Sleep well now, Dad, wherever you may be.*

Kemi glanced down at the book.

'You know what that is,' Willoughby noted. 'It brought trust in a place it was unlikely to be found only a few days ago. I'm pretty sure it'll have the same impact right now.'

Kemi gently ran his fingers along the spine before carefully opening the cover. He cautiously pressed the plastic that was covering the inside pages. 'This needs looking after.'

'And that's what you're best at Kemi,' said Willoughby. 'I can't tell you anything scientific about the plastic cover but I'm assured it's quite good. It has some long, scientific name I've forgotten.'

Kemi was unsure. 'A bribe?'

Willoughby said nothing. He didn't need to. It was already clear enough. Of course it was a bribe.

'Hmmmm,' Kemi mulled it over. 'You would really let go of such a rare artefact just to be granted access to Miss Pettigrew and her collection? You know how much this is worth?'

Willoughby already knew that he had the Assistant ensnared. 'Not quite,' he admitted. 'Such a trade would hardly be proportional, would it now? No, access to Miss Pettigrew and her collection is one thing but there are a few more little things I would see myself needing your assistance with, not least a bit of room and board for a few days. But we can talk about the finer details later, can't we?'

Kemi picked the book up. 'Come with me,' he said. The African led them towards the red cordon that Willoughby had pointed out and then around it and beyond, taking them into the darkness of the cramped staircase. They started to climb, moving past endless rooms full of bookcases, their shelves choked with thousands of books, books that the public were not permitted to access.

Finn waited, letting the others go, so he could be at the back of the group and more importantly so that he could be next to Felicity. Walking side by side, he gave her a playful nudge, knocking her shoulder. 'What yer up to?' he joked, putting on a silly voice.

'I'm walking,' said Felicity.

'Still not talking to me then?' he said disappointingly. He pouted, again playfully. 'That makes Finn want to *cwy!*'

'I think you'll find,' she answered, 'that *still walking* counts as two words which then counts as talking.'

'Reassuring,' said Finn.

Felicity laughed at that. 'You need reassuring, do you, Finn? What's the matter, your head at risk of deflating a little bit?'

Finn didn't enjoy that comment, not one bit. It certainly wasn't flirting. No, it had been too acidic for that. He wanted to retaliate but was neglected the chance by the staircase running out of steps and opening out into a large room. The room they entered was high up in the tower and rather oddly was lit by a number of flaming torches that were mounted on the wall and candles that were sizzling away within an old fashioned metal chandelier that dangled from the ceiling. There was a long wooden trestle table in the middle of the room and twenty chairs surrounded it. Five of the chairs were occupied by men who ate from a variety of plates that were laid out in front of them. None of the men used knifes or forks, trawling through their meals with their hands.

Finn stared at the men, none of whom wished them welcome or even acknowledged them entering the room. They were hairy men, with long, dark beards and longer, unclean hair. Their clothes were dark and dirty, their boots covered in grime and muck.

'I will bring you Miss Pettigrew,' Kemi announced, holding the book close to his heart. 'You will wait here, please.' Then the African was gone, slipping through a door at the opposite side of the passageway.

'Who are these guys?' Finn asked. 'They don't look happy to see us.'

'They're Hunters,' said Devery, who was stood closest. He deliberately kept the volume of his voice low.

Finn was puzzled. 'What exactly can you find to hunt in Bristol?'

'Different kind of hunting,' said Devery. 'They're as tough and as hardnosed a bunch of madmen you're ever likely to come across.'

'Yes, they are,' said Willoughby, agreeing. 'Spend their time wandering around the world, securing precious artefacts for places like this. Not just any old antique either but writings or pieces of art that write about or depict our kind. The Hunters secure them and people like Bronwyn Pettigrew keep them safe, away from the prying eyes of the world. There's a lot more of it out there than you'd think.'

'Almost sounds like an honourable profession, doesn't it?' said Hamish. 'Don't leave out the dirty work, Will. Call it what it is.'

Finn waited for Willoughby to explain but he said nothing.

Devery did it for him. 'Let's just say,' said the Irishman, 'that some people aren't too keen to let go of their artefacts. Others might be keen to show the world what they've discovered.' He nodded at the table. 'These fellas make sure they see sense, one way or the other.'

At the table, one of the Hunters turned to look at Devery as he chewed the flesh and sinew from a chicken leg. In fact it was more than a stare. It was a glare that was riddled with malevolence and ill-will.

Cora had spotted it and she nestled herself closer to her husband. 'He would have to be here, wouldn't he?'

Felicity had spotted the glaring Hunter too. 'Wow,' she said to Devery, 'that one really doesn't like you.'

'No,' said Devery, 'we kinda have a bit of history, me and him. His name is Donitz.'

Felicity was intrigued. 'That sounds like a story I'd like to hear.'

'There's not much to it,' said Devery. 'I killed his dog –'

Felicity was shocked and she gasped. 'You did what?"

'It's not as bad as it sounds,' said Devery, seeing the judgement in Felicity's eyes. 'In my defence the dog was trying to rip out my larynx at the time. I guess you can say we've got some bad blood.'

Hamish chuckled quietly. 'Well ain't that an understatement, seeing as every time you're in the same room you try to kill one another.'

Devery sighed. 'Luckily, I haven't seen him in over fifty years. He always starts it though, not me.'

'They can hear you,' Cora pointed out. 'You know that, right?'

'What kind of dog was it?' Felicity said, still not over the appalling revelation. 'Don't tell me it was a Springer Spaniel? If it was –'

Donitz suddenly spoke, his voice a gruffly impressive growl. 'She trying to be funny?'

Devery leapt instantly to Felicity's defence. 'Hey, she didn't mean any offence –'

'She ain't one of us,' Donitz said, pointing at Felicity with the chicken leg in his hands.

'No, she ain't,' said the Hunter sat next to him, 'so what you doing bringing her to a place like this?'

Finn looked to Willoughby. 'Thought you said we weren't to have conflict in here?'

Felicity was blushing nervously. She took a step closer to Devery and Cora and lowered her voice. 'They're not very cuddly bears are they?'

'No,' said Devery, 'they're not.'

Edgar sighed, scratching the stubble of his beard and looking as though he would rather be doing anything else. 'Must we?' he said to those around the table.

Donitz spat out a greasy shot of saliva at Devery's feet. 'He asked you a question, boy. What you doing bringing a brattish skank like that here?'

Devery wasn't at all intimidated. 'Tell you what,' he said calmly, 'you ask me politely, I might just answer you, *boy*.'

Cora closed her eyes and shook her head, knowing what would come next.

250

Donitz didn't like Devery's challenge one bit and he leapt up from his seat, his chair sliding out violently beneath him and toppling to the floor. But he was prevented from coming forward by a voice.

'My Lord,' said a woman with excitement. Bronwyn Pettigrew had entered the room unnoticed and was staring at Finn with delight and paid no attention to the tension elsewhere. 'It's almost as if a little something from the pages of history has just walked into my world.'

Chapter
Thirty-Four

Bronwyn Pettigrew guided Finn and Willoughby to her private quarters and insisted that the others remain outside in the hall to eat, rest, and by absolutely no means fight. Feeling unable to decline, Hamish, Edgar, and Felicity slotted themselves down amongst the inhospitable Hunters, whilst Devery and Cora took their leave, heading back downstairs to wisely diffuse any tension that was sure to arise.

Bronwyn busied herself with making some tea for her guests. Kemi was close by, standing against the wall like an eagle eyed sentry. Her quarters were on the small but comfortable scale, every last space and surface covered with books. Where it could fit, she had a little table with an old television set, a wooden desk with an ink well, a high-backed chair, a small stripy sofa, a single bed, a modest gas fire, a gas stove, and a kettle. Three more chairs were placed around a little coffee table with a chessboard placed on top of it, a game in mid-flow. There was another staircase in the corner – going up – the existence of which was hard to see in the shadows.

Finn's first impressions of this new friend were positive. Bronwyn Pettigrew had a warm, friendly aura that radiated off her like a scent. She had Settled at the grand old age of sixty two but she had the look and energy of a much younger woman. She wore a long grey dress and a matching grey blazer and despite the dour colour scheme she made it work with an effortless ease, exuding an air of grace through her tall, elegant frame.

'It made me shiver a touch when I saw you,' said Bronwyn, passing Finn and Willoughby their cups of tea. She took her own cup to her desk where she fell down into her seat. 'I felt most of the little hairs on the back of my neck stand on end. I've read all about you of course. You appear in some of my favourite passages. I'd obviously felt your emergence but honestly had no expectations of you coming to visit old Bronwyn.'

'I'd say it's been too many years,' Willoughby said. He placed his tea on the desk and brought across two chairs from the coffee table so he and Finn could sit in front of her. 'I've missed you, you know.'

'Actually, it'll be eleven years next July,' Bronwyn pointed out. 'So it wouldn't appear you've missed old Bronwyn Pettigrew all that much. Don't ask me how I remember snippets of information like that. I've always had a knack for remembering dates.'

Finn sat himself down and as his bottom made contact with the smooth wood he was suddenly exhausted, struck by a wave of fatigue that he didn't even realise had been building. The idea of sleep then entered his brain and took over. He now wanted to find a comfortable bed to such a degree he realised that he would happily trade the promise of more answers for a big fluffy pillow.

Bronwyn however was still talking. 'Best bit about all of this is that, in principle, this cruel weather should break soon, if the writings are to be trusted.' She clapped her hands excitedly and smirked at Finn. 'This is just so very exciting, isn't it? I would imagine you've got a million and one questions?'

The tiredness was starting to take its toll on Finn and he couldn't think of much to say. She was watching him, waiting for him to be polite and speak. 'What power do you have?' he said. There. It was all he could think of and in reality he did want to know. He couldn't help it. The whole situation was amazing but the *power* element of it fascinated him more than anything else.

'Miss Pettigrew,' Kemi answered for her, 'has the gift of wisdom.'

Finn scrunched his face up, not impressed and struggling to hide it. It was hardly an inspiring answer.

'Oh, would you look at his little face,' said Bronwyn. She laughed. 'Would wisdom not be considered to be rock and roll enough for you, young man?'

'Sorry,' said Finn, 'I didn't mean to be rude –'

253

'There's a *but* at the end of that sentence, isn't there?' Bronwyn said. She didn't look at all offended. 'Come on, you don't have to be all shy around me. Say what you feel.'

Finn considered the most favourable way to put it. 'Well,' he said tentatively, 'it's just given the choice, I think I would choose something a bit ... better ... something a bit more exciting. I'd be gutted if I found out I had some power and that's all I was given.'

'It's not a matter of choice,' said Willoughby.

'Do you not think there is power in wisdom?' Bronwyn said.

'I don't know,' Finn answered. 'I mean a guy at my school is the cleverest boy I've ever met in my life, aces all his exams, gets predicted A-stars across the board. He'll be a lawyer or something, I bet. But he's got no common sense and a few weeks back this kid called Jordan found an old hot dog out in the field, had been there for like weeks and was all mouldy, and he made him eat it. So, really clever, but that was really stupid.'

Willoughby's mouth lulled open. He looked down at Finn with a look of utter embarrassment, like a father whose child has just humiliated him in front of a thousand peers. 'Wisdom and intelligence are quite different things,' he said curtly, trying to spare everyone's blushes. 'Bronwyn has lived in this building for four hundred years. Unlike the rest of us she has never had the need to move –'

'Will,' said Bronwyn, 'don't worry about it, please. Do you really think I'm that much of a fuddy-duddy –'

'And why do you think that is, Finn?' Willoughby said. 'It's because of wisdom. She knows how to use mankind like puppets, so that they see what she wants them to see. And they *never* see a sixty year old woman with the gift of everlasting life. You can't put a price on that. It truly is a gift, a damn sight better than being able to heal, let me tell you.'

Finn said nothing in response. He looked at Bronwyn and then Kemi, a little embarrassed, and then stared down at his hands.

'Come on now, Will,' said Bronwyn. 'I really don't need you to protect my honour and besides the lad's just swept up in the drama of all of this. I can see that. He's fifteen. Of course he's going to be more staggered by the thought of punching through concrete rather than having the ability to provide sage advice.' She reached across the desk and slapped Willoughby's hand, a sharp rap across the knuckles. 'That's for you! I must say I don't care for you to describe me as using mankind like puppets. That was a very poor choice of words, shame on you. I didn't like that one bit.'

It was Willoughby's turn to look sheepish. His cheeks went instantly red. Finn found it extremely hard not to laugh out loud, such was the absurdity of the sight. Willoughby looked like he had just been told off by the headmistress.

'Anyhow, I don't see wisdom as a gift in the first place,' Bronwyn said. 'I see it as a quality, an enhanced quality it may be, but a quality all the same.'

Finn started to yawn, a yawn he tried to hide. But it was too strong to go unnoticed.

'Look at him,' Bronwyn said caringly. 'Bless his little cotton socks. I think the hour is a tad late to begin any research tonight. He looks like he could sleep for a year.'

Willoughby rolled his sleeve up and looked at his watch. 'It really isn't late at all. We could easily begin tonight, the sooner the better, in my view.'

'I don't see an energised boy in front of me,' said Bronwyn, having none of it. 'And you look like you could do with a good night's sleep too, Will. I wouldn't say the life of fugitives agrees with you all that much. Kemi will show you to some comfortable rooms where you can have a bit of a recharge. Have a shower, clean your clothes. It'll do you the world of good and I can fetch you the books you need in the morning –' she stopped herself, quiet for a moment, bringing her hands together with her index fingers touching. She was thinking. 'But before you go, perhaps you could satisfy one curiosity. What are you actually looking to achieve from this visit?'

'A roof and a bed,' Willoughby said, 'and access to a few choice books.'

Bronwyn's curiosity wasn't satisfied at all by that answer. 'I have no doubt that's true to an extent,' she said with a knowing frown, 'but I'm all but certain there's more to your visit than simple research. The books are always here. There's something else, isn't there?'

Willoughby nodded his head, accepting that transparency was sensible and unavoidable. 'I've only told Finn the simple parts of the story,' he said. 'What he is, what we are, but the rest I've held back.'

'Why?' said Bronwyn. 'You know the rest, just as well as I do.'

'And I *could* tell him,' Willoughby admitted, 'but he's already been told so much. I don't want this to just be an information dump. He needs to be told the rest with a different, more visual method … your method.'

Bronwyn placed her fingers over her mouth and made a humming noise of consideration. She shuffled in her chair almost as if she was about to stand but then she changed her mind. She removed her fingers, stared at Willoughby and bit her lip. 'I know what it is that you'll ask of me,' she said slowly, still thinking. 'And I have major, major concerns. If anyone else were to find out, it could severely impact on my reputation.'

'You've shown others before,' said Willoughby. 'You showed me once upon a time. I don't see the difference.'

'But he,' she said, gesturing to Finn, 'isn't just anybody, is he?'

'No, he's not,' Willoughby said. He was happy to agree with that sentiment. 'Which makes what I'm about to also ask for a touch awkward. I don't only need you to show him the truth of Obsidian.'

Bronwyn gave him a look that suggested he couldn't be serious. 'You want more?' she gasped. 'What else could I possibly give you, Willoughby?'

'We need Kemi to test Finn,' Willoughby explained. 'We need Kemi. If anyone will be capable of seeing whether he has the powers I believe he has inside of him, it will be Kemi.'

Bronwyn shook her head. 'No, you don't need Kemi. You just need to have a bit of patience. His powers will come to him in time and –'

'Time's a luxury we don't have,' Willoughby said strongly. 'With what we're facing, we need him aware and functioning now, not in three weeks or a year or whenever everything happens to slot into place. There's going to be tough days ahead, you know that.'

Bronwyn thought about that for a long while. 'I don't know,' she said finally. 'If we're talking about impartiality, the ethical argument of what you're asking me to provide gets a little bit grey. We have room and board. To an outsider, if they were to ignore the timing, it could potentially be considered acting with impartiality. If I were to explain to the boy the truth of his prophecy in my own particular way, we're in *highly debatable* territory but perhaps I could argue my way out of it. But allowing Kemi to try and drag the power out of him? Come on, there's no dressing that up as anything other than me helping your cause.'

Finn sat and listened. He couldn't get involved. They were talking about things that were outside of his comprehension. But his instinct told him that whatever it was that Willoughby wanted Bronwyn would grant him. He could sense it. That wasn't wisdom. It was just a gut feeling.

'It's a transaction,' said Willoughby. 'It's as pure and simple as that. Let me remind you, you get the Gospel of Evaine if you help us. That's no trinket, Bronwyn. If you don't want to help there are plenty of other libraries who I'm sure will be more excited to secure that particular volume at any cost. My cards on the table, I don't really feel like doing all the travelling I'll need to get to them. We're already here, yes, but there are things I need and I won't give up the book without it.'

'I already have the book,' Bronwyn pointed out.

'Yes, you do,' Willoughby said. 'And I get why you'd say that. But after all these years I would be disappointed if our friendship came to that.'

Bronwyn turned and shared a look with Kemi. 'What are your thoughts?'

'I think you should say no,' said Kemi bluntly. 'It is always the same with this man. He takes and takes and takes.'

Bronwyn went to sip from her tea but it was still boiling hot. She blew onto the surface to cool it. 'Ok,' she said to Willoughby, 'I'll consider your proposal overnight. It's never a good idea to agree to something on the spot. Why give regret a chance when regret is such a potent force and can cause so many problems? What I would say now though is that if I do agree, you will need to do something for me. It'll be something that maybe you'll need to consider overnight too.'

'I'll do anything,' said Willoughby. 'I don't need time to consider.'

'You've heard of a rare book specialist called Grayson Mellors?' Bronwyn said.

'I have,' said Willoughby.

The tea was finally cool enough and Bronwyn enjoyed a long sip. 'Tell the lad who he is,' she said. 'Bless him, he looks a little bit like a child watching his parents talk about grown up things.'

'Mellors isn't one of us,' Willoughby said to Finn. 'He's a rotten scoundrel. Always been aware of our kind and used such knowledge to make himself a very wealthy man. He's a procurer of rare artefacts and bloody good at it. He's also bloody good at making sure he sells such artefacts at extortionately high prices to the highest bidder, regardless of whether they're one of us or not. He doesn't care about preservation. He doesn't care about secrecy. He cares only about the size of his wallet.'

'Isn't that what your Hunters are for?' Finn said. He shivered at the thought of the answer to his own question. He wasn't actually suggesting the Hunters should go out and kill this Mellors character.

'Mr Mellors is smarter than that,' said Bronwyn. 'He's always made it clear that if anything unbecoming happens to him the world will know of our existence within the hour. I have no doubt he has arrangements in place to make sure that happens.' She took another sip of tea. 'Anyway, there are rumours out there and they say that Mr Mellors has a copy of the Gospel of Iris for sale to the highest bidder.'

Willoughby took a huge intake of breath. 'What?' he said. He was already shaking his head. 'Now, that is impossible! I don't believe it, not for one minute –'

'What's the Gospel of Iris?' Finn said.

'Which was my first reaction,' said Bronwyn, ignoring Finn but addressing Willoughby and the doubt in his statement. 'But Grayson Mellors doesn't do anything without it being of potential benefit to him. If a rumour out there is untrue, he makes sure the players know it's false, especially when the rumour could put him in danger. He hasn't done that this time and by making that claim he *is* in great danger. Taking it as it is, it would seem that Grayson Mellors might just have a copy of the book of all books.'

'It sounds like a trap to me,' Willoughby said, 'or some sort of scam.'

'Perhaps,' Bronwyn agreed. 'But perhaps it's not. If I do decide to grant you your wishes, you will need to go and see if it's true and if it is you will secure that book for me. Then Kemi will test the boy and you are welcome to stay here as long as you need.'

'And if he hasn't got the book?' Willoughby wondered.

'Hypothetically, all you would have to do is go,' said Bronwyn. 'And I would hold up my end of the bargain regardless. My gut feeling is that I just need to know. You'd need to make sure you make no mention of my name. You'd have to make contact with Mellors yourself, from a safe distance so no one knows we're involved. My funding, if he does sell, would have to be transacted secretly. Of course, you would be welcome to see the book, which we both know is something you will need to do. But if it exists, if this is true, I want there to be no doubt. I want that book, Will. It's dominating my every thought.'

Willoughby didn't need to think about it. He extended his hand, confident in his decision, but Bronwyn didn't shake it.

'Exciting times,' said Bronwyn. 'But as I said, I'll give it some more thought tonight.' She stood up. 'Right, it's time for sleep,

Finn. In the morning if we come to an accord, you'll belong to Kemi who will put you through your paces and then in the afternoon we study. Get some sleep, young man. Tomorrow has the potential to be a long day.'

Finn was too tired to argue but he did wonder what exactly they meant by training. He wasn't too concerned however as he was relatively fit and could run about kicking a football for hours. Whatever Kemi had in store, he was certain he could handle it.

Chapter
Thirty-Five

By the afternoon of his second day at Bronwyn Pettigrew's library, Finn considered himself more exhausted than he had ever been at any other point during his fifteen short years of life. He was sat in the raised balcony area of the main library, staring out of the circular window at the people walking down below, wondering if this was what the act of dying might feel like. Some people said you would see a bright light at the time of death, somewhere in the distance or on the horizon, and such was the degree of his fatigue he wondered if he caught sight of such a light whether he just would go ahead and welcome it.

It was a Sunday and the library was closed. He sat alone at the desk, freshly showered and with clothes that had finally been washed. His legs ached. His back ached. In fact, everything ached. Kemi's tests had been intense and bordering on the psychotic. He ached when he sat, he ached when he stood, he ached when he breathed and he ached when he walked. It even ached when he blinked.

The tests had taken place in a secret room beneath the library and in an area that existed amongst the old foundations of the building. The basement of the library was a cold and dark environment, a pitiful place full of cobwebs and odd drips that could be heard but not seen. The area was dominated by a host of strong, stone pillars, the same pillars that could be seen on the floor above in the library itself. Where the pillars had allowed enough room, Kemi had created a modest matted area. He called it his dojo.

Surrounding the mats was a vast array of shelving units and cabinets and within each unit was stored an extensive collection of impressive and somewhat frightening weaponry. The weapons were not modern and were inherently historic – there were no automatic machine guns or rocket launchers here – and consisted of items such as swords from a variety of different era's, crossbows and longbows, pikes, flails, maces, axes, and a selection of plate armour. And the weapons were not just dominated by European culture either, with one large unit reserved specifically for what Kemi described as oriental antiquities. Martial arts were the African's passion.

'This is called a yantok,' Kemi had announced as he walked out into the centre of the dojo for the first time. He had been dressed in simple black gym clothing and was barefoot. He carried two long sticks and he threw one to Finn to catch. 'It's a weapon from something called Eskrima which is a discipline with origins in the Philippines. I will show you how to use it but more importantly how to use it correctly. By means of your first lesson I will ask you to mark these words. Rage and fury are powerful emotions but they have nothing in comparison to effective technique. Effective technique is everything, Finn.'

Finn had been provided with his own matching black gym clothing and he too was barefoot. He also had an audience, much to his dismay. Willoughby, Cora, and Hamish were leaning next to pillars watching eagerly, as was Bronwyn and even the Hunters were in attendance, standing silent and solemn but unable to dispel their own curiosities. The only people missing were Devery, Edgar, and Felicity, who had travelled from Bristol that very morning and before first light, accepting the responsibility of tracking down the infamous Grayson Mellors. He had missed the chance to say goodbye to Felicity. The fact she had gone had underpinned his suspicions that they were slowly drifting apart. But he was glad that she was absent for the training part at least.

'All good things start with a baptism of fire,' Kemi said. 'If the things that are written about you are true there will be specific gifts that will take a little more coercion to reveal. I doubt that applies to fighting. Fighting is primeval, a natural instinct and any raw ability will already be within you and accessible by application of the right brand of duress. That goes for even the most standard mortal man but for you … for *the* child … it will be something much more impressive.'

Finn had looked at the yantok in his hands carefully. He ran his fingers along the surface of the wooden fighting stick. It was perfectly smooth and surprisingly light and made quite beautifully. He had his doubts but he was quite looking forward to unleashing hell. He had always wanted to be a maniac and had the odd dream where he faced down twenty school bullies in the cafeteria, protecting some gorgeous girl's honour and taking down the dastardly bullies one by one. Girls swooned, numbers were exchanged, and legendary status's achieved forever.

'I've never been much of a fighter,' he had felt compelled to point out. He had wanted that fact to be clear. 'I've never used something like this and I'm not even sure what to do with it.'

'That will come with time,' said Kemi. 'It's not about the equipment. It's about forcing your gifts into the open. If that happens you will be even more impressive than I am. I can't wait to see it.'

Finn frowned at that and then he sniggered, almost without realising it. He still couldn't see what it was that was supposed to be so terrifying about the African and his doubts about his reputation were clear in his expression. Even down in the dojo he just looked small and unthreatening.

'Show him!' Bronwyn had shouted, picking up on Finn's clear scepticism. She had gestured towards the five Hunters. 'Please, assault Kemi for me, if you would be so kind. I think our young man needs an illustration.'

The Hunters all sighed in unison like a barbershop quartet warming up for a rendition that they didn't enjoy performing.

'Do we have to?' Donitz moaned in a gruff voice.

'Absolutely right you have to!' Bronwyn barked. 'You accept my lodgings, use my hot water and electricity and you eat my food and stand there barely saying anything to anyone. And do I ever complain? No, I bally well don't. Do something for old Miss Pettigrew for a change!'

Eventually doing as they were told the Hunters acquired their own yantoks from the unit and paced out gingerly onto the mats, spreading out tactically but looking thoroughly miserable. It was all over in less than a minute. They all attacked at the same time in order to improve their odds of success, raining in a vicious volley of blows towards Kemi. But Kemi, almost without breaking a sweat, avoided every effort as if they were feeble and moving like a phantom he struck – five or six swift strikes – straight into his opponents faces and sending them sprawling into the mats, twisting in the air as they went.

'Again,' said Kemi, taking a few steps so that he was back in the centre of the dojo. 'But better! You are all better than that! Don't let me do that to you so easily!'

So the Hunters got to their feet and did it again and this time, fuelled by the previous humiliation, they did indeed attack in a far better and effective manner and with a greater degree of ferocity. But again Kemi was equal to anything they threw at him and almost seemed to be playing with them, allowing them to strike and exhaust their energy before ducking and diving so that their attempts didn't even come close. It wasn't until he started to get bored and when the thrust of a stick almost made contact with his jaw that Kemi asserted his authority and lashed out, once again knocking the Hunters to the ground one by one. Two of them he took out with a strike to the chin, one got a strike in the nose, Donitz had a smack on the crown of his head and the last was taken down by the sweeping out of his legs from underneath him.

The Hunters writhed on the floor in agony and did not get up for some time. They didn't dare. Someone down in the basement was clapping.

'How can you move like that?' Finn asked. Any doubt about his abilities was completely decimated. The man was quite frankly awesome. He was very much impressed. 'This is your gift, right? This is what strength looks like?'

'No,' said Kemi. 'I share a gift similar to Willoughby Carmichael.'

'You're kidding?' Finn said. 'You're a machine. How can you be so tough and quick if that's not your gift?'

'Practice and discipline', Kemi gestured for Finn to move forward and join him on the mats. It was his turn. The Hunters were slowly getting to their feet and clearing the area. 'Eternity gives a man plenty of opportunity to be practiced and be disciplined. Yet I say it again, you should be able to defeat me.'

Finn shook his head. He held his weapon out in front of him. 'I'm only fifteen –'

'Age has nothing to do with it,' said Kemi. 'The same goes for size. You potentially have a strength and speed I could never hope to understand. You have it as a birth right. Come … let us see if we can force it out.'

And so it had gone, with Kemi putting Finn through his paces for the entirety of the first morning. The overriding test was as he had promised, fighting with only the yantok at first, and having been provided with a few basic pointers Finn had failed in almost every discipline, showing no great aptitude for defence or attack. The energy he was also asked to expel was brutally unfair and he found himself jumping, ducking, twisting, jogging, skipping, kicking, he had to do everything and was afforded very little recovery time between each activity.

Finn had no shame in admitting that he became lost and that the melees turned into one long, surreal haze. The *Filipino Eskrima* quickly stopped and the test moved north and onto the Japanese incarnations, to *Kendo*, *Karate*, *Jujitsu*, and a whole host of other variations, most of which Finn had never even heard of. It didn't matter. He was useless at them all. Still Kemi did have some sympathy. Although he had struck Finn everywhere else with the yantok and later his fists, he never struck him in the head or the face.

'What's the point in all of this?' Finn had complained at one stage after a particularly exhausting and epic fail. He was sitting on the mat and nursing a bruise on his shin and dripping with sweat. 'So what? I suck at this! I've not seen it, granted, but I bet you any money the stupid book you all keep going on about says I'm going to be strong, not that I'm going to be Bruce Lee?'

265

'I said I would test you,' said Kemi smiling. He offered a hand and pulled Finn to his feet. 'When did I say that I was going to turn you into a Kung Fu Master in one morning?'

'This isn't working –'

'It's day one –'

'None of this makes sense to me!' That was a lie. Finn had twigged a fair few hours ago. He had realised that Kemi wasn't actually trying to teach him anything. He was simply just providing wave after wave of attack in the hope that Finn would suddenly feel a twitch in his stomach, a knowing explosion of energetic wisdom in his brain or a burst of anger and transform in a split second into a mobile, ruthless, killing machine.

'I've got nothing left!' Finn said, admitting defeat. He bent down and clutched his knees in exhaustion.

Disappointed, Kemi pushed him no further and attempted to move on to a different, less aggressive method. He started by testing Finn's reflexes and acquired a selection of small balls made from leather. He then persisted to launch the balls at Finn at varying speeds and from different angles with the only instruction being that he needed to make contact with the balls using the palm of his hand. He had hit a few but missed far more.

Then Kemi had repeated the process but this time Finn was blindfolded. In the dark he failed to make contact with any of the circular projectiles. On more than one occasion the ball had struck him square in the face.

The flexibility test fared even worse. Kemi had set up a series of boards and towers and with instructions that Finn needed to balance on top of them, he put Finn to work. Again, he failed in every aspect and did not demonstrate any strength beyond what would be expected of a normal individual, which more often than not involved falling to the floor.

In the final hour Kemi had gone as far as to cut his own finger with a small axe to try and drive out the ability to heal but as with everything else he just bled and Finn could offer nothing other than a plaster to staunch the bleeding.

When it was all over they sat together on the dojo mats and Kemi worked his way through a simple pack of playing cards, asking Finn to guess which card would come next. Finn was so tired he didn't care and he put very little effort in and he didn't get any right. He understood that this was a basic test but even the basic was too much.

By the time Finn was permitted to stand he realised that his spectators were long gone. It was by that time Saturday and he had been scheduled to meet Bronwyn upstairs in her quarters but making it slowly upwards he bumped into her on the staircase. Seeing the extent of his fatigue she had allowed him to take the afternoon off and rest. The education could wait and Willoughby had not been happy. For the rest of the day Finn slept and he didn't wake until one day had expired and another had arrived to take its place.

The second day went pretty much exactly the same way as the first. Kemi tested him in exactly the same way and Finn failed in exactly the same way. He could see the change of look in the African's eyes as the morning wore on. Slowly, minute by minute, Kemi was becoming convinced that Finn did not have any powers at all and the light of enthusiasm was dwindling down to extinction. And if Finn did not have any powers this strange prophecy that Willoughby seemed convinced was true was starting to look more and more unlikely.

The fact was not lost upon Finn and it was that thought more than any other that stayed with him that Sunday morning as he sat in the library watching the snow fall down onto the passing public.

He forced himself to move and he got up with a hefty groan, the pain immense in the top of his thighs and around his buttocks. He moved to the window so he could get a better view of the street. He couldn't help but envy those that walked past and he watched them for a great deal longer. They were carefree people living in a carefree world. They didn't have his troubles and his fears. Some of them would have stresses no doubt but none of them could compete with his. They simply got up each morning, went about their business and finished their days without any true demons to keep them awake.

He had been like that *once* and he wished with all his heart that he could be like that again. The initial excitement at his predicament was over. Now was the time for the stark reality and the reality suddenly stopped whetting an appetite and instead left a sour taste.

'Penny for your thoughts?' said a voice from behind him.

Bronwyn was strolling into the library, carrying a stack of books with her and a leather satchel draped across her shoulder. As always seemed to be the case with these people the books were old and crumbling. She was dressed in her Sunday clothes, a baggy pair of trousers and a pink woollen jumper.

She placed the books down onto the table and hung the satchel on the back of the chair. She took her seat. 'I don't think you'll be shocked to learn that I find etymology fascinating,' she said. 'And finding the origins of little sayings *really* is interesting. Still, penny for your thoughts! I can't quite remember where that one comes from.'

Finn didn't say anything. He had nothing to offer anyway. He was aware of how his personality worked. When he was tired, he became silly. He became sarcastic and flippant. He had wondered what he and Felicity would be like on such an occasion. Tired and grumpy, he would give her a run for her money.

'You look a bit more awake than yesterday,' she noticed. 'But a great deal sadder, I would say.'

'I'm failing,' Finn said gravely, the sarcasm at bay for now. 'And I mean I'm failing big time. I don't think I'm the person these people think I am. I can't do anything that Kemi is showing me.'

'I think you should have a bit more patience,' said Bronwyn reassuringly. 'That goes for both you and Willoughby. These things don't happen overnight. And also don't be so quick to bet against yourself. The problem these days is that *everything* is instant and *everything* needs to be had and achieved right now. People wait for nothing. People aren't prepared to. In times gone by you had to save and make sacrifices before getting what you wanted. Now you just get it on credit. When people have *everything* they understand the value of *nothing*. There is a reason why some people used to claim that patience is a virtue.'

'But this is different,' said Finn.

'I don't see it as different,' said Bronwyn. 'No, I would imagine that if you truly are the child that has been prophesised then the truth will find its own way of coming to you and in its own time. Willoughby is trying to force it out of you and perhaps that isn't the way. But come, we can worry about that another time. This afternoon I need to hold up my end of the bargain I struck. Come, sit with me, Finn.'

Finn sat back down but still he found little to be cheerful about.

Bronwyn pulled the first book from the pile and placed it in front of her. 'The book that the others are going off to try and purchase from Mr Grayson is one that none of us here have ever seen,' she said. She ran her fingertips over the cover of the book in front of her. 'This isn't it. But the book I have here was written by a chap who *did* see that book hundreds of years ago and he duplicated a lot of the information in his own work. So the advice in these pages is second hand but I am of the firm belief that it's an accurate depiction of what the author saw. It's all written by hand and in a language very few people will recognise but I can translate easily enough.'

Finn pulled a face. 'My history teacher told me I should never pay much attention to something that is written second hand.'

'And why?'

'Because it's tainted by opinion,' Finn said, 'the position and views can be prejudiced.' He smiled at his own insight, smug, surprised that he had remembered that.

'And your teacher is right,' said Bronwyn. 'But not on this occasion. See, I knew the author of this book. He was a dear friend. He is greatly missed and he was only writing about what he saw, not his views.'

'You all keep going on about books,' said Finn. He yawned. 'But I'm not sure what it is, all these gospels. What is the Gospel of Iris?'

'Now, that is an excellent question,' Bronwyn said. She opened the cover of her book, showing a handwritten title. It was indeed in a strange, unknown language. 'Iris was the name of the first of our kind, the mother of our people. She was born only a few hundred years after the dawn of time.'

Finn seemed to always be yawning in Bronwyn's presence and another was starting to brew. He struggled to keep it under control and rather than trying he just let it rip, roaring like a tired lion. He instantly regretted it. It must have looked very rude.

Bronwyn closed the book. 'People have been talking to you like this a lot recently, haven't they?' she said sympathetically. 'They've sat you down and thrown all these barrages of information your way, haven't they? It must be impossible for you to digest it all. I can't even begin to understand what you must be thinking right now. Fortunately we won't be doing any reading today. No, I have a far more beneficial way of going about this.'

She reached around to the back of the chair and removed a number of items from her satchel, placing them carefully onto the table. There was a thick, tall candle wedged solidly into an iron holder that was shaped like the face of a growling goblin and a large translucent beaker that had a strange liquid floating inside. The liquid was mostly clear but it had swirls of a subtle yellow dilution and floating within were numerous small balls that due to their black colour looked a lot like peppercorns. The final items were two golden goblets that were decorated with a selection of colourful jewels.

Bronwyn rearranged the table into something more suitable. She scooped the pile of books away and placed them on the floor, all but the book she had already spoken about, which she opened up to a particular page and a particular passage. She moved the book so that it was positioned perfectly in the centre of the table, the centrepiece. Then she carefully balanced the candle on top of the book so that it wouldn't topple and moved the goblets so that they were on either side of the volume and in front of both she and Finn.

'I rarely do this,' she said as she lit the candle. 'Paper and fire have never been the best of friends and the same can be said for papyrus. This is also black magic which although isn't quite as bad as it sounds is still something it's never particularly a good idea to dabble with. But this is one of those occasions where needs must.'

The candle safely lit, Bronwyn carefully removed the lid from the beaker and poured the liquid content equally between the two goblets. As the liquid made contact with the gold of the goblet it fizzed loudly and a strong mist emanated from inside. She placed the empty beaker on the floor.

'It looks a little like something from a cheesy horror movie,' Finn joked, peering over the rim of the goblet. Due to the mist he was unable to see the liquid inside. He tried to smell it but it was odourless. 'What is it? Is it safe to drink dry ice?'

'Oh, it has no name,' Bronwyn answered.

'In that case,' said Finn smiling, incorporating the theatrical pizazz of a magician, 'I shall call it *Flame Juice*. If you have trouble remembering it, just think of a juice that's on fire!' Next, he impersonated the announcer of a marketing campaign. '*Flame Juice, puts hairs on your chest or it burns them off.*'

'As good a name as any,' said Bronwyn, happy to play along. 'Flame Juice comes from a very old spell that a friend of mine happened to know. I say a friend, but again I actually mean the author of the book in front of us. I do miss him. It's a very potent potion, Finn, and it is perfectly harmless but put bluntly it enables you to see the past when consumed in conjunction with a certain set of words. I just think that perhaps it will be better for me to show you, rather than read it to you. Willoughby thinks so too.'

'I don't understand,' said Finn. 'How exactly will Flame Juice make me see the past?'

'Does everything in life need an explanation?' said Bronwyn. 'Some things just … are.' She watched his reaction, seeing that he wasn't buying it. 'Ok, people tend to think of time as something that comes and goes and once it has gone it can never be recovered. Strictly speaking that's not actually the case. Let me try and apply some logic. Life and therefore time begins on a blank canvas. Time itself is the artist, the world is the canvas. And as time moves, the canvas doesn't grow or change shape, it just sits there and the artist simply paints over what has gone before it. The past is still there it just can't be seen over what's been painted on top of it, if that makes sense? You can't see it normally but if you scratch the surface of the canvas then sometimes little bits of the past can reveal themselves and you can see them in all their glory.'

'Brain is still frazzled,' Finn confessed. 'I kinda get what you're trying to say but not sure why it's relevant and that was a rubbish comparison, no offence. It's all a bit hippy for my liking.'

Bronwyn tilted her head, watching him. 'Are you always this narky when you're tired?'

'Oh yes,' Finn admitted. 'Give me an hour. That's when I start to get hungry, goes proper downhill then.'

'It is relevant, Finn,' said Bronwyn, moving swiftly on, 'because the past never leaves us. It still exists. It is all around us. And I am going to show you it.' She pointed at the empty beaker. 'And it's a damn sight easier if you're privy to certain black magic. Please, place your index finger on the candlestick holder and keep your hands within the vehicle at all times.'

Finn leaned forward and did as he was instructed. Bronwyn did the same and then she glanced down at the book and fixed her gaze upon a certain passage.

'With your free hand,' she said, suddenly seriously. 'Pick up the goblet and drink. Make sure though that you do not remove your finger from the goblin at any time.'

Finn drank the liquid in one and instantly regretted it. The liquid tasted wretched and was almost acidic and as it funnelled down through his body he felt like his insides were burning. Flame Juice was indeed a good name. He shook and almost removed his finger but through the pain he managed to keep it on the goblin shaped candle holder as instructed.

Bronwyn began to recite from the book. The passage was short and sweet and she didn't bother to translate it into English. 'Render malicore ams thus candour malikay –'

The flame of the candle flickered gently.

'Render mandicore ams thus candour malikay,' she said, a small variation in the wording.

Again the flame flickered, a little more forcefully this time.

'Render semifale ams thou candour malikay,' Bronwyn said next.

The candle didn't move. It started to get brighter.

Finn started to become aware of what was happening but he said nothing and just watched it unfold around him. The room was slowly becoming darker as if an eclipse was occurring outside the window. The darkness kept coming and soon most of the room was cloaked in shadow.

He could no longer see the far side of the room or the staircase. He tried to look out the window. The pedestrians were gone, darkness replacing it. Quickly the table was then absorbed by the gloom and then Bronwyn herself disappeared. All the while the candle kept burning brightly, the focal point, all that was left of the light and the world. The room grew extremely cold and a strong wind struck his face. He heard her voice in the darkness.

'Whatever happens,' she said. 'Don't remove your finger from the goblin whilst it's dark. And we only watch.'

'I feel really silly saying this but I'm a bit scared,' said Finn honestly. 'And I'm really cold.'

'Cold is normal, don't worry.'

'I can feel a wind on my face too! Did you fart?'

'This will sound really clichéd but those are the winds of time,' said Bronwyn. 'And if my example you felt was poor before, try this. This spell treats time like the surface of the water. When the water is calm it is the *present*. Our spell has disturbed the water and caused ripples. The ripples are the past. And we are going to use the ripples for me to show you everything you need to know. The ripples will of course disappear.'

Chapter Thirty-Six

The wind died. Its emergence had been brief, stopping as suddenly as it had begun. Finn wasn't sure what to expect. He waited patiently, still groggy from the power of the liquid, a distant hint of a brewing headache. A small source of light started to glow out in the far reaches of the darkness. He squinted, trying to judge the distance, deducing that it was far away from the warmth of the burning candle and certainly a great deal further than the nearest library wall. The circular light itself, minute at first, slowly started to grow in size and as it got larger the smothering darkness all around it started to react to its touch and dominance. A form of daylight was coming.

He kept his eyes focused on the light. It was getting closer and closer, bigger and bigger, brighter and brighter. Very quickly he was forced to close his eyes to shield them from the painful glare.

There were sounds now, very faint at first but soon loud enough to identify the source. He could make out the tranquil twitter of birdsong and the soothing hum of running water. Then there came the subtle aromas and sensations, the wafts of fresh unpolluted air and the scents of potent, damp grass, and blooming flowers. The senses were certainly not ones that he had expected to be piqued in a dusty old library on a cold afternoon.

'You should open your eyes now,' Bronwyn said softly. She was still with him at least. 'It's time to begin. We don't get long here.'

Finn did as instructed and removed his hand from his eyes. The view that greeted him was so surprisingly majestic that he couldn't help but gasp in awe. The library was indeed long gone, every last inch of it devoured by the power of the potion, and had been replaced by a thick forest of green trees, tall grass, and an array of colourful plants. The tree line was low and the leaves and branches created a natural canopy overhead, the sunlight streaking in through any gaps where it could breach. In the distance and in a clearing a great waterfall dropped down from somewhere up high and out of sight, the water pooling into a luscious lagoon that was as blue as the most impressive sapphire. The lagoon was surrounded by slippery grey rocks of all shapes and sizes and from it there flowed a thin river that weaved throughout the forest.

'Where *are* we?' he asked, unashamedly amazed. A series of colourful butterflies floated past his face. The flapping wings made him dizzy. 'I feel really, really funky right now.'

'We're in one of the ripples I spoke about,' said Bronwyn. The book was still resting where they had left it and their fingers were still placed on the candle holder. The candle was happily sitting there on the open page, lit and burning and showing no signs of going out. The table beneath was the only piece of actual furniture that had survived the transition, coming along for the ride. 'We've disturbed the water now, no going back. Welcome to the past, the oddest frontier you're ever likely to explore. We call these visions, so you know.'

'Where's the library actually gone?' Finn asked, looking all around him. 'Has it actually gone anywhere?'

'We're still in the library,' said Bronwyn casually. 'It hasn't gone anywhere. Anyone finds us back in the present and we'll just look like we're asleep and no amount of shaking will wake us. There's no real way of physically taking our bodies to the past. It's our minds that have brought us here.' She took her finger off the candle holder. 'You can do the same, if you wish. We just need to make sure they're back in place before the end. That's important.'

Finn followed her lead, removing his finger just as a woman emerged from the tall grass in front of him. The woman was dressed in a white robe and her hair was wrapped up in some form of silk cloth to make a neat headdress. A few tufts of deep brown hair escaped, lulling across her neck. In her hands she carried a baby boy and at her feet two further children, another dark haired boy and a blonde girl no older than two or three, walked slowly beside her. Each child's hair was curly and thick. The children were naked.

When the woman got to the water's edge she stopped and tested the waters depth carefully with her right foot. Satisfied she paddled into the water up to her ankles and placed the baby down so he could sit safely. She supported the baby's back with her palm and sat herself down next to the child, her robe floating and resting on the surface. She began to wash the baby's hair, pouring water that she collected with her cupped spare hand. The current was timid and was not dangerous.

The other two children threw themselves into the water and laughed, playing and splashing around with one another giddily, filling the air with the endearing hum of children's delight. The woman started to sing in a foreign tongue as she pressed her fingers through the child's hair, cleansing it. The song was some form of unintelligible but undeniably beautiful, haunting lullaby.

'We need to take ourselves back to places like this,' said Bronwyn. Together with Finn they walked to the water's edge, positioning themselves on the opposite side of the bank to the woman. 'We need to meet some of the people who are going to be of the upmost importance to your future. If I make you understand the beginning you've more chance of understanding the end. Once we're back in the library, I can explain how it all slots together. I won't lie. It will be a lot to take in so you'll need to concentrate.'

'Who is she?' Finn said. He was captivated by the power of the woman's presence. He didn't understand a single word of the lullaby but it was soothing to him all the same. He wished he could translate the language and understand the lyrics, which must have been gorgeous. And he wished he had a similar memory with his own mother.

'Her name is Iris,' said Bronwyn. 'I'm sure you've heard her name mentioned before. She was the first of our kind, all that time ago —'

'How long?'

'Longer than most can ever imagine or contemplate,' Bronwyn said. 'Personally, and as amazing as it may sound, I would put the date around three hundred years after the dawn of time.' She looked to read his reaction. 'Has the potential to make you shiver, doesn't it, that thought?'

'She's so beautiful,' Finn noted. He was too entranced by the woman to shiver. There was just something about her, like she was the epitome of grace. 'Like, really beautiful.'

'She was,' Bronwyn agreed. 'This is my perception of how she looked. She may have looked completely different –'

'I thought this was all real?' Finn said.

'It is,' Bronwyn said. 'For some reason the spell shows you the events, shows you the environments but it doesn't show you the faces. That bit you've got to do for yourself. The faces are imprinted from my perceptions. But I've read enough about all the people we'll see to be confident their images are accurate.'

The woman finished washing the hair of the child in her arms and she wiped some rogue water away from his eyes. Then she placed the child down into the water, letting him play, all the while continuing to support the back so the baby didn't topple over. She smiled lovingly, happily going about her work.

'She's mentioned in thousands of books,' Bronwyn said. 'We've done superbly over the centuries, keeping most of it in our own libraries and out of the public domain. We couldn't keep the Greeks from talking about her though. They were a bunch of chatterboxes, the ancient Greeks. A lot of their stuff is still out there. They spoke about Iris linking the God's to humanity. She's cited as God's messenger and the Greeks honoured her for that. They worshiped her.'

Finn nodded. That part at least, based on the view, made sense to him. 'So she was a God?'

'No,' said Bronwyn. 'They only thought of her as one and wrote about her as one. I guess, back then, they may have had their reasons to think such a thing.'

'Does that not bother you?' Finn wondered. 'That anyone can read about her?'

'Not really,' said Bronwyn. 'They have her as an immortal God, not an immortal woman. She exists amongst the Zeus's and the Prometheus's of this world, simple myths, hence why there's no danger in the books and art staying out there. But she was there, we know that, still alive, walking amongst them.'

Iris looked up suddenly from the water. Finn seemed to catch her eye. She was looking right at him. Or at least that was how it seemed.

'Don't worry,' Bronwyn said. She chuckled. 'She can't see you. She's just looking through you. I think something moved back there in the forest.'

Finn laughed but his expression was sad. 'I'm very used to females looking straight through me.'

'The girl you came here with doesn't look through you,' Bronwyn suggested.

'No, but she hates me.'

Bronwyn shook her head. 'It doesn't take enhanced wisdom to see that's not true.'

Iris scooped the infant from the water and she called for the other children to follow her. She started to walk towards dry land.

'She was the first of our kind,' said Bronwyn. 'She's the mother of us all. I don't know whether she was a mistake or one of God's little experiments. Who knows? I like to think that at the beginning perhaps God didn't know whether to populate his lands with immortal creatures or creatures with a shelf life. So she was his test.'

Finn watched as Iris placed the baby boy on the side of the bank, instructing his brother and sister to look after him. With the baby sat there and content, she walked back into the river, wading into a deeper area. She allowed herself to fall backwards, floating onto her back, the water covering her body. 'Did she have powers?' he asked, still fascinated with the concept.

'Only one,' said Bronwyn, 'that of foresight. That is why the book we call The Gospel of Iris is so important. There was only ever one copy, written by her own hand, and that's why I sent the others to meet with Mr Mellors.'

'Why?' Finn said. 'Why is it so important?'

'The book has three parts,' Bronwyn answered. There was a howl of a wolf somewhere in the trees but Iris didn't flinch. 'The first two parts will be of no consequence, just observations of the world at the time, interesting yes, but not overly relevant. It's the third part that will be so important. My friend who was so good to teach me this whole spell, he saw the book once, long before I was born, and he copied parts of it but he was killed in an accident a long time ago. The book then disappeared. No one living has seen the book in its entirety. The whole third part is said to contain the detail of her foresight. It speaks of a whole host of things that are yet to pass. It speaks about what you were born to do.'

Finn looked away from the floating woman for the first time. 'What I am born to do?'

'Later,' said Bronwyn. She guided him back to the table and nodded for him to replace his finger on the candle holder. 'Let's get through this first.'

There was a distant rumble of thunder. Then, as it had in the library, the world started to grow dark. The darkness came quickly and within a few seconds the woman and her children were gone, the landscape was gone, fading into nothingness and all that remained once more was the light of the candle.

In the darkness, Finn had a question. 'Is she dead?'

Bronwyn chose not to answer. A familiar circle of light was forming out there. The light came quicker than it had before and within seconds the curtain was coming up on a new play.

The scene was vastly different this time around. The landscape was open and as far as the eye could see there were small citrus groves, one after another, growing in small, neat squares. All around the groves the ground was beige, rocky, and scorched. A hedge had prospered despite the obvious challenges to irrigation and it sat at the end of the last citrus cluster, huge and towering, the natural structure sweeping far into the distance in both directions. Beyond the hedge and up high there were three hills of differing sizes. On each hill was a grand castle.

The citrus groves and the paths around them were full of people, hundreds of them. The people were black skinned and they were working the land ardently, harvesting a variety of oranges, lemons, and desert limes and sweating in the harshness of the summer temperature. They used old, small tools that barely seemed fitting for the task at hand. None of them were smiling or speaking as they worked. The land lay eerily silent despite the presence of life.

'You never paid much attention to the children,' said Bronwyn. 'People don't tend to, such was Iris's beauty. But they're just as interesting as their mother. You see Iris accomplished something that none of us have ever managed since. She had *immortal* children, all three of them. And once they had Settled they had powers that were of the strong and fast grades.'

Finn liked the thought of that and it made him feel warm inside. The place they had just left had an impact on him and he was certain the image of the children playing with their mother in the river would stay with him for a long time afterwards and give him great comfort whenever he might need it.

'Here they come,' Bronwyn said. She pointed forward.

Three horses burst through the large hedge. On each of the horses there was a rider, two men and a woman. The woman rode out in front, her figure slim and her long blonde hair flowing behind her in the wind. She wore a sleeveless tunic that exposed her bare arms and a pair of long, leather trousers. The two men who followed could have been twins, their black hair the same long length, their beards the same thickness and their eyes battling each other to be angriest. They were tall men and they rode huge warhorses. They wore similar clothing to the woman and their muscular arms glistened with sweat.

The three riders did not share the skin colour of the people working the fields. They were white. And in their hands they carried long scythes which they allowed to dangle so that the blades only just scraped the surface of the ground as they galloped. It was clear. Slave-owners were approaching.

'They've grown, haven't they?' said Bronwyn. She pointed to each rider in turn. 'Meet Isaac, Evaine, and Tobias.'

Something sinister started to unfold in the fields. The riders charged furiously though the groves and in amongst the farmers. The farmers paid them no attention. They didn't turn around or cry out, even when the riders started to sweep their scythes high and pick their targets, cutting their people down at random with the blades. Within a few minutes more than thirty of the farmers lay dead upon the ground. Their colleagues ignored the bodies, refusing to turn around and check their pulses or offer any form of assistance. They simply stared at the groves, filling their baskets and hoping with all their silent hearts that they would not incur the attention and wrath of their Masters.

Almost as if they had fulfilled a macabre quota, the riders then disappeared, riding back through the hedge from whence they came and back towards their mighty castles on the hills.

A selection of reactionary words stuck in Finn's throat, a throat that had grown dry. He could say nothing and could only stare at the bodies on the ground. He was repulsed. The image that sixty seconds ago he had considered to be a source of comfort now left him confused. The memory had been truly soiled by the violent one that had replaced it.

Bronwyn was reading his mind. 'The greatest monsters in history no doubt didn't look like monsters in the cradle, Finn,' she nodded in the direction of the hills. 'They've gone back to their castles now, back to sit on their thrones.'

'Thrones?' Finn said. 'Who would make them Kings and Queens?'

'They had great power,' Bronwyn explained, 'so they made themselves Kings and Queens. And with their great power came their great madness. Time can do that to you. I've seen it happen many times.'

Finn was about ready to throw up. He forced himself to look away from the bodies. 'Why did they just murder their own people like that?'

'A frequent habit of tyrants,' said Bronwyn. 'What better way to demand obedience, by ensuring that all who stand in your way live in a perpetual state of fear.'

'They looked so cute earlier –'

'What you just saw was sport,' Bronwyn said, 'nothing else. There's a host of accounts that still exist that speak of the sibling's brutality. Towards the end it was said that the two boys became obsessed with the worst of black magic. There are some stories that would give you nightmares. One I recall speaks of Isaac having changed into a shapeshifter, another that Tobias mastered the art of disappearing into thin air. We're talking about the type of magic that hasn't been seen in thousands of years.'

'Are *they* still alive?' Finn asked, fearing the answer.

'I wouldn't have thought so,' Bronwyn said. 'I would say they're long dead. No one has seen any of them for many, many years. The last account of any of them in literature was of Evaine in a book from some time in the dark ages. Tyrants rarely live forever. Fear keeps people prisoner for a time but it usually just gives way to rebellion. Of course every now and again someone will claim they've seen one of the siblings or are working for them, but it's never true.'

A familiar darkness started to creep down from the horizon. This time, Finn was happy and relieved to be leaving this image firmly in the past.

'They all wrote their books too,' said Bronwyn. 'Your father had a copy of one written by the girl. They are so very, very valuable and don't come out into the open all that often, hence our excitement.'

Darkness devoured the world once more. The citrus groves and castles faded into memory.

'Why did you show me that?' Finn said. Knowing the score, he had already returned to the table without the need for prompting, his finger replaced to aid the odd ritual.

'I know it wasn't easy to watch,' said Bronwyn, 'but you needed to see it. You needed to see what power can do to you.

And if, by the very slimmest of chances they are alive, it's likely the siblings will seek you out.'

That was troubling. Finn understood the thinly veiled warnings all too well. He had to have at least some of the sibling's powers. He had been as innocent as the children wading in the water. What could he turn into? And more worryingly of all was the notion of having to face any of the horrid riders.

The light returned and they were now inside the confines of a cold, dark room. The room belonged to the tower of a castle, a small slit of a window showing the tops of trees and rolling hills outside. It was raining. The room was circular and filled with a terrific array of scientific instruments. Bronwyn instantly provided a lesson, showing Finn things he had never seen or heard of, pointing out the armillary spheres sitting on tables, the astrolabe's hanging from hooks on the wall, the astronomical compendium pieces, the celestial globes and the diptych dials lining dozens of shelves, each piece beautifully intricate and shiny. In the centre of the room was a small cauldron, a round table, and sprawled across the floor were hundreds of books.

Two men were in the room with them. Both men wore long black robes with hoods. They appeared to be monks or druids or something of the sort. The first man, the taller man, was standing over the other, having the look of a superior. The smaller man was grinding brittle pieces of rock into a powder within a pestle and mortar.

Finn stepped carefully forward, trying not to stumble on any books. Something immediately caught his eye, an item that stood out amongst the rest as it seemed to have no right to be there. In the middle of the glitz and bling of the other instruments, a simple ceramic pot sat on a shelf. All around the top of the opening the pot had sharp cracks and dents.

'That's a Hessian Crucible,' said Bronwyn. She joined Finn at the shelf. 'They're made to withstand very hot temperatures. I've got one back in the library, I'll show you later.' She pulled Finn around so he could focus on the two men. They watched them go about their work. 'Have you ever heard of something called

Alchemy, Finn? I doubt you'd come across it in a science lesson these days but perhaps history?'

Finn shook his head. He had never heard of it.

'I won't go into it in great detail,' Bronwyn said, 'for there would be an awful lot to tell and alchemy is one of history's greatest practical jokes. You'll find thousands of articles about it on the internet, ninety-nine per cent of which are generally nonsense. But as an overview it goes like this. Alchemy is supposed to be a philosophical belief with three main goals, one, to have the ability to create the Philosophers Stone, two to be able to transmute standard metals into more valuable metals, like gold or silver, and three, to create something known as the Elixir of Life. There were a host of Alchemists who claimed they had managed to achieve all three. They didn't. They either lied or were just quite mad.'

'Are these two Alfimists?' said Finn, referring to the two men working before them.

'Alchemists,' Bronwyn corrected him. 'I'll write it down for you at some point so you remember the term.' She gestured towards the taller man. '*He* is *the* alchemist. There was only ever one. Meet Arthur Huxley. He's one of us.'

Finn wanted to take a closer look but he couldn't make out the man's features beneath his hood. It was most strange, in that whatever angle he tilted or twisted his head the shadows in the room reacted, keeping Arthur Huxley's features perpetually obscured.

'Arthur's gifts were odd ones,' said Bronwyn. She walked forward, hovering a few inches behind Arthur Huxley's back, close enough to watch over the work of his assistant. 'He had a few and they are things that no one had seen before or has ever seen since. Firstly, Arthur Huxley and Arthur Huxley alone could turn metal into gold. For years he thought he was doing it through some elaborate experiment, without realising he had been born with the ability. Beyond that he could also grind a stone into a liquid elixir. Again it was an ability he had from birth. There were no spells. No methods, it was the simple gift that immortality afforded him.'

'That's so specific,' Finn noted. He had picked up on the bespoke nature of the power. 'The rest of us, it's all kind of … general … if you know what I mean. We have strength and speed and things like that. Turning metal into gold seems weird and out of place and a bit pointless.'

'Pointless like wisdom?' Bronwyn said through a wry smile. 'It will all come together later, I promise.'

The smaller monk rose from the table and he moved to a shelf, Finn and Bronwyn moving politely out of his way. He picked up the item identified as the Hessian Crucible. Very carefully he shook the powder from his mortar bowl inside the crucible and brought it back to the table. Arthur Huxley leaned over, examining the work.

'Huxley started using his gift long before he Settled,' said Bronwyn, 'and long before he knew that he was immortal. Thus the concept of alchemy was born from his own delusion. His work was already written about extensively and studied across Europe and Asia before he knew the truth. Arthur was the focal point of the whole movement and after he realised it was all rubbish he still didn't want to lose the credibility that his life's work had given him. So he kept the lie of alchemy going throughout the centuries, popping up here and there when he could. So many people devoted their lives trying to master a craft which could never be mastered. There were never Alchemists. There was only ever one.'

Finn again tried to see the man's face but again was defeated by the shadows. For a split second he thought he might get a good view, as Arthur Huxley took the crucible to the cauldron and placed it inside. But all he saw was the edge of a nose, which gave nothing away.

'Which brings us to the infamous Philosophers Stone,' said Bronwyn. 'The stone is an utter legend, spanning back long before Arthur was born. He used the concept to enhance his own lie. In theory, so it goes, the stone is what is called an alchemical substance with which an 'alchemist' can make their gold but also make the elixir of life.'

'I don't know what that is,' Finn admitted. 'You mentioned that before.'

'Put simply, an elixir is a liquid that is supposed to grant everlasting life,' said Bronwyn. 'It is said that if you drink the liquid in the right place at the right time and within the right cup, you could live forever. The truth was that there was always only one stone that Arthur alone could grind and with it he could make his metals and his potions. Alchemy was simply a ruse so that people could worship him. The concept of the Philosophers Stone was a fabrication so that people would search for it long after he was supposed to have died and keep the legend alive. I would imagine he liked nothing more than to see mortal men toil and waste their lives trying to replicate his examples and experiments.'

'I don't really understand,' said Finn, feeling more than a bit thick. 'I get Iris. I get the kids. Why does any of this matter?'

'This is where we go back to The Book of Iris,' Bronwyn said. She was in her element, clearly loving the telling of her stories. 'Iris foretold of Huxley's birth, of the man who could create gold from his fingertips and life from a liquid. And she went on to say something very significant in the form of three rules for the elixir. The first said that the elixir would grant eternal life if consumed by a *mortal*, the second that it would take life away if consumed by an *immortal* –'

The room was getting darker, rapidly so, the vision coming to an end.

Bronwyn panicked and didn't finish reading off the list of rules. She urged Finn back to the candle holder. 'Quick,' she said, making sure both their fingertips were touching the metal, 'we can't be away from it when the visions end. This is the last one. When the light comes back we'll be back in the library.'

The routine unfolded once more, darkness followed by light. But this time as the circle of light appeared something was different. The light was very clearly a flickering orange.

Finn could make out Bronwyn's face, illuminated by the approaching light. She was transfixed and she was puzzled.

'That's most peculiar,' she said, 'that shouldn't be happening! At least it's never happened before! How intriguing!'

A fourth impromptu vision presented itself with a brutal clamour of noise. The darkness died in a flash. They were back in the world of the first vision, where they had seen Iris and her children. But things were different. *Very different.* Everything was on fire. The grass and plants were aflame and the flames were wild and high, burning with a furious rage. The overhead canopy of the treeline was gone, decimated and exposing a sky that was an overcast grey. Even the river was dominated by the will of the fire, the flames settling on the surface and the water doing nothing to abate the sizzling power. The air was choked with black ash.

Bronwyn was less casual now and looking all around herself with bafflement. This wasn't her doing and she didn't know how to react or what to do. 'I don't know what this is,' she said, having to scream loudly to be heard above the noise of the chaos. 'Don't let go of the candle holder! I don't know when this might fade!'

'What's going on?' Finn asked urgently.

'I don't know.'

'You don't know?'

Bronwyn was silent. If she didn't know, just who would?

They saw her then, both at the same time, Iris. She was in the same area that they had left her, but she was kneeling by the side of the river. She looked the same, still beautiful. But she looked tired and she looked defeated. Her children were gone and she was knelt with her eyes closed. It looked like she was praying.

'*You* are driving this,' said Bronwyn, suddenly realising. 'Never in my wildest dreams –'

'Wait,' said Finn. 'What is the –'

A figure emerged from the burning grass. It was a young boy and he walked out casually and with a look on his face that was both mean and menacing and in his hands he carried a grotesquely large battle axe, the handle a striking black. The boy was very, very familiar.

'That's …' Finn couldn't quite say it at first. 'That's … me –'

That is Finn Carruthers. That is me! What am I doing here?

A strong wind started to pick up and on the wind the darkness of the visions end came, sending long swirling streaks across the sizzling scene. Parts of the world started to distort and shimmer.

'It's ending,' Bronwyn shouted.

Finn had to duck beneath one such thick black streak of darkness to continue watching. He witnessed his doppelganger raise the battle axe high above his head and strike down, ready to remove Iris's head in one swift stroke. The vision ended a split second before Iris's beautiful head was primed to roll across the ground.

Then it was over. They were back in the library.

Finn jumped up from the table, not realising that his legs were wobbly and unstable and he fell to the ground dramatically, ending in a crumpled heap on the library floor. The room was exactly as they had left it but it was now early evening and darker. Outside the round window the snow was falling extremely heavily.

Bronwyn tried to grab Finn by the hand to help him up but he struck her hand away and staggered backwards across the floor, ending up with his back against the wall. 'What was that?' he screamed. 'What the *hell* was that?'

'Finn,' Bronwyn urged, 'please come back to the table and I'll explain –' She reached out once more but again he slapped her hand away. 'I'm not trying to hide anything from you,' she tried to reassure him. 'But you need to calm down a touch. Please?'

'Bronwyn,' he said, making it clear he would go nowhere without an explanation, 'what the *hell* was that?'

Bronwyn saw that she had no choice. 'I think it was a vision from the future,' she said, 'driven by you, not me. I had no idea that could even happen –'

'That can't be my future –' He waited for Bronwyn's contradiction but it never came. 'Tell me,' he said with his eyes wide with horror, 'you tell me now, tell me that's not my future.'

Bronwyn sat down on the floor with him. 'The third rule,' she said, returning to the explanation of the Elixir of Life that she

288

hadn't finished, 'states that when the elixir is consumed by the first of the immortal kind, Iris, it will take away *all* unnatural life and end the line of the immortals forever.' She started to recite a familiar and well known passage. Her choice of wording differed a little from Willoughby's favoured version. 'From a storm of ice and crystal the child shall be born, coming forth, the first of his kind, the last of his kind, the end of the circle, the last circle, the completion of the promise of obsidian. He shall be thy deliverer, thy end, thy peace, thy hope, thy redemption, thy darkness and thy dwindling light.'

Finn recalled Willoughby's earlier words, the night they had met. Willoughby had feared that being told too much would be an information dump and that he wouldn't understand. But Bronwyn's visions had not left him much better off. He had taken in every last snippet of information but still was utterly lost.

'Obsidian has always been the key,' Bronwyn tried to explain. 'Iris wrote about it in great depth. Others saw it and wrote about it so we've always been aware of it. Obsidian, at the beginning was known as God's rock, unique and beautiful. And in ancient times it had spiritual powers that other materials didn't, back when there was more magic in the world. Can you guess which rock it was that Arthur Huxley needed to use to create gold and silver and the Elixir?'

'Obsidian,' said Finn. At least that was obvious.

'Yes,' Bronwyn confirmed. 'Obsidian has always been the spine of the story, running right through the middle of it. Obsidian *is* the Philosopher's Stone, usable by Arthur Huxley alone. Iris knew the significance it would have in the future. She knew what the alchemist would be able to create with it, the substance that would be needed for her to drink to end the immortal gift. That is why she named your mark as the Mark of Obsidian, the one that would be unique and beautiful. It must have seemed fitting for her. And it's what we've known of and some have waited for, for thousands of years. You and the Alchemist are locked to the same destiny.'

'No,' said Finn, 'nothing controls my destiny.'

'Man cannot orchestrate destiny,' said Bronwyn. 'Destiny orchestrates man.'

Finn was shaking his head. He didn't know why he was doing so, perhaps hoping that if he denied the truth long enough it might actually change things.

'What you saw,' Bronwyn went on, 'with the axe and the glade on fire, must have been generated by something inside of you, something intertwined with your destiny, Finn. I had not a slither of control over it. It could only have been a manifestation of the deed itself. That isn't how it's meant to happen and it's not the ritual that will be needed for it to happen. The ritual is supposed to be explained on the last page of the Book of Iris. The book will also speak of the ritual of how your enemies are supposed to kill you. That's why the Brotherhood won't kill you now, for in principle, if the book is to be believed, if you die outside the path of your destiny, another of your kind may be born later on.'

Finn ran his fingers stressfully through his hair. 'Iris is still alive?'

'Yes, she is,' said Bronwyn, 'but no one knows where. She truly hasn't been seen for centuries.'

'But Willoughby,' said Finn, trying to comprehend it all, 'he didn't—'

'He didn't tell you,' said Bronwyn, 'because he's a coward. He didn't want to tell you that together you will try and find The Book of Iris. He doesn't believe Mr Mellors has it but he'll have his own ideas about its location. He didn't want to tell you that next he'll have you find the Alchemist so he can make and provide you with The Elixir of Life. And he didn't want to tell you that when all that is done, he will have you try and find where Iris has been hiding for thousands of years. And when you find her —'

Finn closed his eyes and covered his ears. Even so, he couldn't prevent himself from hearing her voice.

'*When* you find her,' Bronwyn repeated, 'he will have you kill her to end the line of the immortals.'

290

Chapter Thirty-Seven

The rental vehicle was positioned in the bay of a carpark on the outskirts of Birmingham. The carpark served a variety of commercial ventures, amongst them a hotel with a large and garish neon sign sitting atop the roof, an elegant conference centre, and a sprawling office block that was grey, ugly, and empty now that the staff had gone home for the day. Every bay of the carpark seemed to be occupied but very few people could be spotted. No one seemed to be coming and going.

Felicity stared again at the church from the car window. The large stone building sat there in the dark of the night and looked out of place amongst the modern buildings that surrounded it like the bullies of progression. The church was mostly in darkness but the odd flicker of candlelight could be detected from behind the stained glass windows. *Someone* was home at least.

She had been told to sit in the back of the rental car. Devery had decided to drive and Edgar sat next to him in the passenger seat up front. The car itself had been an odd choice. It was a tiny red Fiesta with a small engine that had struggled up the motorway. There was little to no leg room and Edgar in particular looked most uncomfortable squeezed inside, almost as if he had tried to fit into a space that he should never have even attempted.

'What time is it?' Devery asked. He too was keeping his eye on the church.

Edgar looked at the clock on the dashboard. 'Ten minutes past eight.'

Time was slowly getting away from them. The meeting had been scheduled for 7:30pm and Grayson Mellors was already late. They had deliberately chosen to arrive early and had rolled

291

into the carpark an hour before they needed to be there. The plan was to watch the bookseller approach and potentially spot and diffuse any traps that were heading their way. But so far there had been no sign of the infamous book seller.

Devery had been nervous about the whole expedition from the start and he was growing impatient. They had received rigorous instructions from Bronwyn Pettigrew that they must not make contact with Grayson Mellors until they had reached Birmingham. The call they had to make could not be traced. They had to keep both the library's involvement and Finn's location secret. It was all risky business, especially when they should have been doing the opposite and lying as lowly as possible.

'Told you this was a waste of time,' said Edgar. 'Church will be closed in less than an hour. I say we get moving, get some dinner from somewhere.'

'No,' said Devery. 'We wait and we see this through.'

Felicity had been excited at the beginning. It was like being a police officer on an important stakeout. But she had quickly become bored. Sitting in a car for hours on end was not her idea of fun and with time to think she had found her thoughts focusing on Cora's words back in the bedroom of the pub. She hadn't at all forgotten that conversation. And she realised that she had the opportunity to leave now, to open the door and run off across the carpark and disappear. Maybe they wouldn't follow. It had to happen sooner or later.

One thing stopped her from taking the plunge. It was Finn. She had deliberately started to distance herself from him but that didn't mean she enjoyed it. The truth was she missed him, missed the days when it was just her and him. She was doubtful they would ever get that back. It had all changed the moment Willoughby and the others had entered their lives.

'Can I ask you something?' she said, deciding to stay put for a few more minutes at least. 'How do you guys make your money? You seem to have enough to pay massive taxi and car rental fees. I don't really picture any of you sitting in an office for forty hours a week. Do you steal it?'

'You're quite a nosey little thing, aren't you?' Edgar said.

'Nosey is good,' said Devery. 'It's good to be inquisitive.'

'I'm not inquisitive,' said Felicity. 'I am very much just nosey.'

'No, we don't steal it,' said Devery. 'Well, some of us do, I can't talk for all of us. But I've never stolen anything in my life. It's all about a bit of common sense or at least it used to be. I was told quite early on to keep things that were all around me. I worked in my father's law office in Dublin when I Settled. I remember thinking, why am I keeping an ink blotter or a snuff box. What good could that possibly do me? A hundred years later, I got it, when I realised how much it was worth over time. Going to be tougher for the new generations, can't see how there will be any value in an item that's made of plastic in Taiwan and has a billion brothers or sisters.'

'Right, I see,' said Felicity. 'You're basically glorified antique dealers.'

'Will's the master of it,' said Devery. 'He's got a lot of money, believe me. He sold a Fabergè egg a few years back, went for fifteen million. To this day I don't even know where he got it from.'

'And you've really never been tempted to steal a few bits and bobs?' Felicity said. 'God, you guys can be such squares. If I could do the things you do, I'd be doing all sorts of fun things.'

'What would you do?' Devery asked.

'Loads of stuff,' said Felicity. 'If I had strength I'd kick the living daylights out of people. And not even for any particular reason either. I'd do it just because I could. If I was quick I'd use it as an advantage and become an athlete or a footballer or something and make sure I won everything and make millions. Actually screw that, I'd make *billions*, I'd be *that* good. And then imagine if I was invisible or something mental like that. I'd walk in and out of places like shops and banks and stuff and steal *everything*.'

Devery glanced across to Edgar who was shaking his head. 'At least she's honest about her lack of decency,' said the Irishman. 'Most people aren't.'

'Couldn't care less,' said Edgar. 'We're still just wasting time.'

293

'Can I ask,' Felicity said to Edgar, 'why you always seem to be in such a hurry all the time?'

'My wife is still alive,' said Edgar. 'Every day she gets older, she gets further away from me.' He opened his door and started to climb out. 'It's eight-twenty. I can't listen to this nonsense anymore. Let's make sure he's not in there and then get some god damn food.' He slammed the door shut.

The allure of shaking her legs was enticing and Felicity made her way out into the night. She shivered. The night was bitterly cold and she had to blow into her hands before slipping them into the warmth of her coat pockets. She followed Edgar, moving through the small gate at the front of the church quickly and hoping that once inside it would prove to be a little bit warmer.

Inside the church was perfectly quiet. The pews were empty. A solitary Churchwarden, an elderly gentleman, was pottering around on the altar and dusting and cleaning anything that caught his eye. The altar was illuminated by two or three modest lamps and the rest of the church was dominated by deep, dark shadows. The only other source of light came from six long rows of candle stands, three on each side of the church, a number of candles lit in remembrance for souls that had been lost.

Edgar truly did want to get everything over and done with and he guided them into the heart of the church so they could carry out a survey of the building.

Felicity observed her surroundings as she paced up the centre of the aisle. She passed huge pillars of stone, each one adorned with impressively long banners that were hung somewhere from up high and dangled down to the floor like the medieval dressings of a lavish banquet hall. On the curtains there were decorations, ecclesiastical drawings depicting various holy events like the Crucifixion and the Ascension. The internal part of the roof itself was made of an expansive and complex maze of interlocking wooden beams.

She sat down on the wooden seat of a pew in the centre of the building, Devery and Edgar sitting either side of her. The Churchwarden offered a cursory glance but was happy enough to go about his business before disappearing through a side door at the back of the church.

'I don't like churches,' said Devery. To substantiate his notion, he was already looking uncomfortable and fidgeting. 'Don't like the statues either. Feel like they're looking at me.'

'That one definitely is,' said Felicity, pointing at a tall statue of the Virgin Mary by the altar. 'And I don't want to stir but when you weren't looking a minute ago she gave you the finger.'

'You religious?' Edgar asked her.

'Mum was,' said Felicity, 'so was my Nan. We're all Catholics. Nan was really into it.'

'And you?' Edgar said.

'On the fence,' Felicity answered. 'I kinda like the idea of it, especially that we might go somewhere better at the end, but think I still need to be convinced.' She shot the same question back to Edgar. 'How about you?'

'I'm the same,' Edgar answered. 'Think I need a bit of convincing too. Way I see it, it's up to God to prove himself to me, not the other way around.'

Behind them the church door opened and a man entered. Felicity turned to look and she went to ask Devery if it was their man but his expression confirmed that it was. Grayson Mellors stopped in the doorway. With him was a small boy who would have been around the same age as Felicity and who hovered a few paces behind the bookseller.

'This could take a while,' Devery said, 'but he's here. Maybe it's true after all.'

Edgar was narrowing his eyes. 'Interesting,' he said, the appearance not enough in itself to silence his doubts.

Mellors scanned the church and spotting his intended audience he headed straight towards them at a brisk pace. He slipped into the pew behind them. The boy didn't follow him.

'No,' Devery instructed Mellors staunchly. He was all authority. 'Sit in front of us, please, if you would.'

Mellors hesitated momentarily and then did as he was told and moved forward, taking a seat in a place where they could see him at all-times. The bookseller was not a thin man and he carried with him a hefty bulk that sat around the stomach and chin. His age was tricky to determine and his hair was blonde and lengthy and swept back into a ponytail. He was sweating heavily beneath a baggy grey suit and a long green overcoat. He carried with him a black briefcase.

Instinct made Felicity concentrate more on the boy. The boy had taken a seat on the very back row. He was stocky and had a shaved head and an expression that was so dour she wondered if he was the most serious and miserable person she had ever come across.

'Do you know me?' Devery asked the bookseller.

Mellors shook his head nervously. 'I don't know you.'

'My name is Gulliver,' said Devery, adopting a familiar alter ego.

Felicity had a bad feeling about this. *Something* was wrong but she couldn't quite say what it was. A series of alarm bells sounded in her brain. She turned back forward to observe Mellors and noticed immediately the sweat sliding down his neck and pooling on the collar of his suit and jacket and leaving a dark stain. Fear was radiating off the man like a poisonous gas.

'Shall we get straight down to business?' Devery suggested. 'We have heard from –'

'I *don't* have the book,' Mellors admitted without any sort of prompt.

That statement hung in the air a while.

Devery was unsure how to react. 'Do you want to say that again?'

'I *don't* have the book,' Mellors stated firmly for a second time. He twisted his head, his eyes erratic and whizzing this way and that. 'He made me come here! I had no choice! I don't have the book!'

'Calm down,' said Edgar. 'Who made you come here?'

Mellors slipped off the chair and down into the foot well of the pew and covered his head with his hands as though he had just been told that an asteroid was about to strike Birmingham and to take whatever cover he could find. 'He wants to question you,' he mumbled. 'I don't have the book! I don't have the book! I don't –'

'We need to leave!' Devery said urgently. 'Now! It's a trap!'

Devery, Felicity, and Edgar shuffled out into the aisle, leaving Mellors where he was. But when they turned towards the exit they saw that the boy was standing perfectly still out in front of them, blocking their way. The stare he fixed them with was intense and riddled with contempt.

'What's going on, Dev?' Felicity asked. 'Who is this little runt?'

It was the boy who spoke next. His voice was deep and sounded as though it belonged to a much older man. The voice was as evil as it could be. 'You will take me to the child,' he demanded, growling like a chesty wolf.

Felicity paused to think. Was there another way out? She shot a look at the door the Churchwarden had used. Next to it was a second door, one that was bigger and had the appearance of being of more importance. It was an exit alright. She tugged at Devery's sleeve, pointing him towards the possible escape route. But then the door opened inwards and a man moved through, shutting it behind him. She had seen the man before. He had been with a fellow whose nose she had broken once upon a time.

'Hello, Wyatt,' said Devery, also recognising him immediately.

'Hello, James,' said Wyatt. 'I really am sorry for all of this.'

'Told you it was a trap,' said Edgar. He kicked the pew to his left in temper. 'Why does no one listen to me?'

The boy started to walk up the aisle towards them. 'You will take me to the child,' he repeated.

'Can you punch a kid?' Felicity wondered.

'Frowned upon,' Devery said without much confidence, 'but if he punches me first –'

The boy started to run directly at them. He moved with an extreme speed and jumped high into the air.

Devery opened up his body, ensuring his arms were loose and ready and he took his own careful step forward. He was biting his lip, nervous about what would come next. The lights on the altar went out as if they had decided to turn themselves off. The candles nearby were not enough to stop the church plunging into gloom.

Felicity watched the boy disappear in front of her. It wasn't the lack of light that concealed him. He was gone, as if he had vanished into thin air like a ghost.

Devery saw it too and he burst into a nervous laughter shortly before he was smashed off his feet. He landed on the other side of the church, skidding across the floor with a screech towards the altar. Devery recovered as quickly as he could, pushing himself back into a standing position. He bolted up the aisle to go again and was stopped by a force that made him fight. He tried to combat the invisible foe, lashing out with a feverish lunacy, making no contact, but trying again all the same.

Edgar went to assist but Wyatt sprung from the door and intercepted, blocking the way. Edgar threw a punch but Wyatt avoided it easily and threw back a far harder one which connected with his chin. Edgar thumped into the pews behind him, three of them toppling over with the impact of the big man's body.

Felicity was rooted to the spot as it all unfolded. She was helpless but at least that meant that no one had decided to come for her. She had no idea what to do. She wanted to help but couldn't think where to start or what she could even contribute. She urged herself to think but rational thought was hard to come by, especially with the view of Devery being hit all over the church in front of her.

She gasped as the Irishman almost hit one of the candle stands. He was left sprawled on his back and his invisible assailant was upon him in a second, dragging him up by the collar and tossing him once more high into the air.

'Take me to the child?' the boy's voice continued to demand from the darkness.

Felicity's eyes lit up with the power of an idea. There was the opportunity. She had seen it, a slight shadow cast by the light of the candles as the invisible force had set upon Devery. She understood now why the lights on the altar had gone out. The

298

boy had somehow done it so he couldn't be seen. Or at least it was so that his *shadow* couldn't be seen. It was the boy's weakness.

She sprinted to the nearest stand and plucked out two candles from the gratings. Taking them with her she headed to one of the banners hanging against a pillar. She allowed the flames of the candle to tickle the bottom of the fabric. The fabric didn't catch at first but then with a joyous sizzle a thread was aflame and the fire started climbing slowly skywards towards the roof.

'If you think you can hide,' she said bitterly. 'Then try this one on for size!'

Devery was still taking his beating honourably. But he was becoming slower and his defences were more laboured. He didn't have much left and despite Felicity's efforts he still couldn't make out his opponent.

Felicity realised she needed to do more. She got to work, darting around the church and carrying out an identical act of arson at each banner she came across. As she set fire to the final banner she turned and looked out into the heart of the church and saw that it had all got a little bit wild and out of hand. The fire was everywhere. It had spread to the wooden ceiling and parts of it were already starting to collapse.

'I'm *sooooo* going to hell,' she said to herself, both impressed and appalled at her impressive work. 'Forgive me, Father, for I have sinned –'

Devery was on his back and was bleeding from the nose heavily. His eyes were closed and he was one tiny step away from being introduced to a painful and likely fatal unconsciousness. Nearby Wyatt had Edgar on the floor and his head gripped in a tight, dangerous headlock. They were losing.

'Dev!' Felicity screamed, her voice echoing, trying to get his attention. 'Get up! You can see him!'

Devery's eyes started to slowly open. The fires were strong enough that Felicity could see the shadow of the boy in all its glory now. There was the outline, strolling towards Devery.

'Tell me where the child is?' the boy repeated once more. The shadow of the hand could clearly be seen pulling Devery to his feet and slapping a grip onto his throat.

Felicity stumbled down the aisle almost without thinking. There were a series of crashes in front of her as large sections of the roof beams started to plummet to the ground. When they made contact with the floor the timber splintered and the fire cackled and spread out with a wrathful glee through the wooden pews.

She saw her chance. With the shadow distracted throttling her friend she picked the largest piece of beam she could find and she swept forward, bringing the beam down hard on what she took to be the shadows back. There was the crunch of impact and the sound of a furious yell. Devery was loose and he fell to the floor.

Felicity wrapped her arms around Devery's stomach and pulled him up. They hobbled away, trying to find Edgar. They found him nearby, Wyatt slowing squeezing the life out of him. Up above there was a crash and another large beam started to fall. Wyatt saw its trajectory and was forced to let go to avoid it hitting him. Edgar, coughing and spluttering, only missed the collision by a few inches. The collapse created a thick line of fire between Edgar and Wyatt.

Devery rushed to his friend's aid, covering the ground in seconds and pulling him towards the exit. Felicity was already on the same wavelength and she was already in the doorway at the front of the church. She waited until she was certain they were safe and moved outside. As the cold hit her the windows of the church started to blow out. But still the car park was empty. The church had no alarm. There were no spectators. There were no sounds of distant fire engines rushing to help.

'TAKE ME TO THE CHILD?' The boy's voice bellowed from inside the burning church. It was as if the Devil himself was screaming from the fiery depths of hell. The boy was coming.

Felicity, Devery, and Edgar escaped out into the maze of cars, ducking down and hiding behind a large white van, out of sight.

300

'Can you see the car?' Devery whispered. He was wiping the ample blood from his nose onto his sleeve. He also had blood seeping from a wound on his forehead and his clothes were torn from the ordeal. He was a mess and seemed unlucky enough to be frequently getting injured, an unjust reward for his bravery.

'I think so,' Felicity confirmed. She bravely peered out as much as she dared from the bonnet of the van. 'It's over there.' She pointed out, away to their right. 'I can't see him? Maybe if he goes past a streetlight –'

Devery was checking Edgar's condition. 'You ok?'

'Hell, no,' said Edgar. He didn't look well, pale, flushed.

'We go on three,' said Devery, 'quickly, no messing around.' He started his countdown. 'One … two –'

A car nearby was ripped from the car park floor and thrown angrily upwards into the sky like it weighed nothing. The car crashed down with an explosion of metal and shattered glass, as if a giant had been searching underneath the vehicle for something important and then lashed out angrily when it wasn't found.

It wasn't an isolated incident. More followed. A second car leapt into the heavens, then two more, three more, a dozen more. The vehicles rained down as the boy sought out his prey. It was only a matter of time before the van would be selected and then it would be game over.

Devery took two deep breaths. He pushed the rental car keys into his mouth so that they dangled ready and then grabbed Felicity by the hand. With Edgar close behind they burst out from behind the van and made their desperate run for safety.

The boy, wherever he was, must have seen them fleeing. He used the cars as makeshift missiles, throwing them at the running group without mercy to take them down.

Felicity was terrified but she wouldn't stop moving. She could hear the cars coming after her and one particular effort landed directly in front of them, so close that she felt the wind of the zooming metal brush past her face as it fell. Devery took the quickest of sidesteps to avoid it but it had been too close.

The rental car was right in front of them, a tiny red beacon of metallic hope.

Devery had no time to faff around with small keys in small locks. Instead he let go of Felicity's hand and dived through the front windscreen, using his already bruised body to smash through the glass. Felicity went the same way, entering the car through the missing window, as did Edgar, the three of them ending in a strange and unnatural heap in the front seats. Edgar untangled her limbs and pushed her into the back seat.

Devery rammed the key into the ignition. The car came to life and he pushed his foot down hard on the accelerator. The rental car screeched for a moment, the tyres rubbing dangerously against the concrete and then it shot forward.

'Seatbelt!' Felicity screamed. 'Seatbelt! Seatbelt! Seatbelt!' She was unable to find her own and was clutching for it desperately. Her instinct told her it may be a good idea to be strapped in and she wanted at least a modicum of safety in a situation that didn't seem to have any.

An elegant black car dropped down in front of them. Another, a blue estate, fell down next to it. The boy was trying to block their way.

Devery steered urgently and only just managed to avoid the collision, squeezing the car through the smallest of gaps in between the makeshift metal missiles that had now become metal chicanes. The side of the rental car collided and the vehicle crunched and screeched, with sparks spraying out and the metals of the doors rippling and distorting. The Irishman somehow stayed in control of the steering and he desperately ploughed through the gears.

'There goes the deposit!' Devery said, laughing manically.

The church burnt away behind them. There was a loud ringing too, the soundtrack of synchronised car alarms that were blaring and creating a monotonous ballad of damage and discord.

Devery managed to get them out of the carpark and onto the open road, leaving the chaos behind them. 'I think I'm going to faint,' he said, using a free hand to brush the blood and sweat out of his eyes. 'It feels like my actual brain is bleeding!' He turned to

Edgar, angry. 'Just what will it take for you to actually use your god damn power, whatever it is?'

Edgar said nothing. He simply rested in his chair, happy to be regaining his breath.

'What was that *thing*?' Felicity said, peering out through the back window to see if *it* was following. Thankfully and although she could see the orange glow of a burning Catholic church through the gaps in the building, everything looked relatively normal.

'I'll tell you on the way,' said Devery. He was pressing his fingers around his head, trying to take account of every last area of where the blood was coming from. 'Will and I came across something similar back in the Willowbrook morgue. I think it was Tobias.'

'Who's that?' Felicity said.

'Just someone who doesn't exist,' said Devery calmly.

Edgar was shaking his head, his countenance riddled with disbelief. 'He was *just* a boy –'

'He shouldn't have been a boy,' said Devery.

Edgar couldn't let his concerns rest. 'The prophecy says only one child will Settle –'

'I know,' Devery said, 'and that might just call into question the whole prophecy in the first place. I've never read anywhere of Iris's children Settling as children.'

Felicity didn't have the energy to question the men any further. She had her own problems. Cora's warning had arrived back to the forefront of her mind, ready for its stark encore. She regretted not making her escape when the concept had occurred to her. *Next time,* she told herself, *next time I will get as far away from all this craziness as I can.*

Chapter
Thirty-Eight

The library had a far greater number of guests than it was accustomed to and most of them were harbouring similar feelings of disgruntlement and hunger. The reason for their united and negative mood was Finn, although for his part he didn't know that he was responsible. He had been exhausted and feeling unwell from his time with Bronwyn Pettigrew and the visions and had spent most of the evening sleeping as a consequence. She had refused to allow anyone to dine until he woke up and they could all eat together.

As such everyone found themselves eating very late and only a few minutes after eleven pm. The only room large enough to accommodate them all was the balcony in the main library and Finn and the others sat amongst Bronwyn and the Hunters at the long table that had been fetched down from the tower, one big happy family. Kemi alone played both cook and waiter and he fetched various trays of food from a kitchen that must have existed somewhere in the building and he laid out the trays for the guests before taking his own seat.

There was plenty of food to go around, with four trays containing roasted chickens and a vast array of other delicious and enticing treats, including roasted potatoes, creamed spinach, carrots, peas, runner beans, broccoli, walnut stuffing, and gravy that was so thick, rich, and decadent that it was a wonder it didn't clog instantly the arteries of any poor soul greedy enough to consume it.

Bronwyn, Willoughby, Cora, and Hamish shared bottles of red wine and the Hunters refused to drink anything other than an old looking bottle of port that they had brought with them. Kemi, ever the disciplined athlete, would only drink water.

As luxurious and hearty as the food was, Finn found that he hardly had any form of appetite. He cared even less for the dinner conversation. In one sense he should have been at peace and comfortable. In principle there were no more mysteries, Bronwyn having told him everything. He was furnished now with all the facts. A group of *immortals* called The Brotherhood hunted him because they were scared of losing the gift of immortality. A group of *mortals* called The Guild and lead by his mother hunted him, and indeed all their kind, because they wanted to understand and harness the secret of everlasting life. And then there was Willoughby Carmichael. His group had no name. But they had hunted him, in their own way, because they needed him to end the line of the immortals. And more importantly, they needed him to commit murder in the name of their cause.

The last point created a discomfort in his stomach that bubbled away like volcanic lava. Bronwyn had spent a long time after the last vision reiterating that what Finn had seen was not how the whole thing would play out. But it didn't matter. He couldn't shake the image of the swinging axe and the sight of it so close to the beautiful woman's neck.

A piece of chicken breast appeared on Finn's plate. He looked up, seeing that one of the Hunter's had provided him with it. The Hunter was standing next to him with a tray in his hand. 'Eat something, lad,' the Hunter said with a genuine kindness, 'will do you some good.'

The Hunter returned to his seat. His name was Emeric and out of all the hairy Hunters he was the one who seemed willing to speak and interact with them the most.

Finn stared down at the chicken and pushed at it with his fork, a little clear juice leaking. It was fruitless. He just couldn't eat. He instead allowed himself some discreet stares at the others around the table, at Willoughby huddled together with Bronwyn and laughing, at Cora enjoying her food and talking with Hamish about purchasing a new camper van when she got the chance. It was if Finn had seen the light, the truth about all of them. He shared something magical with each of these people but he was

305

not one of these people and he never would be. They were not his friends. They wanted to use him, pure and simple.

There was one person who had never used him. There was one person who was actually his friend. And she wasn't there, instead off gallivanting and trying to be as far away from him as she could, which meant looking for a book that spoke of murder and carnage. When he and Felicity were together they spoke about normal things, about silly, funny and inappropriate things and he couldn't wait to see her again and chat about some form of nonsense and feel like a child again. He was fed up of talking about everlasting life and prophecies.

He understood that he needed to apologise to her and more importantly he understood why he needed to. He had been blinkered by the whole crazy adventure and he had lost sight of what was important. He had no doubt that she would make him work for forgiveness and do more than a little grovelling but he was determined to show her that he was willing to put all his effort into it.

There was also something else he needed to discuss with her. He needed to tell her all about Bronwyn and the visions. He couldn't discuss his concerns with any of the others. He suspected she would be flippant and childish at first but once he told her that he was starting to think about running away again he was certain this would pique her interest. Surely then she would have to forgive him. And she would maybe just go with him.

He tried to hide such thoughts as Kemi cleared the table after everyone had finished their food. It was now after midnight and no one showed any signs of retiring to bed, each of them rendered relaxed by copious amounts of alcohol. Bronwyn excused herself from the table and fetched a book from down in the darkness of the library. She returned and took a seat on the top step of the balcony staircase and read leaning her back against the wall and using the light of a nearby lamp to see.

The five Hunters took a seat on the floor and Emeric removed a small hemp sack from his trouser pocket and they started to play a game with a small selection of intricate metal crosses which they tossed around in a small circle. They were all quite familiar with the rules but to anyone else the game didn't make much sense.

'You've been awfully quiet this evening?' Willoughby said. He was looking at Finn across the table, wine glass in hand. 'In fact, you've barely said a thing since you've woken up. Is there anything wrong?'

Finn shook his head. No, there wasn't anything wrong. At least not anything he was willing to talk to Willoughby Carmichael about.

Willoughby wasn't convinced. He was trying to get into Finn's head with the power of his stare, to read his thoughts and concerns. 'No,' he said, 'there is something wrong. You think I've deceived you, don't you?'

It was Cora's turn to look up. Hamish did too.

Finn didn't want to say a word. Silence was the best answer. Silence would get him in less trouble than the words that he was tempted to utter.

'So, it's to be the silent treatment?' Willoughby said. 'Right, I see. Sometimes, Finn, it pays just to grow up a little.'

Finn swallowed a big old lump in his throat. *Sometimes, Finn, it pays just to grow up a little.* If the comment had been designed to provoke a response, it had almost worked. Not so long ago he had said something similar to Felicity and she had bit within a few seconds. Still, for his part he managed to maintain his silence.

'What's the matter with you?' Cora said to Finn.

'Don't bother,' said Willoughby. 'Maybe we should just let him sulk.'

It was getting closer, the chance of a reaction. The allegation of sulking made Finn twitch and omit a little scornful laugh. *No, Finn, don't let them do it to you. Don't say anything.*

Willoughby wasn't impressed with Finn's sardonic laugh. 'Did I say something amusing, Finn?'

Finn looked away. The Hunters were watching him, their game having stopped. Bronwyn was watching too, glancing up

307

from her book. They were all curious about the exchange going on in front of them and how it would play out.

Cora drank from her wine. Then she started to speak. 'Some gratitude would –'

The reaction was achieved. 'Gratitude for *what* exactly?' Finn said, barking. He was angry and the volume of his voice was almost a shout. 'For what, Cora? Why thank you Willoughby for saving me so you can take me on a journey to murder an innocent woman.'

That shut everyone up. Willoughby was shaking his head as if he already knew what truths the outburst would reveal and was pouring another glass of wine from the bottle.

Hamish spoke first. 'You have to think bigger than that, Finn.'

'Just who are all of you,' said Finn, too far along now to stop, 'to tell me what I need to think? That's all you ever do. I must think this, I must think that, I must do this, I must understand that. None of you have stopped, not even for a second, and asked me what I actually think about any of this. You've never asked me what I want to do.'

Looks were shared throughout the room. There was a serious gravity to Finn's rant and a range of possible consequences that were born from his feelings.

'I'm going to ask you something now,' said Willoughby slowly, 'and I want you to think very carefully about your answer.' He allowed a pause for dramatic effect. 'What exactly *do* you want to do? Why don't you put your cards on the table, young man?'

Finn was suddenly a little unsure. 'I could run –'

'You can't run,' said Cora. 'People want you dead –'

'Then I make it clear I'm no threat to them,' said Finn. 'I make it clear that I don't want to end everything. They might leave me alone. And my Mum, I can hide from her and –' He stopped himself from going any further. He realised he was heading into territory that was unpractised, unchartered, and unsafe.

'I want to make sure that you understand what you're saying,' Willoughby said. 'And I want to make sure that I don't misunderstand what may just be a childish tantrum and mistake it for something else, something that could potentially give us a very substantial problem.'

Finn could sense the eyes of the room focusing on him, burrowing into him like a plague of ravenous vermin. 'What substantial problem might we have?' he said.

Fate fortunately decided that Willoughby's answer could wait. There was a loud click and the lights went out. Everyone stood and groaned.

'I have some candles and torches up in the tower somewhere,' said Bronwyn. She started to head towards her quarters, moving slowly to make sure she didn't trip over any unseen hazards. 'I'll go and fetch them now, will only take me a few minutes.'

Kemi had moved across to the window and was peering out into the street. 'Wait,' he said strongly. 'The power's still on out there and in the neighbouring buildings.'

Bronwyn stopped walking. 'So it's just *this* building that has lost power?' she asked curiously.

Kemi nodded.

'Well isn't that strange,' said Bronwyn. 'The street is all linked up to the same grid.'

Finn couldn't make out anyone in the room but he could feel that someone had moved very close to him, right next to his head in fact and leaning in so that they could whisper. This person gripped him by the top of his arm and squeezed hard. There was a sharp pang of pain.

'Don't you think you've gotten away with that little outburst,' said Willoughby. His whisper was quiet but full of menace. 'You will answer my question and when you do I think it's time you and I had a little chat about how this is going to go from now on.'

'Am I a prisoner?' Finn whispered back.

There was a large crash from another part of the building, a crash that echoed from up high and reverberated around the

309

ceiling voids of the main library. It was the unmistakeable sound of a window smashing.

'You all heard that?' said Hamish. 'I'm just making sure that wasn't my imagination playing tricks on me?'

'I heard it,' said Kemi. He was already on the move and heading back towards the table. He was perfectly calm. 'It came from up in the tower.' He called out for two of the Hunters. 'Emeric, Perris, you two come with me! The rest of you, stay here and keep your eyes open!'

'Kemi,' said Bronwyn, 'there could be many reasons for a broken window and a loss of power.' But Kemi and the Hunters were already gone.

'Do you think we're in danger here?' Cora asked, wondering if the power cut was something more sinister.

'I can't see why we would be,' said Bronwyn. 'I doubt The Brotherhood would be so bold as to come here and I would be very surprised if The Guild even knew about the existence of this place.'

'Hamish?' said Cora. 'Are you sensing anything?'

'Nope,' Hamish answered quickly. 'Not seen a thing!'

The loud scream stopped Cora from needing to ask any more questions. The scream belonged to a man and again it came from the tower. Kemi suddenly burst back into the room, his reappearance accompanied by two flashes of light from torches that he carried in each hand. He had a bag draped over one of his shoulders and although the two Hunters were still with him the one known as Perris was badly wounded. Emeric was dragging him back into the room.

Bronwyn immediately demanded to know what happened.

'There is *something* up there!' Kemi said, giving a vague report. He pointed a finger at the table. 'Please, someone get me a chair!'

Hamish was the first to act and he dragged a chair across from the table.

'Something?' Bronwyn questioned, taking it seriously now. 'That could mean anything, Kemi? Think about what you're saying, please. *What* happened up there?'

'I don't know what *it* is,' said Kemi. 'If I did I would tell you. It's not anything I've seen before. It moved so fast that I barely saw it. But one thing I can tell you is that it attacked us.' The injured Perris was placed into the chair and everyone surrounded him.

Bronwyn gripped her assistant by the shoulders. 'Are the books safe?' she said, her voice trembling with urgency.

'It's not after the books,' Kemi said confidently.

Satisfied to an extent, Bronwyn sprung forward and dropped to a knee in front of Perris, keen to carry out some form of investigation of her own. Kemi provided the torch light. 'Let me see this little scratch,' she said like a wise and seasoned surgeon. She gently eased the torn sections of the trouser leg to one side to reveal the wound. She examined the gash for thirty seconds, pushing parts of it gently and drawing out winces from the victim.

Finn was back to being a passenger, the adults taking over once again. For someone who was supposed to be so important, he rarely felt that way.

'I may have done you a disservice,' Bronwyn noted. 'That's definitely not a scratch. There are three gashes in fact, not one, and they are all fairly similar in length. The skin feels odd too, not like I would imagine it to be. Tell me, did it feel like you were cut with a knife?'

'Was a claw,' Perris stated.

Kemi had opened the bag that he had managed to salvage from the expedition to the tower and removed three further torches. He threw one to Emeric, one to Donitz, and the third to Finn. Kemi kept the two he had been carrying when he returned. They all flicked the torches so that they were on.

Finn watched as Bronwyn pressed her fingers deeper into Perris's wound. When she removed them, her fingertips were stained with a dark substance. 'Can I have some more light, please?' she requested.

Finn moved his torch to the hand she held in front of her face.

'The whole area was quite sodden,' Bronwyn said. 'But it wasn't all blood. There's something else here, some form of black residue, it looks almost like … well, almost like tar.' She started smiling. 'Well I never! As impossible as it may sound, I think it's a Dragwich.'

The faces in the room went instantly ashen at the mention of the word *Dragwich*. All except Finn who true to form had no idea what she was talking about. 'What's a Dragwich?' he asked.

'They're extinct,' Hamish said.

'You can tell her that,' said Emeric, 'when she's dragging you away and clawing at your god-damn face –'

Bronwyn for one was unafraid. 'This would be one hell of a thing to see –'

'Everyone stays close,' said Kemi. He shuffled everyone so that they were together on the balcony, the table behind them, and each person back to back.

They all jumped as a loud rustling sound came from above them, somewhere up high in the roof space. Something was moving up there and it sounded like a rat scurrying from one side of the library to the other. But this would have been one *big* rat. Every one of the torches was directed upwards, searching for something in the darkness.

'Who's controlling her?' Willoughby said.

'They don't exist,' Hamish said once again. 'Not anymore –'

'What's a Dragwich?' Finn asked again.

'Something very ancient,' said Bronwyn, 'of the like we've not seen for many a year. It would appear that dark things are coming out of the shadows once again.'

'I'm getting Miss Pettigrew away,' said Kemi.

'You can't leave,' said Cora.

Kemi ignored Cora's plea and was already guiding Bronwyn, taking her by the hand. She was trying to resist but for Kemi it wasn't up for discussion. Within a second they were both gone.

There was more scurrying. This time however it was not in the roof space but it originated from down amongst the bookcases on the lower level and in the deepest recesses of the darkness. The Dragwich, whatever it was, was stalking them and moving around to test their fears.

'What do we do now?' Cora said. She was terrified. 'That thing is down there, blocking the bloody front door!'

'We go down another route,' said Donitz, 'into the basement. There are tunnels we can access and we might be able to trap it. If not, there are weapons down there too.'

Cora pointed down into the heart of the library. 'Oh dear Lord,' she said, petrified. 'Look!'

Two small red dots appeared in the gloom that hadn't been there before − *two red eyes* − the demonic red eyes of the Dragwich. The creature had a low centre of gravity and was crawling forwards towards the staircase like a wild animal.

'Urgh!' Finn said, deeply disturbed.

The Dragwich started to talk to them from down below in a subtle, haunting whisper. It said a single word, reciting its own name with a raspy relish, the word itself elongated and slivery. It was a slow, malicious taunt that only just about sounded human.

'*Draaaaaaaaaaaaaaagwich!*'

The red eyes made it to the first step of the staircase. That was when everyone started to panic.

Chapter Thirty-Nine

Finn was sprinting downwards through the staircase, a narrow wall on each side of him, panicking people in front and behind. He had dropped his torch in the dramatic departure but there were flashes of light from those with enough composure to had kept hold of theirs. The group broke out into the basement and into the open space of Kemi's dojo. Emeric had automatically taken point and he was aiming his torch out in front of him, searching the shadows of the basement area and checking each pillar carefully for anything that might be moving.

'Is it here?' Hamish said. 'Did it follow us?'

Emeric chuckled. 'Think we can assume it did and –' A dark shadow swept past the light of the torch, making the light flicker. Emeric tried to follow the shape but it was too fast and in a brief moment it was gone.

Donitz was taking his own form of action and was grabbing a selection of weapons from the shelving units. He tossed them to each of his fellow Hunters, arming them with a sword and a crossbow each.

'Where's Perris?' said Emeric, noticing that one of his colleagues was missing. It didn't take him long to realise. 'We left him behind.'

Donitz had no time for remorse. 'You listen to me,' he said. 'Look out for the eyes. We hunt it in groups and –'

The Dragwich flew out from the darkness and straight into Donitz's chest. The Hunter disappeared along with the monster, back into the shadows. His sword landed with a heavy clang and his torch dropped, spinning on the floor where it fell. The light from the spinning torch turned the dojo into a form of strange, demonic disco where no one was dancing.

The Hunters let fire with their crossbows, the bolts flying aimlessly at a target they could not see.

Finn thought briefly about his supposed powers and about those that were in the room with him. He had no idea what gifts the last three Hunter's possessed, but everyone else's were now useless. Hamish hadn't seen it coming. Cora had nothing to move with her mind and Willoughby had no bodies of which to heal, at least not yet. If Finn's powers were ready to make an appearance, he wished they would hurry up.

The Dragwich attacked again, taking a further Hunter with it. This time the Hunter screamed and squealed before a loud tear of flesh could be heard. The poor Hunter fell silent.

The horrid whisper came again. '*Draaaaaaaaaaaaagwich!*'

Another attack, another flash of shadow and another Hunter disappeared from the mats. Again there was a brief bout of screaming and then all went quiet once more.

'RUN!' Emeric bellowed, the only one of the Hunters left alive.

So they did, with Emeric again leading the way with his torch. Finn followed as best as he could and was trying eagerly to keep up. He couldn't fall behind. He heard a sharp rattle of keys and a door get whooshed open in front of him. Emeric was shouting, urging speed, and then the door was slammed shut as the escaping column of frightened immortals made it safely to the other side.

'Are we all here?' said Emeric. He moved the light across each of the remaining faces to check.

The Dragwich was at the other side of the door and was trying to get in, banging away, testing the lock. But the door was made of thick steel and the creature started to smash its hands into the other side with an anger that made an awful racket.

'Don't worry,' said Emeric. 'It won't be able to get through!'

The clamour stopped. The Dragwich must have moved away, looking for another way to get in.

'Where's it gone?' Finn asked, hoping with all his heart that the ordeal was over and that they were finally safe.

'Shouldn't we go back and help your friends?' Hamish said to Emeric, his wavering tone lacking the conviction to suggest he harboured any true enthusiasm for such an adventure.

'They're dead,' said Emeric. 'She'll kill quickly.' He pushed the torch out in front of him, illuminating the long dark underground passageway that awaited them. The passageway was narrow and the ceiling low. The ground was flooded with cold water that was knee deep. The water was coming from above and it flowed down intermittently every twenty or so feet from tunnels that rose vertically to the world above.

'What is this place?' Willoughby said as they walked.

Finn walked a few paces in front of Willoughby, who was positioned at the back of the column. He didn't like not being able to see him, not after the way he had suddenly turned in the library.

'Bronwyn's tunnel,' said Emeric. 'It's an escape tunnel if required and a tunnel to smuggle things in if there's a need to be discreet. There's lot of passageways like this in the city. This one was used for storing wine in a previous life.'

'Where's the water coming from?' Hamish asked. 'It stinks something rotten.'

'A little bit of drainage and sewage I'd imagine,' Emeric said. 'You're welcome to go back up through the library though?'

'I think I'll decline,' said Hamish.

'Sensible answer,' said Emeric. 'And try not to get the water in your mouth. It ain't gonna taste all that nice.' There was a splash as he stumbled before regaining a strong footing. 'It won't take us long and we'll be away from here. We'll come up in the street.'

Finn watched Emeric, Cora, and Hamish push through a waterfall of water from one of the overheard tunnels and as he too walked through the water was freezing cold against his face and it soaked his hair in an instant. His stomach lurched whilst he was underneath, not liking the sensation of the open space above him.

'Something's just occurred to me,' said Willoughby, calling to the group from the rear. 'Did any of the other Hunters have a key to that door?' As if on perfect cue, behind them came the sound of a loud clang of metal against stone. The door had been opened and a familiar voice echoed down the passageway.

'Draaaaaaaaaaaaaaaaaaaaaaaaaaaaaaaaaaagwich!'

That was it. No words were required. They all moved with a more desperate sense of urgency, sprinting down the tunnel, the water splashing up from their ankles.

Finn was exhausted, his muscles suffering from the previous day's ordeal, but he forced himself to find the energy from somewhere. His heart was beating hard, his chest thumping in and out. But then he slipped and fell down into the water. The water coursed into his mouth and nostrils and started to flood into his lungs.

'Get up,' said Willoughby, dragging him back up to his feet.

Finn had lost his bearings but could see that they were directly beneath the next vertical duct, the water dropping a few inches in front of his face. And then he saw her. The Dragwich was coming from up above them, an unhuman face covered with long hair, its body dripping with the strange black liquid. It was crawling down from the vertical duct like a spider, its red eyes shining away.

'Watch out!' he shrieked.

A hand full of sharp claws swept across Willoughby's back, raking and cutting his skin through his clothes. Willoughby fell forward and face first into the water. Then the Dragwich scurried down a little further and gripped him by the ankles and plucked the grown man up into the duct with a strength that bellied its size.

Finn acted immediately and he reached out, latching onto Willoughby's hands. For the briefest of moments Willoughby's body seemed to come back down with Finn's weight but the Dragwich was freakishly strong and it regained its advantage and started to pull Willoughby even further away and upwards. Finn started to move up into the duct with him, his feet leaving the floor. Water gushed into his face like he was taking a shower.

He was crying out desperately. 'Oh my God! Help! Help! Help!'

Hamish and Cora rushed back and together they took Finn's legs, one each, and tried to drag them all back down into the passageway, grappling away like the whole event was a tug of war. But again the Dragwich was too strong and even with three of them involved they started to struggle. Cora lost her grip as Emeric appeared on the scene. The Hunter fired a crossbow bolt up into the duct. It didn't hit and it didn't make any difference.

The Dragwich was becoming more and more vicious and it was yanking with force, trying to pry Willoughby loose from the grips that were trying desperately to save him.

Finn was face to face with Willoughby. He could see the fear in the man's eyes, something he had not seen in the man before.

'Finn,' said Willoughby, grimacing, pained. An instant change appeared in Willoughby's eyes. A look of resignation had now arrived and he smiled and then let go of Finn's grip and disappeared up into the darkness. Finn, Hamish, and Emeric dramatically fell and smashed into the water of the passageway below, one on top of the other.

Cora was already screaming and trying to follow her brother up into the duct. She yelled his name over and over. They could hear Willoughby returning her call, calling out in pain and anguish. He didn't seem far away.

'Cora,' Hamish said, trying to pull her away, 'he's gone! We've got to get out of here!'

'No,' Cora complained, knocking the Scotsman away, 'get off me! He's still alive —'

Willoughby's screams suddenly stopped. Then a moment later his lifeless body tumbled down from the duct, falling into the water. The body was riddled with gashes, bites, and claw marks. He didn't move an inch, perfectly still, lifeless.

A stunned and heavy silence between the witnesses filled the passageway. They all stared at the body, the only sound the running of the water coming down from up above.

Emeric was the first to move and he dragged Cora away from the bottom of the duct. She started to kick and scream but regardless they moved quickly, as far as their dwindling energy and spirits would allow and very soon they emerged out into a

318

second tunnel. The second tunnel was far wider and taller than the first and the water here was waist deep.

The Hunter had his crossbow aimed in the air as he waded through the water. 'It must be moving through the upper tunnels,' he said. 'Keep your eyes peeled.'

'How far?' Finn said.

'It's a few hundred yards,' said Emeric, keeping them moving. 'Once we cover the distance we –'

The Dragwich fell down from above and smashed into the centre of the group. Everyone hit the water at the sudden impact and went underneath the surface. Finn struggled once more to get to his feet but he did manage to shoot his head out of the water. Everything below his shoulders remained submerged. Emeric had dropped his torch and it lit up the water and gave enough brightness to show the image of the creature biting into the Hunters shoulder. The Hunter was frantically trying to fight the creature off but he was failing.

Hamish aimed a punch into the back of the Dragwich which did little more than anger the beast. It flipped around and swept out its hideous arm, making contact with the Scotsman's chin and sending him flying away and landing with a brutal splash.

Emeric took the opportunity to stagger free, clutching his bleeding shoulder. He had lost his crossbow and was trying to recover it from the murky depths.

The Dragwich moved towards Cora with its arms extended, the claws vividly real. Fear and mourning rooted Cora to the spot. She was too devastated to resist. The creature craned its neck back and got ready to attack. It reached out and ran its claws along the skin of Cora's throat, taunting her.

'No!' Finn shouted. He stood up, the water dripping off him. 'Please, no! I will come with you! I will come with you if you let these people live!' He hadn't planned to say it but they had lost and the offer just spilled out of him. They were never going to all get out of the passageway alive and this thing would kill them all to get what it wanted.

The Dragwich stopped. It looked at Finn, its red eyes glaring with curiosity. *'Draaaaaaaaaaagiwch!'* It said, retracting its claws from Cora's neck. Its own name seemed to be the only word of its despicable vocabulary.

'Stop, Finn!' Hamish bellowed. 'You can't –'

'I will come with you!' Finn repeated.

The Dragwich appeared to be satisfied with the deal. But then there was a sudden flash of light and a sharp squelching noise. Time stood still. Everything stood still. And then the head of the Dragwich came away from its shoulders and splashed down into the water. The rest of its body just stood there for a moment, headless and limp but refusing to topple.

Finn didn't know what had happened. He looked across to Hamish and Emeric and they too were flushed with bafflement. But then they saw Devery, striding into the passageway and rushing straight to his wife and wrapping her up into an embrace.

It hadn't however been Devery who had dispatched the beast. The honour belonged to Felicity, who was stood in the water up to her waist and in her hand she was holding a long sword that had black stains streaked across the blade. They had rushed into the building and Felicity had salvaged the sword from the dojo. And with it she had removed the head of the creature in one swift, vicious stroke.

'I think we got back just in time,' she said, 'and this water is going to ruin my boots.'

Finn was dumbstruck. Even though the Dragwich was the most wickedly evil thing he had ever had the unfortunate luck to come across, it still seemed relentlessly violent to see it being decapitated. He was glad and sickened by the graphic beheading, all at the same time.

The standing body of the Dragwich burst into flame. The head, which was now beneath the water, also caught fire. The surrounding water didn't put the flames out and when the body did topple under it rested at the bottom of the flooded tunnel, burning away and lighting up the underground passageway.

'Where is Will?' said Edgar, also appearing on the scene. He had been slower than Devery and Felicity and had only just joined the party.

Cora started to sob loudly, the sound muffled by her husband's shoulder. No one had the heart to answer Edgar's question. No one had the heart to tell him that Willoughby Carmichael was dead.

Chapter Forty

They sat together on the wooden bench that was placed on the hill outside the brick Observatory that overlooked the gorge. At that time of the morning the Observatory's café was closed but someone could be heard inside, no doubt prepping coffee and sandwiches, ready for the day's trading. Before them Brunel's iconic Clifton Suspension Bridge rested behind a moderate mist with only the odd pillar or angle of metal poking out from its foggy concealment. A light snow clung to a light breeze, floating beautifully across the landscape.

It was the first time that Finn and Felicity had been alone in days and so far they had found very little to say to one another. The previous night had afforded them no sleep. They had moved through the night and the spot overlooking the bridge was picked as a place to stop and think. The open spaces of the Clifton Downs were all but deserted, with only the odd dog walker or jogger to disturb them.

Finn glanced across at her from time to time. She was snuggled up beneath her jacket, just staring out at the bridge.

'You know I read once,' she said, finally saying something, 'that people sometimes throw themselves off that bridge.'

'That's a cheery thought,' said Finn sarcastically.

'Morbid, I know,' Felicity added quickly. 'Just popped into my head, I guess because we're here. It's really sad, when you think about it. I mean of course it's sad, that was a silly thing to say really. I can't imagine how that must feel, you know, just falling like that. It would be over in like a few seconds but I wonder how quick or slow it would feel?'

Finn agreed with her. It was morbid. But despite how uncomfortable morbid things sometimes made him he couldn't help but think such a topic was rather apt. Dawn had done very little to dispel the awful memories from the previous night. But what the daylight had managed to achieve was an element of dilution, the light having less terrors than the dark. Calm had followed the storm yet Willoughby's untimely loss had a differing effect on the group that was left behind to mourn him.

It had been Emeric who had risen to the occasion more than anyone else, a man who had been a relative stranger before the Dragwich attack and was now proving to be a new and useful ally. He was the only one who seemed capable of pushing his emotions aside, perhaps because he was not emotionally attached to the quest. He had engaged his brain and therefore had the suggestion for the prudent way to proceed.

A dark shape moved down below on one of the many paths that led up to the Observatory. The shape belonged to Devery and its appearance was only brief before disappearing again. The others were out there too, somewhere in the morning mist and patrolling the area, all except Emeric. The Hunter was off somewhere in the heart of the city, pulling strings and calling in favours from contacts, although the Hunter still had not revealed the full extent of his plan for them.

'You ever seen one of those films,' said Felicity, 'where a group of people are trying to stop something bad happening and then get into a situation where someone has to sacrifice themselves to save everyone else? Sometimes they even have to fight one another for the right to volunteer. 'Please, Sir, let me have the honour of dying!' I've never got that. Do you think it would be like that in real life? You think people would be so willing to let themselves die?'

'I can't say I've ever thought about it,' said Finn.

'What would you do?' she asked.

'No idea –'

'I'm scared of dying.'

Finn hadn't expected that. It had surprising depth for her and she didn't look to be joking. 'Me too –'

323

'Why?' Felicity said. She looked at him as though he had said something stupid. 'Why would you need to be scared of dying, Finn?'

Finn couldn't think of anything to say to that. There was a hint in her tone, a suggestion that he should be ashamed of what he was.

'I'm scared it will just all go black,' said Felicity, returning to her point. 'That's why it scares me so much. If I believed in heaven and all that, would probably be easier. But it scares me that everything might just stop, like someone's flipped a switch and after you just don't exist anymore. You're just ... gone.'

'Do fifteen year olds talk like this?' Finn said.

'Talk like what?' Felicity shot back. 'Do they talk about serious things? What if they've seen a whole load of serious things, like we have?'

Finn sighed. 'Can we talk about something else?'

'I think I'm scared of leaving everyone behind too,' Felicity continued, happy with the topic and not considering changing it. 'I mean I don't really have anyone now but I assume I will one day. I hope I will anyway. I'd be scared of leaving everyone and everything behind and then for everyone to have to go on and I'm just ... well ... not there. I'm scared of being gone and forgotten.'

'People will remember you though,' Finn pointed out. 'Is anyone ever forgotten?'

'Remember me how?' Felicity said. 'Remember me as a headstone? As a hunk of rock sitting on a piece of earth that someone visits once a month?'

He wasn't sure he was following her point and he wasn't actually certain she was trying to make one. She was rambling, her words stemming from the heart and he couldn't help but wonder whether Willoughby's death had bought back painful memories of her own mother dying young.

'Some things just get you thinking, I guess,' Felicity said. She seemed to have finished speaking and she ducked her head further into the depth and warmth of her jacket.

'You hate me now, don't you?' Finn said.

'You got that from what I was saying?' Felicity laughed. 'It's always all about you, isn't it, Finlay?'

'No,' he answered, 'but I've wanted to ask you that for a while. It's just a feeling I've got.'

Felicity didn't provide an answer immediately and she titled her head and fixed him with a strange stare like an architect surveying a leaning building and not knowing quite how to fix it. The look didn't disclose her emotions although there was certainly none of her trademark humour or sarcasm in it. It was real. It was conflicted. It was unsure what to say next.

'I don't hate you,' she said eventually, the shape and delivery of the words on her tongue suggesting that there was more to say. But she didn't add to the statement.

'You paused,' Finn said, not willing to let the question go that easily. 'You were going to say something else.'

'I didn't pause,' Felicity disagreed, 'and I haven't got anything else to say –'

'Liar,' Finn said. He sighed again. 'You *so* did pause. And you so do hate me. You can't hide it. It's written all over your face.'

Felicity fidgeted in her seat. She went to protest but then she altered her planned approach and took a deep breath. She bit her lip and shrugged. 'Ok, fair enough,' she said, 'I paused because I keep changing my mind about it. I think you've been an idiot and not just every so often. You've been an idiot like ninety nine percent of the time. I kept thinking to myself that you'd just use your brain all of a sudden and come round but if anything you've just kept getting thicker. You've just missed so many points. Since they told about what you are, I may as well have not existed.'

'Why have I been an idiot though?' Finn said.

'You shouldn't have to ask, Finn. And it's not for me to tell you –'

'But I've had a lot to deal with,' said Finn, wanting to fight his corner. 'Have you stopped to think about that? I'm not being stroppy, I promise, but have you really *honestly* thought about that? I don't know what to make of all of this and every time I think I know what I'm doing something new comes along to knock me for six. My mind's being dragged like everywhere, all at once, by everyone.'

'And I know that,' said Felicity. 'And that's why sometimes I don't hate you. I know what you've been through and that it's not been easy.'

'How do you feel about me now?'

'Right now … I'm indifferent.'

He looked back at the gorge and tried to hide the sadness that was taking over. He didn't want her to see it for he still had his pride. He swallowed a small lump in his throat that hadn't been there a moment before, sniffed through his nose and composed himself gallantly. There was no point in asking a question if you didn't want an honest answer. But the honesty hurt all the same.

Felicity didn't miss his reaction. 'You know people?' she said randomly, changing the subject a touch to save his embarrassment. 'They're pretty easy to work out, as a rule, aren't they, even at our age? I would say that people all tend to think the same way, more or less, and they also tell each other the same lies. I'm saying this because one thing they'll always do is make you feel guilty about being selfish.'

'I don't get it,' Finn said sulkily. His ego bruised, he didn't want to talk anymore.

'Isn't selfishness a pretty basic thing to feel?' Felicity explained. 'Why don't we just admit it? Why don't we just admit when we're feeling selfish or jealous and not be ashamed of it? Why don't we feel that it's ok to admit that the one person we always put first is ourselves? A woman up the road wins a million pounds on a scratch-card and everyone's like 'I'm so happy for her' and 'oh, doesn't she deserve it' when what they're really thinking is what a lucky cow she is and just why she deserves the luck more than them.'

Finn turned to face her. 'So I'm selfish now? We're going to add that to my bad list? That's really what I need right now.'

'No, I've hated you because *I'm* being selfish,' Felicity said, keen to clarify her point. 'And I'm not going to say sorry for that. Do you know what the very first thing I thought was when you told me what you were? The first thing I thought was how it affected me. And it meant that you and I could *never* be together. Never. It meant that our story, this whole Finn and Felicity thing, finishes here.'

He saw it now and he saw it in colour. He understood and sincerely could not believe that he had missed it, even amongst the chaos. He was flushed with an instant guilt.

'I was as close to my Mum as you could imagine,' Felicity said. 'Like really close. And I've never felt like that with anyone since. I find it hard to be comfortable with people sometimes, even just talking about simple things. I sometimes find it hard to look people in the eye. I don't even know why. I'm just a bit awkward, I guess. I used to think sometimes how can people ever get married and feel comfortable enough to live in a house with a complete stranger? I could just never see it happening. The only people I felt that with were my Mum and my Nan. Then I met this village idiot with gay hair and there was something just there, like straight away. I didn't know what it was, I just felt comfortable with you. I felt I wanted to hug you just as much as I wanted to punch you in the face, which probably makes me sound like a maniac but I don't feel that way about any old boy.'

Finn nodded his head, understanding. 'I'm sorry, Fliss –'

'I don't want you to be sorry –'

'But I am –'

'I just want you to understand,' she said. She reached forward and clasped his hand. 'I have to walk away from you now, as soon as I can–'

That stopped him dead and epitomised the old saying of someone pulling the rug out from beneath ones feet. Felicity wasn't a closed book but she certainly had pages torn, paragraphs smudged by tearful experiences, and whole chapters missing. She was a bit of an enigma. But she had opened up to him on more than one occasion, she had spoken honestly and passionately and this time it had seemed like the conversation was taking them towards reconciliation, not this.

'What are you saying?' he stuttered.

'As soon as I can,' she advised, 'I'm leaving –'

'But … for how long?'

'That would be forever, Finn.'

He couldn't quite believe what he was hearing. 'You can't be serious. Fliss, do you realise how I feel about you, I –'

'Please, don't,' Felicity said it strongly but with tenderness. 'We don't need to say or think like that anymore. Look, as cheesy as it sounds this isn't my journey and I'm not the same as you. No one is. I can't leave you behind in sixty years and I can't bear for you to forget me. It's not going to happen. I leave now and all we will be to one another is a couple of people who knew each other once, for a couple of weeks. That will be so much easier.'

Finn gripped her hand firmer, to show how resolute he was in his disagreement. It wasn't much but it was all he could offer. 'Is that all I am to you?' he questioned. 'That's all I'm going to be to you, someone you knew once?'

'Not right now,' Felicity replied. 'But that's how it'll come to be. This isn't going to help.'

'I will *never* forget you –'

'And that's sweet,' Felicity said. There was the trace of a tear that she tried to hide. 'But I wonder if you'll sound so convincing saying that in two hundred and fifty years?' She leaned forward and kissed him briefly on the mouth. Then moving back a touch she gazed deeply into his eyes. 'Some things are just never meant to be.'

There was a stirring in Finn's soul. Five words started to form. By themselves they were just that, simple words, but put together they became a statement, something that was bold and strong. He had rarely said the first three words before, only occasionally to his parents and once to a pizza, but he knew that he truly meant what he was about to say.

'I love you, Felicity Gower,' he said.

He didn't know what he had expected to happen. He had never had much confidence but he was certain that he and Felicity shared a connection. Whether it stretched as far to be classified as love, he wasn't sure. Still, he had taken the plunge and he waited eagerly for her to return the sentiment.

'Finn,' she said, 'never say that to me again –'

'I will,' he said resolutely. 'I will keep saying it and –'

'I will never say it back,' Felicity said. '*Never*. Things like that won't do us any good. It would mean nothing because we can *never* be together, not while you're like this. So please don't say it again, I'm begging you.'

Finn did not get the chance to argue his case any longer. A group of people appeared in the distance, climbing the hill and within a few moments they could make out Emeric as the leader. He was walking with pace and purpose towards them with the others in tow.

'They look like they mean business,' Felicity said. 'Such a serious group of people.'

'Not sure I like their business all that much anymore,' said Finn. 'I wonder if they're starting to realise I may not be capable of what they think I am and that they've made a big mistake.'

'You still think you're not the child?' Felicity said. He had already voiced his concerns to her the night before.

'I know I'm not,' he confirmed. 'I haven't got any of these powers–'

'You don't know that,' said Felicity.

'What would it take for them to come out?' Finn said. 'They didn't come out when Kemi was kicking the hell out of me. They didn't come out when the Dragwich was trying to slaughter all of us. No, I've got nothing. I just wonder what they'll do with me once they know for sure that I'm just the same as the rest of them.'

The others made it to the Observatory but there were no greetings. Business was too pressing for that. They were told to stand and slowly they all walked across the grass of The Downs, spreading out in a long line so they could walk alongside one another and talk.

Emeric had little need for small talk and he got straight to the point. 'Arrangements are in place,' he explained. 'Way I see it you've no other choice so I made that decision. I won't dress it up. They're not exactly ideal but ideal was never something we could realistically expect in the circumstances. In my view you need to move today.' He pulled a gold pocket watch from the breast pocket of his cloak and gave it a quick glance. 'It's only a few moments after six, any objections to moving in the next ten minutes?'

'Depends on what you're bringing us?' Devery said. There was a natural mistrust in the Irishman's eyes.

'I made contact with an old and trusted friend,' Emeric advised. 'He's not one of us but then he doesn't need to be and that probably works out for the best. He's secured us all train tickets to Aberdeen and the train leaves in an hour. It's the first train of the day. The tickets are in his name of course so they can't be traced. Given last night's ordeal this may not sound vastly appealing but he'll smuggle us into the station using an underground tunnel and we will only board the train at the last moment and he will ensure that the platforms are not being watched. In terms of security cameras, I'm assured they will be facing the opposite way.'

Edgar made an unimpressed humming noise. 'This is the grand plan? Catching a train?'

'My contact will have people at each station we pass through,' Emeric continued. 'They'll make sure that those platforms too are not being watched and will call ahead to inform me if they are so we can take action. It's a long journey, some hours in fact, but no one knows you're here and they can't be watching every form of transport and every form of route up and down the country.'

'They've been one step ahead of us every time so far,' Hamish reminded them.

Cora also had her doubts. 'What's so special about Aberdeen?' she queried. 'Why there?'

'Another acquaintance of mine waits there,' Emeric told them. 'This acquaintance will meet us from the station and transport us to a small dock in the middle of nowhere called Ellis-Roach. It's a tiny dock and certainly won't be watched, that I can assure you. From there he has kindly chartered us a modest fishing trawler, again using alias's, which will then take you across the North Sea and to a Scandinavian port of your choosing. We've used him and that route before to transport our antiquities and it's quite safe. That's where I will leave you. My recommendation from there

330

would be to lay low and think about where you want to go from here. Get some Nordic air, see a fjord, maybe look out for a polar bear and let this all die down.'

'We're catching a train,' Devery said, 'then we're catching a boat. And you want us to hail it as ingenious?'

'He's right,' Hamish said. 'It's not like it's something we couldn't have sorted ourselves. Sitting on a train for hours and pinning ourselves in one place doesn't seem logical.'

Emeric laughed to himself. He cleared his throat. 'Tell you what, you're right, you could have made your way to a station, spent time at a ticket kiosk, afforded yourself plenty of opportunities to smile at a CCTV camera, linger on a platform and take your chances. You could have tried your luck at convincing a local fisherman to transport you incognito somewhere exotic and hope he doesn't question why you want him to do it and talk carelessly. Or you could have rented a couple of cars and spent days and weeks travelling up and down the motorways, trying to work out a way of getting out of the country and away from all this carnage.'

The others shared looks between themselves and even though they didn't announce it out loud it was clear that they grudgingly saw his point.

'This plan,' Emeric added. 'Means that you get to that port with the minimum of fuss and attention and then in twelve hours you'll be on the sea and out of this country. Time isn't on your side, not remotely, and the longer you spend in England the more the enemy will strengthen and the harder it will be to leave. You'll be on a train, in daylight, which will make it harder for any enemies to attack, even if they did work out where you are.'

'What's in this for you?' Cora questioned.

'You mean beyond a simple act of humble charity?' Emeric said. He flashed a wicked smile. 'Oh, that would be money. That's what's in it for me. I haven't told you my fee yet. My contacts aren't cheap, my discretion even less so. But the way I see it, you'll pay what I say.' The Hunter extended his hand. 'Do we have a deal?'

Devery was the one to shake the hand but it was clear he did so with a heavy heart.

Deal struck, Finn lowered his pace so that he and Felicity fell back a touch and followed on the heels of the others. He wanted at least one more moment of privacy.

'Will you come on the boat with me?' he asked. 'You won't leave before? I don't want you to.'

'I think so,' Felicity said. 'Don't think I can stay in England either.'

'What will you do?' Finn said. 'Afterwards, I mean.'

'I have no idea. Maybe learn a bit about Vikings –'

'I meant –'

'I know what you meant.'

Finn stopped walking and he opened up his palm, meaning for her to take his hand and hold it. But she didn't take the offering and continued on her way, leaving him behind.

'I meant what I said,' he called after her. 'I won't change my mind about that.'

She stopped and turned around, walking backwards. 'I won't change my mind either,' she said. 'And from now on I think it's time we start to get used to what's going to happen.'

Finn didn't move for a short time. He watched her move away from him, parting the morning mist. Then, quietly to himself, he said something that she had told him he could not say again in her presence.

'I love you, Felicity Gower.'

Chapter
Forty-One

The wall was dominated by twenty-three monitors that covered the entirety of the plaster. Most of the monitors were on and transmitting CCTV images from throughout the facility, the majority showing empty laboratories, one showing the corridor crammed with a group of unhappy looking rivals, and a single monitor showing a strange image of a man sat in the middle of a room and placed on a chair.

The final monitor, positioned in the centre of all the others like a nucleus, was the largest of all the screens. It showed the image of a man in a fantastic suit.

Agatha Carruthers stood in the surveillance room with the Facility Director. His name was Dr Soames and he was a gentleman in his fifties who had been employed by The Guild for twenty years. He was somewhat foppish and spoke in a posh accent and his hair was long and parted down one side. Beneath his lab coat he wore a patterned shirt.

Her father had been silent for some time. He was thinking.

She was extremely tired but there was not one part of her that longed for sleep. Sleep could wait. She looked at the monitor showing the congregated people in the hallway. Half were her people and the other half belonged to the scientists. They were currently at loggerheads and in debate about the correct procedure in this situation.

Agatha approved of the facility. It was a large building in the middle of an industrial district with three upper floors of offices, sitting next door to the headquarters of a banking titan and a relatively well known medical supply company. The building was an indistinct box of brick and mortar with no architectural pizzazz and had an ambiguous sign at the entrance that read

Huntingdon-Goth Logistics, a title that deliberately made no hints towards what the company actually did. The reception had a single desk and a single receptionist and a row of orange and red soft chairs for visitors that never turned up. A set of double doors could be seen behind the receptionist's desk and beyond the doors was a lift but if anyone made it inside they would see no buttons and no physical way to make it move.

The real entrance to the facility was elsewhere and hidden safely away and it led any real visitors down into the bowels of the earth, to the real rooms and laboratories of the building. The upper floors that could be seen from outside were all empty and had never been occupied. There were at least two hundred of these facilities all over the world, all with different names so that they could never be traced to one another. They were all registered and legitimate with their regional governments and no one ever questioned their existence. They posted profits on the stock exchange, modest profits that never drew any attention to their operations.

Inside the subterranean part of the building the interior was pristine and was made up of four floors of identical corridors that led to a host of identical doors secured with identical digital keypads. The floors and walls were a sterile white and cleaned to within an inch of their life. The lights ran down the centre of the ceiling and were always bright and always on and the corridors were generally empty and silent. At least they were until a Subject was captured. For most of the year the facility was dormant but when the Code was Green, the underground world sprung to life.

Code Green had happened without her say so. Some of her people had intercepted a target and now he sat, in one of the rooms, handcuffed and scared, the scientists waiting to carry out their explorations.

'What's the subject's name?' her father barked suddenly. He wasn't at all happy.

'Stieg Ekström,' Agatha said, 'or at least that's the name he's currently using. Swedish origin but our files suggest he's spent time in the Ukraine, Russia, and Norway over the years. That's if

334

we think it's the same target we've come across through other testimonies. He's never come directly onto our radar.'

'Age?' her father asked.

Agatha nodded. Her stomach did a little flutter. This was a big target to catch. 'Approximately five hundred years old.'

'Ability?'

'Level nine,' said Agatha, 'highly dangerous. We had to shoot him once before our approach otherwise we would never have secured him without losing people.'

Her father was quiet for a long time. Then there was a flash of anger. 'Why am I being disturbed with this?' he said finally. 'The protocol is in place.'

Agatha glanced across to the Doctor and motioned for him to come forward. It was his turn.

'Yes ... Sir,' the Doctor said, his words stammering a touch. 'There ... are some small complications ... er ...well ... in that your daughter ... well the Operatives in fact ... well, they feel the need to question the subject before we can get to work ... and as we stand they are blocking us and preventing us from getting started.'

'Explain this?' The father said that to his daughter. 'What questions need to be asked? He won't talk to you and if he did he would just lie.'

'Quite,' Doctor Soames said smugly. 'I agree entirely.'

'Perhaps I have some new questions in mind,' Agatha said.

Her father was having none of it. 'They do not know what we need to know, Agatha. They *are* what they *are* and only science will reveal the secrets of their origins. I am struggling to comprehend why I would need to tell you this?'

'My staff are all here,' said Doctor Soames, growing in confidence and feeling like his superior was onside. 'We are all here and prepped and ready to go and as per procedure we have suitable explanations in place for our absences from our normal lives. There mustn't be any unnecessary delays otherwise we risk unwanted scrutiny. I personally cannot be missing for days at a time. That is why the protocol is set in stone in the first place and a point your daughter seems to be avoiding. I don't know why.'

Agatha could have laughed out loud and she would have done if she felt it would have been appropriate. It was a huge misstep. And the poor Doctor had been doing so well.

'You are my employee, are you not?' her father asked the Doctor. 'Is it not *your* responsibility to make appropriate arrangements for when you are required, under the terms of your employment to attend the facility?' Her father let that hang in the air. 'Or, so I understand this correctly, are you saying that you are only available at times where it fits in with your family commitments? Are you missing out on a barbecue?'

'No,' said Doctor Soames. 'That wasn't what –'

'I wouldn't dream of speaking for you,' said her father, 'so let me speak for myself and state how I see this. My family has paid you and your people small fortunes for your expertise. You have gladly allowed such payments to sit in your account. I'm sure you live quite a luxurious life off the back of them. I for one would be most put out to discover that you are not perhaps grateful when the time comes for you to hold up your end of the bargain. If such a thing came to pass, I am sure I could dispatch some of my people to your facility to provide you with refresher training in commitment.'

Agatha didn't know whether to be impressed or appalled. It was typical of her dear old papa. He was still a cruel, monstrous man and she didn't doubt for a second that he would be tempted to murder the poor Doctor's wife and fifty percent of his staff just to prove a rather morbid point. Her father despised any whiffs of disobedience and was not afraid to make examples of people.

'I don't care about your home life, young man,' her father went on. 'I only care about what I am paying you to do.'

'I haven't exactly helped the Doctor,' Agatha said, hoping to diffuse the chance of any innocents becoming victims on her part. 'I've not given him my reasons and in a sense he's right. But that's because he hasn't the wit to see the bigger picture. I'm here and I will make sure he carries out the duties we've paid him for once I've finished with the subject.'

There was a flicker in the Doctor's eyes. He was still nervous but he could sense that despite their differing agendas she was trying to dig him out of a very deep hole.

Her father didn't appear to be getting any calmer. 'Doctor, leave us!'

The Doctor took a deep breath of relief and darted from the room as quickly as his legs cold take him, slamming the door shut. Now alone, her father spoke angrily and not veering away from his normal demeanour his next question was sharp. 'I am of the understanding,' he hissed, 'that you have issued an order that prevents your operatives from intercepting those you are tracking? You gave this order the moment they informed you the Swede was secured?'

Agatha wasn't surprised that he knew. 'Theo told you?'

'It doesn't matter who told me. What the hell are you thinking?'

'An opportunity has presented itself and −'

'The child is gone,' her father shouted that at the top of his voice, a fierce growl that made her jump. He took a few moments to compose himself but his chest was pulsating. 'You were instructed to pursue the child as he was unprotected and therefore the subject with the minimal risk. Now that he is in the hands of others that risk has amplified and therefore it would be prudent for you to reassess your overall position. Other subjects are in the area and can be tracked. Bring them in and pass them over to the facility.'

Be strong, Agatha. You've got this. 'There are other factors,' she said.

'There are no other factors −'

'There is more going on here than we understand at present,' Agatha said instantly in response. 'We need to consider the significance of this migration. Why is it happening? A concentration of immortal's in one place at the same time is something that is completely unprecedented. They *all* seek the boy and we need to understand why that's the case. He is the youngest recorded immortal and −'

'Someone has to be the youngest, Agatha −'

337

'But they *all* seek him!' Agatha said firmly, 'and every last one of them. The immortal is a creature of habit, you know that, and their current movements are an utter anomaly. Anomalies can't be ignored. And this Brotherhood, confirmed by Mr Ekström in the room opposite me, well these are heavyweights and they don't come out of the woodwork for nothing. An immortal attracts a Guardian, a single soul, and that is the only one who comes looking for them.'

'They *are* creatures of habit,' said her father. His mood had softened and she knew him well enough to know that she had piqued his interest. 'And knowing their kind they often have little superstitions that drive them. This is no doubt some nonsense that is written in their literature –'

'No,' Agatha disagreed. It was a brave step and one that could certainly backfire. 'This migration is the key. They're scared of the child and we need to know why. We can keep on catching these people and cutting them up, but where has it got us? The child is something different and he may just be the answer to all of this.'

Silence. This was good. He was thinking. He made his decision quickly. 'Question the Swede,' he said. 'You have an hour, no longer and then you report back to Theo who in turn will report back to me. We reassess from there. Are we done?'

'No, we're not done,' Agatha said. There was something she had forgotten to mention. 'I engaged with the child before he escaped us. We spoke at length and it was clear to me that the girl who is with him is very important to him.'

'And?'

'If we do manage to locate the child again,' Agatha said, 'then I fully anticipate that we will not be alone, such is the importance I believe he has. It could prove messy and extremely difficult to secure him. My recommendation is that if the tide doesn't turn in our favour, then we take the girl as the next best option, if that opportunity presents itself.'

'I have no problem with bait,' her father said. He was bored of the conversation and the screen went abruptly black once more.

Agatha spent the next half an hour exerting her new authority and she started by sending the scientists away. They did go to protest but with the blessing of her father all she had to do was look threatening and they quickly backed down. Doctor Soames in particular had lost all his desire to argue.

After she recovered the briefcase that she had left with Theo she made her way across the hallway to the room that held their captive. She punched in a security code to the keypad and a few seconds later she was sat in front of the Swede. As expected he had nothing to say to her. Beyond the flesh wound in his thigh Ekström had not been touched and he stared at her with a brute intensity. His blonde hair was tied up in a ponytail and his hands were secured behind his back with some elegantly bespoke handcuffs that were designed specifically for people like him.

'You've not tried to escape?' Agatha asked.

Ekström was happy just to watch her. He sat perfectly still. He was no doubt fantasising about the malicious things he could do to her if he were free.

'You must be a clever man?' She said it as though it was a compliment. 'Those things around your wrists, they're what we call contingency fetters. They look like standard handcuffs. But no, they're designed for men like you. I know a little bit of metal isn't going to keep you at bay for long. I doubt you'd even break a sweat snapping them in two. It would probably take you the same amount of time to snap my neck, if you could. But of course inside our little cuffs is a chemical called S4TQ, utterly experimental and completely illegal, but should the handcuffs be broken the chemical inside will change with the atmosphere and we'll be spending a good few days picking up all the different charred pieces of you off the wall.'

There wasn't a flicker from Ekström. It wasn't news to him.

'I can't read your eyes,' said Agatha. 'But I don't need to. You're the easiest species on this planet to read. Your species are some of the biggest cowards in the animal kingdom. There's only one thing you care about.'

'Such certainty,' said Ekström quietly. 'You are so sure that I won't break these chains, just to have the satisfaction of taking you with me?'

Agatha hid her smile. She knew his game for she had been playing it for years. He was happy to talk without talking, to speak without really saying anything. A bit of acidic banter was acceptable. But once he opened his mouth he would soon lose control of what came out of it. He just didn't know it yet. Even she was surprised at how quickly she had got her first bite.

'Let me fill in some blanks for you, Mr Ekström,' said Agatha, 'just to entertain myself. You wouldn't dream of killing yourself just to get at little old me. Why? Because you fear Hell. But here's the truth of it. You've already lived a wicked, selfish, murderous life. You're going to Hell regardless of what you choose to do in the end.'

Ekström leaned forward in his seat, careful not to upset the positing of the contingency fetters. 'If that's the case,' he said through an unappealing smile, 'I wonder who it will be that will be sat in the opposite corner?'

Agatha let that fly. She really was in control now. 'Why is the child so important to you?' she asked, changing the subject to more relevant matters. 'What is his significance?'

Ekström reverted back to silence.

'I love a bit of back and forth,' Agatha said. She pointed at the clock on the wall behind her. 'But unfortunately I'm on a bit of a tight time limit, I'm afraid.'

Ekström chose to offer an insult and he spat, the phlegm shooting out and landing near her feet.

'What are your thoughts on torture, Mr Ekström?' Agatha said. 'My views tend to change from time to time. I confess I can be ponderous. It's one of my flaws.' She casually reached down and scooped up the briefcase that was resting beneath her chair. She snapped it open and pulled a small item from within and placed the case back from where it had come from. She held the item out in front of her. 'Do you recognise this?' she asked.

Ekström continued trying to maintain his cold composure but his eyes betrayed him this time. Oh, he knew exactly what it was.

In her hands was the strangest of items. The item was made of straw and hemp and it had been spun and twined into the shape of a small, crudely depicted man. The man had no features beyond two hollow crescents where his eyes would be and his outline was rough and slapdash. The only thing that stood out was a small door that had been carved into the chest of the man and it was a door with the tiniest, black handle. The item could have been nothing but a child's plaything but the sight of it had struck fear into Ekström's heart and he fidgeted in the chair, pushing backwards as though it was evil incarnate and he wanted to get as far away from it as humanly possible.

'How did you get that?' he asked nervously. 'That's impossible –'

'It's amazing what wonders you can acquire from the deceased,' said Agatha. 'Of course normal people may only salvage a carriage clock or some jewellery. But not from your kind, oh no, life is far more exotic from your kind and tinged with those hidden bits of magic from the past. I acquired this many years ago and kept it.'

Ekström started to sweat. He was tempted to struggle before remembering that he dared not.

'It was called a *pontishrek* in the original tongue,' said Agatha. 'But I believe a more popular name, in the dark corners of the world of course, would be a *Devotion Doll.* I love the irony.' She stood and walked slowly over to her captive, placing herself so that she was hovering behind him. He tried to twist his neck so that he could keep his eyes on her. 'Never had this confirmed,' she said. 'And in reality it should repulse me far more than it should fascinate me, but my understanding is that the doll originated from a group of people who existed long before voodoo was even mastered. For me, I've never seen the point in torture. Man always has the capability to lie and conceal, even under threat of the most severe pain. In the end a man who is being tortured simply tells you what he needs to, to make the pain stop and it's rarely the truth. Most output one gets from torture is generally useless.'

She snapped a long piece of Ekström's blonde hair from his scalp. She gazed at it in the light, saw that it would do perfectly. 'And thus there is the wonder and majesty of the Devotion Doll,' she said. She returned to her chair and sat the doll up on her lap like a toy so that it was looking at him. Then she opened up the small door in the dolls chest and placed the hair inside before closing it.

'Please!' Ekström pleaded. 'Don't! You mustn't –'

'The priestesses responsible for this creation,' she said seriously, 'understood that a man attaches more devotion to the ones he loves than he does himself. They understood that a man will sometimes allow his body to be abused and broken and take his secrets to the grave. But flip that on its head, flip it completely, and if you torture someone else, someone this brave martyr truly loves, then he will spill his guts.'

'You witch,' Ekström said.

Agatha impersonated a voice and moved the doll, pretending that it was speaking. '*Please don't hurt my wife or my son or my little baby girl, kind Sir!*' she said. She tapped the torso of the doll and the noise was hollow. 'And all I need to do is place a strand of hair inside the doll and just like its voodoo cousin you can then destroy the doll bit by bit, and someone, somewhere, the *wife* or *son* or *little baby girl*, the person that the captive loves more than anyone else in the world will feel that pain and suffering. The determined torturer will never know who this poor person will be but the captive always will.'

Ekström was shaking erratically now and he stared at her like she was the devil. His face was a mixture of anger, hate, revulsion, and desperation.

'I know you, Mr Ekström,' Agatha said. 'You are not one to bemoan your gift and losses and swear that you will never love again to spare future pain and grief. No, you take wives. You always have. You let them into your secret, you swear them to secrecy and then you watch them grow old and die and then move on to the next one. But while they live you do truly love them. You have someone right now, somewhere, waiting for you, completely unaware of the harsh pain that I could brandish just by pure will. You will tell me you don't have this person but I can already see that you do.'

She twisted the leg of the doll and although it didn't snap away it transformed into a deformed angle. Ekström jerked in the chair.

'Quite the durable little item, isn't it?' she said, taunting him. She twisted the other leg, creating the same cruel angle. 'It's just like plasticine when it shouldn't be. You really can reshape this with regularity –'

Ekström was starting to weep. 'Stop it, damn you!'

'The power to stop belongs to you –'

'No, no, no –'

Agatha pulled at the arm, stretching it angrily and tightly. 'You can even pull a limb right off,' she laughed, enjoying the control she had and pushing it further. 'It can always be stitched back on, after you're finished of course, ready to be used another day for another poor soul.'

'Hurt me, hurt me, not –'

'Who?' Agatha said. 'Not your wife? Not your son? Perhaps your daughter? Maybe we're talking grandchildren? Who, Mr Ekström? Who am I hurting?'

Ekström was turning into a crying mess. He was speaking, no doubt cursing her, but the words were impossible to make out.

Agatha glanced at the clock. She was getting bored now and had no more time to play with her prey. As such she gave one sharp tug and ripped the right arm of the doll clear off.

Ekström screamed at the horrendous sight.

Agatha stood and pushed the doll so that it was almost touching his face. She had not the slightest sliver of sympathy for him. He did indeed have the ability to stop this and he alone was responsible for someone right that moment experiencing excruciating agony. 'Shall I do arm number two, Mr Ekström?' she asked him. 'Number two? Your choice, Sir! Your choice!'

'Ok,' Ekström said. He was beaten. 'I will tell you why we seek the child. Please, just stop.'

There was a loud knock at the door and Theo poked his head into the interrogation room. 'Two minutes,' he said to Agatha like he was interrupting a board meeting. 'Out here, please.'

Agatha could barely believe it. 'Now?'

'Now,' Theo said. 'It's important.'

'I will send someone in to take your testimony,' Agatha advised Ekström matter-of-factly, the game over. 'You lie to him, Mr Ekström, and you know what happens?'

Task completed she joined Theo out in the hallway, taking the doll with her. Her uncle looked almost lively and excited and his cheeks were flushed red, yet she didn't think he had been drinking. 'We've just got a call,' he said quickly. 'You must take it.'

'I've just spoken to my father,' she answered. 'He granted my authority and –'

'It's not your father,' said Theo. His smile was as wide as she had ever seen it and she was not sure that she liked him this way. 'A subject has made contact, just a few minutes ago. It appears that we have ourselves a bona fide Judas. He wants to strike a deal for your son.'

'He knows where the child is?' Agatha was frowning. That couldn't be what he meant.

'He does indeed,' Theo confirmed.

Agatha gasped and had a whole host of instant questions, not least just how this supposed subject managed to even make contact in the first place. She wanted to doubt it. It was a ridiculous concept. It wasn't like the subject could look in the phone book or speak to the operator. What section would their organisation even come under? Did he flick to H for Homicidal Maniacs Devoted to Discovering the Secret of Eternal Life? There was no heading for that in any phone book she had seen.

'You take Mr Ekström's testimony,' she instructed her uncle, more than a little curious. 'You're the best qualified to ensure the correct level of compliance. I will take the call.'

'I've patched it through to the Directors office,' said Theo, placing his hand on the door handle to the interrogation room. 'I have already put mobilisation in motion. They'll be ready to go any time now.'

Agatha felt reinvigoration course through her veins and the feeling was fantastic. She was already motivated but this took it to another level. Theo was many things but one thing she did trust was his judgement in these situations. He was often better outside the *field* than within it.

She had one last thing to do and she ripped the head from the doll's shoulders. Dust floated through the air from the callous decapitation. She tossed the straw head to Theo.

'Get his explanation,' she said, full of unrepentant malice. She nodded proudly at her handy work. 'Then make sure he sees *that* before you hand him over to the scientists. I can't help but love the poetry of it.'

Chapter Forty-Two

The world whizzed by on the other side of the train window, an endless pattern of frozen fields, sleeping towns, and villages. It was snowing heavily again and the sky was an impressive white, the clouds heavy and full of flakes.

Finn had fallen asleep with his head against the window and when he stirred a part of his dream had stayed with him. The dream itself had taken the form of a memory, the memory being from his last family holiday. His mother had been sitting on a tatty red stool next to him in the arcade of the pier. They were laughing together at the daftness of the game they were playing, a novelty game of mounted mechanical metal horses and jockeys that would race from left to right and that you could gamble modest amounts of your money on. Players would press a button, choosing up to two horses, and the numbers would light up and the machine would come to life.

The results that generally ended up being in the arcade owners favour suggested the game may have been rigged but it was still mightily popular, so much so that the arcade even afforded it a commentator, a young girl with pigtails and acne with a microphone who could have been no older than fourteen and looked as bored as she could be with what appeared to be an ordeal rather than a job. It had taken them the best part of ten pounds to finally 'back a winner' and he randomly recalled that it had been Horse Number 6, the bright pink horse with the white cap that was ordinarily the slowest but on this occasion had romped home, coming from behind to leave the field trembling in its wake. They had cheered it all the way, shouting moronic motivational blurbs to the bobbling hunk of metal and once it had passed the finish line they had burst into hysterical laughter and they had even gone as far as to hug.

It was an odd memory of Agatha Carruthers, one of the few where she had embraced something silly. Maybe that was why that particular memory had stuck.

'You look like you're away with the little fairies,' said Felicity, who was sat next to him. They had secured seats on the train with a table and they sat back lazily with their legs resting on the seats opposite. 'What would you be thinking about?'

'My mother,' he answered, without elaborating further. He pressed his head back to the window and started to drift off once again, the zooming landscape taking effect and the monotonous hum of the moving train acting as an insatiable lullaby that he was quite unable to resist. He didn't fall into a deep sleep however and the face of his mother stayed with him. This time he dreamt of her as a child, or at least his own image of what she might have been like as a child, interspersed with what could only have been the cheesiness of a fairy-tale. In the dream she was sat in a tall tower in a cold and windswept land, a neglected Princess playing a harp and singing a song of woe.

Finn awoke with a jolt sometime later and omitted a little snort like a pig.

'That was attractive,' said Felicity. 'Oh, and so is the little bit of dribble running down your chin.'

The train had stopped and was waiting at a busy station. Outside the window the platform was alive with passengers that were disembarking and boarding. No one would be bothering them though. Emeric had taken the sensible step of buying out their entire carriage. At other stations the newcomers had occasionally made an appearance to look for spare seats but when they wandered into the carriage they quickly saw the small monitor above the seats confirming they were 'reserved' and with a huff they swiftly departed to start their search elsewhere.

'Where's Emeric and Cora?' Finn asked, sitting up and wiping the unattractive saliva away with his shirt sleeve. He had noticed that they were missing. Before he had drifted off everyone had been present, Devery and Cora had taken the two seats behind

347

them, Hamish and Edgar the seats opposite and across the aisle and Emeric had been sitting in various different seats all morning and seemed to change at every station they either stopped at or passed.

'I think Cora's gone to get us something to eat,' said Felicity. 'I didn't want to wake you so said to get a cheese and onion sandwich if they have one.'

Finn was unhappy at that. 'Ignoring the fact that I don't like cheese and onion sandwiches?'

'I'm devastated I didn't know that,' Felicity said sarcastically.

There was the sound of a whistle outside and the train chugged and very slowly started to ease forwards. This was good news, another station successfully navigated.

'And Emeric?' Finn asked again. 'What about him? Where's he?'

'I don't know,' Felicity shrugged. 'Think he went to check something with the people he's got outside, or something like that, I wasn't really listening.' She yawned and stretched out her arms. 'It's nearly midday. This train is going to take forever and I'm already really bored. Wish I had a tablet or my mobile or something.'

The train was back to full speed and it hit the open countryside once again. Cora returned to the cabin carrying an arm full of food from the catering carriage. She passed out to each of them a sandwich (which was indeed cheese and onion), a packet of crisps, and a bottle of fizzy drink. A few moments later Emeric too reappeared through the same door and this time he took the first seat he came across, which was far away from the others. Evidentially, after the last stop, the intention was to be antisocial.

'Do you know what I could really do with right now?' Felicity said as she chewed on bread that was very much on the stale side and not particularly nice. 'I'm thinking a full, dirty English breakfast, and holding like nothing back, four rashers of bacon, four sausages, six eggs, hash browns, mash potato –'

Finn sniggered. 'You don't get mashed potato with a full English–'

Felicity wasn't finished. 'Mushrooms, fried tomatoes, beans, toast with full fat butter, ooh and big slabs of black pudding –'

Finn pulled a disgusted face. 'You know they make black pudding from the pig's blood, don't you?'

'We have something called white pudding in Ireland,' said Devery from behind them. 'Now *that* you need to try, it's the best thing in the world, can't really get it over here though. And you missed out soda bread. You've got me thinking about it now.'

'And a wee bit of Scottish whiskey,' said Hamish, 'in a nice milky cup of tea.'

Edgar, who appeared to be asleep, couldn't help but comment on that. 'And they say the image of the drunken Scotsmen is unfair,' he said.

'Best way to start a morning,' said Hamish, 'and it puts hairs on your chest.'

Finn was glad to be talking about something simple again. Breakfast was a random thing to talk about but it was certainly better than the alternative. There was a hot topic that was causing a great deal of concern and had been on the agenda for most of the morning. Tobias had been spotted and Tobias was a child. More importantly he was an immortal who had *Settled* as a child. It was a fact that went against the very prophecy these people had pinned both their hopes and their actions upon and the debate was whether it was enough to shatter the foundation and faith of their entire quest.

Despite his stomach rumbling and complaining loudly in response to the fantasy of greasy breakfast food, Finn thought about taking his third nap of the morning but then he saw a flash of movement between the cabins up ahead. Someone was looking into the cabin from the other side of the glass. No sooner had he noticed it then the door opened and three men walked swiftly into the carriage, one of whom he recognised immediately.

An additional two men entered from the opposite entrance, pinning them in. Again the man at the head of the group was no stranger. He was scowling as he neared and wore a large plaster on top of his broken nose.

Finn closed his eyes and sighed. He wasn't particularly surprised. The last time he had felt truly safe was at Bronwyn's library and he wasn't about to make the mistake of feeling that comfortable again. This journey seemed to be one that would be constantly littered with twists and turns.

Devery had spotted the danger and he shot out of his position instantly. He leapt up and stood high on the seat, his sandwich falling onto the floor and he was ready to resist and fight. But Gilliam Béranger was no slouch and within a split second he had removed a firearm from his jacket pocket and aimed it at Devery's chest. He was ready to pull the trigger if so required.

'You're one of the quick ones, no doubt,' Gilliam said. 'Doubt you'll be that quick with a bullet in your chest. Sit yourself down, friend, there's no need to die here.'

Devery didn't sit and he stared up the carriage. The newcomers were also armed and ushering the rest of the group into the aisle. Only Finn and Felicity remained seated.

Wyatt Eagan walked casually forward and slid himself down into the seat opposite the youngest members of the group. He was the only one not armed. Having asked politely and been rebuffed, Gilliam took control of Devery, dragging him down off the seat and forcing him to his knees at gunpoint.

Finn was already wondering quite how they had been ensnared in this trap. But the answer wasn't far away. Emeric had also climbed to his feet but instead of being a captive he was hovering at the back of the melee and no one seemed to be paying him any intention. And he didn't look like he was likely to mount any form of rescue.

The Hunter caught Finn's stare and looked away, although there was no shame in his eyes.

Devery had worked it out too. Although he had his back to the Hunter he addressed him. 'This your doing, Emeric?' he shouted.

'I have no investment in this quest,' said Emeric, 'but given the choice, I think I'd probably rather go on living.'

Devery was struggling to contain his anger. 'So you know,' he said to the Hunter, 'next time I get the chance, I'm going to kill you.'

Wyatt was looking at Finn. 'These people wanted you to lead them,' he said. 'So it seems only right that I address you, and not them. You comfortable with that?'

'You can talk to me if you want,' said Finn.

Wyatt smiled. The smile was oddly warm. 'My name is Wyatt,' he said by means of an introduction. 'My friend with the broken nose is Gilliam.' He gestured to each of his comrades in turn. Their names were Noakes, Benedict, Speller and Perez. 'I want to start by apologising to you. I want you to understand that I'm sincere in saying that. You didn't ask for any of this, I know that, none of us ever do. And I won't get any pleasure in what we need to do, not a single bit. I'm not sure that's going to be worth all that much to you but I wanted to say it all the same.'

'You think he needs your pity?' Devery said.

'I wouldn't call it pity, Finn,' said Wyatt. 'It's a man showing reluctance at having to undertake something that is forced upon him by circumstance.'

'Have I missed something?' said Hamish, who was on his knees next to Devery, Cora, and Edgar in the aisle. 'When did it change so that you're supposed to feel sorry for the executioner?'

Benedict gave Hamish a harsh thump in the back of the head with his gun for that.

'We only have a few minutes until the next station,' said Wyatt. 'And I think we maybe need to think about how we're going to behave when we get there. We're going to get off the train quietly and without fuss or thoughts of raising the alarm. We can't lose you again now, Finn. That's no option for us. If any of you did happen to scream or run or do something stupid like that we would have to react and that could mean innocent people getting caught in the crossfire. I don't want that and I'm sure you don't either.'

'Where are we going to go?' Finn wondered. He was morbidly curious.

'We are going to go and take you to Tobias,' said Wyatt. 'He's the only one that can perform the ritual.'

Finn was tempted to disclose his theory that he wasn't even the child they were looking for, that he had no power and no ability to end the line of the immortals, that they were wrong. But he could see that it would be fruitless. It wouldn't matter. No one could ever be sure but it didn't mean that he wouldn't need to be eliminated, just in case.

'You're not my enemies,' said Wyatt. He addressed that to the group. 'Not when we drill right down to the bone. But I can't have you following us and I know you will. So I'll keep things simple. We'll get off at the station, find somewhere quiet and all we need to do is slow you down so we can get this done. My thoughts are that two bullets in each thigh should be sufficient. Then when this deplorable task is behind us, I would say that any tension between us is over. I hope you will feel the same.'

'Can I object slightly?' Felicity said. She raised her hand like she was in class and trying to get the teachers attention. 'I'm like fifteen years old. Shooting me twice in each leg seems a little bit over the top, doesn't it? I mean, come on, even for you. I don't know where you come from but shooting kids is kinda frowned upon where I live.'

'You've got a very smart mouth,' said Gilliam. He made sure that his gun didn't move an inch from Devery. 'And seeing as you broke my nose you can have four bullets in each leg for your trouble.'

Wyatt silently shook his head to reassure her. Even though they fought on different sides he wouldn't let that happen.

Hamish started to laugh. It was an unexpected sound and it made everyone in the carriage look at him. It didn't seem fitting given the gravity of the situation.

'Is there something funny about all this?' Benedict said, burrowing the barrel of the gun into the back of Hamish's head.

'Oh, it's not that actually,' Hamish explained, struggling to get his words out through the laughter. 'It's just that something's just struck me.'

Benedict went to strike him again but was stopped by a shout.

'No,' said Wyatt. 'What do you mean?'

Hamish nodded up the carriage. 'Perhaps you should ask Mr Emeric if you were the only people he sold us out to.'

Wyatt's eyes flickered with doubt. He turned his attention to the Hunter, who looked back but said nothing.

'There's a tunnel up ahead,' said Hamish, 'and when we come out of the other side, this train is going to be derailed.'

Everyone in the carriage exchanged looks, taking the threat very seriously. Hamish was not a stranger to any of them and if they did not know him personally they knew of him by reputation, fully aware of the extent of his gift. Hamish had seen something. Something bad was coming.

Gilliam glared at Emeric. 'Is this true? Did you sell us out to *them?*'

Benedict smashed the gun into Hamish's back. 'Or is this some sort of trick?'

'Who are we talking about?' Wyatt asked Emeric. 'Who else did you sell this information to?'

Finn didn't need to wait for the answer. He already knew. His mother was about to crash the party. Things were about to get very interesting. The train entered the predicted tunnel and outside the world went black. The carriage remained lit by the lights running above them.

'Here we go,' said Hamish.

Emeric grinned and chuckled nervously as if he was about to deny it but then his face became stern and he bolted, dashing for the door behind him. He punched the button on the wall and the door hissed open. Gilliam opened fire, desperate to exact revenge for the betrayal but Emeric was too quick and the bullets missed, smashing into the glass and shattering it. The Hunter was gone.

With the sudden clap and confusion of gunfire, all hell broke loose. Cora seized the opportunity and flexed her palms open and the gun leapt out of Gilliam's palm and flew through the air and into her own grip. Speller, standing next to her, tried to disarm her and their hands became locked in a struggle. The aim of the weapon found its way skywards and then went off, firing four quick and loud shots into the ceiling of the carriage and breaking three of the lights.

Devery used the drama and he moved quickly, ducking away from his captor and spinning around the back of Gilliam. The two men started to wrestle and Gilliam ran himself backwards, crunching Devery's body into the wall. Hamish, keen to join in, smashed the back of his head into Benedict's face, catching him off guard, his head connecting with Benedict's chin. Edgar set upon the last two men, punching Noakes in the face and then grappling with Perez's weapon.

Wyatt didn't move an inch. In the American's eyes there was a plea for Finn. The plea said one thing. *Please don't*. But Finn darted forward and hoping that his prophesised strength would suddenly appear he aimed a punch at Wyatt's jaw. The American avoided it with minimal effort and with his left hand he reached forward and clutched Finn by the throat, stopping him from coming any closer.

Felicity attacked at the same time from the right and she too chose the punch as her weapon of choice and although her attempt connected with Wyatt's cheek he didn't flinch and he flicked his free hand into her stomach idly as if she were nothing more than a fly trespassing on his open lunch. But even though it appeared idle, his power sent Felicity smashing up into the ceiling. She came back to earth and slammed into the table, curling up into a ball of pain.

'You leave her alone,' Finn said through the fingers clasping his neck.

'Please,' Wyatt implored. 'Please don't make me hurt you anymore than I need to! I don't want this!'

Gunfire was reverberating through the cabin now, the fight in full throttle.

'We're hitting the end of the tunnel,' shouted Hamish.

The train shot out into the daylight and as soon as it did a line of explosives that were positioned carefully on both sides of the track in front of the train detonated. The detonations spanned a great, expansive length and simply blew the metal of the tracks away so that they no longer existed. The impact on the speeding train was brutal and fatal. It had no chance of slowing down and with the tracking obliterated it thundered on towards its fate. The world around them seemed to rattle and shake.

Chapter Forty-Three

There was darkness. Finn's head was pounding, the pain spreading out in waves and deepening. For a moment he couldn't quite think where he was, although he had little doubt that it was somewhere bad. His eyes were closed and he was lying on his back, that much he could tell, and there was a hefty weight sat on his chest that was making it difficult to breathe.

He slowly opened his eyes. Now he remembered. The weight on his chest belonged to Felicity. Her eyes were still firmly shut and she was bleeding from a small cut on the side of her forehead.

'Fliss,' Finn said. There were sparks of electricity flashing around them. He moved his shoulders as best as he could to try and gently nudge her. 'Are you ok?'

She stirred and groaned. 'I think I'm going to maybe go with no.'

'Are you hurt?'

'God, it was only a tiny little train crash, Finn,' she said. 'Don't be so dramatic.' She raised her head and then rolled off his chest. She sat crossed legged and covered her eyes with her hands. She was very groggy.

Finn took in his surroundings. The train carriage had careered off the tracks, rolled, broken away from the other carriages and come to rest on its side. The chairs and tables were now on the walls although a lot of the seats had come loose with the impact of the crash and were resting wherever they had fallen. The windows, which were now in the ceiling and beneath them, had all their glass missing. There were cables dangling down here and there, broken and omitting dangerous sparks that made them vibrate and spasm as if they were living creatures.

There were the groans and coughs of the injured from every direction. But outside there were also the hollers of shouts. Someone was out there and moving quickly and barking instructions. But it didn't take much to understand that the voices did not belong to eager rescuers. Rescuers would have never got there that quickly. Whoever it was out there, they had been waiting.

Finn got uneasily into a kneeling position and looked up the cabin, trying to locate the others. He saw Cora first. She was laid out on her back a few yards away. Perez and Speller were nearby, both men already standing and searching for their lost guns amongst the wreckage. Cora however was already alert and she opened up each of her palms once more and the two weapons they were searching for skidded out from under piles of metal debris and across the glass covered ground and quickly into her possession. The two men watched them go and tried to grab them unsuccessfully. There was little they could do other than hold their hands up.

'Must we?' Cora said, shaking her head. Armed in both hands, she had the advantage. 'Don't you think we might just have something a bit more pressing to deal with right now?'

There was a series of odd pops from outside like the sound of someone discharging a number of fireworks. The pops kept coming, one after another, and then they fell silent.

'What was that?' Felicity said as she pressed her fingers to her temple. She touched the new wound on her head, noting the blood on her fingertips.

'I think I can hazard a guess,' Devery said. He scurried up the train on his hands and knees. 'I think they're shooting canisters into the other train carriages. They'll knock out the civilians. They won't want any witnesses to see what they're about to do here, too much mess.' He stood, shaking broken glass from his clothes. 'I saw a train sitting on the tracks in the tunnel as we passed it. This is going to be a smash and grab.'

Edgar appeared next, coughing and spluttering. 'I've got a headache,' he said.

Devery started to kick out the remaining pieces of the broken glass in the windows beneath his feet. The train wreck seemed to be at an angle and he was checking to see if there was an escape option available beneath them. But as he kicked through the glass his feet only disturbed grass, snow, and soil. There was certainly not enough room for a man to squeeze through. Dejected the Irishman focused instead skywards, trying to work out a route so that he could get up there safely. He pushed the nearest chair at ground level, seeing if it would hold his weight and making sure it wouldn't break free if he decided to climb up. Satisfied it would suffice he started to climb.

The rest of the immortals too were slowly coming to their senses. Although battered and bruised, most seemed to have survived and for the moment their own battle seemed to have been forgotten. Noakes was the only one who didn't move. The man was stuck underneath two fallen seats. He was clearly dead.

Gilliam for one was watching Devery's ascent with great interest. Wyatt was leaning against one of the walls and catching his own lost breath. He was visibly shaken and bleeding from a wound on his shoulder. Edgar was assisting Hamish and was helping him to his feet. It was Hamish who seemed to have suffered the worst non-fatal injuries and he was in bad shape and finding it difficult to walk. Benedict was simply squatting, rocking back and forth, perhaps injured and looking mightily furious. Perez and Speller still hadn't found the confidence to put their hands down.

Devery had found his way successfully through the strange new geography of the train, using whatever protrusions he could find and then he carefully eased his head up through one of the missing window panes.

'No, Dev,' Cora shouted, filled to the rim with worry.

'They want us alive,' Devery shouted back down confidently and without any trace of fear. 'They won't shoot, not yet. That comes later.'

Edgar led Hamish back to where Finn and Felicity were standing to regroup. 'So are we going to put our heads together on this one?' the big man said to Wyatt. 'Or are we still going to have our little problem?'

'This doesn't change anything,' Wyatt said sadly. However his resolve was shaken and he clearly wasn't sure what to do or say next. The rules of the game had very much changed and this was a game he had not come prepared for.

'Maybe not in the grand scheme of things,' Edgar concurred. He bent down and relieved Cora of one of the guns in her hand. He offered it to Wyatt, handle first, an offer of trust. 'But how about we deal with that once we survive this? Personally, I wouldn't be thinking about the antidote until I've killed the snake.'

Wyatt took the gun and nodded his compliance. Then he looked up to where Devery was spying. 'What's out there?'

'There will be a hill to the left,' said Hamish, reverting back to the details of his vision. 'There's open ground to the right –'

'Hang on,' Devery was getting bolder and pushing his head out further to see. 'I can't see much, and I –'

There was a burst of gunfire. The bullets rattled into the top of the train.

Devery instantly let go of his grip and dropped back down to where everyone else was gathered, disturbing the mosaic of broken glass but landing skilfully on his feet. 'It's one hell of a mess out there,' he said urgently. The gunfire hadn't really shocked him. 'Looks like the whole train's been derailed and there's carriages broken away and all over the place. We're surrounded and they're moving in between the wreckage and getting into an attack position, with lots of trucks and men on foot. They're extremely heavily armed, we're talking machine guns and rocket launchers –'

'What is it with these people and rocket launchers?' Felicity said. She was stuck to Finn's side. 'Do you think they were on buy one get one free or something?'

Devery laughed, despite himself. 'You know maybe they were.'

There was more shouting from outside, closer this time.

'Numbers?' Gilliam asked.

'Couldn't tell,' Devery shrugged. 'But we're very much outnumbered, that goes without saying.'

'Where do we go?' Cora asked.

'It looks like there's some sort of forest in the distance,' Devery said. 'I could definitely see a treeline. If we can get away that seems to be the sensible place to head for, will give us cover, somewhere to hide.'

Finn tried to read the feelings of the people that surrounded him. None of them could hide their fear but they at least had it under control. But there was something in their faces that was relatively new and it was the reaction to the sudden alliance. The dynamic of the alliance hadn't made any of them feel particularly comfortable. None of these people wanted to fight together.

'Ok,' said Wyatt. 'But I say it again, nothing has changed here. Do you understand?'

'Yes,' said Cora sternly. 'We've got it.'

Pop – pop – pop. Three canisters flew into the train, slamming off the flat surfaces and rattling down amongst them like a set of pinballs. Before they had even hit the floor they were giving off trails of gas. Wyatt, Cora, and Benedict took one each and they scooped them up and bowled them right back outside from where they came from.

A second later the first of Agatha Carruther's soldiers appeared. He had climbed carefully on top of the train and was peering in through one of the windows. The enemy was dressed all in black and was wearing a round black helmet, black balaclava, and black ballistic vest. He looked like he could have belonged to a police SWAT team.

Cora was the first to open fire, aiming three shots outside and pushing him back.

A second man appeared at another window. Gilliam decided to take care of this one, shooting a series of blasts up and out of the train. His aim was wayward but effective and this man too was out of sight in a flash but not before firing off his own quick, petulant shot that didn't hit anyone.

Cora looked down, seeing that the man had not fired a bullet but something else. She picked up the discarded item from the gun and held it up to a streak of light from above. 'They've got a plan,' she noted, showing the others the small dart in her hand. The feathers on the end were red.

'Tranquiliser darts,' Hamish noted. He coughed painfully. 'It's like Dev said, they need us alive. They'll only take us down if there's no other choice.'

There was a subtle rattling on the other side of what was once the floor but was now the wall in front of them. Outside, the enemy were up to something.

'They're getting nosey,' said Benedict. He pushed his ear up against the wall. 'And impatient.'

'I'd say they'll try and break through,' said Devery. He seemed to be tapping into a sixth sense to understand what was going on. 'We've got to move now, move and get out there on our terms, not theirs. It's our only chance. My bet, they're placing explosives on the other side of that wall.'

Another appearance above and this time Wyatt and Gilliam shot back, both at the same time. There was a scream as they hit their target. *One down.*

Gilliam was looking up at the windows above them. 'We can't go up that way,' he said. He had noted the many difficulties of the route from where Devery had made the climb. 'Too awkward, we won't get out quickly or smoothly enough. They'll pick us off as soon as we emerge.'

'You need to go out through there,' said Hamish, motioning painfully forward to the train wall in front of him. He kicked the metal. 'You need to break through!'

Wyatt glanced at Benedict and Gilliam, the men with the so called powers of super strength and they all seemed to doubt the likelihood of the success of that recommendation.

'Even if we could bring that wall down,' said Gilliam. 'They'll just fill this carriage with bullets.'

'We smash it down,' said Devery, the only one who saw the logic of Hamish's suggestion. 'And then we run out of here like maniacs before they can get set! I'll go first and draw their fire! Then the rest we leave to God.'

'We can *try* the wall,' said Gilliam, thumping a fist into the thick steel of the train under carriage. The metal unsurprisingly didn't budge and just gave out a solid, unimpressed thud. 'But it's a god damn train! It's thick! I'm not *that* strong! It may take a while, if I can do it at all!'

'You need to move now,' said Hamish urgently. 'I know what that rattling is! Dev's right! They're placing charges on the other side and they'll be going off any second!'

Wyatt was willing to try and he ran up to one end of the carriage, Benedict moved to the opposite end, Gilliam taking the centre section. In unison they started to punch and kick the wall of the train in front of them. It was a race against those outside, to see who could be first to smash down the new wall of the train. Inside the efforts made a hefty racket and caused huge dents and cracks but the wall showed no signs of budging. The train rocked but even with their strength the metal was just too thick. Each man started to tire.

'It's no use,' said Wyatt. 'It's far too thick –'

Devery was watching Edgar very closely as it all played out in front of them, the metal echoing with each failed strike, a rhythmic thud, thud, thud. There was a knowledge and plea in the Irishman's eyes.

'Don't look at me like that,' Edgar said, shaking his head.

'All I can say,' said Devery, 'is if not now … when?'

'Hurry,' Hamish was shouting. 'We're out of time –'

Edgar nodded sadly. He didn't want to but he was in. He took a reluctant step forward and started to remove his jacket.

'I won't be with you,' said Devery, quickly turning to the others. 'I'll draw their fire. You can't group up or you'll be too easy a target. You have to split up and keep moving.'

Edgar threw his jacket aside. He rolled up his sleeves as quickly as he could and looked to Finn and Felicity. 'Either way you two will be coming with me,' he said. 'And no messing about, you stay close to me, and we might just get through this!'

'Ten seconds,' Hamish warned them, 'and then it'll all be over.'

Edgar huffed and then he burst forward and with two almighty punches he slammed both fists into the thick metal before him. There was a tremendous smash and the wall cracked instantly along the ceiling and floor joints, a crack that grew and spread out across the surface like the shockwaves from the world's mightiest earthquake.

Wyatt, Gilliam, and Benedict couldn't help but stare at Edgar with their mouths agape, stunned into silence by the brute show of strength that far exceeded their own and was of a like that they hadn't seen before. They simply didn't know that he had that in his arsenal. No one did. They were dumbstruck, impressed, and daunted all at the same time.

Edgar flexed his head backwards and bellowed out a loud battle roar and with every last muscle tightened in his neck, arms, and shoulders he pushed forward violently with one further punch. The whole metal wall broke off and shot away, speeding outwards and out into the open like a chunky torpedo.

It broke away just in time. As the whole wall took flight the charges that had been placed on the outside detonated in mid-air and the makeshift missile burst into flame. It landed on three trucks that were parked nearby with a sickening crash. The burning wall crushed the vehicles easily and the flames ignited the petrol in the tanks instantly. The whole area exploded, the impressive flames whooshing high into the sky and sending out twisted metal shards and sizzling rubber from the trucks that it had just obliterated.

Devery had one last thing to do and he grabbed his wife passionately and kissed her. When they finished there were tears in his eyes. 'Moving target away,' he said bravely. 'I'll see you on the other side, my love.'

And then he was gone, leaping out through the dust cloud that had been generated from the explosion. As soon as he emerged he was greeted with impolite gunfire from all sides. They may have had tranquiliser guns but they certainly were not using them on James Devery.

Finn had no choice but to follow Devery out into the fray, Edgar leading the way. Wyatt, Gilliam, Speller and Perez split up, heading in different directions. Cora, dragging Hamish's broken body, headed to the right.

Outside was a scene of utter and sickening carnage and devastation. Every single carriage of the Bristol to Aberdeen train had been derailed, just as they had said, and the carriages rested at different, broken angles. Plumes of black smoke shared the atmosphere with the falling snow. It was all but impossible that innocent lives had not been lost.

Edgar guided them to the left, and Finn and Felicity had to sprint to keep up. Finn had Felicity by the hand and it appeared that Devery's diversion was working as they had enough time to make it to the nearest overturned carriage. Hand in hand they dived behind the metal beast for cover just as the first targeted line of gunfire spluttered through the turf near their feet.

Finn looked up from the ground. He, along with Edgar, hadn't realised that there were already two of the enemy taking cover behind the carriage.

Chapter Forty-Four

'Freeze!' one of the enemy soldiers commanded. But Edgar was in no mood to comply. He gripped the nearest of the weapons covering him by the barrel, rerouting the original aim. The bullet that finally emerged shot straight into the second man's shin. Then Edgar ripped the gun from the first soldier's grip and thrust his palm into his chin. The enemy flew up above the train with the impact and disappeared. The wounded man hit the snow.

'We have to keep moving,' Edgar said, 'move amongst the carriages, get to the trees.' He pointed out away from his body and the next wrecked carriage. 'There's our next target.'

Finn was the first to step out but from their previous vantage point they hadn't spotted the five men who were now standing atop the next carriage. They all fired their weapons but Edgar, already committed, ran beneath their fire and thumped a shoulder barge into the bottom of the train. His power was such that it was enough to make the train roll over, the five men toppling off the other side.

Finn shot a quick look behind him, making sure that he still had Felicity by the hand. Thankfully he did and their hands were sweaty with nerves but they made it safely to the next chunk of cover.

Edgar was already behind the shadow of the train and he set upon the five men who had fallen before any of them could regain their footing. He disabled each man until they were all laid unconscious around him.

Finn was already searching for where they might go next. He peered out from the side of the train but more gunfire stopped him from seeing too much. With the little he had seen he had been able to spot Wyatt leaping onto a moving truck and fighting the men that were riding on the back. The truck then lost control, crashing into some wreckage and bursting into flames, Wyatt managing to leap off to safety. Devery was visible too, sprinting through the chaos, disorientating his foes with his speed, gunfire splashing into the ground at his heels. There was fighting everywhere.

Edgar joined them at the edge of the carriage just as a rocket flew past a few inches from his face. In the distance it found its target and exploded. The train carriage they were using for cover rocked but didn't fall over again.

Edgar was keen to move again. 'We stay here we die.'

Felicity didn't want to go anywhere. 'We go out there we die
—'

Three more men appeared, sprinting around the corner of the carriage. The first fired a shot and it thumped into Edgar's shoulder, knocking the big man into a spin and clear off his feet. The next two soldiers moved forward to intercept Finn and Felicity.

Finn was pumping with adrenalin that he couldn't find a way to use. Even in that moment he was a bit insulted at the soldier in front of him casually reaching down to grab him as if he was no sort of opponent. Driven by the insult, he dived in head first, smashing his head into the casual soldier's groin and making him scream with pain.

Felicity was tempted to do something similar but the soldier closest to her, not wanting to suffer the same fate as his underestimating colleague, pulled a tranquilizer gun out from his flack-jacket. *No more messing around.* She screamed, not knowing what to do but Finn came to her rescue and kicked the tranquilizer gun out of the man's grip.

Not impressed, the soldier huffed and punched Finn in the chest. 'Silly boy,' he said. 'Let's stop all this —'

Woooooooosh! The rocket hit the ground nearby, the blast sending everyone in the vicinity exploding into the air, including Finn and Felicity whose bodies flew in opposite directions. As he was taking his flight, Finn saw that it was Benedict who had fired the shot. He had deprived one of the enemy soldiers of their launcher and he was stood on top of a carriage a fair distance away with the weapon strapped to his shoulder.

Edgar was lying on his stomach in the snow and he was crying out in pain. He had been further away from the impact of the rocket but the flames from the explosion had caught on the ground and had swamped close to his face, burning his eyes and blinding him.

Finn, regaining his bearings, instantly wanted to find Felicity. She had landed somewhere less useful, further into the open, beyond the cover provided by the nearest carriage.

Then a familiar face appeared. A huge man stepped casually into view. He was carrying a rifle that looked almost miniature in his grasp and he was moving to where Edgar was reaching out and scratching around into a new and terrifying darkness.

'I know you're there,' said Edgar, sensing the approach of someone who's last intention was to offer a guiding arm. 'You gonna have the guts to fight me?'

Rogen did indeed have the guts. In fact, he saw it as a challenge and if anything seemed disappointed at the blindness. He tossed the gun away and stormed forward. Edgar stood groggily and in the darkness he attempted a punch but it missed. Rogen danced and pivoted so that he ended up behind him, then he smashed a huge barbaric punch into the small of Edgar's back. There was a cry of agony.

Finn could only watch. He could do nothing else. He looked around to see if any weapons were close but he could see none and even if he did he wouldn't know how to use it. Felicity was getting to her feet. She was disorientated by the explosion, not knowing what to do or where to go next.

Edgar was fighting on, or at least he was trying to, but his lack of vision was too much and Rogen was playing with him and allowing him to exhaust himself before launching into a vicious volley of slaps and jabs. The bigger man, knowing that in normal circumstances he couldn't compete with strength and with his ego still bruised from losing to Gilliam in the shopping centre, was now starting to enjoy himself. But Edgar did manage to get one lucky punch in and when he did the contact caught Rogen by surprise and sent him sprawling. Rogen smashed into the nearest train carriage.

'Beaten by a blind man,' Edgar taunted, spitting blood out from his mouth and at least one tooth.

When he returned, Rogen had less humour and within seconds he had kicked out Edgar's legs from under him. Then, having played with his prey for long enough, he pulled a tranquilizer gun from his belt. Edgar Bloom was going with him, whether he liked it or not.

An unlikely source came to the rescue. Gilliam suddenly appeared and before Rogen could fire he grabbed him by the arm. Rogen resisted, grimaced, but Gilliam had no problem with blindness and he fired Rogen's own weapon into his neck. The dart pierced the skin and Rogen's body went promptly limp and fell forward face first into the snow.

In that moment Finn forgot the past and he was already ready to go. He was about to rush to Gilliam, to help him get Edgar to his feet and continue fighting when he stopped dead. Gilliam was walking slowly towards him. He was reloading a dart into the tranquiliser. The dart was destined for Finn.

'Nooooooo!' Felicity cried, seeing what was about to unfold.

Gilliam aimed at Finn, ready to fire. 'Like Wyatt said, this changes nothing –'

A series of bullets prevented Gilliam going any further. The bullets came from afar and slammed into the Frenchman's chest, neck, and shoulder. Gilliam was dead before he hit the floor.

Finn, terrified by the closeness of the gunfire, pressed up against the side of the train, shocked and hiding. More enemy soldiers moved into the vicinity and they hadn't yet seen him. They filled the open area between the trains, descending upon Felicity and grabbing her. There must have been at least ten of them. She screamed again, screamed for them to stop, but they were already taking her away.

The closest soldier was looking urgently at his watch. 'Three minutes!' he shouted to the others. 'Move! Move! Move!' It took two of the soldiers to carry Felicity, such was the fury of her resistant kicks and yells, and three more men went with them, covering the way forward carefully. They were in quite the rush. *Three minutes,* thought Finn. *Why the countdown?* Then it hit him. They had to finish their business before they could expect some sort of relief to arrive. The railway company would have known the train had been derailed. Help would be on its way and when it arrived his mother's people needed to be gone. They would take with them as many of their targets as they could secure.

'Come out now,' a soldier's voice demanded strongly.

Finn could only see their shadows but they were getting closer and about to appear around the corner. Five of them were coming for him. He fell to his knees, feeling the cold snow pressing against his trousers. He could do nothing else. He was utterly defeated. He could see Felicity getting further away and then she disappeared from view. He was losing her and he seethed, feeling the anger and desperation coursing through his veins. *It's over. It's all over.* His expression dropped into utter sadness.

'Finnnnnnnnnnnnnnnn!' Felicity was still calling his name, desperate for him to save her but her voice was getting more and more faint.

'Hands on your head!' The soldier moved swiftly into view. His rifle was aimed at Finn's heart. 'Now!'

A second soldier flanked him and was ready with his tranquilizer.

Finn stopped listening to their demands. Something was building inside of him, an angry series of panic attacks that were pulsating in his beating chest. He suddenly wasn't about to freeze for anyone.

'Take him now!' The soldier with the rifle instructed.

The second soldier fired his tranquilizer dart.

Finn's expression of defeat disappeared and changed. Sadness was replaced with pure fury. He moved instinctively, rolling to his left, the dart missing his torso by the merest of inches and sticking in the ground like a javelin. In his next movement he attacked, thumping the first solider in the face and then without wasting a single breath he gripped the second soldier by the wrist and swept him into the air, slamming his body against the metal of the overturned train. Both men hit the ground and moved no more.

Not content, he was moving again, running from the cover of the train carriage and taking his aggression out on the three men who lingered behind. Not only did he disarm them but he did so with such ferocity that when he struck them they lost their consciousness instantly and landed far away from where they had been standing.

Finn looked at his hands. What had they just done? What had they just achieved?

Edgar was on the floor, rolling around, oddly happy. Although still blinded, he could sense what had happened and he was laughing riotously despite his pain. 'You go, son,' he roared, moving onto his back and lying down. He was slamming his hands into the sodden earth. 'YEEEEEEEEAAAAAAH!!! THERE HE IS! THERE HE IS!'

There he is.

And there he went. Before he knew it Finn was running, sprinting amongst the wreckage and taking out any enemy solider that stood in his way. He avoided their gunfire easily and when he got close he avoided their punches. He avoided every attention, never slowing, moving quicker than he had ever run and bashing and kicking and decimating anyone as if he had been highly trained.

The world and the action moved past in a flash, like he was surrounded by a panoramic version of life and it were being played in fast forward. He saw glimpses of the people he cared about, or at the very least wanted to see come through this unscathed. He saw Cora and Hamish cowering behind a tangled section of twisted metal, three soldiers advancing and pinning them down with fire. Then he saw Devery sprint to their rescue, ploughing into the soldiers before darting off and drawing their fire once more. The interruption was enough to allow Cora and Hamish the time to move again.

He saw Benedict meet his end. The Scot had taken the wheel of a truck and was heading away when a rocket careered into the back of the vehicle. The explosion lifted the back of the truck and flipped it over so that it landed on its bonnet. As it hung there, shortly before toppling over, it exploded.

Wyatt was there too, positioned amongst a group of soldiers. He was running from them, luring them after him and then when the chance arose he took them out. The American was in bad shape though and the wound on his shoulder had worsened and the right hand side of his body was black with burns. But none of these people truly mattered. Only one thing mattered. Only one thing was important.

Finn emerged out from the last section of the wrecked train, back towards the tunnel. Two soldiers were blocking his way and they opened fire with their rifles, the situation having got too serious for tranquilisers. But Finn threw himself backwards, skidding along the snowy ground on his back and underneath the swarm of the bullets. He opened up his chest and punched out the soldier's legs as he skidded past. He could feel their shin bones cracking.

He shot back up and just managed to catch sight of Felicity and her captors disappearing into the tunnel towards the parked train that Devery had spoken of. Time was against him. He picked up an already frightening pace and as he entered the darkness of the tunnel he despaired to see that the train was already moving and chugging away from him in the opposite direction of the wreckage. They were already aboard.

Finn would never catch it. At least that is what he would have told himself during every single day and second of his life so far. But something had changed. *He had changed.* Today was the newest of days and today was different to all that had gone before. A power that he never thought he had, it had come to him. And with that power he was never going to lose the person he now loved more than anyone else in the world. He would not lose Felicity Gower, not whilst he had any trace of life in his body.

He glanced down at the train track and watched as the sleepers shot by one after another beneath his feet. The train was getting quicker and quicker and then he dived, covering as much distance as he could before it was too late, an almighty leap of faith that common sense told him would fail.

Finn's hand made contact with the metal railing at the rear of the fleeing train and he pulled himself aboard. He stood up. His heart was racing and his chest was pumping, in and out, in and out, and a single word was blaring through his mind, repeating itself over and over. *Obsidian – Obsidian – Obsidian –*

The train was far smaller than the one that had been so destructively and decisively derailed and it only consisted of four carriages. It was moving along quickly and emerged out the other side of the tunnel and out into a long stretch of track flanked by tall trees. There was a single large door at the rear of the train, a yellow door with oil stains and pot marks, but Finn couldn't find any way to open it whilst the train was in motion. It didn't help that there were no handles either.

'Let's try this,' he said to himself, digging his nails into the small gaps and grooves around the edge of the door. With a determined yank and still unsure as to the extent of his power he tugged at the door. He almost shrieked with delight as it came away instantly in his hands and he managed to take the sudden weight before throwing it behind him and onto the tracks.

Finn paused for a brief moment. His destiny, the one that everyone had been wittering on about and that he had thought applied to somebody else, had hit him hard and randomly. He couldn't help but be worried that it might fade away just as quickly. It must have been dragged out of him by the seriousness of the situation, enflamed at seeing Felicity taken away from him. But he didn't know how he had been able to do the things he had done. They just happened.

No, shake that off. You pulled a great big heavy metal door off its hinges. You've got this.

He had no more time to dwell on it and he moved inside the first train carriage, which was empty and in darkness. Up ahead the next carriage was bathed in an enticing light. This was where he would find Felicity.

Finn darted up the aisle and carefully opened the door at the other end. He waited in the area between cabins and peered through the dirty glass in front of him. He saw Felicity. Her hands were tied behind her back and she had been positioned so that she was lying on her stomach. They had sensibly put a gag of fabric in her mouth, tying it around the back of her head to stop her making too much noise.

Three of the soldiers who had plucked her from the battle were present. They had now removed their helmets and they all had different colour hair, heads of red, black and blonde, all of the strands matted with sweat from their exertions. The soldiers were surrounded by black bags full of equipment, which was no doubt more weapons, explosive devices, and ammo. All the bags were stored neatly on all the seats and tables.

The men were not the only ones present. There were two additional people in the room. Neither were strangers. The first was Theo and the second was Agatha Carruthers. Both were dressed in the same flack outfits as the others, and they too did not wear helmets and their faces were visible. Everyone was stood up in the passageway, talking.

Finn hit the handle that opened the door and walked inside. The three soldiers all snapped around in shock and raised their rifles.

Agatha glanced up. There was surprise in her eyes but also a look of happiness.

Theo was holding a small gun and he fired a dart. The dart hit Finn in the stomach and the point breached his skin and the pain tightened instantly. Theo, his clothing ill-fitting and making him look like a child dressing up in his daddy's work clothes, smiled in triumph. He was wearing a heavy waistcoat with grenades clipped to both sides like a World War Two commando.

Finn initially fell back into the door and went pale. He could feel the liquid of the tranquiliser coursing into his blood around the wound and the sensation made him faint and weak. But then it was as if his very blood decided it wasn't having that. He could feel his blood pushing back against the alien liquid, diluting it away to nothing.

He stood up tall and proud and plucked the dart out from his body and giving the tip a quick stare he shrugged, unimpressed, and tossed it to the floor.

'My, you've done a lot of growing up, Finn,' his mother said. She was standing just behind Felicity but appeared to be unarmed. She looked at her uncle. 'Don't bother reloading, doesn't look like it's going to have much of an impact.'

Finn surveyed his mother carefully. Her eyes were fixed firmly on him. Beyond her sly grin there was no movement in her face, as though she was trying to ensure that she looked cold, calm, and in control. He started to wonder whether that was true, whether a different story unfolded beneath the surface. He decided to try and change her.

'I'm here, Mum,' he said. 'This needs to end now and you need to let her go.'

'This isn't the end, Finn,' said Agatha. 'Unfortunately, it's only the beginning.'

'What are you doing?' Finn asked. He allowed his pity to seep into his expression. He wanted her to see it. 'I mean, look at what you're doing. People are dying –'

'Sometimes,' said Agatha, 'people have to die to –'

'To what?' Finn said, challenging her. 'To what, Mum? I get it, ok, I get the dude all those hundreds of years ago who went nuts because his brother was staying young. But what about now? Why are you lot all so crazy and all so determined? I mean it's hundreds of years later for crying out loud. Why is living forever so important to you?'

Agatha said nothing.

That gave Finn a surge of confidence. 'I know you,' he continued. 'There were times where I'd be a little embarrassed by you, wondering why you couldn't be friendly and chatty like the other mum's. But I always loved you. I still love you –'

'We haven't got time for this,' said Theo.

'We can never be the same again,' said Finn. 'Not after what you did. But have you ever wondered why this whole thing happened to me? Why it happened to us?'

His mother's smirk softened a touch. 'It's my punishment,' she said quietly.

'Agatha,' said Theo, 'that's enough –'

'Or maybe,' said Finn, 'it isn't your punishment at all. Maybe it's a chance for you to do the right thing, to get some forgiveness for what you've done. Maybe it's meant to be that you and I,' he pointed at Theo, 'stop people like him and stop all the killing.'

He had said his piece and he felt fantastic. He had never had such confidence, such control of his emotions and such control of the words that came out of his mouth. He could see the doubt in his mother countenance, seeing that she had listened and that she was conflicted.

'Let's change it up,' said Finn. 'Come with me, and we can –'

Agatha Carruthers took a step forward, swept a handgun from her pocket and shot Finn twice in his right thigh.

Chapter
Forty-Five

'My men here,' said Agatha Carruthers, 'they saw you out there. They saw you tear through my people as if they were nothing. Which means it's true about what you are. Do you understand what this means, Finn? So many years wasted, trying to find the answers in the wrong places. All we needed to do was wait for you.'

Finn looked down at the wound and was in complete shock. He hadn't expected that. He focused on the small black charred hole where the bullets had entered his trousers and then saw the pool of dark red blood slowly form around the savage nucleus.

'You shot me?' he said.

'Well spotted,' said Agatha. 'Bullets tend to have a different kind of quality to a tranquiliser. I suspect you'll find that a tad more difficult to shake off.'

Finn gave into the pain and was forced onto the knee of the leg that wasn't injured. He had never given any consideration as to what it might feel like to be shot. Why would he? He had lived in a world where he was unlikely to have to face such violence. But now that he had, the pain was the worst thing he had ever experienced.

'It was my suggestion to take the girl,' said Agatha, 'especially if we struggled to secure you within the time allotted. But even I will admit I didn't expect you to come to us quite so quickly. You really do love her, don't you, Finn?'

'Yes, I do,' said Finn, battling through the pain. When he said that, he could see that Felicity was watching him. He didn't doubt that had she been free she would have had something to say. 'But what do you know about love?' he said.

'More than you,' Agatha said. 'I know just how destructive love can be, how it can fool you into feeling something that is completely illogical. I know how it can cloud your judgement and make you do things that you shouldn't. But most of all, I know that love is nothing more than a chemical imbalance in the brain. It is something that the human brain demands that you crave but something that has no utility. It doesn't exist, Finn. It's a figment of the imagination.'

'You don't know as much as you think you do,' said Finn. He tried to move but his wound wouldn't allow it. 'You're just messed up and brainwashed.'

Felicity wracked and writhed on the floor, screaming from beneath her gag, trying to break free.

'You've played with him enough,' Theo said bluntly. 'Secure him now.'

The three soldiers obeyed the command and they came forward, the blonde haired fellow leading the way, pacing up the aisle. He came too close. Finn clasped the barrel of the rifle and pushed it aside. The soldier tried to drag it back so that it was again pointing at Finn but he simply didn't have the strength to compete. The other two soldiers, wary from what they had seen Finn achieve out by the crash, didn't provide any instant support and instead took two wary steps back.

With the poor blonde soldier unwilling to let go of his weapon, Finn swept him off his feet and swung the rifle like a mallet, smashing it down first to the left and then to the right, all the while with the soldier attached firmly and gallantly to the other end and his body crashing into the floor with each brutal impact. By the fifth swing the soldier let go and ended up in a ball, shaking and incapacitated, close to fainting.

Finn had the rifle in his grip. He aimed it forward at his foes but then he remembered Edgar's views on barbaric weapons and he bought it down hard onto his good knee and snapped it in half. He threw both pieces towards his mother. 'You let her go,' he said strongly. He took a step forward. The pain hadn't gone, far from it, but somehow he had still managed to be effective. His power even had the ability to assist recovery from wounds, so it seemed.

Agatha smiled to herself and looked up at Theo, who looked uneasy and unsure of what to do next.

The door behind Finn suddenly opened with a hiss. He turned around and was expecting to see some reinforcements, even though he hadn't seen any hiding in the carriage when he moved through it. But there was no one there. A subtle wind moved past him, as if a ghost had entered the train. The fringe of his hair was ruffled by the breeze and he felt the length of his spine go cold.

Theo went to speak again, to command his remaining men, but he stopped himself. Something terrible had caught his eye. He stared downwards. The pin to one of the grenades under his chin was shaking as if it was alive. Alert with horror he went to put his hand on it but before he could the pin shot out. He looked up to Finn, assuming he was responsible.

'What are you doing?' Theo said.

'That's not me,' said Finn. He already knew exactly what was happening, having put two and two together the moment the cold breeze had found him, recalling the tale Felicity had recited from the burning church she had escaped from. 'You ever heard of the old legend about a chap called Tobias?'

Theo looked quickly at Agatha. She was shaking her head, lost. They were too stunned to move.

Finn smirked. 'He's here.'

There were five other grenades attached to Theo's jacket and the pins quickly shot out of those grenades too, all in quick succession, *clink – clink – clink – clink – clink*. The two soldiers glanced back up the aisle, terrified. Finn watched the pins of the grenades as they hit the floor and rolled down towards him. Theo was screaming and trying desperately to unbuckle the flack-jacket.

'Quick,' Agatha yelled, taking some form of control despite her puzzlement, 'the window!' She fired her gun and shot out the nearest pane of glass.

Theo pulled the jacket off and launched it out through the newly shattered window. But as it disappeared the bottom of the jacket hit the rim of the window frame and a single grenade came loose and thumped down back into the carriage.

Finn observed the small sphere of doom as it toppled down the aisle, heading his way. He quickly lurched forward. He caught the grenade and turned, throwing it away in the opposite direction. The grenade hit the glass in the door behind him and with enough force to break it, flashing through to the other side and landing in the open space between the carriages.

Boom! The grenades outside detonated first but the train had moved far enough along for them not to cause any real damage. The same could not be said however for the grenade that went off inside the carriage. There was a stark explosion and the train shook but luckily stayed on the track. A flurry of black smoke swept in from the hole in the door and filled the carriage from floor to ceiling. Then the fire followed, burning through the door and spreading quickly along the wall and ceiling. The fire instantly found a set of bags filled with ammunition cartridges and they reacted with the heat and exploded, spreading the flames greedily and eagerly.

Finn crawled along the floor and tried to clear his way through the smoke with his hands, seeing very little. He was coughing and spluttering. But very soon, reaching blindly forward, his hand made contact with the hairs on Felicity's head.

'Jesus, Fliss,' he said, feeling around for the gag and scooping it out from her mouth. 'We need to get out of here –'

'What's happening?' she cried.

Finn was grappling around for where her hands were tied. He found the plastic cable tie and snapped it open.

'Is he really here?' Felicity said. She was vividly afraid, having seen Tobias once before and not wanting to see him again.

'I think so,' Finn confirmed bleakly.

Frantic gunfire sounded. Bullets flew all around, swishing through the smoke, scared soldiers shooting desperately at an invisible target. Finn threw himself on top of Felicity and they both covered their heads. The smoke started to clear, pouring out through what were now the many missing windows from the gunshots.

Finn saw the red haired soldier get plucked off his feet and tossed easily out of the moving train. The dark haired soldier suffered a similar fate, finding himself airborne and as if the gravity in the room had suddenly stopped working. His body tilted forward so that he was floating horizontally and then he shot off at a fantastic speed, fizzing past Agatha and Theo, who had to duck, and smashing through the door behind them.

Agatha and Theo returned to their firing, shooting up the aisle. Then their weapons ran dry, running out of bullets, and the carriage fell eerily silent.

'What devilry is this?' Theo said, watching the advancing shadow cast by the fire that was all around them, a fire that showed no signs of abating.

Agatha didn't get the opportunity to answer. An invisible fist gripped both her and Theo by the throat, squeezing tightly, and they were lifted high into the air. She tried to hit and punch whatever it was that was causing this but her efforts yielded no results.

Finn took Felicity's hand and they started to move away towards the back of the train, carefully stepping through the many pockets of flame. But Finn stopped and turned around. He was transfixed by his mother, floating there and having the life choked out of her. Despite the ordeal she was going through she was watching him. She was helpless.

There was a gun on the floor near to his feet. He scooped it up and aimed it forwards, picking a spot where he thought the invisible Tobias might be standing. His mother's eyes started to close and her body became lifeless. He fired a single shot. The shot was met with a scream. The might of the invisible grip came free and Agatha and Theo fell from the air and into crumpled, still heaps on the floor

For Finn the infamous enemy was perfectly visible in front of him for the first time. The successful shot had driven out Tobias's invisibility, shattering the ancient spell, and he was stood there in all his glory. He didn't look remotely happy and was fingering a new hole that Finn had created in his shoulder from the gunshot.

Finn experienced no shock from his appearance. He already knew that Tobias was a child near to his own age, contrary to what he had witnessed during Bronwyn's graphic vision. Tobias, for his part, was no fan of words or talking. He was ready to fight. He pumped out his chest and seemed to levitate and with a ferocity that needed no run up or preparation he flew up the carriage and extended his leg into a savage kick.

Finn had to dive to avoid it and only just managed to be successful. He wasn't so lucky with the second assault and no sooner had he shot back up than Tobias's next kick struck him in the stomach. Finn caught the kick and cried out with the impact, his wounded leg excruciatingly painful, but he held on as he and Tobias smashed up the carriage away from Felicity. Tobias landed on top of Finn and instantly broke free.

The damage in Finn's leg made him bellow out in pain. This was not a good sign. Evidently the wound in his thigh impacted him far more than the wound in Tobias's shoulder.

Felicity, not one to miss an opportunity to get involved, grabbed the closest bag and dragged it off the table. It was incredibly heavy and she dropped it. She bent down and unzipped it and inside was a bag full of black, smooth gun magazine cartridges. She picked one up and lobbed it at Tobias's head. The cartridge was aimed perfectly and it bounced off the top of Tobias's bald scalp. He turned his head and scowled. She had got his attention. Tobias grabbed Finn by the ankle and started dragging him up the aisle towards her.

Felicity plucked up what courage she could and she threw a second cartridge, and then a third, fourth and fifth, more and more, each one hitting the advancing target but none seeming to cause any damage. But she kept going until she emptied the majority of the bag. Tobias stopped in front of her. He just stood there, his expression getting sterner by the second. Whatever he was about to do it wasn't going to be pleasant or polite.

She kicked him full pelt in the groin and when she retracted her foot she smiled at the sheer greatness of her own idea. That was sure to take him down as no boy could take such a punishment. But Tobias didn't move or provide her with a reaction. It didn't hurt him, not in the slightest. 'If that didn't hurt you,' she said, 'then I actually think I feel a little bit bad for you now!'

Felicity reached forward and squeezed his nose and made a little mocking noise as if he had the squeaky nose of a clown. 'Sorry,' she said, laughing nervously. 'I just wanted to see if you were real!'

Tobias got ready to punch her.

Felicity closed her eyes.

Finn stopped it from happening. He used his spare foot to kick his foe in the back of the legs. Then he climbed up and gripped Tobias's armpits and pitched his body up into the burning ceiling. Tobias came back down with a crash and where the thrown cartridges and savage kicks had no impact this had undoubtedly affected him.

The fire was getting out of control and now covered most of the carriage.

'We've got to get out of here,' Finn said as they started running again, heading to the door to the next cabin at the back of the train. He could fight but he couldn't help but run with a limp. He turned around to have a quick glance as to Tobias's whereabouts but he was nowhere to be seen. There was no trace. There were only the ever growing flames. *The coward's disappeared again.*

'You go,' he said to Felicity. 'Get to the next carriage. I'll be there in a moment.'

Felicity shook her head. 'No, we go together –'

'Do it!' he shouted. 'I can't fight him with you here! He'll use you against me!'

'But –'

Finn did something he really didn't want to do and he ushered her to the door and pushed her through against her will. Then he punched the hydraulic button and it let out some sparks and broke, ensuring that the door was sealed shut and she could argue no more. Felicity was on the other side of the glass and she was beating her hands against it. She was angry and distraught.

Finn turned back to the flaming carriage. There was a noise from above. He looked up, quickly realising that the noise belonged to footsteps. Someone was moving on top of the train. He saw the logic. The fire was getting worse and to fight in that sort of oven would be impossible. As such he ran to the nearest window and poked his head outside. The track was running through a particularly thick wooded area and heavy forest whizzed by on both sides of the train, the snow getting heavier by the second and along with the wind storming down his throat. The train was still moving extremely quickly. The Operative who was driving mustn't have had any clue as to what had occurred in the carriages behind him.

There was nothing else to do. Finn clamped his hands on the edge of the window and vaulted out through the gap, twisting in the air like a seasoned gymnast and throwing himself up so that he landed on the roof of the train. He stood up and looked forward. He could see the front two carriages and standing there was Tobias, his arms outstretched. He was watching Finn, motioning him forward.

'Say something?' Finn shouted. His voice was only just audible above the sound of the moving train and the wind.

Tobias didn't humour his demand.

'You utter moron!' Felicity said.

Finn couldn't believe his ears. He flipped around to see Felicity climbing up an external ladder on the carriage behind him. When she got to the top she stumbled out onto the roof.

'Do you never listen?' he said, enraged that she had turned her back on the modicum of safety he had secured for her.

There was a short explosion and the fire tore through the area of the two cabins between them. The flames started to climb upwards and the metal knuckles securing the carriages together seemed to be breaking away.

Finn started to have an idea. He used his eyes to convey the idea to Felicity, rolling them downwards to the separation between the two carts. With the way the fire was evolving, he hoped that it would break the carriage she was standing on away from the front of the train. All he needed to do was keep Tobias exactly where he was. *Felicity, whatever you do, stay where you are.*

Felicity's eyes became wide with alarm. 'Down!' she screamed.

Finn turned instinctively to the warning, flipping around and seeing that they were heading towards a chunky stone bridge. The bridge was low and it was clear that there was barely any gap between the top of the train and the underside of the crossing.

He dived to the floor, Tobias doing the same as the bridge zoomed past overhead, missing them by what felt like only a few inches. By the time Finn had started to get to his feet Tobias was already upon him and he punched him hard in the chin. Finn absorbed the punch as best as he could but it forced him backwards. All the same, he avoided the next two punches but the third made contact with this forehead. He was already losing.

Tobias jumped high into the sky and came back to earth with two further fierce punches which thumped into Finn's shoulders. Such was the power that it knocked Finn's feet through the metal roof, which was breaking underneath him. The flames below tickled his feet.

'Get up!' Felicity screamed, encouraging him.

He was trying but his feet were stuck fast. Tobias was coming though and the kick that followed was designed to knock him out for good.

Finn got out just in time and shifted his head so that it missed the kick. Tobias kicked out again and this time Finn caught it solid and threw the kick away. Tobias lapsed into a somersault and careered backwards but landed on his feet like a majestic ninja.

Another explosion arrived from the carriage beneath them and a huge section of metal came loose in the roof, allowing the flames to start escaping onto the top of the train. A wall of fire burst out, running directly in between the two fighting boys.

Finn ground his teeth. That was enough. He grabbed the closest piece of shattered metal and ripped it free. It was square and flat and could be used as a shield. And he used it as a shield as Tobias leapt through the flames, raining down another range of scrunched fists. The fists thumped into the metal and again the impact drove Finn backwards, pushing him towards the side of the carriage. If he got to the end he had nowhere left to go. All that existed was the open air, the whizzing train track and a painful plummet at a speed that had the potential to kill.

Finn decided to go on the attack and stopped using the metal as a shield. He thrust it forward, trying to make contact, but Tobias was able to twist and pivot and avoid it. Frustrated, Finn lobbed it hard. It proved to be no use. Tobias simply ducked and was on him in a split second. He gripped Finn by the throat, something that he seemed to be pretty fond of, and moved behind him and held him in a terrible head lock.

'I will strangle you,' said Tobias, speaking to Finn for the first time. His voice was deep and demonically old and it seemed to have its own echo. 'But not enough to kill you. I need you alive for the ritual.'

Finn was grappling hard but he couldn't break the iron of the grip.

'Then, just so you know,' Tobias wasn't finished. 'I will go and find your little girlfriend and I will put out her light forever.'

Finn almost pitied his opponent. He had given him all he needed. It returned, the fury, ignited by the threat to Felicity's life. He snapped, cracking his head backwards into a reverse head butt that collided with and broke Tobias's nose. The grip was loosened and Tobias careered backwards, bleeding from both nostrils. Just at that moment the next bridge came shockingly into view and Finn hit the deck as the train funnelled underneath. Tobias however, turning at the very last moment, only had time to spread his weight, bracing himself for impact. Standing tall his body made full contract with the bridge.

This boy however had not lived for so many centuries by allowing his body to show physical weakness and the bridge in many ways came off worse. There was the hollering rumble of obliterated stone as the bridge collapsed and the fractured stone burst out, striking the train and rolling onto the tracks. Tobias was still standing but it was evident that he was severely weakened.

The next explosion shook the train and the two back carriages that Finn and Felicity stood on disengaged. Felicity's image started to move away quickly, the section of train beneath her free from the rest of the locomotive. Felicity's carriage was already slowing, soon to stop.

Something sinister was happening below. The fire had reached its crescendo, reacting with the bags of equipment, and was ready to belt out its final, all-encompassing and impressive note. The whole train was about to explode.

Tobias came forward with his final effort. Bruised and bleeding his punch was as weak as it had ever been and Finn this time was in command and he deflected the assault and pulled him close. Then he pushed out, slamming a generous jab into Tobias's stomach and knocking him through the newly created hole and back down into the train carriage and into the climbing flames.

'Finnnnnnnnnnnnnnnnnnnnnnnn!' Felicity was panicking.

Finn ran. He ran with all his remaining energy and might, forcing himself to push through the spasms of pain in his thigh. The fire rose all around him so that all he could see was a wall of sizzling orange. He jumped, climbing higher and higher as the gap between the carriages got bigger and bigger –

Tobias started to climb up through the gap.

KABOOM! The train burst into a huge, giant fireball, leaping off the track and smashing into the forest to the left, setting a hundred trees on fire. Then it exploded again, the final obliteration.

Finn had closed his eyes for he saw only the darkness. His fingertips were touching something slippery and metal and his legs were dangling in the air. Then he felt Felicity frantically grabbing his hand and she pulled him up onto the safety of the train. She was on her knees and when he was with her he too didn't have the energy to do anything but kneel.

She pushed her hands to his cheeks. The single carriage they were now on was almost at a stop. 'He's gone,' she said thankfully. She was never so happy to have witnessed a death.

Finn was hurting. 'I can barely move –'

'You were amazing –'

Finn shook his head. 'I couldn't have done it without you –'

'Don't be so soppy,' said Felicity. She smiled. 'You're not winning an Oscar, Finn.'

He touched the gunshot wound in his thigh. The pain had ebbed away at moments during the fight, permitting him to function, and now it returned with vengeance. 'I don't feel amazing,' he said. He looked at the fire of the train wreck in the distance. 'Also, I just killed someone.'

Felicity wasn't accepting that. 'You just killed a whack job.'

He sat himself down. The carriage was now completely static. 'I can't believe you squeezed Tobias's nose.'

Felicity chuckled. 'It seemed like the right thing to do at the time.'

Finn laughed in between his laboured breaths. But then he asked a more serious question. 'Did you see my mother?'

'I don't know,' said Felicity. 'I thought I saw a couple of shapes fall off the train a little while back but I can't be sure. It could have been anything. To be honest, Finn, I think she was still on there when it went up.'

'Damn,' Finn said sadly, 'guess that officially makes me an orphan.'

'I had this neighbour once,' said Felicity, 'and heart attacks ran in his family. I remember thinking how weird that was, that something like that could be passed on. But you beat that easily. I don't think I've ever met anyone who's had death by explosion run in the family.'

The sentence summed Felicity Gower up in one beautiful series of words. He should have been insulted but he couldn't help but grin. 'I hope no one ever asks you to speak at a funeral,' he said.

She suddenly kissed him hard, the strongest kiss they had shared to date.

'Fliss,' said Finn when they broke for a moment. 'What I said in there, when it was all going off, it was true. I –'

'Don't,' Felicity interrupted him. 'I told you before, we don't say that.' She kissed him again and when she was finished she pulled him close and hugged him. Then she whispered in his ear. 'But although we don't say the words, don't you go thinking that you mean nothing to me, Finlay.'

They stood up together and she helped steady his shaking, trembling body. They looked back at the pillars of smoke that were billowing away on the horizon from the first train derailment.

'What do we do now?' she pondered.

'We find our friends,' said Finn. 'And we hope some of them are still alive.'

Felicity held him close. 'That sounds good to me.'

Chapter
Forty-Six

The morning air was cold, damp, and tasted of a strong salt. The constant sound of the waves could be heard but not seen and they must have been in a relatively polite and serene mood for the boat glided along the surface of the water smoothly and majestically.

Felicity Gower was one of only two people aboard to be awake at such an ungodly hour, the other accolade belonging to the noble Captain who was steering the ship and tucked sensibly away indoors and within the warm glow of a small cabin behind her. He of course was awake out of duty, whereas her reasons were simply that she had never been on a boat before. As such she had discovered that the strength of her curiosity and excitement made it hard to sleep and she yearned to be outside to soak it all in.

She took her position at the front of the vessel and leaned her elbows into the ships bow, feeling the strength of a moderate wind against her face. She had no idea what time it was but the sky was still extremely dark and the nearest light came from those that were fastened rigidly to the tall masts. Other lights were out there too, in the depths of the darkness and on what must have been the horizon, distant flickers signifying the life of distant sailors, no doubt keen fisherman dedicated to securing a mighty catch.

Felicity was wrapped up snugly in a thick blue overcoat, two black scarfs and a grey wool hat but she still couldn't completely escape the power of the cold. The North Sea was no place for wimps, so she had been told at least four times already, and although she was getting bored of being reminded of that fact, now that she was out here she couldn't disagree with the truth of it.

The thrash of waves, the whistle of the wind, the subtle sound of the ship breaking through the water, they were the only sounds and they were constant and once a passenger got used to them it was almost as if everything else was silent.

She had started to grow fond of the quiet moments like this and recently it seemed there were plenty of opportunities to reflect on what had happened. Everything had grown calmer in fact, mainly due to the fact that they were no longer being chased and they hadn't seen any form of enemy for three glorious weeks. The *battle* on the train had been dramatic and violent and the conclusion was evidently that the ranks of both The Brotherhood and Agatha's Guild had been sufficiently depleted to postpone their efforts. For now, they were safe.

Yet they too had not come through the ordeal completely unscathed. Edgar was in the worst condition of them all and he remained blinded by his injuries. The bullet hole in his shoulder had been dressed and they had covered his eyes carefully with bandages but the brutality of the fight had left him weak and weary and he rarely ventured from whatever bed he was able to rest within. There was hope that the blinding would not be permanent.

Devery had suffered a gunshot wound to his hip area, a wound that he could not get any treatment for as there was no way they could risk arousing suspicion from Doctors who might just ask how he came to be shot in the first place. But luckily the bullet itself had passed straight through and out the other side, so as with Edgar they had cleaned and dressed the wound as best as they could and he was forced to walk with a severe limp in the hope that in time it would heal.

Hamish too was bruised and battered and Cora remained in mourning for the loss of her brother. Collectively the group had grown sombre but they *had* survived and a variety of threats were extinguished and no longer existed, at least not for the time being. Before fleeing they had seen the bodies of Gilliam, Benedict, Speller, and Perez and Wyatt's was the only body they had been unable to find. Still even if the American had survived the battle, one person did not make a Brotherhood and for that, at the very least, they were truly thankful.

So I'm going to see Norway, Felicity thought, preferring to think of more pressing and alluring matters. Despite the thick cover of darkness the foreign country was out there somewhere, waiting for them.

The decision for the destination had been made relatively swiftly. Emeric's plan, although no doubt fake and a ruse at the time, was in fact a pretty good one and it didn't take long to realise that with the enemy out of the fold the passage across the North Sea wouldn't be all that difficult. In addition and having given it more thought, Cora recalled that she had a friend in neighbouring Sweden who shared her late brother's ability to heal and such a skill would be thoroughly welcome, given their ordeal.

Still, they decided to remain cautious and steer clear of commercial vessels and mainstream flights and instead, having ventured through a number of small Scottish ports, they had found a lovely young Captain called Gareth Makepeace-Jones, a new skipper, with a new boat, a double barrelled surname and a man blessed with plenty of money from the rich parents of his passengers who had secured a charter to transport a small group of Science Graduates from a Scottish University on an expedition north.

With a generous donation to their funding and a dubious backstory to support the reasons for their charter (mainly involving dear Edgar requiring urgent medical treatment from a make believe maverick Norwegian Doctor who could potentially restore his sight) the Captain readily agreed to the contract and didn't question the many holes in the story, not least why they didn't just catch a plane.

Regardless in a few short hours the ship would arrive at the Port of Stavanger on the Western Coast of Norway and a new journey would begin for them all.

Life of course was one long journey, so they said, but Felicity wasn't sure that she had ever stopped to truly think about the journey she had only just finished, never mind the new one that rested in front of her. It was all just so insane and her life certainly never used to be so mad. It hadn't been long ago that she had been a touch unhappy living with her foster parents and Finn Carruthers had just been a face she recognised but was a boy who had a name she couldn't remember. He had considered it flirting but she did really think his name was Finlay in the beginning. Things were so different now.

She couldn't escape thoughts of such a near past and she had started to think back to her exams and coursework. She had been excelling at English and History, her Medicine through Time paper having been well received, and she had been making real progress in Maths and Science, subjects she normally struggled with. She had even shown some promise in German, something that surprised even her teachers. But all that was lost and she didn't think it could ever be recovered.

What was she going to do? That was the key question. Should she suddenly turn up in a new town with no parents and enrol herself at a school and book a room in a house somewhere? No, that was impossible. It would never work. She had flirted with the idea of Devery and Cora maybe posing as her parents but she quickly discarded it. They would have no interest in such a scheme. Their paths were always going to take them elsewhere and they would have no appetite to play Mama and Papa. Of course it also didn't help that despite liking the Irishman she really had no great love for his wife. She had never really forgiven her for the things she had said.

Felicity hadn't been lying when she told Finn she intended to leave but she quickly started to wonder where she would go. Where *could* she go? And more importantly how would she afford to live? It was true that she had plenty of money tucked away in a bank account but there was no way of her accessing it now. Her inheritance was not set up in such a way that she could withdraw it all in one go and she already knew that prying eyes would be keeping an eager watch on her account should she slowly filter it away over time.

'You'll have to wait until you're twenty one, I'd say?' said a voice to her left. 'Then when the time's right, go in and take it all out in one big chunk and hope no one's watching and run away as quickly as you can before they realise what's happened.'

She turned to see Finn slowly emerging out of the darkness. He too was wrapped up in a big red padded jacket that he had bought from one of the scientists. He somehow hadn't been able to find a hat and his hair was ruffled by both the pillow he had risen from and the northern breeze.

'Please don't read my mind,' Felicity said sternly, telling him off. 'You know I really don't like it!'

'Sorry,' Finn joined her at the bannister and blew into his hands to warm them.

The mind reading was utterly new and no one particularly felt comfortable with his new talent. Devery had met an immortal once who he claimed had such a skill but as a rule, such a gift was apparently quite rare and not often witnessed. As it happened, it was also rare that anyone would happily allow someone to access their most intimate thoughts unchecked. Telepathy was just one of many gifts that had been bestowed upon Finn since the floodgates had opened.

Felicity allowed her eyes to squint, focusing. 'What am I thinking now then, wizard?'

Finn pretended to be offended and pulled a face, knowing full well that she was insulting him in her head. 'Now that isn't very nice.'

'Well in case you missed it,' she said, 'I'm not a very nice kinda girl –'

'Keep saying it,' said Finn, 'and maybe one day even you'll believe it. I know different.'

'You're flirting is getting more and more lame,' Felicity noted.

'I wasn't flirting.'

He had said it without much humour and Felicity felt herself cringing. Finn had changed, there was no avoiding it. Since he had dispatched Tobias into a much deserved and long awaited grave and embraced the true strength of his power, something had unmistakeably happened to him, like a switch had been flicked inside of him and turned on a hidden part of his personality. She wasn't overly sure what it was but he seemed to move with more grace and stand upright with a confidence that he certainly didn't have before. He was also much more serious and thoughtful about everything. He no longer seemed like a fifteen year old and a big part of her missed the old version of him. She missed the bumbling, unconfident Finn.

'News says the cold snap is ending,' said Finn, looking out at the dark sea, 'just as Willoughby said. Apparently it means I've accepted what I am. The mark on my rib hasn't gone black yet though. Crazy how a book from so long ago could have predicted the whole thing.'

Felicity didn't add anything to that notion. Speaking about this gift had a habit of stroking his ego and when that happened it annoyed her.

'I'm quite looking forward to seeing Norway,' said Finn, changing the subject. 'I guess it's not one of those places you'd think to visit.'

'Yeah, this year we hit Norway,' said Felicity. She wanted to joke and pick somewhere really random. 'Then next year we visit Kazakhstan.'

'Or Iraq?' Finn pitched in, choosing the first random country he could think of that may be off the beaten path.

'I think people do actually visit Iraq sometimes,' Felicity said, shaking her head. 'So that joke doesn't really work. It's not only your flirting that's gone rubbish. Your jokes are lame too.'

'I think people visit Kazakhstan too!' Finn pointed out, defending his ability for banter.

Felicity wasn't having it. 'Not normal people –'

'The mayor of Kazakhstan and the tourist board will be happy with such kind words!'

Felicity pressed her fingers into her temples and stared intensely at Finn, challenging him to read her thoughts again. She had a little smile at the corner of her mouth.

Finn started laughing. The telepathy wasn't about to let him down.

'Charming again,' he tittered. 'I'm also sure the Mayor of Kazakhstan will have no desire to kiss your ass.' He allowed himself to finish laughing at the joke and then became sombre. 'Are you going to let me talk about this finally? I would like to.'

'I came out here for peace and quiet, Finn,' Felicity complained. 'Not to talk about anything.'

'We have to talk about it sometime –'

'We can talk about it in Kazakhstan, yeah?'

Finn scrunched up his face, disappointed.

Felicity moved away and started to head back towards their cabin. She wasn't angry. She just wasn't in the mood for talking. There had been lots of talking and it hadn't done anyone any good.

'Where are you going?' he asked, following her. He was close behind.

'Well if you must know,' Felicity said, 'I'm going for a little poo.'

'You can't hide from it, Fliss.'

'Hide from what?' Felicity wondered. 'The poo? No, that's my point, I'm going to go and drop it off at the pool.'

'Fine,' Finn stated resolutely, not letting her get away from it. 'I'll talk to you through the door then.'

Felicity stopped and made a deliberately loud sigh. 'Jesus,' she stressed. 'Don't you go thinking I'm going to hold anything back. I'm not going to keep all the farts and squirts silent just because you're sat on the other side of the door. I don't care, you know.'

'I'd expect nothing less,' Finn said. 'Farts and squirting I can handle –'

She could see that he was not going to be deterred and she folded her arms and sat down on a small bench that was positioned next to the cabin door. She tapped the surface of the wood, motioning for him to sit. 'Come on then,' she said, finally giving in, 'spit it out, if you must.'

Finn sat down. 'We've been talking about things,' he said.

This wasn't news to Felicity and she had taken steps to ensure that she wasn't included in any plotting. She had kept herself to herself and she was quite happy to allow the mighty immortals to talk amongst themselves and mull over their little plans and quests. But Finn had been trying for a few days to talk to her about it and so far she had managed to resist him.

'We're both orphans now,' Finn said.

'Strictly speaking, I'm not,' Felicity pointed out. 'I've got a Dad out there somewhere but he's just a pleb. He's not dead though.'

He had made that claim to her before and she still didn't think that he could be sure of such a statement. Yes, the train had exploded, but neither of them saw his mother's body and they could not be certain that she had perished.

'But we're both alone,' said Finn. 'That much is true, even you can't deny that. So the way I see it we're in this together, you and me, there is no one else.'

'You're not going to break into song are you?' Felicity furrowed a brow.

'Hamish felt we should lay low for quite a while,' Finn continued, ignoring her jokes. 'And when he says a while, he was talking like decades, so we could wait to see what all the others do and what threats present themselves. They think that moving too quickly will put us in too much danger. I've said no.'

Felicity shrugged. 'Why?'

'Firmly no,' Finn reiterated. 'I'm not hiding anywhere and I'm not moving slowly. I've told them this is how it's going to be. We get to Norway, move to Sweden and find this friend of Cora's, get Edgar back on his feet and then all of us set out to find this Alchemist guy. If that annoys anyone and they come looking for us, so be it, we'll have to handle it the best we can. If we die trying, we die trying. But this doesn't move slowly, it moves fast. We find the Alchemist and then we find Iris and end this forever.'

'And what do the others think of that?' Felicity asked.

'They think that it's rash,' said Finn, 'and they think it's the wrong thing to do right now given what has happened.'

'Then why don't you listen to them?'

'That bit is simple,' said Finn. 'It's because I'm not losing you. I wait, I lose you. You may hate me, you may not have any feelings for me, but I'm not letting you go. Not now, not ever. And if you push me away I'll keep trying and you can have me arrested for being a stalker –'

'In fairness that does sound like the kind of thing I'd do –'

'But what is the point of me doing this,' said Finn, 'if I'm not doing it for you?'

Felicity found that she was speechless at that. *Well said, Sir* was what she wanted to say but she didn't want to give him the pleasure of such a flagrant compliment. It was something that she had been waiting for all along but something that she would never ask for. But now that he had said it and more importantly that he had meant it, the show of commitment meant the world to her.

'If that's the case,' she said, keen to keep her emotions from him, 'maybe we should start talking about just how we're going to find this Alchemist. That's not going to be easy. There are billions of people on this planet.'

'The others have a theory,' said Finn. 'By all accounts Huxley has a reputation of being one of the greediest men to have ever lived. They think that once he finds out about me, he'll find a way to make contact and sell his services for a crazy price.'

'How much?' Felicity wondered.

'Don't know,' said Finn. 'These immortals seem happy to sell out anyone and anything.'

'Which makes me wonder,' said Felicity. 'Do you think they sell these elixir things by the pint or the gallon?'

'No idea about that either,' Finn enjoyed a long morning yawn. When he was finished he pushed his arms outwards and stretched his back. 'Finding Iris may be a bit harder. Bronwyn said we needed to find four mystical maps that will lead us to her. But she's no idea where they are and no one has ever seen them.'

'Sounds encouraging.'

'Doesn't it just.'

Felicity nodded her head and smiled. 'I guess we'll work it out later.'

Finn smiled back. 'You said *we?*'

Felicity reached out and held his hand. 'I said *we.*'

'I love you, Felicity Gower,' said Finn.

Felicity said nothing. Together they sat there on the bench in a comfortable silence, looking out at the dark shadows of the rippling waves of the North Sea that were slowly becoming visible in the dwindling darkness.

Acknowledgements

Gregg Watts, for nailing the brief and creating a cover design that I loved from the beginning.

Jules Hill, for her patience, her contribution, her priceless assistance with software I could never dream of conquering.

To my three amazing daughters who were there at both the conception and the end of this project, for inspiring a great deal of the story's many twists and turns, for hailing the *genius* of a major link in the plot, which for my part I had completely missed and stumbled across purely by accident. I remain unashamed. It was clearly just a subconscious piece of pure inspiration.

Mum, Dad, and Nita, for humouring me, not least when forced to read a great deal of grotty printouts as the tale evolved, for your encouragement throughout.

Finally, thank you for reading and I hope you will return when the story continues in *Elixir.* Coming soon …